LITTLE HORN

LITTLE HORN

STORIES

GEMMA FILES

SW SHORTWAVE PUBLISHING

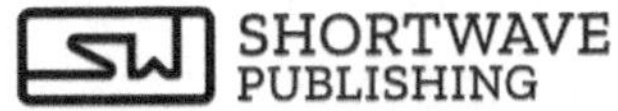

Oh the Larks.

—Joe Orton

STORIES

THE SANGUINTALIST

And the Name said unto Cain, Thy brother's blood cries out to me from the ground.

I wake up covered in blood, but it's not mine; I wake up covered in blood, and it *is* mine. Six of one, half-dozen of the other—take your pick. This is the world I live in and always has been.

I am a forensic necromancer for hire, of a very specific kind. Some of us work with flesh, some with bone, some with what flesh and bone leave behind. I once knew a woman who chased memories along their neural pathways, those electrochemical ghosts that can live on for days inside a corpse, even when its human topsoil is already being furrowed by insects looking for somewhere warm(ish) and easily permeable to lay their eggs, a field their children can eat their way free of. Her gift was a hard one, easy to mangle and misconstrue, like braiding tissue paper. Eventually, she ended up with a headful of other people's voices and a datebook full of the sort of types fragile people really should best avoid, for fear of getting the pixie-dust rubbed off their little wings. I'm not entirely sure what happened to her in the end, but I do keep my eye out for any trace of her, lit or fig.

For myself, I work with the red stuff. It's my calling. And easier by far than so many other things, given the relatively short window of its particular half-life. Accidents and murders, that's my meat: a short stop, a sudden drop, a spatter or a pool. By the time it's dry, it locks me back out, mostly. Or so I tell my customers.

They don't need to know everything about you, after all, not when your relationship's purely business.

————

So, I'm out picking up dinner, and my phone buzzes: ARSEHOLE NUMBER TEN, it says, because you need to be specific. Number Ten's name is Satyamurthy. Murder Squad when he's at home, and even when he's not.

I sigh, thumb working. *What you want?* the blinking text asks him.

Another buzz. *You, obviously. Here.* And an address.

I'm eating. The cursor rests, and then: *Do it fast, then. You might regret it.*

You might be surprised.

Inhale my curry, then I'm off. The site's not exactly walkable, but I grab a cab pretty easily. They don't send cars for you, more's the pity; don't want your name on the record.

Satyamurthy's outside, impatient, waiting to wave me in. His partner, Colville, turns around quick-time as I enter, hand almost twitching in the direction of that gun neither of them is supposed to have.

"Don't step on the evidence," she barks.

"Try my best," I reply. It's a challenge, all right—stuff is everywhere you look, splashed up high, probably from carotid *and* jugular at once, given how wide the corpse's second mouth gapes. But she knows that.

The body's nude, and basically faceless. Looks like someone did it with a brick? Everything's all mushed up, red stuck with shards, shattered bone-bristles, the occasional tooth; hands are gone at the wrists, possibly for time's sake, dumped somewhere they'll end up similarly deconstructed. If it weren't for the dick, lying snug and slack up against one gore-smeared thigh. . . ah, but that doesn't always mean much, does it? Or less than it used to, anyhow, as I should know.

"You want a name, I take it?" I ask Satyamurthy, not looking up to watch him nod. Because my gaze is all on this one, now—that blank ruin, equally dented all over, only a rough geographic idea left to tell you where the eye-sockets should go. Yet there's a pull to it nevertheless, a sort of gravity; I can feel it, even from here. It's telling me bend down, get closer, ask my questions. It's telling me it *wants* to tell me, so come meet it halfway, before its time runs out. Before the blood it's still trying to shed finally goes cold.

You damn well wait your turn, I warn it, as I do.

Down on my haunches, a deep squat, arse to heels. I rummage through my pockets, slipping on my thumb-rings—antique bone, fossilized, worn so thin with use my skin tints them from the inside. Iron reinforcements so they don't break under pressure, with sharpened horn set in a deep groove across my knuckles: right, left, curved like beaks, points extending well past my nails. Set them to the pads of my forefingers and they dent the skin; no scar tissue, see? I don't have to break the skin to draw blood, never have.

Not when it comes when I call it.

Cruentation, that's the old term—blood evidence. Bring a corpse with traces of violence into the presence of its suspected murderer and watch to see if it starts to bleed. Root of the word comes from the Latin, *cruintare,* to make bloody, and they really did use to not only pull that whole rigamarole, but bring it up in court afterwards, way back before proper forensics. Back when the intersection of maths, physics and biology, alchemy, religion and magic was a sight more slippery than it is today, and the same people who'd just learned you could see little bugs swimming around in a drop of water under a microscope's lens still thought women's wombs wandered around their bodies, getting all clogged with rotten sperm and producing fumes that made them go hysterical.

My blood to yours, then, and your blood to mine—cry out, make your plea, your last appeal. I'll help you, if I can; justice isn't always possible, but I'll try my best. Hear you and remember from now on, either way.

This promise is an old one, older than old. My mother taught it to me, like hers taught her. It goes back forever.

We were priests and kings once, Lala, my little one, my Nani used to tell me, and still does, even when I don't want to listen. *Long before Kukkutarma became Mohenjo-daro, for all its name reflects our former glory. Before the glaciers grew and retreated, even, in the very morning of the world, when everything was equally unstable. When all our cities were graves, and all our graves, cities.*

(Yes, yes. But this ain't then, is it? And I'm on the clock and time is money, theoretical square root of this whole bloody late-stage capitalism barter system. I scratch Satya's back, he scratches mine...)

That's how it should go, anyway; almost always does. Even if we don't often itch in *quite* the same places, him and me.

I close my eyes, feeling my fingertips pink and bruise as the drops start forming: all that tiny life, forever swimming and fighting, eating and dividing, without rest, or pity. Each globule a secret universe caught in the moment of creation, utterly unaware of its own precariousness, dim and scarlet and salt.

There's a thrum in the air when the corpse's blood recognizes mine, sparking, a struck string. A red mist rises from the body's pores, sending out feelers, and I can already hear Colville draw breath behind me, give out a disgusted little grunt. It doesn't break my concentration. I know my business better than that.

Now, I say, silent, tongue moving against my teeth, the roof of my shut mouth. *Tell me now. Show me, if you can't form the words. Let me see it.*

Let me see it all.

————

Turns out, Satya takes notes on his phone, same as every other wanker working on a screenplay down at the local coffee shop. Probably helps to be able to send them to himself via email later on, though I doubt whoever manages Murder Squad IT security likes it much.

"*Eithne* Morden?" Colville repeats, reading over his shoulder, to which I don't bother nodding.

"En-ya," I correct her pronunciation. "Used to be Eustace, till she had it legally changed. You really did miss diversity training day, didn't you, Detective? It's all right; lots of Old Girls on the job these days, I'll bet, now the Old Boys Network's finally dying out. You'll all have to catch up, eventually."

She opens her mouth, but Satyamurthy waves her silent. "Skip the vinegar, Ms. Mirwani. Anything else we need to know?"

"She was down from the North, couch-surfing, staying with pals in Stepney. Came out to have a good time and mainly did, till she didn't. The last place she remembers being is the Five-Pointed Star—dropped her phone in the washroom, but the person she left with stepped on it, 'by accident.' They said they'd pay to get it fixed, then dropped it down a drain, after. She was drunk enough by the time they got here, she can't recall exactly how it happened, which I suppose is just as well. Last clear thing in her head is a really nice kiss, then getting spun 'round and rammed into the wall, face-first."

"And her clothes?"

"Like I said, she doesn't know. I'd assume whoever did it burnt them, maybe in one of those cans over there." Adding, as he raises a brow: "That's what *I'd* do."

"Hm. I'll keep that in mind."

Behind him, Colville sighs, crossing her arms. "Don't reckon you caught a look at the bugger's face, after all that."

"Not how it works," I tell her. "I see what they see, how they see it. You've watched me work before."

"Ah yeah, cert. 'Cause that'd be *far* too easy."

Now it's my turn to shrug, stone-faced, even as the red ghost of Eithne's memories hangs heavy in the air around me, refusing to dissipate just yet—a heady mixture of thwarted desire and terrible surprise, disappointment, familiarity: this was always a possibility in her life, one she'd accepted early on, same way I had to. Though I do like to think I'd fight harder at the end, if and when I find myself here. I *like* to think I've lived long enough not to walk into it with my eyes wide open anymore, glitter-encrusted and high on hope, led on like a lamb to slaughter by some toxic combination of dumb youth, drugs, and alcohol.

"It was a woman, I know that much," I tell Colville. "Eithne wouldn't've gone with her, it hadn't been. And not some straight woman putting on a show to pull a bit of the new, either, or a lady who goes both ways—girls don't hang 'round the Five-Pointed Star unless they're queer through and through, no matter their accoutrements. It's a bi-phobic bloody dive, that one."

"Been there a lot, have you?"

"Enough to know."

"And why does this not surprise me?"

"Well, you do look a bit hard to surprise, Colville, sad to say. Rather a disappointing way to live, I'd think."

And here the banter ends, thank fuck. Satya puts his hand up, reins her in, gives me the nod; the both of them sod off, leaving me with Eithne. Not really a place to hang around much longer if I don't want the hangover I'm courting already to last into tomorrow, but there's still a few loose ends to clear up—you have to be polite, always, when dealing with the dead, especially those killed traumatically. They appreciate gentleness.

Need to go now, love, I tell her, slipping my finger-rings back off again. *It's a cold place, this, and there's nothing much left worth seeing. I'll do my best to make sure things go right, from here on in.*

From her blood's dimming tide, eddying ever downwards, I can still hear the last few rags of her voice issue, so small and sad. Asking me:

But why, sis? She really did seem like she liked me.

They all do, darling, in the moment—that's the hard bloody fact of it. But it isn't your fault, you have to know that. Or hers either, if you can believe it.

. . . why not?

I shut my eyes and take a breath before I answer, long enough to settle myself so I can be dispassionate about what I have to tell her, circumstances notwithstanding. Seeing, as I do, one more awful flash of Colville's face seen through Eithne's cunt-struck eyes, caught in that split micro-second of transformation: desire to calculation, lips reshaping in a wolfish sort of half-grin that doesn't quite reach her gaze, because someone else's has just. . . dropped over it, like a filter. Two phantom fingers hooked through her medulla and poised to twist, turn down the empathy, turn *up* the all-too-human atavistic urge to rip and rend and tear. That crossover point where kiss becomes bruise, becomes bite, adding a vile cannibal savour to the sauce; *lustmord*, that was the term, back when old Sigmund Freud was first slapping his dick-centred psychological worldview together before inflicting it on the rest of us poor sods, no matter how nature, nurture, gender, and anatomy might admix.

Colville, completely unaware of how exactly she woke up feeling so sore this morning, but still with that tiny little bit of a shine about her, the after-trace of someone else's magic. Hadn't known if I was right until Eithne showed me, but here it is in all its former glory, a sigil set to flame between her brows like a tiara's centre-stone—something roughly triangular, point down to signal malign intention, a signpost to the Left-Hand Path. And inside it, shimmering, a filigree made from lines and loops crossing over each other at odd angles, impossibly compact.

I study it till I've got it down, then file it away for tracing in my memo book, once I'm done with the immediate; think I know the right person to take it to, difficult though that'll be. But one way or the other, it's nothing I'd ever bother Satyamurthy with, even if it *didn't* point directly to the bitch who plays his backup.

She's just a tool, after all; innocent, at least of this. And maybe she really did find her target beautiful for those few flirtatious minutes, if only because whoever turned her on poor Eithne told her to. Maybe the something new she's learned about herself will even keep on resonating away under the hood, albeit subconsciously, formal lack of gender identity jargon aside —I mean, I don't ever expect apologies, or anything like that. But considering how she and Satya come linked at the hip, be nice to get through a few of these meetups without her constantly trying to point out how I should feel shite about the way I'm made, even by implication.

Because she was used, that's all, I tell Eithne, finally. *Used and thrown away, just like you but worse, 'cause she's forgotten all about it.*

"But worse?" I'm *the one who's dead, sis.*

I know, love. I'm sorry. But. . . you're the one who's free *now, too, free of it all. And her, until she knows the sin she's committed. . . she never will be.*

Does that help, though? Probably not; wouldn't for me, if our places were reversed. Still, Eithne seems like she's a better person—*was* a better person. Better than I'll ever be, by far.

I'll make it right, I promise again, rage washing up over me from my deepest parts, poisoning myself from the inside-out with it, against everything my Nani ever taught me: need to be hard and sharp, from now on, considering who I'm going to be dealing with.

Because *We stay away from each other, Lakshmi-child,* she always used to tell me, even back when my Mum still insisted my name was Latif. *Especially those who deal with the living, not the dead. . . stay clear, let them damn themselves in their own ways, and meet their own punishments. When magic calls you take note, but do not answer. It will call you to your doom, if you let it.*

And God knows she had the right of it too, as I well know myself, from almost every time my path's crossed another magician's—but who else can we trust to police each other, if not ourselves? Who else is qualified?

(*No one can say, Lala; no one knows, or ever has. Not even me, or you.*)

Exactly, granny. And since I'm gonna die either way, just like everyone else. . .

Eithne gives one last sigh and leaves me. I stand there alone in the dark, trying not to shiver; above me, there's a skittering from the rooftop, the unseen rafters. Birds, or rats, or bats.

You do what you must, my Nani whispers inside my skull, the curl where ear meets cartilage meets bone, making my jawbone thrum in sympathy. *Only be careful, Lala, when you do. There are so few of us now, and you. . . you are one of the last.*

"Not dead as yet, though," I say out loud, like I'm making another promise. And turn to go.

———

When you're born something people don't expect, you learn to value being valued, and pretty damn quickly. That's the core of what attracted me to Caelia Asperdyne, in the first place—I mean, beside her being beautiful, and sexy, and posh. Besides her being at least as outstanding in her chosen field as I ever was in mine, if not more so.

There's a tradition of *hijra* in my family, spoken or not; if you're born to the blood, no one much cares how your bits dangle or don't, unless there's literally no one left to breed more little necromancers. But there's not a lot of women, cis or otherwise, who choose the path of Haute Magie; plain truth is, the High Hermetic Arts appeal mostly to detail-obsessed system junkies who get off on getting all the bells, whistles, flourishes and correspondences right for their own sake, and that almost always means blokes. The women I've met who took up a Path did it either 'cause they wanted something right away, too badly to bother with a learning curve, or 'cause the magic wanted *them* too badly to leave them alone.

I never asked Caelia what made her different, that way— that's just etiquette. A worker wants to tell you their story, they will; they don't, you don't ask. We had plenty of stuff to do with each other in the meantime, anyway.

Caelia and I met when her lawyer, who works for one of these five-name third-generation family firms whose hourly rates start at three digits, approached me on behalf of his client —he'd found me through Satyamurthy, pursuant to some questions Caelia needed answered. *About what?* I asked. *Blood,* he said, unsurprisingly. Turned out, she needed to know whether a particular sample had come from an honest-to-God virgin or not (it hadn't), and whether the donor was still alive when it was taken (she was and still is). And since there's basically no one who'd want to know this sort of detail aside from someone else working the magical side of the street. . . well, I got interested. All the more so, once I actually met her.

Not that the alive-or-not part had anything to do with scruples, mind you, as Caelia herself later told me, *I can use it either way*, she'd murmured in my ear, trapping me between her black steel wine cabinet and her tall, lush body. *Just need its correspondences, so I can know* how *to use it. That's all.*

Really don't think that matters as much as you think it does, I remember gasping.

It does, to me. Those are the rules we play by.

You *play by.*

Exactly so.

Which is magic in a nutshell, right there. Doesn't matter *why* it works, or how, so long as it does. It's surprising how far you can get, in fact, without asking those sort of questions at all. Certainly explains why Caelia and I got on as well as we did, for as long as we did.

For people, though, the *why* of it very much does matter. Which is why we don't get on anymore, her and me.

Still, I can't pretend I don't like having an excuse to see her again, no matter poor Eithne had to die to make it happen. Can't pretend I haven't missed brushing up against Caelia's whole world, really. . . that lovely place where bills were a joke, the fridge was always full, and you could say *fuck you* to anyone who looked at you sideways. Can barely keep from jumping her, in fact, when the doors to her condo's private lift roll open for the first time in two years just to show her already standing there waiting for me, arms folded over a red satin dressing robe with nothing much on underneath, and smiling her old familiar half-smile as she watches my eyes widen at the sight.

"Lala Mirwani," she says, upper-class drawl touched with just a hint of Welsh music you could feel against your skin, like being stroked with fur. "Fancy a drink? Or is this just business?"

Only Caelia could make a word as dry as "business" sound that dirty. Have to make myself look down where her shadow meets the imported marble tile, to remind myself what dangers lie hid inside that gorgeous package of hers.

Because yeah, there it is—harder to spot when she isn't moving, but if you squint just the right way it becomes obvious, even when you don't know exactly what you're looking at: a second layer of darkness fitted almost-but-not-quite over the first, lapping it less like water than like flame. Her angel's black halo, edged in corner-of-the-eye UV flares like static, telling you whatever you'd just caught a sidelong glimpse of was inherently. . . *wrong*, neither good nor evil, simply far too much and definitely not right. Nothing that should exist, at least not here, not now, not yet.

I mean, we're all a bit more than baseline normal, those like Caelia and me. . . but the thing that distinguishes Haute Magie from almost every other type of working lies in its practitioners' willingness to call on pretty much anything that'll get the job done, no matter what that entails. Some stick themselves inside circles or stick what they called down/up inside there; some ink wards on themselves and conjure spirits into objects or other people (dead, alive, whatever), assured they're far too well-protected to worry about possession if the item in use suddenly goes boom.

What Caelia's done, though. . . that was the opposite, basically. She's invited something in and let it live there rent-free; didn't even ward herself after, to keep it from leaving. And by allying herself with this *thing*, she's made herself over into something almost as powerful, as improbable; by taking it inside herself, she's signed a bargain whose after-effects shed contagion, a radiance no one but her could live alongside, without starting to change in ways they might find troubling.

Never did figure out whether it was an actual big-A angel or just some poor elemental brainwashed John Dee-style to think it was, but either way, being with Caelia was always a package deal. I think I was just the first one she'd ever stayed with long enough for that to get to be a problem.

So: "Business," I force out. Then adding, not quite too low for her to hear, "Business first, anyway." Which gets me an even wider smile and a step forwards, till I hold up my memo book: "No, not yet—safe room, then we'll discuss it. Please."

That shuts the charm off. "Of course," she replies, coolly. And leads the way.

Caelia's safe room used to be her penthouse's smallest guest bedroom, before she remodelled it into a hermetic workspace: long tables along all three back walls, floor retiled in slate that would take chalk markings easily, oil lamps to back up the ceiling fixtures, extra ventilation ducts laid in, and—most importantly —the door remounted with hinges on the outside, plus an extra layer of warding runes round it. *So, if worse comes to worst, I can seal whatever I can't deal with in behind me with one slam,* she'd explained. *Until someone opens the door, anyway, but by then I'll be at least three cities away, living under a completely new identity.*

It wasn't a joke, so I hadn't laughed, and she'd noticed. That might've been the moment things started to change between us, now I come to think.

Still, it's a comfort to feel her wards go up all 'round us both, as the door closes behind us. Caelia listens, attentively, then takes my memo book and pores over the sigil I've drawn, her finger tracing its lines. The movement stirs memories.

"Not your classic alchemy, I'd guess," I note, to distract myself. "But you're the expert, so. . . what is it, *Transitus Fluvii?*"

Caelia shakes her head. "Looks to me like a recursive acrostic —you write the spell down as an acronym, laying all the letters on top of one another; maybe do it in Enochian or Hebrew and then translate it numerologically first, for extra oomph. Almost impossible to decipher, unless you already know what it's meant to do, and why."

"I know the *what*," I tell her. "Not sure about the *why*, yet. Though I have an idea." She raises an eyebrow, waiting for me to elaborate. "This is too much effort for something that isn't personal, and no way a sweet little girl like Eithne made this kind of enemy. So, my guess is, it's about Colville—ruining her life, turning her into what she hates, every way you can. And timing it so she'd be the one to catch the call, after? That's twisting it, right in the soul. Exactly what a bastard like this'd laugh about."

(A bastard like this, a bitch like you—or me, under the right circumstances.)

It isn't anything we've had to say to each other, not out loud. And one good thing about Caelia, even if I did, she wouldn't be too insulted.

Caelia nods slowly. "Given she and her partner are familiar with our community,they may well have made enemies in it, or one who at least knows who to hire."

"You, for example."

"Or *you*." She gives me a meaningful look. "You do realize, the people most able to answer that question are going to be those least interested in doing so."

"Yeah, yeah, I know," I mutter. "Thin blue line, etcetera."

"Quite. And still. . ." Caelia taps the glyph. "If your reproduction here is accurate enough, I should be able to follow its traces to its maker, for at least a little while longer." She pauses, then takes my hand. My insides lurch. "But Lala, listen to me here, love—anyone who could do *this* is as good as I am, maybe better. They'd be dangerous even if all you wanted was information. If you want to make them answer for this, however. . . be aware going in, you may not be able to."

It rings true, or true enough—worry, on my behalf. Gets under my skin in a way I can't guard against. But I make myself remember Eithne—how bewildered she'd looked, even at the last—and Colville, who doesn't even know to be. This is worth the risk.

"Never mind me," I say. "Just do it, or don't, whichever. Let me make my own call, after that."

"Lala, please. Of course, I'll do it." She lets go of my hand, and I sigh—then freeze as she cups my cheek. Her voice is soft; her eyes hold mine. "You *know* you were the only person I couldn't say no to."

I clear my throat but can't hide the rasp. ". . . that's flattering. . ."

"Yes, I'm sure."

". . . but since you said we had a narrow window, we, um—ought to get started soon, I'd think."

She leans into me, then, and the movement of her lips against mine lights up my body from scalp to groin. Whispering: "Not *that* soon."

———

Oh, Lakshmi-child, my Nani's voice groans a few hours later, the second I cross the threshold of my shitty little no-bedroom apartment. *What's this smell about you now? What've you done?*

I roll my eyes in the direction of my bed, where a carved wooden box sits atop a set of bookshelves made from plastic milk crates, remembering now how much I've always hated coming back from Caelia's place to mine—it feels like falling from a luxury hotel room window straight into a garbage skip. "Nani, enough. This is not like before, and not your business, anyway."

That girl again, isn't it? Nani replies, not at all put off. *She's no good for you, Lala.*

"Fwah. Like I don't know *that.*"

Do you, though? Ah, well. Children.

"Just doing what I have to, like always. You were the one always told me to, remember? If it was up to Mum. . ."

No answer. I sigh, go to the bookshelves, take down the box and open it.

"Nani," I repeat, addressing the object within, tone gone all conciliatory and respectful, "I made a *promise, hai?* To one dead, and to myself; to Her, beyond us all. Please don't make me break it."

From inside, cradled on a nest of scarves, my grandmother's shrunken, mummified head seems to squint up at me through the wrinkled slits that are all that's left of its eyes—and though it doesn't move, memory alone supplies the wry, toothless smile.

Hum, I see; fair enough. But none of us ever knows as much as we think we do, and it's what we don't know kills us, Lala. Don't forget.

I swallow, nod, then shut the box back up on her and go to take a shower. The hot water's actually working for a change. I step under the spray, close my eyes, and try to stop myself from overthinking things so much.

———

"This's him," Caelia tells me a few days later, scrolling her phone to show me a snap of some semi-handsome bloke, bald and bearded, a haematite stud in either ear—pure Guy Ritchie hipster-gangster, aged about twenty years past his sell-by date. "Don't let the smile fool you, he's a dangerous, powerful man, and a lot older than he looks, for all he knows not to look *too* young. Goes by the name of Dominic Traeger, these days."

"Sounds like you know him."

"*Knew* him, yes; he's. . . my type. My *other* type."

"Oh, ta."

Caelia shrugs, beautifully, and rolls off of me; I lie there tangled in her ridiculously high fibre count sheets, buzzing everywhere we've touched thus far, though my groin's obviously got the brunt of it. *Stand down now, fool,* I tell myself, harshly. *Fun-time's over, back to business.*

Can't quite keep myself from admiring as she pads glory-naked to her dresser, though, with both shadows following like a live-action blackwork tattoo designed to highlight her effortless desirability, never quite in sync. Plucks a parchment scroll from the top drawer's secret inner compartment and unrolls it, holding it up: I recognize the calligraphy even from here, though not the glyph itself.

"This is what tipped me off," she says. "His style's. . . memorable, if not that particular sigil. And no, I still don't know what the other one says, aside from 'find a complete stranger and fuck yourself over, Detective.' presumably. This, though—he had it *everywhere* at what used to be his place, back when I went to him for a short course in hard-won life-hacks *vis à vis* our mutual hobby. Probably has it somewhere on his body too, just for good measure."

Like you don't know, I think, but don't say; just sit up, instead, immediately interested enough to not bother taking the sheets with me.

"Ah. So what are they, wards?"

"The *ultimate* ward, or so he thinks—an anagram designed to protect him from everything, living, dead, or otherwise. Nothing gets past it. *I* certainly can't, and I was there when he wrote it."

"This doesn't exactly sound promising, Caelia."

"Doesn't it, darling? Ah, but think about it just a little harder, for half a mo'; a working like that only has one limitation, the same inherent weakness *every* magician has, by nature. And definitely, every man."

As she glances southwards with a knowing smirk, I feel my brows half-raise—not sure if I'm meant to feel insulted—then pause, considering it further.

"You're talking about imagination," I say finally.

"Oh, I very much am. It's the Achilles' heel of all hierarchical magic, you see, a sadly heteronormative tendency to separate everything in the universe by nature and degree, even those which share qualities that make them far more inherently liminal, not to mention interstitial. Much like your own sweet self, Lala. . . you, and your little trick. The one you don't tell most people about, unless you really, *really* like them."

And here it comes, fast and hard, a slap in the mental face made from equal parts memory and embarrassment; me and Caelia swapping stories in the dark, me all lax and happy enough to be far more post-coitally stupider than usual, while she used every charm she had to pry from me the secret even my Mum made sure to warn me should *never* be told out loud, ever, especially to outsiders. The most primal use of blood-based necromancy, which only we Mirwani—supposedly—have ever been able to master; that much-lauded skill which set us apart from every other dead-worker in a whole city of the same, a whole nation. The thing pilgrims would travel thousands of miles for, paying us in prayer and dread and riches untold to perform it upon their behalf, so long ago that the very fortunes we'd reaped from them had all long since crumbled to ash and dust, just as surely as the pilgrims, their justice-seeking dead and the necromantic city-state, which once gave birth to my family itself.

So: ". . . ah yeah," I say, at last, without much emphasis at all. "*That* trick."

———

The blood cries out, and we answer, taking on their grief, their anger, their hunger for revenge. Their blood sinks deep inside us, becoming ours. We gather it together and send it out, seeking justice. It isn't easy; it costs, a lot. But it can be done, and—so far as we've been able to tell, after yea these many millennia (two, maybe three at the most)—only by us.

Like a tulpa, or a golem? Caelia had asked me, there in the dark. *Sort of,* I'd replied, like the fool for her I've always been.

Because a *tulpa* is a thought given flesh and sent out, half fantasy, half detritus; because people are dirt and blood is dust, you only wait long enough, and a golem is dust brought to life by magic, by the literal application of God's own word. But no, it's not really like that at all, like either of those things, except metaphorically.

We call it *Peccai-ji Madam*, this thing only we can treat with —Queen Blood, That Lovely Red One, Justice's Price. Her titles built around one catch-all word for many different things, but always with an affectionate diminutive applied as though it's just one more member of our family, a female one: a sister, a cousin, an auntie. Or perhaps someone even further out, a person whose kinship is entirely more difficult to define: a good neighbour, a respected elder, someone we know we can turn to when all other avenues are blocked or lost. Something that will always answer *our* prayers, if no one else's. A literal court of last resort.

Does it come from inside you, or outside?

Both. . . maybe.

Do you control it, or does it control you?

Both. Neither. I don't know, *Caelia.*

Then who does?

Nobody, Cee. Doesn't work like that.

I remember her lying back, eyes on the ceiling, studying the lack of cracks. Saying, eventually: *It'd drive me bloody mad, that sort of magic—no language, no control, no rules. How do you stand it?*

I shrugged. *Because it's mine,* I told her.

(Mine. Ours. Its own.)

You accept what you're born with, I might have said—but that's not exactly true, is it? Or it is, but it's complicated: I was born knowing I shouldn't be male, after all, and eventually I was able to make everyone else accept it, without even having to resort to surgery (thank you, modern medicine). Which is a sort of magic on its own, I suppose. . . and like every other kind, you do still have to pay for it, once you've figured out the cost.

That's why Caelia's arts and mine remain truly antithetical in the end, no matter how much we enjoy one another's company; on some fundamental level, the Haute Magie crowd think so long as they find the right middleman, they'll never have to pay for anything. It's just contract work to them, everything done at a safe remove, all neat and tidy. No crossed lines, no *mess*. Sex magick aside, even their sacrifices usually involve something else's precious bodily fluids.

Not how I was raised, let alone what I've learned from personal experience. Because what does the price matter, so long as the right thing gets done? There has to be balance in this bloody world of ours, or nothing's worth a good goddamn.

You'd really think the people who made up the phrase "as above, so below" would have already figured that part out, wouldn't you? And yet.

———

So here I am now outside Mr. Calls-Himself-Traeger's office tower, waiting. Or not *me*, rather: Her.

The version of Her She lets me be, once all the necessaries have been done.

Real me still lies at home inside a ring made from rings, corpse-posture assumed, naked.

Covered in blood—all mine, this time, up to a very tiny yet important point. The biological grit cocooned around a single red liquid pearl of Eithne's blood-memory, hidden away inside me somewhere. . . left resonating, one more note in an endless scale, a raga that never quite stops skittering beneath the beat of my own pulse.

I can't ever completely let go of any of these people, that's the truth. Their cries keep on resounding, thin though they might dim, with time; that's only as it should be, considering their grievances. So, we absorb their hurts, let them sink deep and scar over. . . which is why, much like the dead, the *Mirwani* never forget. And why, in turn, when you learn how to fuel your magic with pain, it becomes that much harder to hurt you enough to make you stop what you're doing, once the judgement's been agreed upon between all three of you at last—by which I mean you, the client (the corpse whose final pain you share, whose inconsolable cry you ride), and *Her*.

Never let yourself believe the gods can't be bargained with, my Lala, my Nani says, *both ours or theirs, or anyone's. But again, remember:* Bargained *with, only. Not* cheated.

So yeah: 'it's a tricky dance, the blood-walk, even with all six theoretical feet going in tandem, tracing a chart that changes with each fresh client's complaint. Summon the blood, theirs and yours, then slip it like a skin, stepping disembodied into the psychic shell held in every erythrocyte's genetic memory; feel it rise up and swirl around you in a glinting red torrent, forming a new self only held together by will, power, grief and loss, the four hands (or so Nani always said) of Kali Herself. Thus, becoming something both real and unreal, neither ghost nor living, neither golem nor undead: indestructible, untouchable, unstoppable. . . as long as you can keep the balance.

To walk with *Peccai-ji Madam* is a gift, and it bears a price. It has to. When you do it, your flesh is made of blood and fire and anguish, and it burns. Oh, you can push it down if you want, let the power numb you; have to, really, at least a little bit, or you lose your grip. Then it all falls apart and you wind up slamming back into your true flesh like some ham-fisted stunt wrestler's clotheslined you. *Not* fun. But push the pain too far down, you forget you have flesh at all, and you'll wander blissed-out and blind until your heart gives out from dehydration. Every journey with Queen Blood is a fresh test. Just how much pain can you bear, and for how long? And most importantly of all—is what you're doing it for really worth it?

That part, at least, you usually know the answer to by the end. One way or another.

By itself the blood-shell looks exactly like you'd expect: a wet, shiny, scarlet image of its worker's body, like you've stripped down, plunged into an abattoir's catch-tank and come up streaming crimson. But it doesn't take much practice before you can make it look like what you want, or even nothing at all if you don't feel like being seen, though that takes effort. I'm playing it simple; I'm huddling in the mouth of an alley across from the skyscraper, unglamorously glamoured up to look like your average out-of-their-head hobo, mumbling and shivering and cursing in filthy rags. If Traeger's the sort of person Caelia says he is, he won't even notice me. . .

. . . and I guess she really *wasn't* lying, after all, 'cause he doesn't; comes strutting down the street like bloody Willy Moon, swiping a bright gold keycard to let himself in without even a glance in my direction.

Owns the top three floors, Caelia told me, *with his workspace in the penthouse; means home's at a safe remove, but it also means he has to go there regularly, after dark, to renew the wards that need that kind of working. So, he'll be there tonight.*

Suppose his schedule changes? I'd asked.

It won't have. A very thin smile. *It can't.*

Don't know why it bothered me she was so certain. Jealousy, I thought, at the time—not that I have any claim on her, really, any more than she does, over me. And not that that's in any way what tonight's about, either.

If I needed to breathe, I'd take one, deep. But I don't, so I just rise instead, hobo-guise shucked off on the instant for a no-filter selfie-image, nearly forgetting to remember to make myself walk after him rather than simply glide a half inch above the asphalt street, smooth as if I'm skating. No keycard needed on my part. With a mere flick of the will, I pass myself through the glass, reach the elevators, slip between steel doors, pop the ceiling hatch, and leap up. Spark up the cable like a charge along a fuse, right to the top, a fizzing (in)human bomb.

Then I pour myself out through the crack those still-shut outer doors slide along and eddy back to "normal" height, following the fading heat-ghosts of Traeger's footsteps through empty corridors till they disappear beyond a set of double doors carved from what looks like whole slabs of black oak, each rimmed with half of some mediaeval Satan's gaping mouth: lips and teeth, concentric rings of fire spiralling inwards and down-wards to those great bronze half-tongue braces in the middle, worked all over with bas-relief images of sinners in hell that'd make Hieronymus Bosch puke.

Stuck together, both doors lock fast into one huge rune, same as the one Caelia sketched for me. Its power seems immense, blazing, threads linking out through every brick in the workshop wall, hot against my lack of face like hatches thrown open into a furnace at full roar. If she's wrong, trying to pass through will tear me apart, so fast and hard the backlash might reach all the way to my real body. Landlord won't like that, considering how it'll make it nigh impossible for him to ever rent my place again. Be a good way to kill me, if she only wanted to—so I'll just have to trust she doesn't, as of yet. That I'm still right in that assump-tion, now I'm out of her lovely warm bed and back into the World Invisible, where everything I do (or don't) brings a hundred unsung dangers, at the very least. . .

Sod it, though; Eithne needs avenging, not just grieving. Colville too, for that matter.

I think about closing my eyes, for all I can't. *Think* about stepping forward. And—

—there I am on the other side, all of a sudden, no safer than before but none the bloody less, either. With that giant ward still quite intact behind me, and barely a flicker to mark my etheric wake. *Never been quite so happy to be made to feel like I don't exist before,* I think. *Not in the flesh, nor out.*

Inside is what rings like a repurposed boardroom, with three whole walls of windows facing east, west, north. Doesn't even have the drapes closed, though I can see the gold tracks of their runners framing each bank of panes and each gold-shot red carpet-weight mass drawn back to either side of the door, heavy as a Doric column: ooh la la, look at *him,* quite literally.

'Cause there's the man himself once more, just like I figured —Traeger, tracing his chalk from point to point of a massive pentagram on the tiled floor, kneeling stiffly down at each juncture to murmur incantations. Not sure if he's spotted me yet, since I probably register most as a vague blur against the tiny screaming faces carved underneath his All-Ward, but I already know how things will change once I move further inside. How the air all 'round me will start to smear, colours gone prismatic and deformed, caught on the blood-shell's aura. How Eithne's almost-gone Kirlian signature will tangle with my own astral body's silvery trail, both of them snagging and scattering in polluted shards around Queen Blood's incandescent, inverted halo. Quite an effect, 'specially when it takes you off guard.

But none of us have time for all *that,* really. Do we? Nah.

I flare all the way up, therefore, glamour whipped aside fast as a shed cloak, Jean Rollin sex-vampire sudden entrance style: crackaBOOM, you naff wanker! See him jolt a bit right where he's squatted, halfway up and halfway down, knees cracking like twigs; his voice rises, incantation pace doubling but not pausing, let alone stopping—it *can't,* like Caelia said. There's far too much at stake for him to get thrown off-course, after all, what with all those para-dimensional mind-worms and what have you nosing hungrily all along the edges of his personal defences, blindly seeking for a crack to stick their toothy tongues through. One second's inattention, or distraction, and he's gone—devoured. Consumed beyond recall.

Time it right, Lala, you won't even have to fight him, Caelia'd told me, her eyes glittering. *Just. . . interfere.*

I can't lie: 'it's a rush, seeing that realization of helplessness shoot through him: helplessness, confusion. . . fear. Things he probably hasn't felt for years, if ever. Even more of a rush, knowing it's me causing it.

I slide up to him, moving as he moves, red hand lifting to cup his throat, red fingers poised to clamp shut and choke off the binding words; his eyes bulge wide and white. Around us, the aether crackles like bacon frying, twisting as forces both mind-less and sentient nuzzle hungrily at this world. I think about saying something like, *This is for Eithne,* but that's pointless; he won't know who she is. And I can't really get angry enough about Colville to posture on her behalf. Maybe it's the best karma of all, now I think about it, that he won't even know *why* this is the moment when he ends. . . *Karma.*

Shit.

Nani's voice comes back to me, her first lesson, and her last. *We hear the dead, my girl; we help finish what they've left undone, to send them on. Lay them down, when they won't rest. But one thing we don't do? We don't decide who's fit to join them. We don't pass judge-ment on the living, no matter how deserved it seems. That's not what the Gift is for. Forget that, and we'll answer for it.*

I hear Caelia laugh, short and sharp. The way she's always laughed when this sort of talk comes up. *Childishness,* she called it, in the last and bitterest of our fights. *There's what you want, and what you don't want. If you don't know the difference, Lala, you've got no business with the Art.*

There's a different anger in me, now.

I ease my hand back from Traeger's throat. Not all the way—close enough to still be dangerous—but enough to make it clear what I've decided. His fear recedes; the panicked babble slows, his voice firms. The queasy-making shimmer in the air subsides. When at last he finishes, standing from the pentagram's final point, he turns and looks at me. Sigils of poisonous violet light ripple through his skin, jellyfish current-eddying.

When he speaks, his voice is hoarse enough an accent leaks through, more like mine than I'd've guessed; one he worked a long time to lose, I'll bet.

"Dunno which t'ask first: how the hell you did this, or *why*."

"Haven't done anything just yet, have I?"

I've blurred my face and form to vagueness, made my voice a sexless croak. But his eyes narrow nonetheless as he looks me over, all too sharp.

"You spent power to get here; more'n a little, I'd say. Means you want *something*." He takes a breath, forces his tones back into learned poshness. "Want it bad enough to need me at your mercy, but not enough to kill me—not right away. Which means you need to know something only I can answer or need me to do something you can't." He smiles, the sort of thing a foolish, hopeful little snip like Eithne would've probably found charm-ing. "Either way, I'm perfectly willing to talk terms."

I don't move but flick my red right hand into claws and thrust them to prick his throat, five scab-black scalpels cupping his larynx, freezing him where he stands. The smile collapses; he holds very still. I shudder in a breath.

"Fuck your terms," I growl. "Just tell me why."

"Care t' be more specific, luv?"

The words are insouciant; the look in his eyes isn't. I like— *She*—likes that.

"Blood cries out," I tell him. "From the ground, where Eithne Morden fell. And off of Colville's hands, after."

He swallows. "Still. . . not quite getting the reference, darlin'. I mean, I'd *like* to be helpful, but—"

"Petra. . . Colville," I say, very clear. "Detective Inspector. Same one as you geased into murder, so I fucking *know* you know the name. And workers like you don't believe in karma, mate, but right now? Only thing between you and permanent payback is whether or not I buy your reasons, so spill it."

His eyes narrow. "'Workers like me,'" he repeats, softly. "Meaning—you're not, or you couldn't have gotten in here. But you know someone who *is,* someone who had to untangle this spell for you, this geas you say I laid. . ." His mouth twitches like he's about to smile again, before he visibly stifles it; so earnest, I almost want to laugh. "Now I think on it, p'raps you're right. It *is* about reasons. Just not mine."

"What—" I cut myself off an instant too late; he's heard it, and the doubt behind it. He relaxes, as I kick myself.

"Just think it through," he says, and I still want to gut him, just for the condescension in his voice. "Eithne Whassername, this cop who killed 'er—catspaws, all the way down. And now you, playing judge-jury-hangman on a stranger, just on someone else's word? You telling me it never occurred to you, even once, how maybe I'm not the mage you're lookin' for?"

I want to scream, but I don't. Just point out: "The sigil, though. It's yours."

"I'm hardly the only bloke in my craft who uses sigils, for all we're *mostly* blokes; Magick-with-a-K 101, that is. But there's at least one who isn't, so ask yourself—"

I want to tear off Traeger's head and wallow in the gush. I want to smash this pentagram and let in every invisible horror it's keeping out. But however good that rage tastes, I know—*She* knows—its target isn't here. Which sets Madam and me all a-tremble, both: called Her up for retribution, so that's what I owe her; the punishments for abusing our links to Her made for some of Nani's most horrific bedtime stories, back when. But if I'm wrong and he's right, the mistake I've made, not to mention why I've made it. . . oh, hell.

"—who was it identified that particular work as *mine,* exactly?"

The dead don't lie, though it's not like they can't, more like they don't want to. Why would they? *People* lie. Bloody people, like Traeger, though he's not lying now—not when I can see inside him, through Madam's eyes.

No, he's not the liar here. Neither of us are. The liar. . .

. . . she's somewhere else, entirely; in her own studio, probably, bent over a bloody black mirror, eagerly scrying to see what I do next. While already having metaphorically washed even the faintest trace of the blood she sent me to shed from her beautiful, long-fingered white hands.

And meanwhile, Traeger, too blithe now to be anything but innocent—of this, at least. He keeps nattering on, obliviously.

"Don't think I'm not grateful, mind. Never averse to knowing about a gap in my work, even if you're likely to be the only one I ever heard of could fit through it—" He brightens, suddenly. "Wait a bit: Bloody *karma,* yeah, which makes you that Paki corpse-fiddler Caelia's taken up with. Venus over Mars, Scorpio rising. . . the last *Mirwani* in London, as I live and breathe." His grin is wide and malicious. "*Thought* I smelled curry."

All that steadies us is Eithne's soundless whisper, somewhere deep within: *Not finished yet.* So, I master the blood-golem with a final tremor of will, letting myself float backwards, towards the door.

"Got my eye on you, arsehole," I tell him, no longer bothering to cloak my voice. "Remember that."

He shrugs. "You and a hundred others, luv."

Bastard.

Peccai-ji Madam allows me one tiny indulgence, for the disrespect. I spit at him. The blood sizzles on his cheek like eggs hitting a smoking pan; he bellows in shock and fury, and I take with me the immensely satisfying sight of him slapping at his face and dancing like a circus monkey, before I snap back out to the street in a flickering whirlwind of power.

I almost lose my shape in the process, spiralling over the city in a crimson cloud, but rage is still holding me together. I know where I have to go.

The Five-Pointed Star is still open, and I barely need to wait at all—like magic (ha)—before I see who it is I'm here to find, stumbling out, piss-drunk: Colville, alone this time, looking torn between laughter and nausea. I swirl 'round her, nudging her into an alley mouth, where she finally gives in to the latter. Only when the spasms are finished does she realize there's a figure standing over her. Give her credit, though; once she knows she's not alone, her gun comes out and up with *amazing* speed.

"*Back* off, assho—"

But then her eyes rise further, meet the gaze of the Red Madam, and her jaw drops. The gun wavers in unsteady hands. *Peccai-ji* and I take it from her, almost gently, tossing it aside. Then we spread our arms, as if to embrace her.

Threads of blood, fine as spider silk whip out from the Madam's face, lash across the air between us and sink into Colville: her eyes, her nose, her lips, her temples, her ears. She tries to shriek and can't; her head goes back in spasm, and her arms fly out and lock stiff. Memory kicks awake the buried echo within, turning over a folded layer, and we all three watch together as Colville stares slackly into the mirror of a ladies' bog while *someone* reached over her shoulder from behind, traces the sigil on her forehead. Can't really see the face under that blur of moving light Caelia's angel's halo makes when she's wearing it instead of it wearing her, but it's a mere instant's work to substitute Traeger's self-satisfied mug before showing Colville how the rest plays out, in full surround sound and Technicolour.

Give anything to avert my eyes from Eithne's suffering again, but the Queen makes me stay steady; I'm here to be a witness for Colville, this time, and pay the price for my own blind trust at the same time. Briefly, I wonder what's more awful for a copper —the realization of what she was made to do, or just how easy it was to make her do it. By the end, Colville's on the filthy ground hunched up, bawling like a baby, and I'm feeling sick at myself for wishing I could still hate her.

"*They will come for you,*" *Peccai-ji Madam* tells her, with my voice. "*Stay or run, as you choose. But now you see how it was done and might be done yet once more.*"

('Cause who's to say Traeger's never run this game on anyone, after all? And better yet. . . now I see why Caelia sent me this way, at him. He deserves *some* sort of justice for the part he's played in all this ruin, even if it's only the kind Colville dishes out when she's mad enough.)

Oh Lala, Nani would sigh, disappointed, if she saw how easy it is for me to point any human being at another, like a gun. But not our Madam.

She simply licks her teeth and laughs.

Without warning, then, Her power disintegrates around me in a burst of blind dark. There's a sickening plummeting sensation in my guts, horribly familiar, right before I slam back into my circle-bound body, the hot slick blood covering me gone instantly to cold, dry powder. And all the strength goes out of me at once, a blown-out candle flame, as I topple over, with barely time enough to close my eyes.

When I wake, hours later, my hair is matted redly to the floor by that ghastly bruise-slash- scrape 'cross the back of my head, throbbing like a hangover times twenty. Even my teeth hurt.

I failed, Nani, I think through the pounding ache. *I failed Her. And you.*

(But: *No, child,* comes her sweet, dry voice, full of awful understanding. *No, never. You* were *failed, is all. As so often happens, amongst humans.*)

And: *Yeah,* I think, lying there, beyond exhausted. *True enough.* Fuck if I wasn't.

———

Caelia's waiting for me again when her penthouse lift doors roll open, but fully dressed this time, and not smiling: no surprise, there. What hurts more than I expect is that she's carrying her walking stick with her, polished oak carved with charcoaled runes—whimsical fashion accessory to the normies, deadly weapon to anyone with the Sight to see it for what it is. I look at it, then her.

"Bloody really?"

"Had to be sure," she says, without a flicker of shame. She steps back, gesturing me to the living room. Two glasses of wine are already poured, waiting. I sink down on the couch and pick up one, but only moisten my lips with it, wondering how far it'd go if thrown. Caelia sits beside me, carefully, the stick still close enough to reach. She's studying me like she's never seen me before, or not quite *this* clearly.

And all the while her angel-shadow ripples back and forth over the carpet beneath us, a cat's tail twitching, if that cat was made from power; turns its black outline of a head towards me now, though Caelia's gaze has shifted to my glass instead.

"Not in the mood for red, for once, I see," she notes, so coolly the joke barely registers. Which makes the shadow tilt its head even further, same way some people do when they're smiling, if it only had a mouth to smile with.

"Not sure if you knew it was a possibility, Cee, when you first set this thing in motion," I tell her, still looking at my wine, "but you almost got me killed last night. Very badly."

"That was never my intention, Lala."

"Yeah, well, even so." I really do take a sip, this time, just for luck, before setting the glass down, gingerly; delicious, of course. Expensive too, probably.

Too bad it tastes like blood.

"Not to mention how Eithne *is* dead, still," I point out, meanwhile. "Always will be."

"Yet Traeger's still alive."

"Was when I left, yeah—still is, far as I know." I angle myself to face her, letting the rage

inside me show, if only just a bit; enough to sting, but only if she ever really gave a damn. Suggesting, as I do: "Maybe *you* should do something about that, this time, it bothers you so bloody much."

She doesn't flinch, not quite. "Maybe I would, if I could."

"Oh, I'll bet *that* would, if you asked it," I snap back, pointing down. "But then. . . there'd be a price, yeah? One *you*'d have to pay, personally."

"Yes," she agrees, and looks away, voice very small. "There would be."

"So. Better to geas some mundy into murder and set up some poor bitch to get killed; would've happened sooner or later, anyhow, the way they were both going. Better to lie to a. . . *friend*, make her almost break the only bloody law that *matters*, aside from gravity. . ."

"Lala, for Christ's sake, I never meant to hurt you. Not *you*."

"But you *did* hurt me, Cee, quite a lot, as it turns out. More than I expected, if I'm honest. And all that stops now."

I get up, and Caelia follows, stepping back. The cane's in her hand. Around her high heels, the angel-shadow coils and puffs itself, trembling with anticipation: *Use me, oh use me, let me go. Let me fly at this creature who dares to question us and teach her a lesson that will burn her to the soul.*

All it would take is a twitch of those skillful fingers, but she doesn't do it. Just dips her head a bit and replies, without preamble:

"Would it help if I told you what he did to me, as part of my apprenticeship? How he. . . broke me, as payment for teaching me?" Here she stops and swallows, wincing in what looks like actual pain, something I've never seen her register before. "I can't remember the person I used to be, Lala—and no, I'm not overstating it; that's just the truth, plain and simple. I'm *owed* vengeance for that, surely."

I surprise myself with my own calmness. "Absolutely. But so's Colville, and Eithne—so'm *I*, for fuck's sake. You fucked us all to collect on your debts when you could've just done it yourself, you'd really believed it was worth the risk."

"If I could have attacked him directly, don't you think I would have? He made sure never to teach me anything he couldn't already ward against. I've spent fifteen years trying to find something he didn't know, and nothing ever worked. Until. . . until you."

"Then why didn't you just *ask* me? I'd've done it for you, myself, you just *asked*. If you'd told me the truth."

At this, she gets up and starts pacing, cane still clasped, now for comfort.

"I was afraid," she finally says. "That you'd be angry, at first —that you'd think all I wanted you for was the trick. And then. . . then I was afraid you'd say no; tell me I'd survived, so I should be grateful, and move on. I couldn't've borne that."

"That's someone else you're thinking of, Cee."

"Is it?" She turns on me. "You walked away! Left him upright even though he'll come after me next, now he knows I set you on him. . ."

"Because it would have damned my soul, I hadn't!" The spark burns hot, but it fades fast: all I feel now is tired. Numb. "I have *laws* I follow, Cee, just like you; magic's no different than the rest of the world that way. You don't get what you want, ever, if you're not prepared to pay. So again, if you want him dead so badly, why don't you just run him down, like a normal bloody person? Buy a gun, a knife—buy a man *with* a gun, or knife?" Caelia clenches her teeth, aggravating me further. "Or is that too messy, too personal? Too up-close-and-risky?"

"I'd end up in gaol."

"With *that* following you 'round? Seems unlikely."

The angel-shadow punches up even higher, fawning on her, lapping at her calves: *Let me, oh, let ME.* But she just shivers, eyes tight on mine, till just looking at her is enough to make me tired.

"Okay, then," I say, quieter. "Then I guess you'll just have to do what the rest of us do, when somebody kicks us in the teeth for fun and pisses off, laughing. . . learn to *bloody live with it.*"

For a second, I almost think I see what might be a flicker of shame cross her face, but it's gone long before she looks away. Then her voice goes cool and light once more as she shrugs, blonde hair swinging. Asking, as she does—

"Very well. So. . . what are you going to do about it?"

"Not much I *can* do, can I? I mean, take away the whole magic angle and the whole thing sounds like I lost my mind— you're still white, still cis, still rich; my word against yours won't mean much, 'specially when they search my flat and find my Nani's head. I'm just a grimy little foreign fortune-teller from a long line of such, buggering idiots out of their dosh with tricks— exotic, but untrustworthy. Must've been what you liked about me."

"Oh, Lala. It was so much more than that."

I almost believe her.

And: *You know nothing*—something—says suddenly, inside my head: a voice that's nothing like one, plucked and tingling like a harp-strung nerve. I barely manage to control my start, glancing back at Caelia, who hasn't moved. Can she really not hear it, even with the thing it's coming from rising to darken her thighs, sending reversed wing-pinions up to graze her shoulder-blades and shrug themselves around her like a wrap, a not-quite-living clasp, pumping power into her through her pores?

You who ask no questions except of raw meat, of dripping juice, opening your flesh wide to the Queen of all Decay. How dare you touch my vessel, whether or not she allows it? Half childish sneer and half echoing roar, a fleshless waterfall of contempt. *At least* this one *knew the terms of her bargain when she made it, well enough to not make more.*

You're welcome to her, is what I want to tell it, in return. But even now. . . even now, I don't believe that. If Caelia ever asked me to help her shuck this awful thing from her, I would.

But: *Be grateful she has never thought to,* the thing whispers back, growing even further, eclipsing Caelia's outline till she narrows all over, an air-starved flame. *You would. . .you will. . .die trying.*

And she doesn't even seem to notice, that's the truly terrifying thing, just leans forward, smile returning, sadder than it's ever been. And tells me: "I know you don't believe me, but it's true. And I did miss you too, Lala. I still do."

I lean forward as well, kiss her slowly, let my tongue taste hers and suck her breath deep inside me one last time, drunk on it in an instant. But when she finally lifts her hands to pull me against her, I just back away.

"Good," I say. "Keep on missing me, then."

And turn, punch the elevator's button, never looking back. It's harder than I expected.

Maybe she watches me, maybe she doesn't. The angel-shadow stays where it is, folding around her like a cloak, humming its satisfaction at my departure. But already, inside Caelia's mouth, the drop of blood I worried from the inside of my cheek which holds Eithne Morden's last memory will have already vanished through the mucous membranes underneath her tongue, its transit powered by the heat of our kiss. Within days, its colonization of her cells will be too advanced to stop. It will spread and spread, reproducing as it goes, turning the insane complexity of Caelia's microcosmic interior universe against her, slow but steady, impossible to alter.

Because here's what I know, the wisdom of mere meat and juice, the Fleshly mantra: How we're all one vast intersection, a decay-bent machine that runs on balance, a series of interlocking systems, chaos theory in action; so incredibly easy to disrupt catastrophically, with so little effort. So maybe it'll be cancer, or a thickening of the blood, an aneurysm, a heart attack; maybe her immune system will detonate in a cytokine storm. By the time she understands what's happening, it'll be too late; her angel will desert her, flee the sinking ship like a mutiny.

This is the problem with a separation of magics, all drawing what must surely be the same basic power, but for very different things.

Very, very different.

———

The next text I answer from ARSEHOLE NUMBER TEN, Satya comes to get me himself, gesturing me into the passenger seat of his car. Colville isn't with him. When I get in, he doesn't pull the car out right away. Doesn't seem able to look at me, either.

"Did you know?" he asks me eventually.

"Wasn't her idea, mate," I tell him, already knowing it won't help. "I can't prove it, but. . ."

"Whereas forensics *could* prove she did it, no matter why. And did." He sits there a second, considering whether or not to tell me the rest, as I just wait. "She wasn't there when they came to arrest her, so they tracked her phone to some office building and found her just sitting there on the steps outside, another corpse at her feet. Some nob named Traeger—a 'consultant,' that's all his cards said. I asked her why she did it, when they brought her in. 'Didn't like his face,' was all she said."

"I'm sorry, for what it's worth." A pause. "Don't guess I'll be seeing you again, hm?"

No reply. But—he just keeps on. Sitting there.

Until I suggest, delicately: "Unless. . . you have something for me."

A long moment crawls by, before he finally meets my eyes, and I can see his answer.

A lot of corpses in this city. A lot of dead people with no name, and no one else to ask them for it. Their blood, crying out from the ground.

"Please," he says. I sigh.

"My pleasure," I reply.

———

By which I mean, my duty.

ECHO
CHAMBER

From: Creepgal1991@gmail.com
To: ross.puget@freihoeveninst.ca
Re: TRYING TO TRACK THIS DOWN, CAN YOU HELP

You don't know me, and I don't know you, but we have friends in common through the Freihoeven Institute, which is how I got this email (obviously). I have a podcast transcript, but no podcast to go with it—the podcaster appears to have deleted the file and disappeared, so I can't get in touch with them. Everything else is still up on the website, except that episode. No one's answering the main contact email anymore, and the company hosting the podcast isn't responding either. It's not a big deal, but I'd like to be completist (again, obviously).

Not sure if you've ever heard of The Weal, but it started out as a sort of alternative to a shortwave "college" radio show done over at Mundiplex (scare quotes around college, because Mundiplex is a straight-up diploma mill specializing in whatever lures Ontario HS grads to take out government educational loans —music production, CGI, SP/FX, etc.), but in podcast form, ostensibly because the team couldn't go into the studio anymore due to COVID. The host/deejay, Meander Denny, also has an ASMR YouTube channel; that's not updating either, now.

I started listening to her there as self-care when my anxiety was spiking, blah, blah, blah. So, while I was binging through those, she started cross-promoting The Weal, and I subscribed to that too. Liked it a lot, especially since she seemed to program most of it out of her personal music collection, and I'd never heard most of the stuff she tended to fall back on (all this late '80s, early '90s stuff, on vinyl and tape? Her producer must be some sort of old dead tech addict too. Or was).

I don't know much about Denny, aside from what's still available online. Not even if that was really her name. The whole website is super-rudimentary, like they just heard a bunch of Pacific Northwest Stories ads for Squarespace.com and ran with them (check out that shit they set up for The Black Tapes, you'll see what I mean). And just like with TBT, the actual transcripts are done by somebody else on Reddit, probably the same person who moderates r/TheWeal. Which *also* hasn't been updated since they posted this, come to think, hidey hidey hoooooo.

Anyhow. I guess I just tend to get obsessive (that's why they call it OCD, ha ha), but if you could help me out with this quest of mine, I sure do need some. People speak highly of your Weird Crap Locating skillz, and I'm gonna shut up now; read the attached, tell me what you think, yes/no.

All best, stay safe, whatever.

Ulee Schaw (you can get me here or by DM on TwitterX, @Creepgal1991, that's me)

PS: . . . Carra Devize says to say hey, so hey.

———

@rpuget hey, got your email. you want me to find a copy of the episode, that it?

@Creepgal1991 oh hey hi!!!! yeah that would be cool, but if you can't then maybe just the song shes talking about???

@rpuget sorry, what song was that?

@Creepgal1991 dude seriously did you read the attached or what???

@rpuget you know you can use just one question mark, right?

@rpuget okay, sorry, bad night last night. i read the first couple of pages. tell me what song you're talking about, i'll look.

@Creepgal1991 millennial much? don't feel like you have to humour me.

@rpuget kid, c'mon.

@Creepgal1991 fine, okay. its called sheetshake by yseult haight. dont bother googling her discography, she never officially recorded it. its actually not even supposed to exist.

@rpuget okay, that's never good.

@Creepgal1991 :D :D :D i know, right?! seriously, go read what meander says about it. ill wait.

@rpuget don't doubt it.

———

TRANSCRIPT: "THE WEAL", EP. 73, *orig. broadcast 2/11/2021*

DENNY: Hi, kids. I'm Meander Denny, and this is The Weal.

As you all know, or should, I'm a huge fan of musical oddities, especially ones from female artists. And one of the oddest ladies to ever make music may have been Yseult Haight, former British child model and actress turned self-taught multi-instrumentalist, music producer and performance artist. Over the course of her surprisingly long and completely unsuccessful career, she and various collaborators recorded under a variety of band names: Night Mouths, Blood Spire, Corpse Medicine, Arsenic Sword; Wolf-Whore and Glad of War and Prey for Worms; Sweat Trench and Plague Box and We Are All Made of Blood. As London rock critic Jo Gaiters once put it, back in 1999 (TERRIBLE COCKNEY ACCENT): "That girl changes bands more often than she changes her underwear. . . and considering how rarely she performs wearing anything else but lingerie, that's sayin' something."

. . . sorry about that. (LAUGHTER)

All of Haight's projects read as some subset of goth; she was doom before doom, gloom before gloom, and consistently occult-referential. The one I want to talk about today was supposed to be included on her final album, *Memento Vivere*, the one that came out after her disappearance from public life; half the critics out there think it's her best work and the other half call it a spectacular public flameout. My own impulse is to say, "Both, both—both are good." Well, not *good* in this case, but true, anyway, because even if you don't remember the album, you just might have heard of this song—the song which isn't supposed to exist, the song the record execs pulled from the album before it came out, the song that *Rolling Stone* critic said was—hang on here, I wrote this down: "Based on the description alone, I'm confident it will prove the *ne plus ultra* of either sheer genius or pretentious bullshit."

(LAUGHS) It's called "Sheetshake".

Odd title, right? Haight said it derived most directly from a song called "The Shaking of the Sheets," possibly written sometime in the seventeenth century, and eventually recorded by classic British folk-rock band Steeleye Span. Themed after the mediaeval *danza macabra* or Dance of Death, it was a meditation on basic human existentialism through the lens of the Black Death, the Great Mortality—the bubonic plague, brought via flea-infested rats, which raged through Europe from 1347 to 1351 and killed either seventy-five or two hundred million people, with no distinctions made between saints or sinners, aristocrats or peasants, old or young, hale or lame, beautiful or ugly. The sheets being shaken here are winding-sheets, grave cerements; the central image is an endless parade of corpses dancing in a huge circle, spinning round and round, but always willing to make room for one more.

"As you are now, so once was I; as I am now, so shall you be." Sound familiar?

Haight being Haight, though, there are loads more influences at work here—a lot more resonances, or perhaps assonances. During the Black Death, for example, penitents who believed the plague was an apocalyptic God's punishment for humankind's wickedness roamed from city to city in an ecstasy of self-harm; they'd whip themselves bloody and march until they died of shock, infection, exsanguination or starvation, tranced out and singing hymns to the very last—like a crowd of naked, bony, musical zombies, the literal Walking Dead.

And after that, you get another odd phenomenon: In July 1518, a woman named Frau Troffea suddenly began "to dance fervently" in the middle of a Strasbourg street, in the heart of the Holy Roman Empire. Not only did she keep it up herself for weeks, others began to join in—over four hundred at final count, many collapsing, even dying from heart attack or stroke. Most psychologists believe this "Dancing Epidemic" was an incident of stress-related religious mass hysteria, though other people have since blamed things like demonic possession, epilepsy or convulsive ergotism—the same thing that *might* have caused the

Salem Witch Trials. One way or the other, it seemed to start tapering off after sufferers made a pilgrimage to the shrine of Saint Vitus, which is why convulsions of any sort have sometimes been called St Vitus's Dance.

Here's the really weird thing, though. At the height of the Dancing Epidemic, not only were the main symptoms dancing—jigging in place and flailing a lot, at any rate—but the recommended cure was *also* supposed to be dancing. By September 1518, Strasbourg's government had set up a stage in the town square where musicians would continually perform to help the shuffling, bone-weary "infected" keep going without succumbing to fainting or seizures. And what was the music they played to make these people dance? No one knows, not for sure. Could it have been something like "Sheetshake"?

Or think about this: We all know the one about how that old familiar kindergarten rhyme "Ring Around the Rosies" is *really* about the Black Death—how the rosies are buboes, the pocket full of posies are herbs and flowers used to ward off either infection or the smell of rotting corpses, and "ashes, ashes, we all fall down" is about how bodies would be collected in carts, dumped into plague pits and then sprinkled with quicklime and ash before being buried. But what about the "ring around" or "ringa ringa" part? It almost sounds like a description of infected people dancing in a circle, so long and so intensely that they eventually fall over and die. . . and then what? The others just keep on dancing over them until *they* die, and so on, and so on? Until there's no one left?

————

r/lostmusic [PRIVATE] • 1 day ago
by **creepgal1991**
COMMUNICATION THREAD FOR YH SONG PROJECT

Hi, whoever gets the login information to post to this thread, I'm really looking forward to meeting you and getting started on the project!

mlhenderson • 19 hours ago
I'm assuming from the alias that this is Ulee Schaw? My name is Morgan Henderson, Ross Puget gave me your contact details and suggested I could be of use to you. Touchy stuff first: I charge £20/hr for my services, plus expenses, three-hour minimum, and if I need to go into risky areas of the dark net, I ask for a £2,000 deposit for emergency legal expenses up front (returned if not needed). Nowadays that should be roughly $2,500 USD.

creepgal1991 • 19 hours ago
Wow, okay, that's more of a commitment than I expected. Is the deposit necessary?

mlhenderson • 19 hours ago
No, but it may limit my ability to find what you're looking for, especially if the original file is extremely old and obscure, which Ross's description suggests it is. There are some servers it can be legally dangerous to find your login credentials on, even if you never touch a single file.

creepgal1991 • 19 hours ago
It's just a song. Where do you think it's going to turn up? On an ISIS web forum?

mlhenderson • 19 hours ago
It's data. It could be anywhere. You have to decide how much finding it's worth to you.

creepgal1991 • 19 hours ago
You get right to the point, don't you?

mlhenderson • 19 hours ago
I'm trying to save us both time. I've had people try to back out of paying before. For what it's worth, I'm more inclined to believe you *because* you're balking at the price. People who plan on cheating me from the beginning tend not to protest.

creepgal1991 • 19 hours ago
Well, you know what? Okay. It's more than I expected, but I'm serious about this, and Ross says you're really good, so it's an investment, right? Send me the e-transfer address.

mlhenderson • 19 hours ago
Will do

mlhenderson • 18 hours ago
If it's any reassurance, your request piqued my curiosity. Mostly my clients are ad companies who want me to find lost copies of '60s and '70s commercial jingles, so they can make sure they're not breaching copyright somewhere. You're an intriguing change.

creepgal1991 • 18 hours ago
Thanks, I think?

———

TRANSCRIPT: "THE WEAL", EP. 73 (*cont'd*)

DENNY: In woodcuts, murals or bas reliefs of the Dance of Death found in churches all over Europe, the skeletons are often depicted playing instruments as they lead freshly-dead humans through the *danza macabra:* flutes, violins, drums, bagpipes, hurdy-gurdys. Interestingly, these are all instruments Yseult Haight could—and did—play, looping individual tracks through playback rigs and layering them around her vocals as she performed live. She was also fascinated by ancient musical traditions such as mouth music, vocal percussion, and drones, as popularized by Real World Music artists like Sheila Chandra, Iarla Ó Lionáird and the Tsinandali Choir—and this is where we get another one of those weird, maybe not so coincidental parallels. Because sadly, much like Sheila Chandra's, Haight's career would come to an abrupt, screeching end in 2011, when she suddenly announced she'd been diagnosed with "burning mouth" syndrome.

What BMS consists of is exactly what the name suggests, basically—a constant burning or scalding sensation in your mouth and throat. Sufferers report that it makes speaking above a whisper, let alone singing, unspeakably agonizing. However, it primarily affects postmenopausal women and is defined by its lack of identifiable medical cause, so strangely enough, it doesn't grab a lot of headlines or research attention—the word "psychosomatic" gets thrown around a lot. Why doctors think people like Chandra or Haight would give up their music if they didn't have to—or why they'd need to make up an excuse, if they decided they *wanted* to—is beyond me, but God forbid we take women at their word.

Anyway, after Haight announced she'd developed BMS during the recording sessions for *Memento Vivere*, and that it would be her last album, ticket sales for her last concert performance went through the roof. . . which doesn't sound good either, does it, in terms of "oh boy, THIS isn't some sort of scam."

Still: cynicism's easy, sincerity's hard. And nobody goes to the sort of effort Haight went to while putting "Sheetshake" together without being *very* sincere indeed about. . . something.

Maybe just about going out with a bang, if nothing else.

"Sheetshake" is one of what Haight's fans call her Ghost Tracks, the songs that she liked to perform by improvising around what she claimed were actual paranormal "ghost box"

EVP recordings that she'd play as a backing track. For extra punch, she liked to do this in venues she and her groups claimed were haunted; I don't know if any of them *were*, but I can tell you there is a documented incident of Haight applying to play in the famous Winchester House and getting denied. *That* would have been a concert worth paying a couple thousand bucks for; fuck you, Taylor Swift. (LAUGHTER)

One early Ghost Track, for example, was layered over an EVP supposedly recording the last breaths of an Englishwoman who died giving birth to an equally dead baby in what had formerly been a tuberculosis hospital during the post-World War I influenza pandemic. I'm amazed the entire audience didn't run out of there puking pea soup when she played *that* one, and I don't even *believe* in EVP.

Anyway, getting to the point: when Yseult Haight held her very last performance, ever, she held it in the French cave system called La Grotte des Chuchotement—the "Cave of Whispering," a series of caverns near Dordogne where French peasants went to hide from, guess what? That's right: the Black Death. Motifs coming full circle, here.

Even that isn't the end of it, though. See, some archaeologists think this may have also been a site for pagan ritual, going back all the way through Celtic France to prehistoric times. A sacred place where certain people sacrificed themselves to the spirit of whatever might be threatening their tribe—famine, plague, predators either human or inhuman—in order to save everyone else. Because deep inside the caves, you see, they've found full and partial skeletons laid out in painstakingly excavated rock shelves: young people, strong people, their bodies excarnated by hand and then re-encased in mud mixed with yellow ochre, surrounded by dried flowers.

Even stranger, each skeleton was apparently buried with a polished quartz stone inside their lower jawbone, where their tongue should have been. Proof that the tribesmen and women thus interred might have actually competed for this honour. In that the stones swapped for tongues might have been 'drawn' in some sort of lottery. . . but this is all theory, obviously; I might be letting my freak flag fly.

Well, whatever—I don't believe it, necessarily, but Yseult Haight might have. So, from her POV, if there was ever a place you could listen to the dead, those caves would be it.

And this is where Haight played "Sheetshake" for the first and last time, a ballad she wrote based on—as she put it—"a long history of plague songs and poems," layered over an hour of ambient tone they took the night before. This, they assumed, couldn't fail to include various EVP. "Whatever we pick up, we'll use," Haight apparently told her fans, in what would become her final tweet. And the thing they hoped to pick up was a trail of plague stuff going back, back, back, possibly forever.

Okay, right now I can hear you all saying, "But Meander, if nobody ever *recorded* this song, how do you know she played it there?" Well, there *is* a recording, supposedly. Something claimed to be one at least. The story is, a fan had one of the very first smartphones with them, one with a good enough mic and camera to record live music, and snuck it into the Grotte, intent on capturing not so much the *song,* as the moment—Haight's last performance. And the .mp3 that came out of that has been floating around odd corners of the internet for nearly fifteen years, copied and recopied, remixed and resampled, until God knows whether anything from the original's left of it at all.

I keep saying "last," don't I? That's because while everyone who attended Haight's performance at La Grotte has clear memories of rocking out until they essentially fell into some sort of trance, waking up the next morning either still shuffling or at rest where they fell, none of them seem to have any idea what happened to Yseult Haight—not even her own musical cohort. I guess it's not hard to vanish off the grid if you're barely on it to begin with; whatever fame Haight's name comes attached to has always existed mainly in the minds of those obsessed with her, after all, like me. And yet: Here we are, left behind, with only a song to tell us where she might have gone. An impossible song.

Ever notice how when people say you can't have something, that's when you start to want it most? Or how just the fact that something's known to be lost makes you utterly *determined* to find it?

Well. . . I did, I think.

And in a moment or so, I'm going to play it for all of you.

———

From:Morgan Henderson mlhenderson233@yahoo.co.uk
To:Ulee Schaw Creepgal1991@gmail.com
Re:YH Song Project, Report #1

Dear Ms. Schaw,

I've attached the itemized report for the first week of my investigation—you'll see I've discounted the first three hours as a gesture of good faith, since I reassured you in previous emails that I expected to be done well before this. I still believe a telephone conversation would be useful to us both, but I understand the time zone difficulties.

You'll also note that I've attached a second file; this is a transcript of an interview I had with a historian at a London college, someone who specializes in mediaeval music and the communities who fetishize it. You may or may not find it relevant to deciding whether to continue.

Regards,

Morgan Henderson

———

TRANSCRIPT P 2/3
MH/DR L BRAZDA, NEWCOMB COLLEGE 5/9/2024

LB (CONT'D): must understand, it is misleading to think of a "song" as a specific performance or arrangement. It is more useful to see a piece in terms of its, let us say, its DNA—its position in a line of descent, like a set of mitochondrial markers, connecting different versions to each other throughout age after age. In terms of the particular piece of music your client is looking for, there are works sharing its heritage in nearly every era since the Black Death, or even before. In Elizabethan England it was a drinking song called "The Dancing Girls." In Germany, during the Thirty Years' War, it was a funeral lament called "Sie legte morgens ihren Kopf hin," which means roughly, "She lay down her head in the morning." Then there's a nineteenth-century ragtime tune, sometimes credited erroneously to Scott Joplin, called "Putting On the Devil's Shoes."

And the line goes on, through Tin Pan Alley, some blues tunes from the '50s just before Elvis Presley hit it big, even samples in some music from the '80s and afterwards. Like a taproot system, underlying and connecting all the trees of the forest. One never simply "listens to music," Miss Henderson. Every song carries history with it. More than most people can, or will, ever know.

MH: And the folklore around it is part of this. . . this root system? This DNA?

LB: Well, yes, if you believe in that sort of thing. Many of my friends in the historical recovery communities do; others do not. I wish to stay friends with both groups, so I take no position.

MH: But you'd no doubt agree that the number of deaths and

disappearances reported around performances of these songs is. . . atypical, if true.

LB: What is "typical," Miss Henderson? Music was doubtless playing in proximity to nearly any death or disaster in history. "Amazing Grace" is played at thousands of funerals every year. Is it cursed?

MH: That isn't an answer, exactly.

LB: No. It isn't, is it?

———

TRANSCRIPT: "THE WEAL," EP. 73 (*cont'd*)

DENNY: Our special guest today is sound engineer Mike Purvis, who I've invited in to, in his words, "fuck around with this track and see what we end up with." Say hi to everyone, Mike.

PURVIS: Hi to everyone, Mike.

DENNY: (LAUGHTER) Dude, you promised.

PURVIS: Yeah, I promise a lot of things.

DENNY: So I've heard. (LAUGHTER) Okay, enough banter. Tell us about exactly what you're going to do here.

PURVIS: Well, the first step is basically to start the song playing, then run it through what we call a separation filter, which should give us the ability to pare the song back to its, um. . . formative layers? Remove the ambience, the crowd sound, remove the instrumentation and/or looping level by level, remove the vocals, until we disclose whatever's at the bottom of everything.

DENNY: The Ghost Track. The EVP.

PURVIS: Yep, that's the one. You down?

DENNY: Always.

————

FINAL INTERVIEW WITH YSEULT HAIGHT, *Palimpsest* Magazine, August 2010 (unpublished, due to magazine going out of business in June of that year):

HAIGHT: There's a line in a song I like—"Kala," by Bill Laswell, from his album *City of Light*. It's about watching bodies being reduced to ash on a ghat in Varanasi, about giving up your flesh and embracing impermanence: *Once the breath goes out, it's fit to burn.* And this is something I've come to accept, as a singer, as a musician—that breath is the centre of human existence, not just physically, but creatively. Breath can heal and breath can harm. It allows you to manipulate other people's emotions—to soothe them, to seduce them, to enrage them, to provoke fear and confusion. When people talk about psychic vampirism, I truly believe what they're often actually talking about is this sort of vocal work. They just don't realize it.

INTERVIEWER: Like a cat sucking a baby's breath while it's asleep? Or like SIDS?

HAIGHT: You may very well laugh, and yet.

INTERVIEWER: Miss Haight, I'm not laughing.

HAIGHT: Aren't you? (PAUSE) It's been proven there are certain tones the mind finds extremely difficult to deal with, and while they're hard to reproduce vocally, it's not impossible. Throat singers do it, for example, especially in unison. Shamanistic meditation employs it as well; breath is used to invoke and evoke, to create a numinous, ritual state in which the performer convinces those around them that they're entering an alternate dimension where spirits might appear. At any rate, breath keeps you going, and at the end, it's all you have left. One last, long exhalation. That's why live performance is so important— because you're all sharing a breath, together. The crowd responds to you, and you respond to them, and something is created that otherwise would never exist except at that moment.

INTERVIEWER: So a song played live becomes a different song, is that what you're saying?

HAIGHT: *Part* of what I'm saying, yes. It becomes something that can only be understood in that exact context. Something impossible to reproduce, under any circumstances.

INTERVIEWER: You're not a fan of live recordings.

HAIGHT: No more than I'm a fan of bad taxidermy.

INTERVIEWER: Tell me about "Sheetshake."

HAIGHT: Ah yes. "Sheetshake" will be played once and once only, by design. What it becomes in that moment will be *very* interesting. And the rest. . . will be silence.

———

@mlhenderson found it

@Creepgal1991 the ep????

@mlhenderson obviously, yes

@Creepgal1991 holy shit dude how????

@mlhenderson contacted mike purvis' partner, as it happens

@mlhenderson he himself is in hospital, but the other gentleman was very helpful indeed

@Creepgal1991 in hospital?? why??

@mlhenderson some sort of mental breakdown, I believe. and exhaustion

@mlhenderson they found him in the mundiplex studio, passed out, marching fractures to both feet

@mlhenderson his partner says there've been surgeries scheduled

@mlhenderson attaching the .mp3 to my bill

@mlhenderson do tell me what you think, after

@Creepgal1991 thanks, will do!!!

@Creepgal1991 did mike say what happened to meander????

@mlhenderson miss denny? I believe not

@mlhenderson his partner says he hasn't said anything about anything, thus far

@Creepgal1991 but it's been like a year?!?!?

@mlhenderson even so

@Creepgal1991 well okay

@Creepgal1991 thanks again!!!!!

@Creepgal1991 ps

@Creepgal1991 did you listen???

@mlhenderson absolutely not

———

From:Creepgal1991@gmail.com
To:ross.puget@freihoeveninst.ca
Re:FOUND IT AND NOW I'M GONNA LISTEN

Hey man, just wanted to dash this off to you first, because I'm so! Excited!!!! (Sorry not sorry, back on my Zlennial bullshit again;)) Morgan was a trip, cleaned me out for sure, but it's gonna be worth it. And it's all because of you, you grumpy M-word you (I don't mean motherfucker;))).

Oh shit, my texts are beeping. Is that you????

———

@rpuget hey Ulee, yes it's me, hold off a minute PLEASE

@Creepgal1991 wtf????

@rpuget listen, you know how I know carra, right? You know why?

@Creepgal1991 freihoeven inst creepy shit yeah yeah

@Creepgal1991 fckin SO?!?

@rpuget Morgan got hold of me, she's worried about you

@rpuget and she doesn't GET worried so that worries me

@Creepgal1991 sweet I guess???

@rpuget SHUT UP ULEE

@rpuget MPs bf sent her his emails theres this stuff he and MD talked about beforehand about how MDs mom died of covid, she had COPD lived in a building full of people who wouldn't mask, MD thought YH maybe wanted to use the performance to cure herself but if she did it wouldntve worked because you can only use that place la grotte to cure others by sacrificing yourself ANYHOW ARE YOU LISTENING

@rpuget MD told MP wouldnt it be great if everyone who heard this could be rendered immune to or cured of covid and he said but one of us would have to disappear/die and she said shed be fine w/ that

@rpuget so even if it only makes you dance till you pass out that doesn't sound like anything you want to hear man

@rpuget ulee

@rpuget ulee

. . .

. . .

. . .

@Creepgal1991 already pressed play sorry

————

TRANSCRIPT: "THE WEAL," EP. 73 (*cont'd*)

(MUSIC)
(BEAT)
(BREATH)
(VOICE)
Hmmmmm
Hmmmmm
Hmmmmmm
Hmmmmmm
In and out and round and round
In and out and round and round
Take away the young man take away the old
Every one in his degree
When you hear the music everyone must dance
The shaking of the sheets with me
Low and high together everyone must dance
The shaking of the sheets with me
Hmmmmm
Hmmmmm
Hmmmmmm
Hmmmmmm
In and out and in and out and innnn
and out and in and out and innnn
and round and round and round and round
and round and round and round and round

Adieu, farewell, earth's bliss;
This world uncertain is;
Fond are life's lustful joys;
Death proves them all but toys;
Rich men, trust not in wealth,
Gold cannot buy you health;
Physic himself must fade.
All things to end are made,
Brightness falls from the air;
Queens have died young and fair;
Dust hath closed Helen's eye.
Mount we unto the sky.
I am sick, I must die.
Lord, have mercy on us!
Hmmmmm Hmmmmmm Hmmmmmm Hmmmmmmmmm
and in and out and innnn and round and in and out and innnn
and rrrrrrrounnnddddddd
As. ye. ar. Nou.
So. onc. vas. Ay.
As. Ay. am.
So. Sal. Ye. be.
Remembre. Man.
That. Thou. Mist. dei.
Hmmmm Hmmmmm Hmmmmmm Hmmmmmmm Hmmmm-
mmmmmmmmmmmmmmmmmmmmmmmmmmmm

MEANDER: (UP UNDER) plagues, there's plagues all through
history, and every time a plague happens someone redoes the
song—disease to flesh as distortion is to sound, something that
changes it, sets it against itself, breaks it open, breaks it down.
And La Grotte, the cave is an echo chamber, reverberating—if
you bend a note it becomes something else, in and out and round
and round and in and out and round and round, Pied Piper
plague legend, opening a door through a mountain through

sound

(MUSIC, BEAT, BREATH, VOICE, UP OVER, TOGETHER)

Young
Old
High
Low
Shake
Shake
Shake
Shake
The breath the life the breath the spark the breath makes life
keeps life alive the spark nurtured the air consumed breathe out
breathe in breathe in breathe out
In for fuel and out to heal
Out for song the sound that fuels
The fire that burns away the weal
The weal the weal the weal the weallllllllllllllllllll
and at the moment of death we release the sound that lives
forever that moves forwards backwards into the spaces between
all things the vibrating nothing that makes up everything pure
potential the universal pulse an overlay a retuning a returning a
trance a seizure a frequency no human ears designed to hear
It makes you a receiver
It makes you a speaker
It makes you an echo chamber
The skull the skull the skull the skullllll
Open your jaws and let it come through
Open your jaws and speak
Channeling
Channelllinggg
Channelllllinggggg

The note the beat the beat the note the cut throat's note the skin
drum's beat
And break the skin wide open break the sky wide opennnnnn
the skin the sky the sky the skin the skin the sky the sky the skin
Dance
Dance
Dance
Dance
Dance
DANCE
DANCE
DANCE

ONLY CHILDREN

This morning I woke up blind, face-down; I emerged, thrashing, out of a nest of ghosts. Outside, it was blowing snow; inside, the windows were condensation-frosted and dripping at the base. The dehumidifier blasted. I got up, peed out all my juices, then drank two huge glasses of replacement water. The daily cycle. Lights on everywhere, burning through the night. None of yesterday's chores done. I loaded the dishwasher, started it up, loaded the washer-dryer and did likewise. This whining, uterine churn and slosh against metal walls. I don't know if it's the level best way to start a day, but it's mine.

Busywork does distract from fear, though, if nothing else. And on some level, I'm still afraid—on some level, I'm *always* afraid. Everyone who has a kid knows about that.

Everyone who ever *was* a kid knows about that.

———

No matter where you live, anywhere around the world, there's a story that gets told about something coming to take your kids. Google that shit, if you don't believe me.

In Algeria, it's the H'awouahoua, his body composed of different animal parts and eyes like blobs of flaming spit, plus a long, dragging coat made from clothes from all the children he ate. In Germany it's the Butzemann, both noisy and faceless, a cloak-wrapped corner-darkness dweller that jumps out to attack kids who stay up past their bedtime. In Spain, parents sometimes give their naughty children away to the Hombre del Saco, while in Indonesia bad mothers and fathers get theirs taken by Wewe Gombel, who keeps the kids safe in her nest and leaves the parents to waste away without them. And then there's the Haitian Métminwi, an incredibly long-legged spectre who walks around scooping up anyone still roaming the streets after midnight. Nobody knows exactly what he does with them, but since they're never seen again, it's probably not so great.

"These are all boogeymen," I tell my son. "That's a very specific kind of monster."

"Boogeymen like boogeyman, bugge, boggart, boggeldy-bo," he agrees. "Bugge's probably the oldest—it's from, like, Anglo-Saxon times. Just means 'something scary.'"

"That's right."

"And they all eat kids."

"Sometimes. Sometimes they just steal them."

"But *only* kids, right?"

"Right."

My son loves monsters. He takes them very seriously, just like I do. So, he takes a moment, thinking long and hard, before he asks the next question.

"How old do you have to be before you're not a kid anymore, Mom?"

Ask your Dad, I want to say, but don't. Answering, instead: "Legally? Up here, you're an adult when you turn nineteen—that's when you can drive, and vote, and drink. But I think you're probably not a kid once you're a teenager, personally. I mean, you can have sex when you're sixteen, right? With another sixteen-year-old."

"Uck! As if. So. . . twelve, then."

"Pretty sure."

"Kinda need to be more than *sure*, Mom."

"Well, I agree." I smile. "That's what the monster drills are for."

———

When I was eight, there was a friend of mine who knew everything, or seemed to. I think we've all had a friend like that, probably.

He was small, skinny. Never at school. He only came around when the parents weren't there, outside, usually. On the playground; at the park. We had a great set of parks around where I grew up, on either side of the ravine. You could get off at Summerhill TTC station, start walking and get right within reaching distance of home before you ever had to get onto the street.

There's only one park where I live now, and I do take my son there when he asks, but he knows the rules: how he has to be situationally aware, 360 degrees, from the time we enter to the time we leave. Can't just get caught up in shit. Has to keep with me, flank my stride, neither too close, nor too far away. And take photos as he goes, with his phone, just like I do.

"How do you know what to take photos of?" he asks.

"I just feel it. You can too, I bet—try snapping anything that interests you, anything that makes you want to look at it twice. That's a good place to start."

He nods, internalizing the idea; I can see it rumble around inside him, hitting against the sides of his mental pinball machine, ringing up points. God, I love that guy.

"Think I could be good at it someday, like you?"

I shrug. "Well, you're smart enough, and you don't wear glasses yet, so. . . good enough, I guess." Then, tapping my own specs, and smiling: "Better than me, eventually."

"Mom, you know what I mean. Like. . . people *paying* me for photos-type good?"

"Sure, why not? It's more about luck than anything else—being in the right place at the right time. Or the wrong one."

"What?"

"Don't worry about it, baby. Go run."

I hold back, watching him, tracking him with my lens. Thinking about that friend of mine from when I was eight again, the same way I so often do; how I could never quite determine what he looked like, aside from being so thin. Like his face was just. . . blurred, a vague smear of pink on beige even in the most direct sunlight. He *had* eyes, obviously, since I recall how sly they were, how they slid away from mine in a manner both flirtatious and unreliable; he had a mouth, always quirked and smirking, lips pulled back over narrow teeth. But what colour his gaze was, whether or not he had braces like Em or a widening gap between the front bottom two like Peter. . . to this day, I don't know. Not even if his hair was dark or blond, or dark blond (as my hairdresser calls mine, even though it's straight-ass brown, and always has been).

An impression of a person, that's how I remember him. He was good at that, even closeup.

Better than other things I've seen trying to do the same thing since, by far.

———

Because yes, my son's right: people *do* pay me for my photos, well enough to keep us in a nice little one-bedroom downtown, at least with his dad chipping in on child support. We came together quickly in university and blew apart just as quick, though less explosively than my word choice makes that sound. It doesn't matter, much; I always knew I'd have a child one day, more likely a boy than a girl, according to some strange inkling in the pit of my mental stomach. So, I guess my son's father was just a means to an end in some ways, but it's not as if I didn't say I loved him at the time, and not as if I didn't mean it. I just didn't really know what love *was*, yet.

That only happened when our kid was born—*my* kid. Mine.

I don't talk about monsters with my ex. He doesn't believe in stuff like that, and getting him to the point where he did believe in it would take far too long for him to be useful. That's okay, though. I have my son, and he has me. He will always have me.

Most people find my photos disturbing, even the ones who pay me for them. They think I've made them that way. Some-times they want to know how; sometimes they tell me not to tell them, because that would spoil the effect. I stay quiet, either way.

I mean, it's not like I *can't* mock up photos, obviously. That's actually how I make the *big* bucks, every once in a while—emer-gency money, accident money, bug-out money, fuck-off money. It's always good to have, even if all I usually do is stick it in a Tangerine account and let it accumulate. The equivalent of hands-off sex work, by my artsy-fartsiest friends' standards, but I don't care what they think. Not so long as they get me what I need.

I'm the only person in Toronto who specializes in arranging photo spreads that look like crime scene photos, so far as I know, let alone in taking pictures for people with a death fetish— people who fantasize about what their love-objects would look like if they were dead, or about what they'd look like if they were dead themselves. I source out all the stuff I'm not qualified for to a select crew of models and effects artists, people who can't get work this high paying any other way. One of them is this awesome self-taught body painter who does YouTube videos, for example, making herself into a series of living optical illusions; another's her favourite muse/hookup, a woman who's six foot six and 123 pounds with extreme body tissue laxity due to Marfan Syndrome. I set up the scenes, my friends prepare or pose in them, I take the snaps and we all get paid, never knowing who wants them or why; it's all done anonymously, over the Web, with the help of yet *another* friend. After which I modify them enough to be unrecognizable outside of the wank-book of their commissioner, superimposing the facial features and bodily signifiers of whoever the customer wants to see. . . like that.

"It's *creepy*, Sera," my ex used to complain. "Hell, it's not even consensual."

"Sure, it is," I'd reply. "Mainly."

"Seriously? Then so is necrophilia, I guess."

"Oh, come *on*, Tolliver. Necrophilia's a legitimate health issue —*this* is like Halloween makeup, just a bit more hardcore. You know, like the Zombie Walk."

"Nobody's *fucking* at the Zombie Walk, Sera."

"Nobody's fucking in my *pics*, either, Toll. Where d'you see anybody rubbing uglies here, exactly? Show me."

And: "Mom, Dad," our son would say, not looking up from his crayons, "please don't use the 'f' word."

"Sorry, buddy," Toll would agree, automatically; "Sorry, baby," I'd chime in. Then half-wink, half-smirk at him, over Little T's head.

Yeah, we made a pretty good team, once, all three of us—still are, on occasion. But Toll was right to get out when he did, in the final analysis, by which I mean while he still could.

He always deserved somebody just a little bit nicer than me.

———

Here's one from my latest show, *Where They Didn't Find Her*. Long shot of a completely different dump site, double-exposed with collage elements culled from Toronto Police Department photos gotten via that third friend of mine. The body in question was found 02 October 2019, in a shallow depression on the weed-fields between where Coalsack Park backs onto the Don River's west-side hiking trail. Skeletonized almost entirely except for the hands and feet, lumpy inside socks; prints were gone due to decay, wet leather gloves over bone and mush. Forensic odontology used for ID. Cause of death determined by stab marks through clothes—twenty-one stabs, clustered on torso.

But like I said, the site I photographed for wasn't hers. It dates back far further, to August 1990.

To the summer when I was eight, in fact.

————

"There's a thing that lives down there, you know," our friend who seemed to know everything told us, that day. "Under the bridge."

"What, like a troll?" Em asked, still braiding a dandelion chain. Her hands were covered in sticky juice and green smears, reflected yellow dancing underneath her chin.

"Not like that, no."

"Ooooh, you mean like the *boogeyman?*"

This from Peter, who always had to have the last dig in. But our friend just turned to smirk at him, replying, with laudable contempt—

"The boogeyman is bullshit, dummy. Parents made him up. 'Go to bed, or the boogeyman will get you.' *This* is *real*."

"No, it isn't."

"Sure it is. I know where it lives. I can show you."

Because here's the truth, okay? Kids don't want a house made out of sweets; kids don't want a van full of puppies, or a moment's taste of grownup status. Kids don't want money dropped down a sewer—well, I mean yeah, they do want all those things, obviously, given how many purely human predators have caught kids by dangling these things in front of them. But more, much more than any of the above, kids want *a secret.*

". . . guess that could be cool," Peter admitted, finally, trying to sound diffident. "Hey Em, you in?"

"Mm, okay. Sera?"

They all pivoted to look at me, then, in the bright sunlight. It was a hot day, not just August, but *late* August, the grass around us buzzing with activity, our clothes scanty as we could get away with and still wet to our skins, blood-warm, twisting uncomfortably closer every time we moved. Yet in that moment, I remember, I felt a weird kind of chill: internal, fluttering 'round inside me, an implication of infection. A sense of wrongness which almost seemed to whisper: *No. Don't.*

"I can't," I said. "I have to get home." And I didn't, but. . .

There was simply something *about* that kid, is all I can think, even after all this time. There always had been. Like a rattlesnake lazing in a cool burrow, fascinating mixed with dangerous in just the right balance. . . so long as you knew not to get too close. And when to back away.

I watched the others go, and then I went to the library and read until six, and then I went home. And in the morning, I went to school, and those kids weren't there. My friends. They never were again.

They never came back.

———

I'd gotten my first camera earlier that summer, one of those throwaway ones from the drugstore counter, the kind they sold to tourists. Took a lot of snaps with it, clicking and clicking till it wouldn't wind forwards anymore, and then I kind of forgot about it, aside from the blister I'd raised on my thumb. So, it wasn't until afterwards—after all the fooferaw with cops and the journalists, the hysterical news coverage, neighbourhood parents forming a scrum both in front and in back of the school for weeks, refusing to let us anywhere near that down-sloping gulley inside which they'd found what was left of Em and Peter, coiled together like some slack-sucked, boneless chimera—that I finally got the film developed. Because I wanted memories of my two bestest friends in all the world I could pin on my walls, ones that would make me forget the porous newsprint spectacle of that browned-up, withered dandelion chain still hanging around what used to be Em's neck under her tarnished, braces-girt permanent gasp of pain, or Pete's split teeth jutting up from his lipless bottom jaw like a pair of dull little eyes, something small and terrified trying its level best to burrow down and hide inside his mouth from something bent on its destruction, and failing miserably.

All the photos showed us in the park, like usual. No surprises there. Except for the last one, in which another figure could be glimpsed crossing up from the ravine towards us, using the path that led down under the bridge. . .

A thin figure, back-lit, small enough to be another child: skinny limbs, face blurred as if someone had scraped a nail across it, trying to erase the features. And all of it swirled together into what wasn't quite a lens flare halo, more a blob of darkness gradually dimming until whatever resemblance it had ever held to a human being simply. . . disappeared. Until it began to drip downwards into the ground, eddying like smoke run backwards, like five different kinds of equally bright paint in water muddying inevitably to brownish-black.

I still have that photo. I keep it in a safe-deposit box, under Little T's name. But it doesn't matter who has it, really—I know what it means, what studying it taught me. Which means I can recognize the effect in any photo I take now, and so can he.

I've made damn sure of that.

———

Tolliver isn't the most observant guy in the world, but even he could see something was off when he came by to pick up Little T for their weekly used-bookstore crawl. "You look kinda walloped, Ser," he said, low but frank. "Listen, do you want me to take him for the weekend? I could even do the week, if you wanted. It just seems like you need some rest."

I couldn't tell him he was wrong, but I couldn't tell him what was wrong, either. I could hear T bustling about in his study-nook-turned-room, picking out completed books to try reselling; the noise somehow sickened and reassured me all at once. "No, Toll, thanks, but—we've got a special day tomorrow. I've just had some late nights planning it. Seriously, I'm okay," I emphasized, when he looked dubious. "We'll both be."

Inside, I winced at how that had come out, bracing myself for Toll to say something like *wait, you'll* both *be okay?! Is there some reason he might* not *be?!* But like I said—not the most observant guy in the world. Or maybe he was going out of his way to show he trusted me, I don't know. It isn't important. All that mattered was that he sighed, nodded, and didn't ask to look at the photo print I'd been spasmodically turning over and over in my hand. He just took our son and left.

I waited ten minutes before looking at it again, just on the off chance they'd come back for something T had forgotten. It hadn't changed. I'd gone to the park by myself, walked around. Enjoyed the sound of kids running over green grass, under trees, chasing and being chased by dogs—I like watching dogs play, as long as it's at a distance. Taken photos intermittently with my phone. Surfed through them on the subway ride home, not thinking about anything except what might make a good back-drop for the next corpse-face collage. And then I'd made some strangled, startlingly loud noise and jerked in my seat, shocking the elderly Punjabi woman next to me into a spasm of her own that snapped her elbow against mine and sent the phone clattering to the floor.

Oh, no, I've damaged it! she'd said after picking it up for me, genuinely upset. *The screen must be bent. Is that your son? I'm so sorry. Please, give me your contact information, so my husband can repay you. . .* In the end I had to show her other photos, to prove it wasn't anything she'd done.

She asked to look again at the last one and was silent a long time. *Something is very wrong with that child, isn't it?* she asked, quietly. *No child should be that thin.*

It's not a child, I told her.

I should delete that picture, I think. If I were you.

I plan to, I said.

And I did. But not before getting home and printing it out, where I sat, staring at it for hours. Thinking.

———

Because I have a kid myself, now, I watch him pretty close. Closer than my mom watched me, for sure. They call it helicopter parenting, tell us how we're curtailing social development, or some shit. But I watch him, and I watch out for kids who hover around him, whispering. Kids who seem like they know everything.

Skinny kids.

I didn't even notice the kid in the park that day, when I'd been taking the photos. Just a vague memory of a blurred form, glimpsed from the corner of the eye, noticed more for his ragged clothing than for a sly look or obscured face. Looking at the photo later, it was some kind of black, bleak miracle that somebody hadn't grabbed him and called Child Services, or the police. Or someone. Those limbs were too long, too wire-thin, too pallid to look human even for a second. Skinnier even than I remembered my old friend being, thirty years ago.

But people do watch their kids more closely these days. Families are smaller; they go outside far less. There's more fear. Less trust. Less. . . opportunity. So maybe it's no surprise that whatever that thing is, it's getting thinner.

Must be pretty fucking thin, by now.

Pretty desperate.

And now I'm going to tell you something that will *really* make you dislike me.

I've told you how I always knew I would have a kid, someday. That I would *have* to have one. But can you guess why?

Oh, I think you probably can.

And none of that means I don't love him, though the tensile strength of that love has certainly surprised me, over and over again. It still does. He's taught me so much about myself, Little T has. Who I am. Who I can be.

The other day, when I thought I'd finally found that old "friend" of mine, I sat up straight. Not because I really thought my son was in danger; he wasn't—isn't. I've taught him better than that. And not because I thought that thing who killed my real friend might know who I was, aside from T's Mom. I don't think he'd recognize me now, not the same way I know I'd recognize him. I've changed a lot, and not just from growing up.

No.

It was because. . .

. . . even now, I don't know if I can kill a kid, not even if it's just something that *looks* like a kid. But for *my* kid? *Mine?*

I damn well know I can try.

And the thing is, Little T won't be in danger forever—he

knows that too. I've shown him the statistics. These things hunt within a narrow age range, and he's almost past his eat-by date.

Still, if it doesn't happen soon—if it doesn't work *this* time—there's nothing at all that says we can't try again. He's a handsome boy. He'll be a handsome man.

————

I look forward to being a grandmother.

PELICAN

I found a book on animals once, stuck between shelves to prop 'em up, all stiff with dust. Remembered enough from when my gram taught me my letters on Dr. Seuss to sound the text underneath the pictures out aloud, after I finally got bored just looking at 'em. One was of this bird perched on a stump by water that had a huge flap of skin hung down from its beak, big enough to shovel up fish in and swallow 'em whole: *Pelican*, it said underneath. *Waterfowl, extinct.* Like most've of the rest've them things wasn't extinct along with everybody else who'd touched that same book by the time I got hold of it.

Anyhow.

In the Middle Ages—*when?* somebody'd writ in the space next to it, like they was waiting on me to tell 'em—folk thought pelicans fed their kids by ripping open a vein in their chest and letting them suckle on it, so's the chicks would drink till the momma bird died. Maybe 'cause they'd noticed birds didn't have tits, or maybe 'cause they just couldn't make 'emselves believe chicks get fed when their mommas puke meat they already ate back down their throats, once it's all ground up to liquid. People think all sorts of dumb shit, now same as then—I've sure had the hard proof of it this far, like all my damn life.

But my gram was Bible to the day she died, so I understood what the next part meant, when others might've not. That this whole pelican thing was a parable, a sidewise way to bring in Jesus Christ Almighty, who shed his blood on the cross so we might live forever: salvation through sacrifice, *self-*sacrifice, and all that happy crap. Like how if we had any extra food, we should give it away, just on hopes somebody else might do the same, things ever happened to fetch up the other way 'round. Like they wouldn't be far more inclined to kill her, rape my momma and me, then take every other thing we had 'fore setting the whole place on fire 'round us and leaving us to pull ourselves out 'fore it burned down far enough to kill *us* too.

Can't blame my gram for wanting to believe that Bible shit was true, I guess, though I sure enough did, after. I mean, she was only eight when the world ended—that's what she claimed, anyhow. Told my momma everything she remembered hoping Momma'd tell it to me, but I don't think Momma much believed her, 'cause she kept on changing the details till she forgot what exactly Gram said first. Trying to make 'em sound more likely, maybe; that's the nice version, one I used to tell myself, back when I still cared. Before I figured out she didn't really give a shit, either way.

Didn't matter much, as it turned out. Took Momma two months to find out she was carrying, five more before my brother killed her; she bled out in a swamp, passed him in pieces after punching herself in the belly with rocks, trying to get revenge on the one who squirted him up inside her. And I just sat there watching, waiting for her to die so I could take her pack, 'cause I was so sick of getting beat on for not being pregnant too. Never did get my courses, turned out, probably an account of being torn up so bad that first time, but it wasn't like I felt sorry over it

—even then, I knew if you'd nothing else to trade, sex was always the fallback.

And motherhood? From what I'd seen, that shit got you nothing but dead.

Sometimes the best thing you can do for your kids is to kill 'em 'fore the pain starts, my momma used to say, as we staggered through this ruined world together. *Sometimes it's kill yourself, and let them eat your corpse.* Not like I ever believed she'd've done either, no matter *how* many times she said it; that was my gram talking, not her. The second part, anyway.

And besides: the real trick is knowing which.

Or when.

———

How I found the kid? Like this: wild as hell and twice as ornery, so much he snapped and scratched at me between bouts of puking; sick from eating rotten meat and sleeping in a corpse-nest, clutched tight to the one must've been his momma, once. Thumb deep in his mouth, even then.

The place was a campsite, fairly well-covered. Parents'd made 'emselves swamp suits from grass and such, muddied up their faces—couldn't make him do the same, so they just let him run free instead, counted on him to roll in the dirt like a dog and go animal, which he'd sure done well with since. But they'd been found nevertheless, no matter how well they hid, or fought. I saw the end of it clear. Took down two more as they died, and the rest must've run, not even bothered robbing 'em after.

Think he might've been eight, maybe, by the time I fell across him. Just like my gram, when *her* world went black. 'Cause things do go 'round and 'round, and that's the fact.

(One of 'em, anyhow.)

As to why I kept him, well... he was way too sick to be worth the effort's killing, like I said. Would've made for bad meat himself, as I'd learned that first year. Pets can be useful, though. Good for scouting and backup, for clearing track; good to trip traps first, so you don't. Good for company, extra warmth on a monsoon night. I'd sure fucked people for less, and at least that wasn't likely to come up—not for years yet, I was lucky.

There's worse things by far I could've done to tie him to me than I did, but it ain't like he was innocent either; that's how I thought of it, at the time. I watched him a while, to make sure.

He was a good little predator already, just like me. And I guess—

I guess I thought: why not?

———

Didn't take all too much to tame him, soon found out. I had fresh water, weapons, a bit of food; still had some meds left from my last pass through what my momma'd called "town," those knocked-down knots of too-big houses where gangs set up markets and drink-holes, lying wait for lone fools to screw with. So I tempted him in, tied him down, fed him up and got him well. Held him while he shook, stroked his hair. . . even sung to him a bit under my breath, so's he could feel the burr of it through my skin. By the time he was well he was looking at me all bright-eyed with his mouth a little open, same way dogs used to, back when I still found 'em. Before they came too close, that is.

Pet 'em with the one hand, cut their throats with the other. Dogs are easy; they never even saw it coming. Dumb creatures.

He wasn't that, at least.

We moved on, once he was able. I made him take the swamp suit off his momma, mud it up twice over, inside and out. The smell was good to keep sharp-toothed things away, or make roamers want to look elsewhere. We'd crouch down in the muck, follow 'em soft for a while, then he'd take 'em low and I'd take 'em high, get the voice box so they couldn't scream out; he went straight for the back of the knees till I taught him to slip his blade in between the ribs or slash inside the groin, nick all those places where something popped and blood sprayed out. Butcher 'em quick, get the parts that stayed good longest, and disappear.

Nights I heard him trying to sing sometimes, his voice all raspy; I'd kick him quick, make him stop, 'fore somebody heard. But I did recognize the songs, same ones I'd sung him in his fever. Same ones my gram sung me.

One time he tried to hug into me without asking, so I punched him right in the gut, made him whoop like he was going to heave; he knew to do it quiet by then, and made sure to. Told him: *Don't try cuddling up, boy, not if I ain't said so—I ain't the same one dropped you.* Knew I had him trained good by that time when he just nodded.

And if I woke up next morning to find him close enough I felt him, no matter how careful he'd been not to let us touch? Well, that was all right. Just meant he knew who kept him fed, was all.

I didn't ever ask the kid his name—didn't want to know, in truth. Just in case things went bad, later on. Never told him mine, either.

Not that I could remember it by then.

———

The pelican. Why do I keep thinking about it? Been years since I stopped looking at that picture, and I know the words by heart.

Maybe 'cause I passed the book on to the kid, back around the same time he finally started talking. . . answering when I told him stuff, though not answering *back*; I knew he knew better. Made sure of that myself. 'Cause I showed him his letters and left him to it, the same way Gram showed me.

I sure didn't have anything else to give him, not 'less he grew the balls to kill me in my sleep. Which I knew—hoped—he would, someday, and sooner rather than later.

Already felt the sickness on me, you see, thickening up my blood. Microplastic Syndrome, that doc in Essboro called it, when I took the kid in to get him checked for radiation and bioplague, after we crossed the outer edge of where St. Louis used to be; where Gram lived was bad for it, or so said the CDC map.

Biggest place I ever been, Essboro. They had generators, WiFi access, greenhouses. Ate a tomato for the first time ever there; the kid ate a whole apple one nibble at a time, so slow it turned brown 'fore he reached the core. Ate that too.

You can stay, the doc said, after he told me what I could expect, going forward. *Be glad to have you, no matter what you might've done. We all know what it's like, out there. And the kid could stay too, of course.*

But we moved on instead, the both of us. I sure wasn't gonna leave him behind, not by then. Not when I was used to him.

Not when he was *mine.*

———

I taught him to be me, 'cause that's all I knew. And that's the problem.

Started to cough a month back, maybe. I can feel my heart skip. This tightness in my chest, my muscles. I ache all over; getting slow now, slower than either of us can afford. And I can see him watching me from the corner of his eyes, but not like he's getting ready to take my shit and skip, like any normal asshole. More like he's getting ready to nurse me till I die, then lie down and hug me till he does too.

And: I don't know why I should care 'bout him being that kind of stupid, if he is, so long's he waits till then. So long's he keeps me fed and safe, like I kept him, till it's not like I'm gonna know anymore if he doesn't. . . fuck, I shouldn't. Not with all I seen.

Nobody should.

He shouldn't, it was the other way 'round.

I dream about the pelican, chewing up food till it's soft enough to swallow. Chewing it up and dripping it into their chick's mouth, just the way I did into his back at the start, when he was too sick to know he was starving.

Ten days since we found the family, living in their swamp-side squat—little house like a tent wove from reeds and grass, popped up on top of a cave they'd dug out under the earth. Has a chimney made from cans with a wet stump 'round it for cover, smoke seeping up slow, like it's part of the fog, smart. Saw the momma hunting rats with a spear, the poppa picking fungus with a baby slung under his some sorta cape he made from old plastic to keep it warm, dry and muffled, but with a scarf on top to make sure it doesn't smother. Smart again. And there's other kids hid back in the cave while their folks are out, one maybe my boy's age keeping watch, good enough with a sling. I saw him pick a bird off a tree twenty feet away, even in the rain. Heard my boy give his grunting laugh at that and knew why: I'd've beat him good for doing something like that, he was mine. 'Cause you never do know who's around, no matter how long you've been where you are. Safety's a lie.

They're weak, my boy told me that night, huddled in our hide. *We could take 'em, easy. That could be our house. We could eat off them for weeks, dry the rest. Live there a year or more.*

Too many, I said. *And a man too.*

We took men before.

Not with a woman and kids for backup. Not when we don't know how many might be back in there, for sure.

He went quiet then—nodding, but not like he agreed. More like he knew I was hurting too much to move just then, so he'd wait, and try again later.

Felt my chest squeeze again then, and twice as hard. Thinking: *that's my voice comin' out of your mouth,* as it did.

So, we keep on watching, for now.

That family love each other, I think. Close as I've seen since my gram died, since my momma turned mean. And they're *not* weak, not so's I've noticed. Poppa and momma done their share, here and there, keeping roamers away; know to keep out of sight if there's more than one, and make sure they're dead 'stead of trying to run 'em off. They cut up the corpses, but don't butcher 'em. Spread 'em around for the stink, or use 'em to bait their traps instead.

Think if they just found my boy, they might do him the same way, 'specially if he threatened 'em. But if they found us together, if they killed *me*. . . if I *made* them kill me. . .

If they saw him cry over me, like I think he might. Like he might still be dumb enough to.

I think they might take him in, even if they had to treat him the way I did, at first. Like a dog too wild to let in the house or leave your kids alone with. But—

—tameable, if you feed it. If you pet it. Set water out for it. Give it a name and call it, till it comes. The way I never would.

The way I never could.

———

Tomorrow. I'll make 'em kill me tomorrow, then it'll be up to them. And then. . .

. . . well, I won't know, will I?

Either way.

HAGSTONE

Jourdemayne Project > INBOX
Nathalie Seguin **nat@nseg.org** 11:47 p.m.
to Alec Christian **achristian@gmail.com**

Alec, thank you again—I can't tell you how grateful I am for your help on this. I mean, you know how much work this is going to involve and you were always better at the people stuff than I was, but I think we both know the truth: after the past few years, I don't see me getting on anything other than the mainland ferry for a good long while. Maybe ever. That's not even a sad thought, you know? It's quiet out here, and beautiful, no matter how cold it gets in January. The next time you come to stay I want to show you a new trail I found, right across the island. (Don't worry, I'll make sure it's in summer. Or spring, maybe; summer gets muggy.)

The restoration's going well; I should be most of the way through the first reel by the end of the week, and it's all there: the prologue with the coven in the woods, the sequence where Oswald and Christina desert camp after the battle, the deal with the Witchfinder and the raid on the hut, right through to where

Milady orders Oswald to retrieve her property. (I see what you mean about the F/X, there's some really trippy rotoscope work in there.) I'd be happier about that if I didn't have this lingering feeling the client's doing this as some perverse kind of test. It's never been hard to find usable copies of reel one, and I told the agent right up front that if they weren't going to turn over everything at once, the best approach was to start with the *poorest-*quality source material, so we could get the most time-consuming part done first. Instead, I feel like I'm jumping through hoops. I'm only the expert with twenty years' experience, why listen to me? But the client gets what they pay for, and they're paying for my exclusive availability no matter how quick I turn things over, so I guess I shouldn't complain.

I'm looking forward to hearing how things went in Marseilles. Sorry I got on your case about it last time, I know you know what you're doing, I just worry that sometimes your style won't go over as well in that crowd as it does over here. Hope you're enjoying France.

--Nat

SEGUIN RESTORATION LTD.
Returning Lost Images To Light
www.nseg.org/info
P.O. Box 1011, Ashford Is., BC, V2V 4L8

———

Re: Jourdemayne Project (2) > INBOX
Alec Christian **achristian@gmail.com** 1:16 p.m.
to Nathalie Seguin **nat@nseg.org**

Hey Nat,
Well, I was going to get annoyed with that crack about my

style, but I spent last night in a drunk tank, so I don't have a foot to stand on, do I? Yeah, turns out the direct approach doesn't always work, even if it's supposed to be an open pre-festival publicity party. Don't worry, I didn't say anything about you—far as Barztegui knows I'm just another Gen X-slash-Millennial film nut who doesn't grasp the idea of boundaries. The minute I started asking him what kind of supplementals he was planning for the *Hagstone* BluRay, he turned red, started shouting and basically forgot how to speak English. Must be true he does this a lot, though, because both the security guards and the cops were pretty laid-back about hauling me out of there. (At least, I think they were. Full disclosure, I *may* have been a few sheets to the wind myself at the time.)

Still, not a completely wasted night; that reaction pretty much proves Yves Barztegui *is* your anonymous client, which means his grandmom ("Loopy" Lady Lil Jourdemayne-Barztegui, aka the current Jourdemayne estate-holder) must *finally* be planning to break radio silence about that freaking film. I think your gut's probably on-target too—Barztegui strikes me as exactly the kind of purist asshole who wants everyone who works for him to prove themselves personally, no matter how good a rep they bring to the table; it makes sense he'd want to compare your work to what others have done first. Then again, what do you expect from a guy who's aristocrat on both sides, one Basque, one Norman?

That said, I think it's actually good news all 'round: once he sees how good you are, the rest of this job is in the bag. And now I can head back to London, where I'm gonna get started tracking down anyone left over from the production crew/cast (you know the whole cast was composed of crew members doing double duty, right? 'Course ya do.;)). Let you know who I find.

Keep chill, kiddo!

--Alec

PS: Love to see what you've got as a beginning, if you feel like sending it over—gotta have something to read on the Chunnel express.

———

HAGSTONE: *Recovering a Forgotten Dream*
Restoration Introductory Essay by Nathalie Seguin, (C) 2024

- 1 -

What do we mean when we say a film is "lost?" Films planned but unmade, made but mislaid, or deliberately buried? The incomplete, or the censored? Sometimes they fall into holes attached to obsolete entities, or obsolete technologies, their stories trapped in canisters of Super-8 film moldering away in a forgotten storage unit, formerly owned by some out-of-business studio, unwatchable because nobody keeps the right kind of projector working any more. Sometimes you have to seek them out, never knowing where you might find them, like Ken Russell's *The Devils*, which *still* needs a non-PAL, non-bootleg, non-censored release. Or maybe you'll only ever get other people's impressions of having seen them, through old books, stills, lobby cards, or anecdata about that one public screening people might or might not have attended, like Henri Cotillard's supposedly endless review of Hans Backovic's *Le fin absolue du monde*.

They haven't been digitized; they aren't being streamed. There's no network through which they're being illegally shared. No one knows enough about their existence to demand they be allowed to see them.

A film without an audience, after all, might as well not exist.

And then there's the question of ownership. Though the filmmaker may claim ownership over his or her own vision, in the days before file-sharing entities like YouTube, alliance with a distributor was an absolute necessity; said distributor could then claim ownership over the *product*, and bury it if they felt they weren't likely to make money off it being seen. In this way, a film being "lost" can become a form of freedom—especially if there's no one left who might legitimately claim they have a "right" to make money off it being found again. Copyright protection, after all, only holds if it's being defended; once one version of a film escapes into the infoscape "wild," it isn't long before it spawns offspring, whose resemblance changes with every iteration-slash-generation.

All of this brings us to the case of *Hagstone* (1975, Canadian-U.K., co-written and directed by Maren Carbray and Ashbet Lamp), a film that—while it can now be viewed once again, in whole or in parts—can nevertheless be said to "not exist." Even though the names on the credits are matters of public record, were those people really the ones who "made" *Hagstone?* Who owns whatever *Hagstone* is now? Who was *Hagstone* first made *for*, and why would they want to see it? And how can audiences today hope to connect with the vision and the audiences of nearly fifty years ago, in a world so drastically different from any those filmmakers could ever have foreseen?

Though I can't promise to answer all of those questions, I *can* promise that the journey we're embarking on, our voyage through the process of restoration and recovery, will dive farther into the source material than anyone else has ever been able to, thus far. So, if things do remain lost by the time we're finished, at least I'll know it's not *my* fault.

- 2 -

First things first: What is a hagstone, anyway?

Sometimes also known as an adder stone, a hagstone is any stone with a naturally occurring hole worn through it, most often made of flint, and found on coastal shores or in caves. Such stones are traditionally believed to have magical properties, ranging from protecting the bearer against all sorts of dangers (nosebleeds, lightning strikes, foot rot, swine fever, snakebite) to revealing all sorts of hidden knowledge if the bearer looks through it (the true faces of fairies, which of your neighbours are witches, or even—as with the one used by the legendary Seer of Ban—visions of the future). The hagstone legend is thought to have inspired the superstition about looking through one's wedding ring in order to reveal lies, and is known in English, Welsh, Scottish, and even Russian folklore—to this day, the English town of Hastings is said to be under a curse laid by notorious occultist Aleister Crowley, who is reported to have magically bound any native of the town to always return to it unless they could find a hagstone on the Hastings beaches to take with them when they left. But in the context of the 1975 film—and unsurprisingly, given film's nature as a visual medium—it is what can be seen through such a stone that drives the story.

Following an eerie prologue in which a coven of elderly nude women disport themselves in the woods, and which ends with the coven leader holding up the titular artifact to the unnaturally large moon, *Hagstone*'s story proper begins when Oswald, a Roundhead soldier in the English Civil War, deserts his company along with his camp-follower lover Christina in the aftermath of a victorious battle, while his comrades are viciously sacking an unnamed English town. (This sequence is one of the film's more infamous aspects, often described as rivalling Russell's *The Devils* for its explicit brutality and implications of gang rape—a fact which becomes even more disturbing when one remembers that all the film's main characters are played by women, as were the majority of the extras.) Oswald and Christina's flight nearly ends in their recapture, and Oswald's likely execution, until they are offered shelter on the estate of the mysterious noblewoman Milady, who speaks only through her Moorish servant girl and never removes the white vizard mask she wears beneath her cowl.

Days later, a witchfinder covertly visits Milady's estate, and Oswald panics, thinking himself betrayed; he takes Milady's servant girl hostage, but surrenders when Milady (through the girl) tells him secrets of his past not even Christina knows. Milady reassures Oswald the witchfinder is working for her, and poses no threat—he's been hired to recover a powerful artifact from a coven dwelling in the nearby forest, and cannot betray Oswald's presence without revealing his own double-dealing. All the same, Milady suggests, it would be well if Oswald accompanied the witchfinder to both confirm his compliance and provide assistance if needed. Reluctantly agreeing, Oswald joins the witchfinder. . . and quickly discovers that the witchfinder is not what "he" appears to be, either—"he" is in fact a woman, the original witchfinder's sister, who assumed his identity after the witchfinder died of pneumonia following a trial-enforced ducking. (This is particularly interesting when you remember that Oswald deserts to protect Christina's secret, the fact that she was born male, while the secret Oswald's been keeping from Christina is that *he* was born female.)

"The only thing real about any of this," the "witchfinder" tells Oswald, "is the gold that fool woman's paying me to take away a toy from a crowd of starving beggars. Help me and say nothing, and half of it's yours." Her cynicism is soon proven fatally mistaken, however, when they find the ring of huts where the coven dwells. Dispatching most of the coven with pistol shots and quarterstaff blows, the witchfinder demands the coven turn their object of power over, only to be told mockingly, "Herself won't like what she sees through it." Then a creature—never clearly seen, but long, low, black, and (possibly) hairy—bursts from the trees to attack the witchfinder. Fighting back, she breaks her lantern across the creature's skull, setting it on fire, and the rampage of its blazing agony ignites the coven's huts and burns them to the ground. Oswald flees, only to discover that Milady and her servant have followed them and are waiting just outside the tree line, with Christina bound and helpless; Oswald is ordered back into the clearing to "get what we came for!" or Christina will be slain. Having no choice, Oswald waits until the fires have burnt out and ventures into the ruins of the largest hut. There he finds the witchfinder, still alive but horribly burnt, the familiar creature lying seemingly dead, the blackened skull of the head witch, and the artifact for which all this carnage was enacted—the hagstone itself, a disc of grey flint with an eye-sized, smooth-edged hole worn through the middle.

Ignoring the witchfinder's moans of pain, Oswald retrieves the hagstone. As he lifts it, the witch's skull suddenly speaks aloud: "*Do not trust the Lady, soldier,*" it tells him. "*What she seeks will destroy her, as she will destroy to gain it. So, flee now, before—*" But the skull is cut off when the witchfinder, in a final agony of rage, smashes it with her quarterstaff. . . and the familiar, in turn, springs to life and tears the witchfinder's throat out, spraying blood across the ashes. In horror, Oswald watches the dead witches' eyes open, and the ashes rise like a grey wind, whipping through the trees; he flees in panic, still clutching the hagstone, and is pursued back to the treeline, where Milady, the maid and Christina wait for him. Another nightmarish chase ensues as they follow Milady and her maid's lanthorn towards what turns out to be a huge manor surrounded by a ring of salt. Once they cross this barrier, the ash-wind dissipates, revealing the familiar, who roams back and forth, waiting to spring on anyone who tries to leave.

"She says you must wait until dawn," the maid tells Christina and Oswald, who link hands, exchange a fearful glance, and reluctantly follow Milady inside.

Then a thunderstorm descends, rain threatening to wash away the protective barrier within minutes. Milady proposes a ritual seance, during which they will be protected as the maid looks through the hagstone, which may reveal a permanent solution. Desperate, Oswald and Christina agree. The maid brings them to a ritual chamber whose walls are hung with black velvet, seating them at a circular table set with candles whose top is made from blackboard. As Milady scribes a protective circle on the table-top with white and red chalk, the maid lays another circle of salt around the room's perimeter. The familiar enters the house, but slams up against this secondary ward, trapped, growling in the doorway. Then the maid sits, handing Milady the hagstone.

"She says I must write what I see," the maid says, bringing out a roll of paper and a piece of charcoal. Milady removes her vizard mask, revealing a face scarred by smallpox and syphilis, and raises the stone to one blind eye.

At once, in the film's most surreal sequence, the 'hagstone's visions show first the end of the night—the storm's end, the sun rising, the familiar blinking out, Oswald and Christina leaving, walking away from both manor and forest—followed by the end of the Civil War itself: the restoration of the monarchy, Oliver Cromwell's coffin dug up and his head on a pike, various dissenter groups rolling, shaking, quaking, and dancing like witches or revelling soldiers, the Puritans aboard-ship on their way to America, the maid's fingers scribbling words from Abiezer Coppe's famous *A Fiery Flying Roll: overturn, overturn, overturn.* Things begin to bend and blur, soundtrack turning electronic. . . and what we see next is obviously the England and London of 1975, depicting incomprehensibly vast crowds, swarms of roaring vehicles, pictures from famous crime scenes, sexual decadence, war-zone carnage, addiction dens, industrial pollution, and everything else that would break the mind of a seventeenth-century person, Roundhead *or* Cavalier. Inevitably, it ends with the sound of an atomic explosion, screen turning white.

We return to the ritual room, where Milady sits motionless.

The maid has just replaced her vizard mask. She offers Oswald and Christina their sack of silver, and steps backwards into shadow, disappearing; they take it, and leave. Finally, Milady removes her own mask once more, as the camera closes in. Behind it, Milady's face is nothing but a single skull-sized black hole; Milady has become, herself, a living hagstone. Closing in further, the camera's lens and that awful hole become one, and in the final darkness—held for what seems an amazingly long time, but is probably only a full, silent minute—we begin to convince ourselves we can faintly see things moving in the dark, coming towards us. Then the bright gold letters of "THE END" come up, copyright information shown at the frame's bottom, and the film is over.

Or is it?

————

Re: Jourdemayne Project (3) > INBOX
Alec Christian **achristian@gmail.com** 5:25 p.m.
to Nathalie Seguin **nat@nseg.org**

Dude. I mean, *dude*. Seriously, Nat, if you ever want to give up the film restoration business, try going into copywriting, right? I've only seen like one knockoff-grade version of *Hagstone*, and it didn't come off anywhere near as creepy as you make it sound—though in hindsight, the transfer sucked, it was a late-night replacement showing at a film festival, and the audience was mostly drunk. Plus this is the generation that's grown up on *Game of Thrones* and the latest *Chainsaw* remake, so I don't think they get how much of an accomplishment it was for a shoestring crew in the early 1970s to pull off what they did. Fucking Millennials. (Yeah, I know, I'm only Gen X myself. Sentiment still stands.)

So. Started at the BBC, just in case—I mean, they *did* fund it (partially) and show it (once, before flushing it down the drain along with all those old *Doctor Who* eps and Nigel Kneale's *The Road*). But no joy, which is why I spent the last few days going back and forth in London between different film archives and the PR office of Ellstree Studios, and I don't know what's worse—cheerful kids who don't recognize anything I tell them, or retirement-age archivists who act like they're guarding the royal regalia. But—drumroll, please—one of those archivists did turn up something that should be "congruent with your interests," as the kids say: a letter from Maren Carbray, the co-director, where she talks about the movie! Downside is, it's mostly about what's *not* in the script, but it still strengthens some of your theories—I got the archivist to scan it as a PDF and I've attached it. Let me know what you think.

———

April 16, 1973

Dear Roland,

Pleased as I was to hear that Chris L. spoke so effusively of our project, I think you may have come away from that conversation with a somewhat mistaken idea of the nature of this production. Won't lie to you—I never did make Miss Lamp aware of your. . . suggestions? Recommendations? Requests?—but only because I knew without asking what she'd say: "There will __not__ be any orgy scenes in this film, there will __not__ be any love scenes involving an innkeeper's nubile daughter, and there will be __no__ climactic sword duel on the battlements of a fortress." So, if all that's going to make a difference to your investment decisions, best to make that clear now, hm?

I don't mean to come off as more obstructive than I must, obviously, and to soften the blow, I'll share something that's been kept under wraps until now: at least one rumour is true—Ms. Lamp is, in fact, using the mediumistic technique of automatic writing to compose her script. Or at least, so her "dear friend" Lady Lil assures me; I'm deeply skeptical, though I suppose I've no idea what a blind woman's writing process would look like to begin with. Still, she is helping secure most of our key shooting locations by offering her Staffordshire property, so it's not worth challenging. The script pages are all properly typed by the time I see them, anyway. Hope that's piqued your curiosity sufficiently to retain your involvement?

If not, I understand, and shan't take it personally if this no longer sounds like a viable opportunity for Lionmouth Films—Chris L. aside, this is probably no one's idea of a commercial product. I mean yes, the basic tone skews to the horrific (somewhat), and it definitely involves the occult, but. . . we're not exactly talking about Dennis Wheatley territory here, and though Miss Lamp swears by the idea that it's based on historical fact, I don't think we're going to be able to sell it as a costume epic, either. Hannah Glaive and I have actually been working on a backup production model I'm quite excited by, even though it may get a bit tight by the end. Either way, I'd very much appreciate it if I could hear back from you by 15 May at the latest, as we want to begin shooting as soon as practically possible.

All best,
Maren

———

Re: **Jourdemayne Project (4)** > INBOX
Nathalie Seguin **nat@nseg.org** 9:02 p.m.
to Alec Christian **achristian@gmail.com**

Alec: Thank you, thank you, thank you! I don't think you realize just how useful that letter actually was—it not only confirms the automatic writing rumour, but it proves Lil Jourdemayne *was* a friend (or more?) of Ashbet Lamp, not just a dilettante whose father lent out his mansion for the prestige of being in a movie. I wonder if she was the person who typed out those notes, or whatever? (PS: Any chance you can find out who the guy at Lionmouth was? Not critical, but every hole we can fill in helps. PPS: "Chris L." is Sir Christopher *Lee*, right? Squee!:))

Anyhow, what I'd really love would be if you could talk to anyone who worked on the film who's still alive. I know that's a long shot, the youngest of them would have to be in their seventies by now, but it might be worth trying, especially since the IMDb.com entry's got more holes than a sponge. Sir Michael Caine can't be the only working actor still around who remembers that decade.

Oh, and extra good news: the next shipment of source material arrived today, along with the next installment of my contracted fee. Barztegui/Jourdemayne money, I guess. So, I can carve off a chunk of that and send it to you right away if you need it. Same PayPal?

Nat

———

Re: Jourdemayne Project (5) > INBOX
Alec Christian **achristian@gmail.com** 3:37 a.m.
to Nathalie Seguin **nat@nseg.org**

Hey, cool! Yup, always the same.

New elements, huh? That's gotta be exciting as shit. If there's anything like the rumoured "lost clips"—the flashes in the future-vision sequence where you can see things like the Berlin Wall falling, or headlines about Princess Di's death, or footage from 9/11—then you know you need to tell me, right? ;) Or at least confirm that rumour Soraya M. was telling me about, that they actually shot footage that was meant to go *after* the film's "real" ending. (Some people even say you can see your own death in the hagstone darkness, eventually—but then again, they would.)

Still tracking down cast and crew; a smaller pool of names, thanks to the double-duty overlap, which makes it quicker to get through but also means hitting a lot of literal dead ends in very short order, which is about as depressing as you'd expect. All the actors are dead except for Georgie Spack (Oswald), who has Alzheimer's, and fuck is *that* a sad case—a coalition of LGBTQI+ activists had finally just managed to get him out of that place his family and the psychiatrists had him committed to for getting an "unnecessary" double mastectomy (because there's no such thing as being a trans man, dontcha know) when the new diagnosis came down, so he had maybe a month of freedom before they had to get him placed in a completely different care facility. Much the same on the non-performer crew side, unfortunately—Maren Carbray got ovarian cancer in 2000, the others were mostly self-taught amateurs who sort of dropped off the map, etc. Between Thatcher, drugs and AIDS, the 1980s did for a lot of UK peeps. . . plus the drink, man. Fuck, film types love to drink. As we both know.

So, now I'm following three potential loose ends—four, if you count Lady Lil, who I somehow doubt is gonna give me shit: Hannah Glaive, the cinematographer, plus the two roles with no names next to them—Milady and her maid, the black girl. Glaive's last record of residence is in Birmingham; as for the other two. . . well, we'll see.

Keep safe, and tell me everything!!!!

--Alec

————

HAGSTONE ESSAY NOTES, Notebook Eleven, N.S.

How was Hagstone put together?

Ashbet Lamp, "consultant"/co-writer and co-director, became a psychic after being blinded in World War II at the age of sixteen (massive keloid cataracts on both eyes). She was raised as a Spiritualist and had always practiced automatic writing but began conducting her own séances after she claimed her "spirit guide" visited her in hospital during her convalescence. Claimed the guide helped give her knowledge of the backgrounds through which she "saw" the script's events—lost history, forgotten history, women's history.

She was contacted by Maren Carbray, who would become her co-director and the film's producer, while visiting the Des Esseintes Circle in Ontario, Canada, where Lamp gave a lecture about the visions she had during her séances—the fact that the automatic writing she produced was always markedly different from what she "received" or channelled while answering clients' questions. All the writing was in the same handwriting, very different from her own, using archaic grammar and vocabulary eventually dated to the 1600s. At the time (1973), Carbray was making a documentary about the DEC's attempts to reconstruct Kate-Mary Des Esseintes' famous ectoplasmic "helper," using tulpa-making methods. (Maybe reference the 1972 Philip Experiment, during which a Toronto parapsychological society tried to "create" and communicate with the fictional ghost of a Civil War soldier—did the DEC know about that? Confirm, if possible; cut, if not.)

After filming the lecture, Carbray started to have dreams she believed were sparked by Lamp's automatic writings and claimed she recognized them as "the other half" of Lamp's narrative, so she went to Britain, bringing her core crew with her, where Lamp conducted a series of séances that led to the script being written, the shoot planned, the setting chosen and the Jourdemayne family approached for support. (Confirm exactly when Lamp and Lady Lil met, if possible. Carbray seemed to think they were intimate; true? Probably irrelevant.) (I do seem to recall something about Lady Lil's own grandmother being pretty "loopy," in her time—the 1930s? The reason the Staffordshire estate was so great for shooting *Hagstone* was at least in part due to *that* Lady J.'s commitment to "rewilding," long before the term got popular. She supposedly had to pay massive taxes to keep the Crown from taking even part of it for war effort farming, for example.)

Current available versions

The remastered BluRay release from NoneSeen [2015], made from a shitty VHS dub with burnt-in Dutch subtitles that popped up in Canada during the 1980s and began making the rounds at fan conventions. Rumours of a Korean DVD version with extra footage cut to make room for TV commercials, as well as a hybrid edit that sometimes turns up on YouTube which someone involved in the original film might have put together. Finally, there's the maybe-myth that a rough cut made from dailies was stolen at some point, possibly by someone who worked for either the Canadian distributor or the post-production studio where it was mastered, then matched with the soundtrack afterwards. This version shows things captured by the camera during scenes cut later, as well as various background action and alternate cuts. All the extant versions have the same problems: recurring fuzzy focus, intermittent sound drop out, clunky pacing that feels like a bad editing job—mine has to be better. HAS TO BE.

Tweak the existing print. Clean, patch the missing elements. Cut them back in. Restore the whole thing. Burnish till shiny.

That's the plan.

———

Re: **Jourdemayne Project (6)** > INBOX
Nathalie Seguin **nat@nseg.org** 6:16 a.m.
to Alec Christian **achristian@gmail.com**

Alec—sorry it's taken me so long to get back; the new material I'm working on takes a lot more time than the earlier print, partly because the quality's much worse, but also because of other issues. I'll explain, but I have to start with a brainwave I had last night, jotting notes.

You know how everybody who's ever seen a version of *Hagstone* complains about how bad the pacing is, how the editing makes the story feel hiccuppy and jerky? It just hit me: once you account for broadcast cuts like the Korean DVD and the changes made in the fan-edits, most of the really disruptive edits are in every version across the board—which means they were present in the studio's original, now lost, theatrical master. But I can't make that make sense. Limited budget or not, Maren Carbray was a CBC rising star—she wouldn't have let a film school freshman job like that out of her edit suite, and Lamp couldn't have done anything about it either way. So, either someone else *chose* to hack the story to bits before the public ever saw it, someone no one knows about, or. . . I don't know what.

Which brings me to those other issues: these new source elements? They have some *seriously* strange stuff wrong with them. Don't even know if I can call it "wrong," it's not interfering with restoration or transfer, but the film itself just *feels* weird when I touch it—like a different set of chemicals was used for development, maybe, or a different base polymer. And periodically, in three- or four-frame chunks that occur every minute or two of run-time, it looks like somebody's used some kind of translucent staining process to mark the film up in deliberate patterns. *Weird* patterns too; not letters or numbers or time-codes, more like zodiac signs, except I can't find anything online that looks like these. The exposure's too faint and short for anyone to see at proper running speed—well, to consciously notice, at least—but the fact that the client didn't mention it? That bothers me. I don't know whether I'm expected to include these subliminal sigils in the final transfer or edit them out, and if I get it wrong, I could get hit with a lawsuit that'd basically destroy me.

(Why didn't I ask my agent Suz, the third party involved here? I did. She didn't see how it was relevant.)

(Fuck.)

Also—believe me, I know this is going to sound ridiculous coming from someone who moved out of a city to cut down on her panic attacks, but I'm beginning to get freaked out here, and not like I used to, not like any way I've ever felt before. Panic attacks I get; I recognize that shit. This is something else. It's like I'm being watched, all the time. When I'm working, it's like the *movie*'s watching me.

I know you know I hate pressuring people, friends especially, but—whatever you can find out, it just got a lot more important. Please tell me whatever you find.

Nat

———

Re: Jourdemayne Project (7) > INBOX
Alec Christian **achristian@gmail.com** 4:10 p.m.
to Nathalie Seguin **nat@nseg.org**

Fuckin' *sigils*? Christ.

Nat—if you were worried about sounding crazy, don't. I believe you. Not the first time I've had to take some pretty unbelievable shit on faith.

Good news is: I found Hannah Glaive—she's in her nineties and in a nursing home, just like Georgie. Difference is, her mind's still with us. Didn't seem at all surprised by some of the questions I asked her, either. The stuff she said. . . well, it's not reassuring, I guess. Best I can suggest is that it does provide evidence you weren't given critical information about the job, which might protect you from breach of contract if you need to bail. But one step at a time.

I recorded the interview; file's attached. Have a listen.

Alec

———

TRANSCRIPT hglaive-20240913.mp3

AC: I'm grateful for your time, Ms. Glaive—

HG: Hannah, boy. No gratitude, either; any other matter I'd be grateful to *you*, just for breaking the monotony. Can't be happy *this* finally happened, though.

AC: You were expecting me?

HG: You or someone like you. I've my own phone, you know. Can see what everyone's raving about, on Reddit and what. Been rumblings before, 'course, but this time felt different. So Loopy Lil's trying to bring it back, is she? (PAUSE) Oh, don't waste my time. *Hagstone.*

AC: Well, her grandson's spearheading it, but he'd need her permission, I guess. I have a friend working on restoring the last few reels right now, and she's run across things that've, uh, provoked some questions.

HG: Mm, I'll just bet. She seen the signs on the film, yet? Ashbet

Lamp drew those. Used a Chinese writing brush and some kind of chemical, to mark up the daily negatives in the darkroom. One day I turned out the work-lights, just to see what'd happen. Didn't slow her down at all—don't think she even noticed. (Beat) That's a joke, son. Her bein' blind, and all.

AC: Ms. Glaive—Hannah—look, I really need to know if my friend is in any kind of trouble here.

HG: Might be. Might not. I mean, the film. . . ah, hell.

AC: Is there something in it? Like—is it haunted, cursed? What?

HG: I don't know. I really. . . I really don't.
(LONG PAUSE)
Who else've you talked to?

AC: Nobody. There's nobody left.

HG: And why don't that surprise me?

AC: Okay, um—well, let's start with something else, then. Who came to you first?

HG: Maren, obviously. Hadn't worked together before, but we knew each other from the Ceeb and the Beeb—both of us'd been back and forth, doin' co-pros and the like; she fucked my ex, I fucked hers. Was pretty good with a camera herself, but when you've already agreed to let a woman who can't even see share credit for your direction. . . well, you need another pair of eyes. That was me.

AC: You don't sound like you liked Miss Lamp, much.

HG: Pffft. She brought in Lil, so that was good, and all—Lil and her money, Lil and her land. But no, I didn't have much respect for her kind. Thought she were a faker, at best. At worst. . .

AC: Do you know how she and Lady Lil first met?

HG: Sure. That Basque fella she married threw parties, hired all sorts to entertain—magicians, rock stars, strippers, tarot readers. Ashbet Lamp was one of those. Helped the stories she told reminded Lady Lil of ones she'd heard already, old family tales, old secrets. . .

AC: What?

HG: Didn't you know? Milady—the courtesan who married a rich Cavalier lord with an interest in occultism, gone blind from the pox, both kinds. . . what'd you *think* her last name was? And who better than Miss Lamp to play her, from Lady Lil's point of view?

AC: Ashbet Lamp played Milady, that's what you're saying. (PAUSE) So. . . who played the maid?

HG: Hm, well. That's a whole other can of worms.
(LONG PAUSE)
You know much about Miss Lamp's work, after the War? After she lost her sight?

AC: Uh, all right: I know she graduated from automatic writing to mediumship, if that's what it's called—

HG: 'Cause she "found her spirit guide," yeah? Ever read much about spirit guides, boy?

AC: Dude, I'm almost forty. (GLAIVE LAUGHS) They're like these. . . ghosts who help a medium out, right? Pet spirits that connect them with whoever clients want to hear from. Usually kind of racist stereotypes with super-exaggerated accents, y'know, um— "me big Chief Red Cloud, come from Great Plains Beyond, tell-um heap good news of life after death." That sort of crap.

HG: That's about the size of it. Well, Miss Lamp's spirit guide said it was a little black girl. . . a "Moor," she called her. Said she was dressed in black, like a maid. And her dress looked like it was from the Civil War.

AC: So that's how you guys ended up casting the role.

HG: Ha! Maren never cast anyone for that; Ashbet Lamp, either. Show you the sides, but I burned 'em. You'll just have to take my word for it.

AC: . . . I'm sorry?

HG: Not as sorry as I am.
(LONG PAUSE)
All the scenes with Milady, we did those on a closed set: me, Maren, Miss Lamp. Nobody else. We cut 'em in after, matched 'em up pretty well with the other stuff, I dare say so myself. I mean, there was a bit of the old herky-jerky, here and there. . .
(PAUSE) Not much to be done about it, though. And Maren claimed it added to the effect.

AC: What effect?

HG: Was obsessed with all that subliminal shite, our Maren. Just like Ken Russell, and that Hollywood hack who did *The Exorcist*.

Inserts, jump-cuts, parallel imagery—your friend's probably seen her fair share of 'em, by now. Anyhow.

AC: The girl.

HG: Like I said, we shot them scenes on a closed set—me, Maren, Miss Lamp in all her finery. Even her costume smelled weird to me, y'know. . . like dust, rot. The vizard mask was yellowed. I think Lady Lil might've loaned it to her, out of some old trunk in the attic. (PAUSE) So, we'd set the lighting and block it, Maren would hold up the clapperboard, call it. And then—

(LONG PAUSE)

AC: Ms. Gl—Hannah—are you saying. . . ?

HG: You tell *me* what I'm sayin'.

(LONG PAUSE)

AC: (Finally) Could you *see* the girl, when you. . . filmed her?

HG: Not then, no. After. When we developed the rushes. She'd just step out onscreen, like. . . out of a shadow. Maybe that's what the signs were for, on the film—to make sure other people could see her, the way Miss Lamp always could. (PAUSE) Could *hear* her, though.

AC: The girl—like on set? During shooting?

HG: Yeah, that's right.

AC: How the fuck was *that* supposed to work?

HG: Well, I thought herself—Miss Lamp—were a ventriloquist. I mean, I don't believe in mediums, or such. . . didn't. Then.

AC: I mean—a vizard mask, right? Doesn't even have straps. You hold it on with, like, a knob on the inside, between your teeth. So Ashbet Lamp *couldn't* have been talking, no more than Milady does. . .

HG: Aye, well, I thought she were a *good* ventriloquist—expert, with tricks no one'd seen before, outside of the spook-show. Had to be. She were famous, after all.

AC: And—you never said anything? To anyone?

HG: What would I have told, and to who? "Oh, you just watched a film starred a ghost?" Used to be they frowned on shite like that, even in Cannes. (PAUSE) Know what Maren used to say, when people asked why *Hagstone* got so trippy?

AC: Yeah. "It's history; they believed stuff worked differently, back then. To them, what we find mundane would be science fiction. That's why a movie set in another time period can only be approached experimentally, through a series of shorthands, because they're aliens to us, the same way we'd be aliens to them."

HG: Ha, you *have* done your research. Or think about it this way —once upon a time, there was no such thing as physics or UFOs; nobody knew how disease worked, or how every drop of water was full of things too tiny to see. But they still knew if you got drunk as fuck, chewed a few wild mushrooms and lit a candle in a dark room, ghosts would start dancin' on the walls. Already knew long since how the eye can trick itself, from campfires, from caves. How it can show you whatever you want to see. . . or what you *don't* too. Far more of that last part, depending on who held the flame.

AC: Gods and monsters, huh?

HG: Aye, lad. Now turn that bloody thing off, will you? I'm done.

————

Transcribed from SMS text message chain, smartphone of N. Seguin

Tuesday, May 13, 2024 8:22 p.m

> Alec—Im scared
> Really really scared
> No fucking clue what to do
> U there?

8:25 p.m.

> Been stuck outside my house for 2 hrs

8:33 p.m

Clock got turned around. Working till 6 am, falling asleep at my edit desk, waking up when it's dark again. Having nightmares where Im wkg on the future vision sequence, and I see things I KNOW in the cuts, from my LIFE. PEOPLE I

8:34 p.m

> Sometimes see characters in my dreams too
> Oswald, Christina
> The Witchfinder all burnt black, one eye bugging out

Milady's mask
Sometimes just floating by itself, or on someone else's face
Sometimes on ME, in a mirror

8:36 p.m

Never saw the maid till today
and I WASNT SLEEPING
I fucking swear I was awake

8:39 p.m.

Woke up round 6 pm, went to kitchen, made coffee
Looked out the big bay window doors to the deck
Saw her right behind me in the reflection
Close enough to touch
She was reaching to put a hand on my shoulder

8:52 p.m

Sorry, had to pause there to throw up
Not joking

So, I screamed, threw my mug, of course she wasnt there when I
looked but somehow I knew she WAS still there, dont ask how
and I ran

Been walking up and down the beach ever since
Forgot my shoes
My feet hurt

8:53 p.m

Ran back in once to get my phone

Didnt see anything, but I wasnt staying to look

I dont know what to do

No ferry to the mainland till 7 am tomorrow

8:57 p.m

God Im so stupid

Youre still in fucking England

like 4 am there probably

FUCK

9:16 p.m.

Moved out here because I thought itd be more peaceful ha ha

———

Re: Jourdemayne Project (8) > INBOX
Alec Christian **achristian@gmail.com** 4:10 p.m.
to Nathalie Seguin **nat@nseg.org**

Hey, Nat. Good to hear you're settling in at your friend's place—again, I'm so, so sorry I didn't connect with you when things hit the fan out there. Thank God it's spring, right? If you'd had to spend the night outside in January. . . No, you know what, I don't want to think about that. Bet you don't, either.

I haven't had a chance to reach out to anybody I know about your contract questions, yet, but I have to say, supernatural shit isn't a generally accepted cause for contract negation. Better news, however—I may have found something useful, though I don't know how, yet. But.

Long story short: I went to Jourdemayne Manor myself. I didn't get in, of course. But I yelled into the gate intercom that I wasn't going away until I spoke to Lady Lil, and their security guy threatened to call the cops on me, and we shouted at each other until I told him to tell her, "The Moorish girl's back!" No answer to that for a long time, and next thing this polite, creaky-sweet voice like Dame Judi on a snort of helium asks, "Young man, is this about *Hagstone*?" And I said, "Bet your ass, ma'am."

Couldn't get the conversation on record, 'cause the gate speaker was too crappy for my mic to pick up. But I got the salient points. Apparently, the whole *Hagstone* story goes back to an actual Jourdemayne ancestor around the time of the (English) Civil War—blind Milady, possibly once a sex worker, who found one of these stones and (being both a superstitious old fart *and* an asshole aristocrat), made her little enslaved maid look through it for her, so she could find out when the Civil War was going to end. Well, the maid did this and promptly died, and Lady Jourdemayne was *awfully* put out, because the girl had grown up in her family. . . ever since her client-turned-hubby Lord Jourdemayne bought her from some Portuguese traders out of Morocco, just so she could be a helpmeet for young Milady, who was already dealing with—"issues," was how Lady Lil put it, above and beyond all that syphilis he probably gave her in the first place. So. Yeah.

I asked her how Ashbet Lamp had gotten involved, and her voice gets a bit more quavery, but it's still weirdly cheerful; she says something like, "Oh, that's an old, old story. Let's just say I'm not the first person in the world who took a great interest in a fascinating new acquaintance, only to find that the acquaintance was less interested in me than in. . . someone else in my life. For a while I thought I was willing to settle for what I could get. But then, finally, I realized everything I'd done for Bet thus far all just added up to a stepping stone—what she needed to do in order to get to what she truly wanted, whatever the cost."

And I asked her what that was, and she sounded surprised and said, "Well, the hagstone, of course. The power of its vision, infused into the spirit of that poor dead girl who'd been flittering around her since the Blitz—some dreadful image of the future, the last war, humankind's final destiny. Do we survive whatever we do to ourselves, or not? That's why Bet stole the final master of the film, the *complete* master, from Maren Carbray's studio back in 1975, took it home and screened it for herself, somehow. Perhaps because she needed it as the final step in some ritual she'd been designing for—oh, years at least, maybe her whole life."

"Did it work?" I asked, probably sounding like a complete dumbass. And her voice goes very dry, and she says, "I very much doubt the way she hoped. Not since Maren and I found her body on the floor of her flat with the front of her skull gone, the entire inside scooped out, and the edges and inner surface of the bone charred black."

Well, I didn't know WHAT the fuck to say to that, strangely enough, but that didn't stop her. "I suppose you're wondering why we sent any sort of version of the film out into the world," Lady Lil says. "*I* would if I were you. Well, my husband was already on the hook for almost twenty-five thousand pounds, which he did *not* appreciate, and we had to give the distributor something if we wanted to make any money at all. So, she checked the master over by herself—didn't even tell Hannah Glaive—and chopped out anything she said she thought 'looked odd.' I was young and sentimental enough that I asked if I could keep the leftovers, even though I intended to reconcile with Henri; no idea what I thought I'd do with them, after. But, well, life goes on. And if my pretentious *cinematiste* of a grandson hadn't stumbled across those reels in the same attic where Bet and I found Milady's outfits, none of any of this would be happening now."

"My friend is restoring it right now," I told her. "She feels like she's in danger. Is she?"

"I think not. Unless she's a medium, that is."

"She's seen the maid."

"Anyone who's watched the film, cut or not, has seen the maid," she said. So, I told her some more about your situation; her basic advice was take everything new you were given and burn it. I told her her grandson would sue you into bankruptcy, and she said she'd try to get him to change his mind but couldn't make promises. "I'll also ensure that he never hears about this visit," she said. Which was unhelpful, but kind of nice.

And that was that.

So, night's fallen, and I'm walking back to my car, feeling like I didn't accomplish all that much (beside getting creeped the fuck out and genuinely nauseous, at least for a minute or so there). I took a little detour through the woods, looking for the remains of the witch's hut set. Didn't find it. It's a beautiful place, very peaceful, though I'd prefer to go there during daylight hours.

Anyhow, just as I get back to the road, I step on something that sort of squeaks under my foot. I moved my boot and something glinted. So, I dug around and found this.

[SEE ATTACHED PHOTO]

A hagstone. Not THE hagstone, obviously, but. . .

I wrapped it up and FedExed it to you, yesterday. You should get it by Monday.

Get back to me, man. And stay safe!

Alec

———

Re: **Jourdemayne Project (9)** > INBOX
Nathalie Seguin **nat@nseg.org** 6:00 a.m.
to Alec Christian **achristian@gmail.com**

You know I had to go back, right? All my shit was there, and not just the professional stuff. So, I did, like a fucking dope.

I've NEVER been that scared in my own house. Ridiculously scared—I mean, there was nothing there, and I checked the whole place. But man, I wish I'd asked my friend to come with me.

Hair on the back of my neck was standing up like quills, my whole body slick with cold sweat. I grabbed my laptop, the deck with everything I'd digitized thus far, my hard drives. . . the place smelled weird, like vinegar. Old emulsion. Like I could still smell those elements, even though they were all back in their cans. Which I did *not* take with me, BTW. . . not that I could've, those things are huge, really heavy. I'd've wrecked my back. Not to mention

(I just didn't want them anywhere near me)

Now here's the weirdest thing: I hadn't read your email yet. WiFi went out at my friend's place, like it often does (and mine too—this happens a lot on the island, because it's an island). But as I'm going out the front door, locking it behind me, I notice the mailbox is open, something sticking out of it. Better get that, I think.

And I don't know why, but next thing I know I'm opening it up right there, ripping off the wrapping like I might find a golden ticket inside; we have litter laws out here, but just drop that shit like it's hot and watch it blow away, staring at what I've found. 'Cause hey ho, it's a stone with a hole through it. Flint, looks like. About the size of my palm. I can see my life-line through the hole, cut in half by its edge.

Better not look through *that*, I think. I remember thinking it.

I guess you know what comes next.

Call me.

———

TRANSCRIPT OF PHONE CALL BETWEEN ALEC CHRISTIAN /
NATHALIE SEGUIN
chrisnat-20240914.mp3

AC: Are you okay?

NS: Define "okay."

AC: Nat, for fuck's sake—

NS: Look, I'm just being an asshole. Yeah, I'm all right, I guess.
Back on the mainland, in hospital. . .

AC: (INTERRUPTS) Fucking *hospital*? Nat, Jesus—

NS: Calm down, man. Let me talk.

(PAUSE)

AC: You looked through it.

NS: Seemed like the thing to do, at the time. Why the fuck did
you send it, otherwise?

AC: . . . yeah.

(PAUSE)

NS: One minute I'm just staring at it, and the next. . . shit, I don't
know. Literally. I'm back at my friend's place, and she's
screaming something at me, like: 'Oh shit, Nat, what the fuck did
you do? What's with your face?' And I didn't know what she was
even talking about. Just that there was this bright light behind
me, and this weird noise, and the wind was hot on my back. . .

AC: Did your—was that your *house*?

NS: It burned down, yup. Everything I had, except the stuff in my pack. (A BEAT) Which means I'm not getting sued, at least; that's the good news.

AC: The reels.

NS: Yeah, they're gone. Weird symbols and all.

AC: Just as well?

NS: That's what I'm gonna tell myself, from now on.

(LONG PAUSE)

AC: . . . why're you in hospital?

NS: They think I burnt my eye, somehow. Scorched the cornea.

AC: That doesn't sound good.

NS: It's not. (A BEAT) Thing on my face was a burn too, apparently. Second degree. The doctors say it'll go away, with time. Say I was lucky.

AC: . . . fuck.

NS: You got that right. (A BEAT) I saw the maid again, just for a second, when I turned around. Before my friend dragged me off towards the beach. She was standing up the road looking down at us, fire behind her—man, that was a shot and a half, right there. Wish I'd had a real camera on me, not just my phone—

AC: (INTERRUPTS AGAIN) You took a *picture*?

NS: No, Alec, I didn't take a fucking picture—I didn't have time.
Fire spreads fast on an island; we just beat it down the beach, ran
like hell, waded out into the water. Threw the fucking stone
away and kept on going. (A BEAT) By the time the fire ship and
the ferry got there, I thought I was going into shock. But they got
us on board pretty fast, warmed us up, took us straight over.
Bandaged my face. . .
(LONG PAUSE)
Hope that girl likes island life, though—that's all I can say.
'Cause I'm not going back, anytime soon.

AC: I don't blame you, man.

NS: I know you don't. But thanks.

(LONG PAUSE)

AC: So. . .

NS: So.

AC: . . . when you looked through the stone. . . what did you see?

(LONGER PAUSE)

NS: I can't remember.

AC: Would you tell me, if you did?

(EVEN LONGER PAUSE; THEN)

NS: No.

POOR BUTCHER-BIRD

"Down here," he says, and I nod, like it's not obvious. Dip my head like I'm nervous, but a little shakily too. Like I'm as excited as he is. You have to be careful about these things; he's dumb, sure, but nobody's *that* dumb.

You'd be surprised.

I had to work hard to hook up with this guy, who claims his "name" is Shrike93, just like his email. These Web handles really crisp my arse-hairs, which I know makes me sound old—old enough to know what a Luddite actually was, any rate. The main good part about having once been a factory girl in the 1890s is, it keeps me small and weak looking. Not a threat, supposedly, 'specially when stood next to some bro like the Shrike, all swole up with hormone-saturated meat and childhood vaccines. Nothing like. That, and I know not to sound how I think, either, when I speak out loud. Worked hard on that over the years. So much so, it holds pretty well, except when I get riled up; lucky how none of this posturing is quite enough to rile me, though. Not as yet.

He always picks two, and one of 'em doesn't tend to come back—that's the rumour. That's why I wasn't surprised I found another potential initiate waiting for him, when I got to our IRL meet-point; made sure to bristle a bit, then waited for the Shrike to step in once it got truly heated. Can't waste that precious red, now, can we? And he was quick enough to make his move; the minute this other wee pixie haircut bitch pulled a flick-knife out. Which was just as well. . . for her.

She thinks she'll be the one gets picked, all right. But I *know* I will, and that's the difference.

Experience always wins; that's my motto. So down we go, the three of us, the Shrike leading the way, with me and Pixie-Cut trailing after.

It's almost always down, with these sorts. The house is an abandoned two-story box on a high-fenced lot somewhere in the Annex, thick inside with cobwebs and mouse shit and dust, except for the lane these slags have cleared between the kitchen's back entrance and the door to the basement. And at the bottom of those stairs, there's another door—brand-new, very fancy, normal on the outside but heavier than it looks, with a neat little combination smart-lock built into its knob that has to be keyed from the Shrike's iPhone, using his thumbprint. He undoes it on one side, then does it back up on the other.

Note to self: need to get hold of that thumb.

Inside, another stubby flight of stairs, going down half a story to some sort of sub-basement; might have been meant as a wine-cellar, maybe, or a bomb shelter. There's lit candles stuck in bottles everywhere, half-melted into wax stalagmites, and the air heavy with incense like it's 1969. Whole floor's paved with bare mattresses slicked in dark plastic on either side of a clear area, three feet wide by thirty long from the door on inwards, mosaic-tiled in red and gold—a ritual path to that joke of a shrine they've set up along the back wall. And there, at last, is that big red lacquer cabinet, inside which I can only assume they've got the thing—the person—I want.

The rest of the cult are all lined up on either side of it too, not that they probably think of themselves as such: twenty of 'em, all told, unless somebody else is hiding in the bog somewhere. Not that they seem to *have* a bog down here, that I can see.

They've all got names he insists on telling me, which I forget almost immediately, 'cause it makes it easier. Instead, I file 'em under characteristics: Blue Hair, (too much) Face-Metal, Green Highlights, Snatched Brows (with scarification), Needs More T. Not to mention Bare Midriff, Assless Chaps, and straight-up Topless (girl *and* boy), plus a variety of other mock-Goth costuming; leather, studs and vinyl, too-large hoodies paired with artfully ripped fishnets. There's even one in the back seems to be wearing a blood-stained fake fur-suit, bright pink, splotched all over like some naff bunny-leopard hybrid. Think I'll call him Anime Chimera, if and when it comes to it.

This is church night for them, I reckon. Get together with like-minded individuals, share

something meaningful, go through the ritual celebration that gives their dull little weeks a goal—all dressed up with some-thing to pray to, not to mention somebody to kill over it. And so blessed, blessed sure, in their black little hearts, how no one else ever does the same. Bloody children.

Still, kids can be tricky, 'specially when they're high, and armed. As I know from hard experience.

They're passing 'round bottles now, probably scarfed from parents' liquor cabinets: tequila, scotch, bourbon, vodka, red wine. I take a swallow or two, enough to make sure my breath smells like theirs, and mime the rest, while Pixie-Cut gleefully chugs whatever she's handed. By the time the Shrike stands up by the cabinet and loudly claps his hands, she's well and truly plastered.

"Brothers and sisters!" he shouts. "The moon's gone 'round again. It's that time!" Yells and cheers and hoots. "Time to renew ourselves, once more. Time to be *more*." More noise. I clench my jaw, holding my cardboard smile still. "Anyone have a story to share?"

A beat.

"I did it!" Green Highlights, a girl, yells abruptly. "I found my boss. Told him I'd changed my mind, and when we were alone, I broke his nose and I knocked out his teeth—" this gets more cheers "—and then I carved PERV into his forehead, and I wham-mied him so hard he's never gonna know who did it! *Ever!*"

Howls of triumph fill the room; people hug Green Highlights, slap her back, hoist her hands into the air like she's won a boxing match. She's actually crying now I look close enough, poor cow.

Still, I'm sure it feels good, while it lasts.

Up by the cabinet, Shrike's grinning like a preacher tallying up donations in his head. Calls for other stories, and gets them: all much the same, though none quite as righteously vindictive as Green Highlights's. Petty grudges, gleeful sadism, conquest-notches; the sort of selfish that people dream about in bed or in front of a bathroom mirror, through clenched teeth, tears, or panting, between the short strokes. The *I Deserve This* rag, I call it —high on their own drama, the sweet bile backwash. Pixie-Cut looks pretty much like she's already halfway to getting off herself at the spectacle, what with those big eyes and that flushed face, rapid-breathing through her nose; me, I make sure to keep on trembling just in case. Not that anybody's really looking.

Finally, Shrike calms the crowd down with a gesture and beckons me and Pixie-Cut closer, both of us shouldering past each other down the red-gold road to Paradise. Because tonight's the climax, right? The end of a months-long seduction waged over every form of social media available, led down a trail of whispers about transformation, transfiguration, apotheosis, *power*. Some new kind of kick, or—just maybe—a very, very old one, all dressed up in post-Millennial drag.

"Other people talk about confidence, or love, or tapping enneagrams," he tells us. "But we're not like that. Our shit isn't bullshit, it's *real*. Gotta be ready to handle it, though. . . to show

how you're willing to pay the price. That you can *stand* knowing this sort of secret."

The crowd's stepped back by this point, clustered to hide exactly what's happening with the cabinet's slick red doors; behind them, I can hear a couple of flunkies wrestling with the gilded handles, grunting in effort as they heave it open and pull out *something*, heavy enough to scrape the floor beneath. The ones in front grin a bit to themselves, eyes studying our faces: oh, they want a reaction, can't wait to see it, that first moment when —whatever it is we're gonna end up looking at—registers. Not that Pixie-Cut even seems to notice, her gaze still riveted to the Shrike's own, chest heaving pornographically.

"No rituals," Shrike goes on, smiling even wider. "All you need to do is see it. 'Cause when you do, I'll look at you, and I'll just *know*. That simple."

I nod, slightly; Pixie-Cut swallows, quick and dry enough I know she's going to ask, which means I don't have to. Blurting out, a second later: "Know *what*?"

"If you're one of us, of course."

He turns, smoothly—like he's rehearsed it. Steps aside to show what's standing there: a triangle of tarnished brass, three coiled legs topped with a wide, flat metal bowl big enough to wash in, and who knows, maybe that's what it was originally meant for. There's a half-mirror set above it, after all, fanned out like a glass ruff behind the thing that sits inside, haloing its awfulness in sullen, splintered light.

A gasp, from Pixie-Cut. While from everyone else—even the Shrike—comes a long, slow breath, drawn out rather than in. Half religious awe, half physical pleasure, admixed with just a hint of happy recognition: so *beautiful,* this artifact, this thing we serve and own. This thing that owns *us.*

It's really hard not to laugh, watching the other girl's face change. Watching her suddenly grasp that this isn't a joke or a piece of ego-boo, simple playacting. That when they crow about violence wreaked on anyone who pisses them off, they actually *mean* it, and the only right move for any still halfway sane and moral person who finds themselves in this particular situation is to scream and run forever.

Neither of which she has the brains to do, of course. Instead—

"That's a *head*," she blurts out, yet again; can't stop herself from doing it, poor bint. Like she genuinely thinks maybe someone in here just hasn't noticed yet and needs to know.

"It is," the Shrike agrees.

"A head. . ."

"Yes."

"You guys. . . *killed* somebody. . ."

The Shrike smiles, slightly. "Not exactly," he replies.

Which is when the head opens its eyes and blinks at us, blearily. Like we just woke it up. Like it's *pissed.*

Around us, the crowd whoops and claps. One of them gives this weird crooning laugh, a baby's crow of pure delight. The head opens its mouth, lips drawing back in a snarl, the corners slightly torn—think it'd be hissing, if it only still had a voice box instead of that ragged bit of gristle and skin where the neck's been sliced through right underneath the jaw. The slightly uneven mixture of bone, tendon and sluggish black grue prevents it from standing straight up, like it's on a pedestal, so it has to sit cocked sidelong instead, off-kilter.

Pixie-Cut is shocked silent now, for which I don't blame her. The head in the bowl rolls bloodshot, ice-coloured eyes up at us, lids flickering spasmodically—I see its pupils narrow horizontally, u-shaped, cephalopodal. Its filthy mat of hair is snarled to the point I can't tell its original colour, let alone whether it's supposed to be curly or straight; the face, both gaunt and flat, has skin like black volcanic beach sand, cheekbones like napped flint. The teeth are stained brown, serrated edges sharp enough to glint in the candlelight. Its jaws work up and down, trying to bite at empty air. Its nostrils flare, eyes snapping back and forth between me and Pixie-Cut, who's started to make a noise like a balloon deflating. I raise my eyebrows.

"Someone's not too good with surprises, is she?" I ask the Shrike, as his cult explodes in laughter around us. He doesn't reply, though, only sighs, like he's seen this before. Then he glances at me—I try to look thrilled, or not disgusted, at the very least—before nodding to the others.

They're on Pixie-Cut before she's even finished taking her first step backwards, one on each arm, one behind her; Green Highlights yanks her head back and cuts her throat with a big kitchen knife, while the other two shove her hard, backwards, into the cast iron clawfoot bathtub they dragged up behind us during the Shrike's little speech. She trips over the edge, hands still trying to staunch her wound, quick enough her head slams into the tub's metal floor, ending her struggles instantly. And then there's only the sound of liquid, hot enough to steam a bit, glugging into the tub.

There's an odd little beat of silence, as if even the Shrike's startled how fast she went down. It sets me back a moment myself, truth told. Can't feel too much sympathy for Pixie-Cut; she wanted what these gobshites are selling, after all. . . just couldn't reckon the real price, not till it was too late. But it still hits hard sometimes, seeing life end like that: so sharp, so sudden, a blank face on a mound of cooling meat. Meat which used to be a person.

I'll probably go the same, one day—too fast to see it coming, let alone feel it happening.

The Shrike recovers himself, with a little shiver. He leans down and grabs Pixie-Cut's belt, hauling at the corpse till he folds her into one end of the tub, making room for her blood to pool at the other. Then he turns and reaches up, carefully, to lift the head from its dish. Hooks his fingers through knots of hair over its ears and makes sure to stay well shy of the teeth, slow and steady, same way a smith uses tongs to carry a casting cup full of molten metal. Gasps and whispers ripple through the crowd; they back away as he brings it within sight of the tub, which sets its jaws working even faster; the teeth grind against each other, making an eerie sort of *zizzz*, so much like flint striking I almost expect to see sparks fly from the mouth. But all that comes out is a slice of tongue, liver-coloured, torn where hunger's made it chew at itself.

"Who drinks first?" the Shrike asks, that same hyper, cultish, too-happy tone back in his voice. To which all the rest of 'em yell back, pretty much as one—

"*She* does!"

"That's right: her first, then us. Blood in and blood out, blood come 'round and back again like every full moon, every time, forever." Turning to me, then, with a return of that oh-so-charming smile, of his: "And you drink too of course, if you want to. Because. . . you *do* want to, don't you?"

And me, I don't even spare Pixie-Cut a blink, since that'd put me in the tub right along with her, most likely. Just hold his gaze instead, coolly, and reply, as I do—

"Wouldn't have bloody well come here in the first place, would I, if I didn't?"

"Smart girl," he says, approvingly. And lowers the head into the blood.

The moment he withdraws his hand, they all surge forwards, gathering 'round with avid eyes and panting mouths. I let the crowd carry me, let *my* mouth hang open too, trying not to breathe too deep; can't let the scent get to me. Not just yet.

The change starts the instant the head sets down. Swollen threads of reddish-purple tissue crack their way through the sand-black skin, spiralling up jawline and cheekbones like time lapse footage of vines growing, inflating out of nowhere. The eyes widen, their slotted pupils rippling, blooming circular; irises darken, sclera flushing abruptly clear—alert, aware, *human*. The lips plump out, tongue soft instead of shrivelled, blushing from purple back to pink the way jerky soaks up water. Beneath the black outer crust, smooth brown skin wells up, splitting it apart and shedding it in a rain of dark flakes; dust powders off the teeth, bleaching to old ivory, new ivory, salt white. Even the hair thickens, darker and sleeker under its entangling slick of dirt.

Suddenly, the thing in the tub is a living woman's head, face distorted with rage, eyes flashing around to glare at all of them, mouth shaping curses none of them would understand, even if they could lip read. The sight only makes them laugh and applaud. Metal-Face actually leans down and mouths a version of her own words exaggeratedly back at her, like he's imitating a bad kung fu movie dub. That just gets *more* laughs, making me sigh in disgust, if only on the inside: these bloody kids. No respect for anything, them. Not even themselves.

"Is that safe?" I distract Metal-Face by asking, when I can't stand to watch any more. "I mean. . . you're not supposed to look 'em in the eyes, right?"

He makes a raspberry noise, scoffing. "Nah, bitch can't tell you to do shit, not without lungs—just glowers at you, way she's doin' now. It's kind of a turn-on, actually." He grins at me, confidentially. I make myself grin back, choking down the spiky knot of fury in my gut. "'Sides which, sometimes if you get close enough, you can even kinda tell what she's thinking. . . you know, like all the stuff she wants to do to us for cuttin' her up in the first place, and yadda yadda. Like sharing somebody else's dream, and you're starrin' in it. Know what I mean?"

"I think so."

"You'll find out soon enough. It's trippy as hell."

The Shrike grabs the head by her hair again, lifting it high; the throat's ragged, severed edges have lengthened, strands of tissue twining down the way an avocado grows tendrils if you stick it in a glass of water, still soaking up red drops. I can see the white of bone amongst raw flesh—half a new vertebra straining to form itself, maybe—and the twin holes of trachea and esophagus. It's fascinating, if queasily so.

The Shrike holds her above his face and shakes the drops into his open mouth, gulping

them down, shuddering like it burns him good. Blood like scotch, like tequila, like mescal. Like Black Death vodka. Then he brings the head back down and smiles, right into her raging, champing face.

Next to him, Mr. Anime Chimera hands over yet another knife; no ripped-off cooking tool, this one, but a big, ugly thing with an ulna-length blade and a handle made from antler, fit to gut a wild boar. The Shrike takes it, spins it like some hibachi grill chef at a teppanyaki restaurant. The head snarls at the sight.

"Open up, baby," he tells her—practically purrs it—before he jams the blade in between her jaws, stabbing through tongue and soft palate alike with a squelch, then slicing back and forth out through both cheeks with a flourish deft enough I know the son of a bitch must actually have *practiced.*

Her mouth rips open in a soundless scream, tearing the wounds wider; I can see the helpless agony in her eyes before the Shrike drops the knife, forces the lower jaw shut and slams his mouth against her ruined lips, sucking up the spurting blood the way one of my old factory-floor mates might've slurped up the froth off the all-sorts keg's spigot when no one was looking— that hideous mixture of dregs sold for whatever pittance got offered at the local boozer's, right between the rat fighting pit and the hanging meat. The bottom half of his face is a crimson mask by the time he's done, white eyes glaring through the spatters above it.

He raises the head high. His teeth are sharper. His nails have sprouted into claws. He howls, and his flunkies all howl back at him. For the first time, there's a note in their voices that sends ice over my skin. They're stupid petty slags, these infants, but they're still monsters. Can't go forgetting that.

Shrike-boy turns the head so the mouth is facing away and holds it out, like an Aztec might show off a fresh-cut heart before throwing it into the flames. These blood-junkies all scramble up to it in a line, each one gulping down as much as they can before the rush knocks them crazy-eyed and reeling, stumbling away to make room for the next. Every few drinks, there's a pause as the Shrike reopens the gaping wounds in her face, which keep trying to close. And then it's my turn, right at the last. Bastards actually start chanting like it's a frat party, while Shrikey-boy lifts the head towards my face.

I tip my head forward, touching foreheads with the thing like we're old friends. Through slitted eyes I see the head's nostrils flare; it can't breathe, but this close, my scent's got to be in its nose all the same. Any luck, that'll be enough.

I'm sorry, I think, trying to will the words inside her skull. *You've suffered so much, taken so much insult, such. . . indignity. But this is the last time, I promise.*

(We *promise.*)

I press my mouth to the hot, sodden, shredded lips and smear my own with the run-off, forcing dry-swallow after dry-swallow to make as if I'm drinking. Trying not to think about how, if the Shrike relaxes his grip an instant, she could take my nose and lips off with one bite; *probably* won't, if she's recognized whose spoor lies on me, and yet.

At last, I pull away, do my best job of screaming at the roof like the rest of them, and then suddenly they're all around me— hugging me, pounding my back, kissing my cheeks and forehead and red, dripping mouth. I grin back and let them kiss me, let the orgy take me, even though I want to puke.

———

Finally. I slip my panties on, quick and quiet. The rest can wait. I step over the Shrike, heading for the cabinet; he blinks after me, clearly taken aback by how fast and steady I'm suddenly moving, but too blood-drunk to quite realize what's going on. And then, before comprehension can hit, I'm back, his big fancy gutting knife in my hand. Down on my knees, free hand slamming his arm down, *whack.* It's a good knife, no denying that. Takes his hand clean off, quick as a guillotine.

Shrike's mouth opens ludicrously wide, his eyes bulging; he grabs his spurting wrist, so choked with shock he can't even get a scream out, only a kind of rattling gasp. The blood dulls pain, but I think it must just be plain failure to understand what happened—he's gotten far too used to invulnerability.

I don't give him time to recover. I grab up his iPhone from where he left it, on a cabinet shelf, then weave deftly through the rest of the junkies to the door. His thumb activates the phone, and the security code's pre-entered on the app.

I shake my head, amused. "Sloppy, sloppy," I murmur, triggering the app as I toss the Shrike's hand over my shoulder.

The door unlocks with an audible clunk. I pull it back.

The woman who stands there is—as ever—the most lovely thing I've ever seen: Angel-tall, her eyes and hair the same shiny black, skin the colour of rose gold buffed with silk. When she smiles at me, I feel dizzy, lit from within, ready once more to beg to be drained to death's point again and again, living forever in that moment just before my heart starts to stutter and my breath to catch, my blood mainly plasma, sucked transparent. I start to kneel, but she lifts me back up, effortlessly.

"Not tonight," she murmurs, and I know it must be true. She always knows best, after all. "Milady," I agree, instead. And bow my head. The Shrike's roar cuts through the air, shocking the ghoul-junkies to their feet, turning the post-orgy haze instantly into a cold blast of fear and fury; they're all on their feet, crouching with claws out, sharpened teeth glinting through snarls. He staggers towards us, and I can see that his wrist's already begun healing—give him a couple of weeks and he'll have his hand back, not that he'll ever get to see it.

"Who's this bitch—?"

"She's my boss." I grin at him, this time, feeling like I'm washing away a week's worth of sweat. And then I point over their heads, at the cabinet behind them. At the head in the dish. They turn like they can't help themselves, and I finally let myself laugh as they see what I see. They gasp, swear, a couple even shriek.

The head is smiling. And its eyes are wide with joy, even as tears spill down its cheeks, trickling into the rotten grue around its throat.

"My boss," I repeat, "and *her* sister."

Milady smiles, close-mouthed, and shrugs off her cloak; it puddles to the floor, leaving her body nude and shining in the candlelight, like polished wood. Her eyes throw back the candle-light in a yellow-orange glitter. The ghoul-junkies instinctively shrink back, wide-eyed and slack-jawed, looking as much dismayed as terrified—like children about to cry, thinking only, *Oh shit, someone caught us, they caught us, they* caught *us!*

And then Milady lets her mouth spring open, and a forest of dripping fangs bursts forth. A long, purple tongue lashes out, whipping back and forth; drops of smoking spittle fly across the room. One hits Green Highlights' face. She screams in flabber-gasted agony and staggers back, hand over her cheek; when she takes it away, her smooth, pretty skin is a raw patch of oozing lesions, like leprosy gone mad. That *really* freaks the shit out of them.

Except the Shrike. I'll give him this, he must have been the only one with enough brains to think about this possibility.

He moves fast enough, even I can't follow, scooping up his knife with his remaining hand and flashing across the floor. In the next instant the knife's sliced almost spine deep through Milady's neck, in and out, while his wrist-stump smashes into her stomach and drives her backwards. She grabs her throat, genuinely surprised, as blood slicks her breasts in a crimson flood. I can't repress a gasp. The Shrike pins her against the wall with his stump and poises the knife over her breast, point first.

"Head and heart, bitch," he rasps at her, panting. "Everything else in the stories, it's all bullshit —but the one thing they all agreed on? Head, and heart, and spilling your blood. How do you think I got hold of that thing in the first place?"

A jerk of his head, back at the cabinet. Then turns his head, slowly, to glare at me, and asks exactly what I know he's gonna ask:

"... the hell are *you* laughing at?"

It takes a second to master myself.

"Well—you, obviously," I finally force out, revelling in being able to use my real voice for the first time since this whole dance began. His eyes narrow. "Regular Van Helsing, you, eh? But I don't suppose it ever occurred to you that some vampires, they come from places *outside* Transylvania."

His flummoxed look only makes me laugh harder. Adding, as I do—

"Yeah, that's right. Like... *this.*"

An unearthly noise rips through the air, between us: a sickening wet *crunch* like a hundred bones breaking at once, followed by a glutinous, bubbling, drawn-out squelch. Milady lifts her head, seeming to stand up taller—and taller, and taller yet, even taller still, as her blood-smeared body slips downward out of the Shrike's one-armed wrist pin and thuds to the floor. The torn skin of her sliced-open neck stretches wide, like a sphincter, shitting out a viscous tangle of pink and scarlet, purple and yellow; the acrid sour stink of acid billows into the room, so strong the Shrike stumbles backwards and half a dozen of the cultists double over, retching. Down against the wall like some cast aside doll with her skull popped off, legs slid out in front of her beneath, an abandoned toy made from flesh. And then...

Then, Milady floats free, glorious as some bee-orchid floating on the tide, her beautiful head sat proud atop a hovering mass of slimy, shining viscera. Flowers of breast fat cling to her fluttering lungs, her unshelled heart hammering fast enough to spurt blood with every beat, a thready red halo, jet upon jet upon jet. Her nude spine whipping like a wet glass snake, a legless lizard, all scales and tail.

Penanggalan, *they named my kind, in my homeland long ago,* she told me, the night we met, laughing at my fumbling attempt to shape my Southwark-flavoured lips 'round the word. Still can't really pronounce it, even now, but she never did make me try again after that night.

Just the sight's enough to break some of them. Metal-Face is one, exploding into a frantic screaming sprint for the door, face stretched and blind with the terror the vicious little idiot thought a god never needed to feel again. He's not as fast as the Shrike, but he's still faster than a human—and it's not enough.

Milady's tongue whiplashes through him like a razor, turning off his scream in a gurgle; he hits the floor in two pieces, body fountaining blood and his piercings clacking as his head rolls away. Howls, wails, and screams drown the room once more; this time, though, there's no triumph, no joy.

None but hers.

Milady floats forward as the blood-junkies cower away, sobbing, trying to push themselves back into the walls. I slam the door hard behind me, hearing it lock—should've kept the hand, shouldn't I? Ah, well, spilled milk; find it later, easy enough —and bend down to scoop Milady's abandoned body up by hooking my arms under hers, dragging it after her. The head is still grinning, still crying, as Milady draws up before it and lowers her eyes, her own tears welling up in sympathy.

"*Sister,*" she says, voice gurgling like vinegar through old, slimy pipes. "*I am. . . so sorry we could not be here sooner.*"

Gives a sigh like bagpipes tuning up and cuts her wet eyes

my way; I carry Milady's skin-suit to the cabinet and set it down, seated against the side, empty neck gaping upwards. Then I lift her sister's head—no need to be careful now—and set it onto the hole, positioning it carefully. Within an instant, I feel it jolt and twist in my hands; see the skin rippling as tissue weaves to tissue, sealing fast.

The body jerks, hands thrown high, grabbing at the head to make sure it's on tight. A second of startlement, right before she knows she's truly free once more. Then she throws her head back, mouth wide in soundless laughter.

At that, Milady laughs too, a sound like a tar pit swallowing something helpless. Sister turns to me.

Can you still read lips, little one? she mouths. I nod. Her grin turns savage. *Then tell them this.*

She gives me the words, and as she stands, her fangs sliding out, I turn to the cowering crowd and say: "You owe this woman a *lot* of blood."

It's a different sort of orgy after that. Milady lets her sister do most of it, though she joins in when the ghouls start fighting back at last, terror supercharging their strength and fury rather than sending them running; if they knew how to fight, or fight together, even Milady might have trouble with these numbers. But they don't. I go back to the door and stand guard, meanwhile, the Shrike's knife in my hand, making sure none of them escape. Which is why I get a great little surprise bonus when the boy himself comes at me, having managed to grab his iPhone again—I hear the door unlock behind me, as we struggle.

Well, I've earned a little fun for myself, haven't I? So, I step aside, let him by, watch him use that same blinding speed through the door and up the stairs—

Which is when I show him *my* speed. My strength. Catch him by the ankle just before he reaches the upper door, and with one hand I twist and whip him back down into the subcellar, hard enough to bounce him a yard high off the mattresses when he hits. Then I jump back down onto him and hamstring him in both legs, flourishing the knife the way he did when he carved up Sister's face— not that he'll appreciate that irony, but I do. I flip him over, then sit back down on his stomach, crushing the remaining breath out of him.

Most people when they know they're beat, they just crumple. Credit where credit's due, the Shrike isn't one of them. He glares up at me.

"You *bitch*," he rasps, repeating himself. "Go ahead, kill me. I'll still die something you'll never be: *free*. You work for monsters. I. . . made the monsters. . . work for *me*."

Believes it too, even now; well, well. Some prats, they never learn.

So, I cup his face in my hands and lean down, suddenly not angry anymore. Just tired. "We're all monsters to somebody," I tell him, and twist, *hard*.

Still got enough of Sister's blood in him the broken neck won't kill him right away. Nor will what I do next, which is to chop off every limb at elbow and knee; his boosted metabolism's sealed up the first amputation before I finish the last. He doesn't feel the pain, but I can see it in his eyes: inside, he's screaming. And he'll scream until Milady and Sister finish him.

I take a deep breath, then, and let myself collapse sideways, finally resting, not moving as warm blood slowly pools 'round me like a comforting bath. Nobody left alive that's capable of running, not anymore. And as always, my mind goes back to the past. . . my past, long past, a hundred years and more. When I made my choice, the choice *he* thought was such a joke, and why.

Milady wasn't the first monster I ever met, you see. But she was the one who changed me.

On the factory floor, we were all of us just meat to the owners, one mere mistake away from being maimed or killed, lit on fire or sliced apart by machinery gone wrong. I once knew a girl who licked matches for a living, ha'penny a week, and called it good; she died with her face gone soft and her teeth rotted out, unable to eat for fear of choking on bits of her own phosphorus-poisoned jaw. Just like the hat makers who went mad from mercurous nitrate fumes, or the dyers who puked themselves to death turning out yards of arsenic green just because it was that year's most fashionable shade, or the poor Radium Girls in their turn, glowing in the dark while their bones decayed from the inside out.

But me, I was lucky; Milady took me away from all that. Fed me her blood, and fed on mine, though never enough to turn me. Only enough to bind us together and keep us bound so I could do her daytime work throughout the years, the centuries. Till I knew myself older by far than almost any other ghoul in North America, if not the whole world.

I never had to give up the sun, or the taste of bread, or anything else most true humans think make their tiny, fragmentary, mirror-shard fragile mockery of a life worth living. I never had to give up nothing I didn't want to, did I? And I never, ever will.

The Shrike thought he'd got it made, breaking the chain like he did: all the perks and none of the labour, none of that hunger to love and serve and be mastered. Bloody child, like I said. But I'm no Renfield, nor is Milady any sort of Dracula. It's far more like being an apprentice than a mere employee. Far more like being someone's adopted child, loved for her dreams as well as her skills, her capacity to love and *be* loved. And no human gets in the way of that, ever.

I'm something else now—a monster, a god. Servant to a god, sole priestess of She I worship. It's a better life than any I ever hoped to have, back when, or could ever hope to have, in future.

Milady comes—mother-lover, endless fount of knowledge, strength, power. *Eternity*. Who raises me back up now from where I lie cocooned in these false ghouls' blood, her rescued sister at her side, and kisses my cheek, my forehead, my mouth.

Who licks the excess from me like a cat cleaning her kitten only to take my lower lip between hers and nip it lightly, tattooing it with the sacred symbol of her bite. Who lifts me high in her cold embrace, her guts twining 'round me like tentacles, digestive acids burning at my skin, and cradles me against her doubly naked bosom, pumping with stolen blood.

"My little London sparrow, my soot-grimed dockyards orphan," she calls me, knowing how I can't help but shiver with delight at her voice. "My lovely, faithful, poison-hearted little cannibal girl."

"Always, Milady."

Stroking my face, thumbing my eyelids closed, as the ecstasy comes on me—that deep, slackening, satisfied sleep which always comes after true slaughter. These fools thought they knew it, but they didn't know the half; couldn't, could they? No human ever will.

"My sweet, poor little butcherbird."

I close my eyes and dream, glad yet once more how when death finally did come for me, it had nothing at all to do with industry. And in the dark behind my eyes, I see only red, the same endless hot salt sea that laps inside Milady's skull, the same thing that will surely drown me, eventually—take me down, drag me deep and ingest me, never letting me surface again until my flesh has changed to sharp-edged, quartz-toothed pearl, fit to stand at her side instead of kneeling before her.

The same thing which will finally lick the last sad taste of my humanity from me forever and spit me back out, reborn into darkness.

PEAR OF ANGUISH

Know what a pear of anguish is? Imogen asked me, that last day we spent together, and I shook my head. *I'll show you. Take a look.*

She opened up her book and thumbed through it quickly, spreading its dog-eared pages open to display two illustrations set next to each other, one a sketch, the other a photograph. Both were indeed roughly pear-shaped, as advertised; the one on the right spread out in petals, weirdly organic, while the one on the left was black iron, spiked all over, sharper outside than in.

You use the screw, here, she said, pointing. *Tamp it down, tight, and thrust it up inside, anyplace that's big enough to take it. Could be the mouth, like a gag, that's why people in Holland called it the choke-pear. . . but other people, they say they used it during the Burning Times, on women. Down there.*

Jesus, that's gross, I said. *Seriously, what—why? Why would anybody—*

—stick that inside someone and pull the screw, let it open up, see what happened? Her eyes were still on the page, half-slit and dreamy, like she was hypnotized. *It's no different than cutting yourself, Una. . . all on the inside, though, instead of the outside. No scars. None that show.*

And somebody else doing it to you, instead of you doing it to your-self, I pointed out. Cutting, I could have said—would have said, later on, when I finally knew how to say things like that out loud —was all about control in a world without it. Hurt yourself to dim or stem the pain you already knew was coming. What kind of control would shit like *this* give you?

It's dumb, I told her, finally. *That'd* kill *you. Totally different.*

Imogen smiled then, her smile that looked more like a snarl, skewed left and upwards, in a way that made her look as if she were having a stroke. *Like you've never thought about it,* she replied. *Steal your Mom's booze and a bunch of pills so it wouldn't hurt as much, slit your wrist the right way and let them find you like that. I used to plan on setting myself on fire with the gas can my dad kept in our shed, back in Gananoque, but it's harder here.*

Why not throw yourself off the bridge, you want it that bad?

Maybe, one day. Maybe.

Around us, the Ravine wasn't quiet, so much, as full of a very different sort of noise. As part of a system of watersheds down-town Toronto sat overtop, the section we knew best ran under-neath the St. Clair Ave East bridge, bisecting our shared neighbourhood for a mile in either direction—trace it far enough south and it blended into Rosedale, eventually becoming part of the Don Valley Parkway, which an enterprising hiker might trace almost right on down to Lake Ontario. The trees grew so close they strangled the sky, and the creek rushed by at full flood over rocks and trash, striking liquid against the run-off tunnel's concrete walls. Green dusk here at the bottom of the slope, true dusk starting to show up above. The insects sang and the leaves rustled, and for half a heartbeat I thought I heard a cicada whine so loud it cut through my skull like a skewer.

Seriously, I said, at last, *don't be so fucking stupid; don't pretend like it even matters* how. *You'd still be just as dead.*

Sure. But think about how they'd all feel, if we did.

From "me" to "we," in one small slide. That was Imogen, all over.

They'd laugh at us, Im, is all, I told her, after a long minute. *Look sad in public and make fun of us in private, for being weak-ass losers who couldn't stay alive long enough to get into high school. Like usual.*

But Imogen simply sat there studying those horrible pictures as if she thought somebody was going to test her on them later, ignoring me entirely.

————

The very first day I met Imogen, I followed her down under the St. Clair West bridge without even thinking twice, straight into the Ravine's heart. She let herself out of the recreation yard through a crack in the fence and moved downwards into the green shadows through weeds that grew big as bushes, clumps of nettle and deadly nightshade, scrums of birch with big torn strips of bark hanging down from their trunks like loose bandages. There was a path, but she avoided it, preferring to make her own.

I'd been coming back from lunch when I spotted her, still reading that book she'd been nursing under her desk all day in the corner of the recreation yard, ignoring a clot of "popular" girls discussing her from near enough to make it obvious, yet far enough away to make objecting to being discussed more work than it was worth. I didn't know any of their names yet, but I recognized their faces from earlier; I didn't know *anybody* here yet, given I hadn't known I was changing schools until Mom had told me the week before, when she'd picked me up at the airport after coming back from Melbourne only to take me "home" to a completely different house from the one I'd left a month before.

"You'll like it, Una," my mom told me; "it's a whole fresh start."

"Sure," I agreed. No point in arguing.

Arguing never helped.

1:00 p.m. on day one at the new school near the new house, and the only one in class whose name I'd managed to learn thus far besides the teacher—Miss Huergath, roughly my height but twice my width, sporting red plastic frames and a big cross at her neck—was Imogen, who nobody seemed to like and everyone seemed to be afraid of. She didn't seem all that scary to me, but then again, why would she? Usually, *I* was that kid.

That alone made me want to follow her, to see what all the fuss was.

"And what did you do over the summer, Imogen?" Miss Huergath had asked that morning, after the national anthem was over and we'd all sat down again. I followed her gaze to see who she was curving her mouth at and found it was a girl sitting almost beside me, head cocked and long, pale hair half-shading her face, eyes glued to whatever she had in her hands. She barely looked up, flicked her eyes back and forth, before replying.

"I spent most of my time reading mythology," she said. "Norse, Greek, Egyptian, Aztec, African. Christian."

"Christianity isn't mythology," Miss Huergath said.

Imogen twitched one shoulder, not quite a shrug, but not quite *not* one. "All right," she said.

One of the other girls snorted. "But *why?*" she asked, as if the answer implied: *Because you're the most giant geek who ever geeked, obviously.* And for a minute she seemed like she might go on, but Miss Huergath raised her hand instead and snapped her fingers at the same time, silencing her.

"Jennifer Diamond," Miss Huergath said, "do we talk out of turn in this class? No, we do not." And then she was turning my way, scanning the attendance sheet. "So," she began. "Mmm. . . Una, is it? And how did you spend *your* vacation?"

Everybody looked at me, then, the way I'd been praying they wouldn't, freezing the breath in my lungs and thoughts in my brain together at once, for one painfully long moment, as I struggled to form my next sentence.

"In Australia," I told her, at last, when I was able. "My dad lives there." Which drew a snicker, of course, courtesy of what sounded like the same girl as before: *Australia? But* why?

I felt my face heat, all my pimples flaring up at once, and tried to distract myself from the strong, immediate urge to throw something at her by looking back at Imogen, whose eyes were back on her book. That was good; I remembered thinking how I'd wanted to know what the title was, whether it was one I'd already read, and tried to crane my neck to see. But the light on the spine was too strong for me to make anything out, even if she hadn't had it opened so wide.

Around us, the class went on with Miss Huergath's Q & A, a steady drone, busy-dumb as bees in a hive. And I was able to sink back into myself, invisible, or at least as much so I ever could be —me, with my adult height and full pubertal shift at age ten and a half, almost eleven. Me, so gawky and inconveniently well-developed, my face painfully sunburnt from that last trip to the beach before boarding the flight back to Toronto; I still wore the horrible navy blue acrylic turtleneck I'd spent a day and a night travelling home in, if only so nobody had to gape at those long strings of red-brown skin working their way off the back of my neck and into my cleavage, let alone the scars on the inside of my wrists.

Which was uncomfortable, but no more than anything else, really: the glasses with lenses so thick they sometimes fell off when I leaned too far; the braces, rubber bands linking my top to my bottom canines, tending to snap when I yawned. The stretch-marked C cup breasts I'd somehow grown over those last two weeks of August, so fast I had to wear one of my mom's bras until we could take a trip downtown to the Eaton Centre, with her underwire cutting into me every time I slumped.

And all that fucking blood, that was the worst of it. The way it always seemed to catch me by surprise after that first time, with an acne flare-up, a pre-migraine squint, and a general feeling of having been punched in the crotch as heralds that I'd yet to get used to tracking. Not to mention the rage that came with it, stronger than it had ever been before, which is saying something.

I hated it all, hated my body, hated myself. Didn't help I'd always felt like a monster, long before looking like one—never in on the joke, not until I figured out the joke was always me. Like a bomb with a timer anybody could wind up, a storm made from screams, thrown fists, and broken furniture. Like anyone could make me explode by looking at me the wrong way. Like everyone *would*, eventually, because it was oh so fun to watch, when I did.

My last school had been like that, from grade one on. *You make it so easy for them,* Mom used to tell me, and I guess I did. I guess I always had.

So yeah: if there was someone else who already filled this new class's mockable outsider slot, I'd love to make sure she was the person I had to make fun of in order to keep the roving eye of social malevolence securely away from *me*, for once.

Down into the ravine, therefore, trailing after Imogen. I didn't even know her last name then, and it didn't matter—I wanted to see what she'd do. My plan was to spy on her, take notes, carry stories back to the clot of "populars." Be practical and start out on the right side of things, for whatever good that turned out to do me.

Didn't work out that way, though.

———

You've been hanging around with Imogen, Jenny Diamond said as I put my glasses back on after drying my hair, still huge and naked from my post-swimming lesson shower—I surfaced blinking, taken aback to find her there and horrified to see she had the whole fucking pack with her, all the "populars" at once: Fazia Moorcroft, Nini Jones, Peri Boyle. *I mean. . . we wanted to make sure you knew about her, before you made a mistake. It's not too late.*

I already knew I was blushing again, probably all over, clutching my wet towel like a shield and wanting to hit her so hard she'd cough blood, so hard I had to breathe a moment, deep, before I spoke. *Too late for what?* I asked her, finally.

Nini and Faz grinned at each other. *You know she's a witch, right?* Faz asked.

Witches aren't real, I said.

That's what a witch would say, Nini told me. *You a witch too, Una?*

No, I snapped back, already knowing it was the wrong answer.

Later, after they'd gone—after I'd screamed at them until they left me alone, at last, hard enough to hurt myself, hard enough that swallowing felt like something scraping the inside of my throat—I retreated to the toilet and crouched there crying slow, hot tears, rereading the back of the cubicle door top to bottom like a litany: *le freak c'est chic, heather sucks dick, frig your-self, imogen = witchie-poo.* Pretty soon my name would be up there too, probably misspelled. So, I bit into my thumb until I could taste salt, until the toothmarks were deep enough to sink an entire nail into, until I knew I'd still have bruises two weeks on, purple-grey in yellow. Like swearing blood-brothers, I guess, but without the other person.

When Imogen saw what I'd done, saw the marks I'd made on myself, her otherwise unreadable eyes got all wide and soft, as if I'd handed her a ring or something. And: *I knew it,* was all she said, quietly. *I knew you were like me.*

Nothing to say to that but *yes, obviously,* so I nodded, instead. Knowing that from now on, we'd be the same in everybody's eyes. Kicking myself for thinking I could ever avoid it.

———

I know why I am the way I am now, and part of me managing to figure it out eventually involved teaching myself to forget—to place that time, those events, my entire childhood, at one remove, behind a scratched and dirty porthole through which I could either view things without actually having to feel them, or feel things without remembering what caused those feelings. To recall my experiences without getting caught inside them, forced to relive them on loop for what seems like hours, pinned in an endless, useless churn of postdated embarrassment and rage and hate.

From where I am now, my adult perspective, I can see that what I once thought was spite on others' part was actually fear that if they let me get away with being abnormal, then what use was the standard of normality they kept their own status by clinging to? We were all women, at least prospectively. . . but since puberty made me the only one with overt female characteristics, I was the one who stood out. So why not be a cop instead of a criminal, the "populars" must have thought, policing the tall poppy for crimes we'd all share a year or so later? Slut-shame the girl who thinks of herself as a brain on top of a spine, who barely notices boys except as noisy distractions; raid her locker for maxi pads because she never remembers to bring her lock, then stick them to the inside of her desk so she'll find them when she flips up the top, a mocking message written underneath with shoplifted drugstore lipstick: *These belong to you, hee, hee, hee.* Since they all purported not to know what these things were, because none of them had to, yet.

Similarly, I can see that what I used to think was my own innate evil—the evil Imogen obviously shared, which called her to me, and me to her—was simply a long-inculcated belief I'd been somehow born *wrong*, a bullied bully, book smart but street stupid: Violent from puberty on, but always uncontrollable, an egotistical liar who could never be relied upon to do the right thing, mainly because she was incapable of understanding what the right thing was. After years of therapy and some chemical help, I now understand I wasn't *bad*, different, blind to what most people apparently came into this shitty world knowing about how to fit in, how to get along.

But even only glimpsed through the porthole, the feeling sometimes comes back without me even knowing what it's about, in waves. A tidal wave submerging me, but it's all faceless, formless, attached to nothing. It's like I'm being haunted by the ghost of a feeling; I don't know who I'm angry at, or why; I don't know what I hate them for, just that I do, and that seems illogical, selfish, weird. So it turns into me hating myself, being angry at myself, for being weak enough to want to trust, to make friends, to find *love* somewhere outside the divorce-broken ring of my own family in the first place. For laying myself open, so stupidly, again and again and again.

My parents thought they were each other's best friends too. That's why they thought they never needed anybody else, till suddenly they did, but didn't have anybody to turn to. And while I told myself even back then that I'd never live like that, if I could help it. . . really, how could I have ever expected things to turn out differently? They never taught me how to manage to live with other people without hurting them, not even by bad example.

You scared them, Una. (Good.)

You made them scared of you. (*Good.*)

(They fucking should be.)

Things I did in the moment that passed through me like a storm, so fast and hard I could barely remember I'd done them, later on. Like: oh yeah, *that* happened. I cut holes in other people's clothes. I pissed in other people's shoes. I stuck someone else's Barbie's head up inside me, then put it back on the doll for her to find. I smeared my own blood on the wall, wrote things in it. The same year I met Imogen, I picked up a cat by its tail while listening to a record on headphones, then couldn't figure out how my Mom could have known what I was doing; even after I left Imogen behind, I strangled a girl and knocked her head on the floor because she said my whales looked more like tadpoles. Later, in yet another "new" school, I got sent to the principal for interrupting class by describing how to do a lobotomy in detail, which I'd picked up by reading a biography of Frances Farmer, then threatening to do it on one of my classmates with a compass.

I know why I am the way I am now, but only because I've managed to live long enough to figure it out. That's the simple truth. And I wish—I *do* wish, even after everything she did, I did, *we* did, together—that Imogen had been able to do that too.

Eventually.

———

"Come out," Imogen told me, that first day, as I crouched in the bushes, watching her. "You're Una, right? Think I can't see you? I can see everything."

That seemed unlikely, but I instantly felt dumb for being there, so I stood up, instead; crossed my arms and scowled at her, *fuck you* face screwed on hard, expecting her to be frightened. Which she very much obviously wasn't— beckoned me over, peremptorily, and showed me what she was doing: how she'd set creek-washed rocks in a circle with a baby doll's detached plastic face in the middle, looking up, blue eyes blind in the green-dark diffused sunlight slipping down around the bridge.

"The fuck is *that* for?" I asked, and she giggled.

"You swear like a boy," she said. "Is that because you're so tall?"

"I don't know, I fucking like it. So, what *is* that, anyway?"

"I'm making a scrying mirror. Watch."

She turned it over, then, showed me a small, round mirror she'd carefully fitted inside the face, probably from somebody's makeup kit. "First you have to cure it, see—take a flame and melt the edges so it won't fall out, the sign of fire. Then leave it all night where the wind can get at it, especially if it's blowing past a graveyard; the sign of night, the sign of air. Then wash it in the creek and leave it down here under a bunch of leaves, looking down into the dirt, the sign of earth and water. One thing left to do now: anoint it, and see if it works."

"Anoint it with what?"

Another giggle. "What do you think?" she asked, pointing to where my sleeves had rucked up, glued with sweat, to show off the scars inside both my wrists—those scratches I always told people came from the cat, if they asked, which they mostly didn't. Not to mention the deeper cuts, treated with Bactine and Band-Aids, which I never told anybody about at all.

I had a hook I'd stolen from my Nana's embroidery kit once, meant for ripping seams; Imogen had a pen knife, the kind that folds out, its handle wrapped in tape she'd coloured black. She stuck its point into the pad at the base of her pointer finger, between heart- and head-lines, and twisted till she had to pull it out sideways, freeing a drop of blood the size of a dime. "Now you," she commanded, and I didn't even think to disobey. I was far too interested at that point—I wanted to see if it would work. Nothing I'd ever tried by myself had up to that point, and I'd always wondered why.

(*All little girls try practicing magic, eventually,* my first girlfriend would tell me in second year of university. *That's because magic offers power, and they don't have any. . . magic tells you things can change, if you want it bad enough. They haven't figured out yet how that's a fucking fairy tale, and fairy tales aren't real.*

(And I remember nodding, but that was mainly because I was drunk and she was beautiful, enough so I wanted to agree with her. Thinking, as I did, how I could sure tell her some stuff to the contrary, if I wanted. If I felt like I had the right to.

(*I used to have a friend who'd disagree,* was all I ended up telling her, though, so low I don't think she actually heard me.)

Imogen squeezed her wound until she'd painted a triangle on the mirror's surface, point up. "Now you," she said, "but widdershins, opposite, other way 'round. Point up."

"I know what widdershins is," I told her, grumpily, sticking the hook between my index and middle fingers. To which she laughed again, full-on this time, loud enough to startle a nearby pigeon.

"Of course you do," she said.

———

And what did you see in the scrying mirror, Una? A voice asks, from deep inside my mind—that first psychiatrist Mom sent me to, maybe, with her sad, smart eyes. To which I answer, internally: nothing. I saw nothing. I never saw anything at all. Not even when I said I did.

And what did Imogen *see, do you think?*

I can't know that. I only know what she *said* she saw, over and over: a way out, an escape. A door to somewhere better than this shitty world we both knew we were trapped in, the place where one step forward always led two steps back. Where everyone else got away with everything and we got away with nothing, not even with being two similarly inclined weirdos lucky enough to find each other, to share an affinity, to make up stories together and lie our way into believing them. . . acting like we believed them, anyhow. On my part.

And yes, we hurt ourselves; we hurt each other. Why not? Pain was already a constant. Imogen's fairy tales at least promised that pain could be harnessed, used as currency. They promised it could be bartered for entry into the numinous. No different from any other religion that way—any other mythology. All the ones we'd studied and discarded on our own, before finding each other.

I mean, pain really *should* count for something, don't you think? Considering how much it hurts.

Think about it, Imogen told me. *Why do other people hurt us? To get what they want, which is for us to hurt. Cause and effect. So, when we hurt ourselves, Una, what do we want out of it? What can we possibly want?*

. . . to. . . not hurt, anymore? She didn't answer, simply waited, which is how I knew she must be disappointed in my reasoning. *Okay, no—no, obviously, that's too easy. To hurt, so long as it hurts them too. Like they hurt us.*

And? she prompted.

And get away with it.

That's part of it, sure. . . witchcraft, all that. Baby steps. But I want to go further, as far away as possible. To a place where my pain makes me queen, empress. To a place where my pain makes me—

—what, fucking god? Good luck with that, man. She wouldn't look away, which meant I had to, eventually. Asking her, after a beat: *And besides. . . what about me?*

Well, you too, Una—come on, did you really think I didn't mean it like that? We're sisters now. Of course, you too.

(*So long as you're willing to pay the same price, that is,* she didn't say, and didn't have to.)

———

This thing we were after didn't have a name, but we knew we'd know it when we saw it. It felt like. . . some prospective culmination for all that leprous, un-channelled pubertal fury I felt, that crazy rage to procreate held completely separate from true sexuality, never thought about in conjunction with other people, because they all hated me and I hated them. All those "hunky" boys whose attention Nini and Faz competed for, never understanding they knew even less about the whole shebang than *they* did; I'm not saying I didn't think about sex at all, but not with *those* idiots. I mean, I already knew how to masturbate—"gouging," I called it, for some reason, probably because everything that appealed to me at that age was about secrecy and humiliation, revenge and freedom from consequences, a toxic antique glamour wrapped in blood and gold and jewels. And power, power, power, like my girlfriend-to-be would say.

I remember how I used to stand in the bath looking upwards into the shower's spray and touch myself till the blood rushed so far out of my skull, I blacked out: *That*'s how it felt, the thing Imogen wanted us to find, together. I'd wake up in the tub, cold and wet with the back of my head ringing against the porcelain, and believe me, it's not like it never occurred to me I was probably killing brain cells, or risking I might crack my head. . .

But because it felt so good, I kept on doing it—chasing that high, the mounting buzz and pixelation, the letting go, the refreshing dark. Even more like dying, I suppose, than the little death itself.

"Blood's what opens a door," Imogen used to say. "Did you really think you wouldn't have to pay for something like that? Something *wonderful*?"

"No."

"No, that's right. I knew you understood. That's why we're friends."

So, every day we'd go down in the Ravine, look in her scrying mirror and try to find a place where the world wore thin, a crack through which to reach somewhere else. We looked for it everywhere. Under the bridge, through the trees, inside the downwards slope of the walls, the deepest part of the creek. We mapped things out in either direction, a mile or more south and north, down towards Rosedale, up towards the Mount Pleasant Cemetery. We broke through thickets of willow-whips and blackberry thorns to emerge into what had looked promising from below, only to have it turn out to be yet another slice of some too quiet side street lined with twin garage houses and speedbumps, its offshoots all cul de sacs, for absolute minimum public access.

Imogen would always be the one to see it first, of course; she'd cry out, point with her free hand and set off running, pulling me along. Hand in hand with our wounds pressed tight, grating, throbbing: the lope and the stagger, faster and faster, lungs burning, until it finally blinked out almost as we reached it. And I'd bend at the waist to spit on the ground, coughing as Imogen cursed, damning everything she could think of.

"It shut again," she'd say, finally, once she'd calmed enough to form new words. "We weren't fast enough. We have to be faster."

And I'd nod, still gulping. "I know," I'd reply. "Next time, maybe. Maybe next time."

————

A third voice, now: Imogen's, of course. Who else?

You never saw anything, *Una? That's not what you told me.*

Well, no.

Because sometimes. . . sometimes, I did. Almost.

Probably a shared illusion born of mutual self-hypnosis, or whatever—but I got scared after a while, because increasingly I fooled myself that if I squinted at the exact right angle, I eventually might be able to catch something forming in the air, superimposed over whatever supernatural beacon Imogen was leading us towards. Because, on one particular day, at the very moment dusk turned to twilight, I genuinely thought I could see the threshold. . . a thin, bright line starting to trace itself around what could only be a frame, hanging high in the air with light from another world spilling out as the door it came attached to began to crack, just a fraction. Before it slammed tight once more.

A fingernail of new moon shining down on us where we stood, and stars, so many stars, caught in the trees' darkness like glitter in a woman's hair. And Imogen grinding her thumb into my wrist, wringing my already-stinging hand so hard it spasmed: *Fucking* faster, *Una, goddamnit. It's like you don't even want it.*

I do, though, Im, I swear. You know I do.

She gave a long sigh, then, almost a snarl. Ragged and ugly. It scraped me inside, like sandpaper.

You'd better, is all she said.

———

Here's what I *do* know: when someone disappears, no matter the reason, they leave a hole. Wait long enough, and that hole is all you have—it's all you're left with. The assumption that they're gone, and they're not ever coming back. It creates its own gravity, like every other anomaly; everything left over revolves around it, forever.

It's like a scratch on a record; it leaves a groove. It'll never play right again. So, every time you hear this wounded song you associate with that gone person, you'll remember she *is* gone— remember she might be dead—and it'll hit you all at once, everywhere, over and over again. Shake you like a bag full of rocks. You'll be one big bruise.

The dead hate the living. We have what they want: time. We have choices, chances. The dead are hungry, always. They resent us everything, even our pain.

By remembering what you've forgotten, by trying to see what it is that happened objectively, what is it that you invite back into your life? Do you open a door, summon a ghost? Do you announce yourself as open to being haunted?

The past is a trap and memory is a drug.

Memory is a door.

———

Blood holds the door open longer, Imogen realized, after we'd not quite done it enough times to have some statistics to work with. *We need* more *of it; that's the key.* Which is how we ended up poring over *A History of Torture and Execution,* which—in turn—is where Imogen found her pear of anguish. And it wasn't as if I really believed she'd be able get a hold of one, but who knew what she was capable of, or what she assumed *I'd* be capable of? I really didn't feel like stabbing myself (or her, or both of us) in the vagina as part of some *Let's Go! Narnia* craziness, any more than I felt like throwing myself from the bridge with her on the off chance a door might open in thin air, halfway down. . .

I wouldn't tell on her, though. That was never an option.

That evening, however, my body decided things for us. I stole an empty jar from the kitchen and squatted over it for an hour after lights out, reading *Salem's Lot* by the streetlight leaking through my bedroom window. The result was clotted red-black, thick and dreadful; I'd filled it halfway by the time I stuck the lid back on and screwed it tight, wrapping it three deep in plastic bags before stowing it away at the bottom of my backpack.

Suffice it to say, nobody ever told me that much like any other sort of dead flesh, shed uterine lining really does need to be refrigerated.

———

Nini Jones. If someone had given me a gun, even at age twelve, I truly think I'd've shot that bitch right in the face. The strange part is that when I think of her now, I see her as she was—plain, not pretty: rake-skinny and dishwater blonde, weird eyes, weird angles. But back then, she was really, really good at convincing me and everybody else that she was perfect, the righteous social arbiter of everything "in" or "out." Jenny Diamond had money, supposedly from the fleet of cabs bearing her last name; Faz was born glamorous, a lovely brown girl centre-set in a bright white trio of semi-pro assholes. And Peri Boyle, I eventually figured out, simply trailed along behind all three of them, avoiding censure through protective coloration. A low-grade trick, I guess, but I sure couldn't manage it. . . Imogen, either. So good for her.

"The hell's this?" Nini drawled, the next day, down in the Ravine—and grabbed the jar from Imogen, who'd barely started to twist its cap. The force of the move alone was enough to make it spring the rest of the way open, releasing the worst stink I'd ever smelled, a whole hot summer day's worth of fermentation. Nini sprang back, dropping it; the jar shattered against the ground, sprayed rocks, dirt, and glass shards coated with decaying menstrual blood everywhere, including across her white canvas shoes.

"Jesus, *uck!*" She screamed, kicking out at Imogen with one stained foot, who kicked back, hitting her in the knee. Nini started to fall and caught onto Faz, who flailed, almost upsetting them both, while I saw Jenny Diamond retch in the background as the wave reached her, coughing: "Oh holy shit, fuck *me*, is that —? Una, *God,* you *freak.*"

I laughed long and loud, hyena-harsh. "Medical waste, bitch-es," I growled, "same as your mom throws out every month. You stupid fucking retard *children.*"

To which Faz replied, too loud, at almost the same time, with her one arm wedged under Nini's now and the other hand tugging at Jenny's skirt-waist, trying to pull them both away: "Seriously, guys, c'mon—what do you want, like. . . some *disease,* courtesy of the St. Clair coven? A serious case of Tampax cooties?"

"Cooties don't exist, you dumbass," I threw back. "Or witches."

"Yeah? Tell that to *her*."

I glanced over my shoulder, in time to catch Imogen in mid-crouch, coming up with two fresh handfuls of creek-bed rocks, wet-slick and twice as heavy. She flung them at the "populars" underhand and barely aimed, as if she was pitching the world's worst softball game. One glanced off Nini's shoulder to whack Jenny in the chest, both of them squeal-braying in protest as Faz broke into a run, dragging them with her, straight past Peri Boyle, who'd been hanging back all this time behind a nearby tree; she whirled to yell after them, but I didn't hear what she said.

That was because the other rock collided with the side of my head, opening a gash in my scalp that ripped open the top of my ear and sent my glasses flying, leaving me face down in the dirt with blood in my eyes, functionally blind and howling. Already in half-Hulk mode to begin with, I felt myself *go off*, top of my head exploding into metaphorical flames; I rounded on Imogen with both hands clawed, ready to rip, to tear, to knock her head on the ground until it broke.

"I'M GONNA FUCKING *KILL* YOU!" I vaguely remember roaring, even as Imogen saw my face and cried out like some weird bird, half in guilt, half in ecstasy. Like. . .

Fresh blood, Una. That's exactly what we needed. Not that old stuff, that garbage you brought—fresh. *Because it doesn't count if it's too easy, right?*

(Right.)

It has to *hurt*.

———

It was Peri who found my glasses, in the end, and gave them back to me in the nurse's office, once I'd blundered up out of the

Ravine with Imogen still screaming after me—Peri, who was never really my enemy, and became my friend after both of us ended up in the same Alternative High School, a few years on. Her mom was a French teacher who thought she was extraordinarily cultured, I later found out, always rabbiting on about Yeats and Robert Bresson, and married to this asshole writer, penniless but culturally approved; he was award-winning, her reward for putting up with Peri's dad all these years, a "mere" journalist. The two of them would go after Peri tag team style, work her like a nine to five, trying to convince her that because she was physically rather than mentally inclined, she must be genuinely stupid. And while I do think Peri might indeed have had a learning disability, she had more heart in her finger than her bitch of a mom had in her whole body.

For a while, every time we met as adults, Peri would always end up reminding me how brave I was, how much she'd admired the way I wouldn't lay down and take it back in school, even if she'd never done anything about it. And every time she'd tell me this, I'd wonder what exactly she was on—until the night I finally made myself peer back through the past's dirty porthole at it, and remembered a dinner with Peri's mom and stepfather during which I'd spent three courses smouldering at the way they baited her before finally erupting, yelling at them both at the very top of my voice: "She is *not* dumb, but *you* are a pair of assholes who deserve to die alone!"

They don't know, though, do they? Imogen sometimes asks, from inside my scarred ear. *That you're not brave, never have been, but get you mad enough, and you'll leave anyone behind. People can count on it. You make it so easy for them, Una, after all. You always have.*

Fuck you, Im.

Like that, yeah. See what I mean?

Which is when I see her, or think I can, through whatever door her own blood eventually opened, smiling at me sweetly from whatever black-jeweled throne she sits on, pointing a finger at me with its long, gilded, cormorant-claw nail. Then shrugging, and returning to whatever duties she has, on the other side of the crack: organizing a library made from cured rolls of human skin, maybe. Writing new spells in gold-dust and quicksilver. Mummifying her enemies alive, or flaying them, or flaying some to mummify others. A twelve-year-old sociopath with a crown serving gods who run on rage and hate and pain, never quite grown old enough to bleed herself, except with a ceremonial knife: powerful, finally, enough so she can probably order rain to fall and mountains to rise if she wants to; a suitable reward, no doubt, for all her effort. But alone, now and forever, in every way that matters.

The same way we both are.

———

So, the school nurse called my mom, and the look on her face when she saw me. . . I don't have to try to remember *that*. She made me tell her who all the other kids were, marched to the principal's office to tell him she was keeping me out of school for a week, and booked us an assessment at the Clarke Institute for Psychiatric Health. After it was done, the doctors told Mom they thought that if I actually believed I was a witch, I might have anything from narcissistic personality disorder to early-onset schizophrenia. They recommended she commit me for observation, to be sure.

"We're not doing that," Mom said, which is why she's my hero. Instead, they gave her the name of a child psychiatrist I ended up going to for the next five years, as well as suggesting I should stop seeing Imogen. Mom agreed.

Then it was Monday again, and I was coming back to school for one last day, essentially to pick up whatever stuff I might have left behind. I walked across the bridge and through a side route I often took in order to avoid the "populars," a wind tunnel triangle between the Ravine's west slope and two residential apartment buildings in an L-shaped arrangement, following along the Ravine's side until it blended into the yard's back fence. But today, this path wasn't empty, like usual. Instead, it was crowded with kids, teachers, even janitorial staff, all pressed up close to the fence and staring down through the trees, the green shadows, the close-knit weeds and bushes. An ambulance was parked at one edge of the crowd, flanked by two police cars, their lights on and blinking; someone had strung crime scene tape through the fence from one end to the other, suturing the hole Imogen and I used to go down through shut.

I couldn't see what they were looking at, not from where I stood. So, I edged my way around the outer rim of the crowd instead, a loose arrangement of younger-grade kids in clumps of two, three and four apiece. There I eventually found one boy I didn't think I'd ever seen before and approached him.

"What's happening?" I asked, quietly. "What are they all doing here? Are those the cops?"

"Yeah," he said. "Somebody called them this morning, after they went down through the Ravine coming to school. I hear they found a girl's clothes down there, all covered in blood, like she'd had her throat cut or something. No girl, the clothes."

"No body, huh?"

"Nope." He paused for a moment, not even looking at me, before adding: "The cops think it might have something to do with this girl whose mom reported her missing last week, Imogen, the one everybody thinks is a witch. They think maybe her friend Una did it."

I don't have a lot of memories I'm never quite sure I didn't make up after the fact, but this is one, if only because I've thought about it so long as a series of descriptive sentences—no emotions attached, not even images, simply a string of events: this, then this, then this, then this. I know I must have found out the facts of what happened to Imogen, at least so far as anyone else knows them, but I might as well have read them in the papers or seen them on TV. I do know I switched schools almost immediately afterwards, though we didn't move house until three years later, and the new school came with a new bus route that went literally in the opposite direction from my old one—it meant I never really had to interact with any of these people or places again, not unless I wanted to. And I had no reason to want to.

I do think it happened, though. Maybe the very flatness of it proves that it happened.

I certainly don't have any reason to doubt that in real life, things aren't as dramatic as either Imogen or I would have liked them to be.

————

I'm still here, and she's not. That's all I know. And I know myself, the way she never got to. And whatever happened, I wasn't there. It had nothing to do with me. It still doesn't.

Nothing, or everything.

So, if I slip my fingernail down the inside of my wrist some-times, along the closed seam of a long-healed scar, what does it matter, as long as I leave it shut? So long as I only *think* of unpicking it, of shedding blood and seeing what might happen? What light might leak in, and from where, over the lintel of the invisible? What door might begin to form, haloed in shared wounds, opening at last to let me through, even after I left her alone to make her own key?

Pay the price, make it hurt; reap your reward, fast or slow. That's how magic works, or so I've always heard.

Isn't it.

Bb MINOR
OR THE SUICIDE CHOIR
AN ORAL HISTORY

B major: harsh and plaintive
B minor: solitary and melancholic
Bb major: magnificent and joyful
Bb minor: obscure and terrible

Key and mode descriptions from Marc-Antoine Charpentier's
Regles des Composition, ca. 1682

KAYLA PRATT, HELP LINE VOLUNTEER

Tell me about the call.

How it happened was, I was volunteering on the Keep It Street-Safe vandalism tip line, the one they set up to find out who's been knocking out all the RESCU cameras in the area around where King Street East turns into Cherry Street, past Front Street down to Lakeshore—you know, that big development where they're building what's gonna be called the Canary District. Red light cameras mainly, but they've also knocked down a couple of traffic monitoring cameras, some ATM cameras. . . it's like they're trying to turn the whole area into one big dead spot. It's hard enough to get an idea of what's happening down there anyhow, because it's pretty much either construction sites or a whole lot of old, semi-industrial spaces like the areas under the Gardiner Expressway, buildings no one's bothered to demolish yet.

I didn't get the call myself, because I was monitoring for control that night, but I saw out of the corner of my eye that Sam seemed to be having trouble, so I cut in, took it over. It took a minute to figure out what was going on, because it was two people and they were talking really quietly, whispering right up close to the phone, like they were afraid somebody was going to hear them. There was a lot of echo, a lot of noise; they told me they were in a bathroom, but I could hear stuff coming in through the walls too, like people singing, or—you know that thing really hardcore Baptists do, like at that church up near Pearson International Airport? Speaking in tongues—glossolalia, they call it. It was like that but singing. Singing in tongues.

These people, these *girls*, they sounded really young, like kids. One of them had a bad cough, wet, rattling in her chest. The other one sounded stronger, but her voice was still so hoarse I could barely make out what she was saying.

What was *she saying?*

Uh, like. . . "Help us, please send help, we need somebody. Our moms are going to die, the Mouth says they have to do it to themselves. She says everybody has to." Just like that, over and over again. She never stopped. Not even when the phone cut out.

Didn't you think maybe it was a prank? I mean—

—if it was real, why didn't they call 911? Yeah, that's what my boss wanted to know too. "Why would they call *us*, Kayla?" Like I could give a fuck about *that* question right then. . . not that I said it out loud, obviously. Not like *that*, anyway.

Because you believed the call—the callers.

You'd've believed it too, if *you'd* heard it.

I have, actually. The recording.

Oh yeah, okay. Well—she sounded pretty fucking convincing, right? Like they were both scared out of their minds, like they were gonna start crying any minute: a hostage situation, somebody being held against their will, maybe a bunch of people being coerced into. . . murder, suicide? Mass suicide? (PAUSE)

Minute I heard the one with the cough talking like that, I knew we needed to kick this up to somebody who was a lot better equipped to deal with it than us.

The Emergency Task Force.

That's what they're there for.

————

ARSHAN NAJI, ETF STAFF SERGEANT, SPECIAL WEAPONS TEAM SUPERVISOR AND NEGOTIATOR, TORONTO POLICE SERVICES

Tell me about what happened next.

Well, we couldn't get a hold of the landlord immediately, because it was a weekend, but the building manager said they'd been there since before she applied for the job; it was a condo, fully paid off, and the owner lived there, along with a bunch of her friends. Zusann Groff, that was the owner's name—and she was a lawyer too, so there was nothing they could do to force them out, not even with the occasional complaint about noise or overcrowding. . . well, *suspected* overcrowding. Nobody really knew *how* many friends Groff was cohabiting with, exactly, till we got inside.

Why not?

Because pandemic, that's why not. Remember how fast people started inviting other people over, basically the minute they could prove they got vaccinated? No big parties, just keep it to one or two at a time? Well, it took a pretty long time for Groff's neighbours to figure out none of the people coming to "visit" ever actually left, especially when we went into that second lock-down, the Rho variant scare one. She was the only person who ever came and went, or people *saw*—or when you knocked on the door, she was the only one who ever answered. But when you live close by you can tell when there's people next door, even when they're hardly talking to each other, at least not very loud; lots of moving around, lots of flushing the toilet. An incredible amount of food deliveries. And that was a long time before choir practice started up.

Choir practice?

That's what Groff's nearest neighbour called it, uh. . . Ada Sagao. Groff was the last unit on that floor, down a little hallway, just past the stairs; Sagao was right around the corner, but she could hear it through her bedroom wall. She was working out of her home, like everybody else—said she asked Groff and her guests not to do whatever they were doing in the evenings, so she could sleep, but then they started doing it in the mornings instead, which woke her up way too early and gave her panic attacks. Then she asked Groff if she could maybe not do it every day, and Groff said they had to, because they had something coming up—Sagao thought it was a performance of some kind, but when we interviewed her later, she couldn't say for sure Groff ever really called it that. So Sagao complained to the manager, and Groff told the manager she'd do something about it, make alterations that'd help them keep it down.

Did she?

Brought a bunch of guys in, almost immediately. They worked quick. Things did get quieter, after that.
(PAUSE)
Until we showed up, I guess.

———

ADA SAGAO, COMPUTER TECHNICIAN

Tell me what Zusann Groff's choir sounded like.

I don't know it *was* a choir, as such. Not officially.
It's. . . hard to describe. Singing, I guess. If you could call it that.

What else would you call it?

I'm not a music expert. All I know is, it was disturbing. It disturbed me. And—no, forget it.

What were you going to say?

Well. . . afterwards, when I read about it in the papers, they said there were thirteen people living next door to me; the woman who owned the place—Zusann—plus twelve others. Which is crazy in and of itself, really, considering how small these units are, but. . . whenever they started singing, it always sounded like more. Like, a *lot* more.

Was it always the same song?

"Song. . ." (LAUGHS) Yeah, I guess it was, eventually. I mean. . . yeah, after a while they'd hit something that sounded. . . familiar. It always *felt* the same, somehow. Like—

Like what?

Like—cold, and high, and lonely. Awful. Like everybody was singing in two different keys, two different voices. And one went so low it droned, and the other went so far up it—yelped, shrieked? But it was still *music*, somehow. And sometimes, when they hit that pitch. . . sometimes. . . it was like they weren't even human anymore.
(PAUSE)
You ever hear of Nusrat Fateh Ali Khan? Sufi devotional singer, did some stuff with Peter Gabriel, back in the nineties? He sang *qawwali*, this incredible stuff full of yearning and heartbreak, pure vocal pyrotechnics. I think it's supposed to sound like you're in love with God.

Okay.

Seriously, Google him, it's worth it. Well. . . this was like the opposite of that.

Could you make out any words?

Most times I don't think it even *had* words. Not by the end.

I heard you recorded some of it.

Not me, no. My friend, Kika—she's a musicologist. You'd have to ask her.

Can I have her contact information?

Uh. . . sure.

————

ARSHAN NAJI, ETF STAFF SERGEANT

Initially there was some back and forth over right to enter, but we were finally able to push through on the idea of child welfare endangerment. I mean, "push through" sounds like we were doing something shady, but it was a legitimate concern—the threat sounded imminent, plus we didn't have any sort of idea how long we had before things were likely to kick off, just the phone call itself and a whole lot of weird noise from inside the unit.

The choir.

The singing, yes. That was already going when we got there. It never stopped. (PAUSE) So we knocked, asked for Ms. Groff, called through the door that we were there to run a welfare; no response. Repeated it three times, asked for permission to enter: still no response. Eventually, the Crown got a warrant to us, and we were able to move forward.

How so?

We tried negotiation first, obviously—opening channels,

etcetera—but. . . basically, they just ignored us. Kept on singing, louder and louder, to the point where we thought we heard screaming. That's when I gave the order to breach.

Was there any resistance?

No. It was a clean entry, minimal damage. Nobody anywhere near the door. We cleared the place room by room, without incident: kitchen, living space, one bathroom, two bedrooms. The place was spare, totally stripped down, barely any furniture left. Both bedrooms were nothing but Ikea bunkbeds—that's where we expected to find the kids, hopefully alive.

And did you?

No. There weren't any kids, turned out. There never had been. It was just. . . somebody, a couple of somebodies, pretending, I guess. I hear some of Groff's friends used to be actors.

Why would they have done that?

Basically? I think to get us to come over and break in on them in the first place.
(PAUSE)
Anyhow, we were stumped there for a few minutes, still couldn't figure out where the singing was coming from—not until we checked the floorplan, saw the unit used to have *two* bathrooms.

The alterations.

That's right. They'd knocked everything out, made a whole new room, hid it behind a fake wall at the back of bedroom number two. It probably used to be an *en suite*.

So that's where they all were? Thirteen people?

Yes, it was pretty tight, especially with the soundproofing. And it must've been just loud as hell for them in there too, considering. . . I mean, we could hear it all the way outside, like I said, right through the front door. Once we got in, it was just—at what seemed like *assaultive* levels of volume, even with all our gear, the noise we were making ourselves: flash-bangs on entry, yelling, what have you. Made you want to. . .

Staff Sergeant?

Excuse me.
(PAUSE)
It was my second-in-command who spotted the hinges, so we could open it up that way; if there was a lock on the outside, we never found it. We went in with Halligan bars, tore up the plaster, knocked out the pins. It sprang open quick, right at the same time the singing stopped. . . I *think* that's when it was. It was definitely over when we saw—what was in there.
Who. Was in there.

Ms. Groff?

Her, sure. Along with everybody else.
(PAUSE)
When we opened the door at last, pried it open, there was this. . . you know that kind of noise when you open a can of coffee? Vacuum sealed? It was like that. And then this rush of cold coming out, *intense*, like dead of winter. Cold enough to crisp your ass hairs. Plus, this rush of. . .
Well, I know it sounds insane, but. . . air. Coming in past us. Almost strong enough to knock me off balance.
(PAUSE)

I don't think I ever told anybody that before.

Casualties?

Not by our hands, ma'am.

————

WINSTON JONAS, PARAMEDIC

Oh my God, man, you don't even know. I never saw anything like that, and I've seen a lot, like, a *lot*. Enough so's I can't sleep without medication, you get me? Yeah, it was bad.

Can you give me details?

I'd rather not. But that's what you came to me for, right? Yeah, you and everybody else.
(PAUSE)
So, there was this secret room at the back, flush to the wall, no windows. They'd built it themselves. Had no lighting inside it. Just a triangular, black space—totally black, I mean like they'd painted it black themselves: The walls, the floor, the ceiling, all covered in this foam stuff with a layer of black paint slopped over it, for soundproofing. Thirteen adult human beings crammed in there, all standing with barely enough room to breathe, all staring upwards and singing, apparently, *real* loud. I don't know how they could bear it.

Why do you think they—?

Not my business. Not my job. I leave that to the experts.

Which ones?

Ones that specialize in *crazy*, lady. You feel me?

I do.

Uh huh. So—they were all dead when we got there, probably since ETF popped the door. I mean, they must've been, right? Because of the singing. Glad I didn't have to hear any of *that* shit, I can tell you.

They were so close-packed, we had to take them out one by one, lay them down on the body bags and zip them up for transport. FIS Scenes of Crime needed to get in, take their samples. But we pretty much knew how they'd gone out, after the first few. Cyanosed lips, petechial haemorrhaging, orbital distension, second-degree burns over all the exposed skin—but not heat burns. *Cold* burns. Only thing came to mind at the time was, maybe if you drowned them all in liquid nitrogen, all at once, like they do to flash freeze fancy snacks. . .

But that obviously couldn't have been feasible.

Yeah, no shit. I mean, later I did think of something else, but—

But?

. . . Hard vacuum. Decompression. Except even straight vacuum doesn't freeze you right away, you know? No air in space, so no, what's it called, convection. Whatever took the air out of that room took all the heat out of it as well, and out of everyone in it.

Still no fucking idea how.

———

KIKA RIOS, MUSICOLOGIST

Tell me how you got involved.

I was brought in to analyze the Choir's. . . work, I guess. Their style.

By whom?

By Ada—Ms. Sagao, their neighbour. We've been friends for a couple of years; we met in a community choir ourselves, ironically, a downtown women's group. Stayed in touch over Zoom after rehearsals shut down. So one night I actually heard them over Ada's speakers, and I said, "What the hell is *that?*" and Ada told me the story. Well, I was fascinated on a professional level.

"You tell me," Ada said. "Is that even music?"

"Oh, I think so," I told her.

I asked if I could hear more. "Come over," she said, "pretty much anytime, and just wait. You can't miss it."

So as soon as I'd got my latest booster and was clear to go into other homes again, I went over to Ada's place, ran some recordings, then took them home and tried to figure it out.

How would you summarize your findings?

Well, I—oh, can I ask? Am I going to get in trouble, for the recordings? Privileged communications, or something?

At this point, that seems. . . unlikely.

Okay. Good. Well, I recorded like three hours' worth over a couple of nights, then processed it through my editing suite. Have you listened to it, yet?

No. I was hoping to.

I'll send you some files. It's. . . just *insanely* complicated. The base is done in the same atonal style you get in throat singing, or death metal, where it's all about speed and force and the harmonics are accidental at best, all percussion and dissonance. Syncopation, speed riffs, ululation like you get in tribal music. But then, they'd layer in some operatic tremolo, real Mozart's "Queen of the Night" aria stuff, combined with sounds like gongs and flutes and kanglings, and they'd punctuate it with roars and shrieks. Very. . . animalistic.

Were there lyrics?

Uh, yeah. In the beginning, most of what you heard where actually vocables, stuff that just *sounds* like language: you know, like "doo wah diddy, diddy dum diddy doo." But other stuff turned out to be real phrases in weird, archaic languages—I had to get a university colleague to identify some of it. He said he recognized Sanskrit, Aramaic, plus some other thing he thought might be actual Proto-Indo-European. And some he didn't recognize at all.

Could he translate any of it?

It wasn't clear enough, no matter how I cleaned it up. Or— that's what he said. Thinking about it now, maybe. . . I mean, it was just this look I caught on his face, but I wonder if, maybe— he understood more than he said. Just enough to, uh. . . know he didn't want to understand the rest?

I don't know. That could just be me.

One thing you have to understand, though, is. . . I'm making the Choir's work sound like just random chaotic noise. But it wasn't. It was very carefully structured. Like, Bach-level complexity. Deeper, even. At full volume in that tiny space, it must have sounded like a cross between a battlefield and a voodoo ritual. Those decibel levels, that close-quarters vibration, it's almost. . . well, it's the kind of thing they're trying to make directed-energy weapons out of. The kind of thing that induces religious ecstasies. Altered states. Hysteria.

If that woman, Zusann Groff, if she wrote and arranged that herself, then she was either the biggest musical genius I've ever run across, or she was completely psychotic. Or both.

"Both" sounds about right.

Yeah. I mean, given.

———

HAL KASHIGIAN, FORENSIC PSYCHOLOGIST

Tell me how you got involved.

I was contacted by Zusann Groff's mother, Akela Halloway. She wanted. . . to understand, I suppose. How this could have happened.

"This."

The Suicide Choir.

Hm. And how did it?

You want my report, basically? Well, it's true that privilege doesn't apply, not with Ms. Halloway *or* Ms. Groff—they were never my patients, nor did I ever sign any non-disclosure agreement. I always make it very clear to clients that in order to make an assessment after the fact, I have to be free to use whatever evidence I gather or conclusions I reach in my own work later on, and Ms. Halloway had no problems with that. So...

(PAUSE)

... all right, then.

The Choir didn't leave any sort of testament, no bible, no diaries. Zusann Groff was their host, which probably made her their leader, but that "Mouth" epithet, in the initial hot line call? Much like the implication there were children in danger inside the unit, this appears to have been fiction. Groff didn't rename herself or give herself a title; she was no Shoko Asahara waiting to happen, any more than the Choir was Aum Shinrikyo. The only people they ever seem to have threatened were themselves.

Though she trained as a lawyer, Groff had always been interested in music. She was what you'd call an auto-didact on the subject. In particular, she was fascinated by the idea that some vocal musical performers could produce not only emotional effects on their listeners but also physical effects on the world around them: opera singers hitting notes so high they shatter glass, for example, or the theory that certain vibrational frequencies can cause hallucinations—the "fear frequency," they call it. How a standing wave of nineteen hertz in the infrasound decibel range, right below the bottom end of human hearing, can make people feel like they're either seeing ghosts, or about to see a ghost.

What do you mean?

Don't worry, we'll get there.

In or around November 2019, Zusann Groff first began advertising for participants in a "musical experiment." She auditioned over a hundred people, picking twelve: Lila Dabney, William Rhoads, Jenny Birthwell, Myung-Jin Heo, Holt Werkheim, Sarai

Goshen, Morgan Morrison, Alena Rostova, Tegan List, Geza Heliot, Michael Young, and Victoria Spurling.

Why those people? What did they have in common?

They could all sing? And they took Groff seriously too, I can only assume—that would have been the real deal-sealer. They believed in what she was trying to do.

They wanted to see ghosts.

In the beginning, maybe. But later on. . .

Anyhow: the Choir members all met in a common space at Birthwell's condo, up until Toronto citizens were asked to socially distance themselves as of March 2020, and meeting publicly became impossible. As the government's plans to deal with the global COVID-19 pandemic became more and more restrictive, they were physically separated yet drew emotionally closer. They rehearsed by Zoom, continuing to work on the music they'd been developing. Each became the subject of noise complaints from within their various buildings.

At some point, however, something happened. What, exactly? Again, hard to tell. We only know the results.

They started moving in with Groff.

Yes. They moved in, one by one; they committed to the next phase. And so, by degrees, they changed from a choir—a community—into a cult.

Is that what they were?

What else? A cult doesn't start out like a massive pyramid scheme, you know, or a super-church—a cult can be a family, an office. . . thirteen friends in a condo who build themselves a windowless room, pack themselves in like sardines, sing until they pass out. All that's required is that they believe something for which they have no immediate proof.

They didn't leave anything behind, though, like you said. So—how can we know what they believed?

We can't, not thinking normally. So, the only way we can try and reproduce their train of thought is by thinking, um. . . *abnormally,* metaphorically, poetically. Magically.

Magical thinking?

Of course. Like any other religion. Doing the same thing over and over, absolutely believing you'll get a different result from the one that logic, science, the basic rules of physics say you will —I mean, that's *faith,* isn't it? That's the very definition.

Most religious conversions still need some kind of catalyzing experience, though.

Sure, absolutely. These were people whose image of the world had already been undermined by Groff, her ideas, the possibilities of impossibility. And then things start to change all around them, without warning—a pandemic, a plague, "alternative facts," Fake News. Panic, depression, zealotry on all sides, and they realize they have no power to affect any of it, no power over anything but themselves. So, they did what they thought they had to, and believed whatever made those choices sound. . . well, not *logical,* exactly, at least to anybody outside the magic circle. But inside. . .
(PAUSE)
Tell me that doesn't sound at least a *little* familiar.

But it's. . . ridiculous, isn't it? To think that—

Think what? That horse dewormer cures COVID? That pedophile Jewish vampires who secretly run the world keep stables full of kids they torture for their adrenochrome? That if you only stand in a closet and sing long enough, hard enough, a door will open in the ceiling—a door to somewhere else, *anywhere* else? Because given the current situation, "anywhere else. . ." no matter how unspecific. . . starts to look pretty fucking good.

All of that, yes.

Hey, don't tell my uncle. Without QAnon to fall back on, he'd probably drink himself to death inside of a week.

How does. . . something like this start, though?

How does anything? Someone got an idea—Groff, probably; she heard a voice, or she had a dream, or whatever. And she told two friends, and they told two friends, and so on. . . it spread like a meme, because everyone she told was equally afraid of the same things she was afraid of. Fear makes for fertile soil.

Look, these were lonely people, just like the rest of us. They wanted to get together and do something special—like church, like bowling, like a mosh pit. Remember going to clubs, how stacked it used to get? Swaying on the dancefloor, like a single huge, giant hug? Breathing in each other's breath as you sang along to whatever was playing?

Yeah, I'm old, I get it; I lived through AIDS, kid. When every-thing—everyone—you love is suddenly infectious, you have to choose your options, take your chances.

Not every kind of worship is summed up by a monk praying in a cell; not every kind *can* be. People need to touch, to share, even if all they share is the same delusion, even if it's something that could kill them. If staying alive means letting go of human contact entirely, then what's the fucking point?

They're dead now, though. That's the point.

Is it? Maybe. Maybe.
(PAUSE)
Do you know there was a dead man's catch on the inside of the hidden room's door, rigged to open if whoever was closest to it went slack? Heo was a contractor; she probably designed it. So, I don't think they were looking to die, necessarily. Just. . .

Why didn't the door come open when what happened—happened, then?

Maybe it would have, if Naji's team hadn't broken in.
Oh, and one more thing. Did you know the Choir all had retinal damage that *predated* their death injuries? The same kind of damage they all showed afterwards, but less of it—little dots just over the pupil, tiny sections of intense degradation, seared there by extreme cold. If you look at them close up, very close up indeed, they look like little galaxies.

Which means . . . ?

No idea.
Listen, you're an adult—I'm sure you've already noticed none of this "means" much at all, in context. A lot of times, life. . . and death. . . seems utterly inexplicable, to the point of cruelty. Like: "This was just a thing that happened, make of it what you will." Whatever the Choir ended up with, is it any better than what we're left with, or worse? A dying earth and a plague in

progress, melting ice sheets, rising water levels? Dead fish, bleached-out coral, garbage islands?

So, I'll tell you what I told Ms. Halloway, if a little more bluntly: I can tell *what* I think happened, but not why. . . never why. Because if any of us are looking for answers, one way or the other, I think we're going to end up disappointed.

So, you don't know why they contacted the hot line, then. Why NFT was brought in.

. . . My best guess? Witnesses.

Witnesses?

Even Bible-less cults want to proselytize.

BLACK COHOSH

For Willow Dawn Becker

It begins where it ends, for him, for them. But not for me, or for us.

That's the whole point of the exercise.

———

Women take what's beautiful and make it horrible, they said, back in Salem Times. . . you know how we are, we just can't help it. We're weak and wicked, born sinful and inclining to sin; we can't be trusted, not even with ourselves. Our brains are small, wombs wandering and full of evil spirits. We steal men's penises and hide them in birds' nests. We smear ourselves with the fat of unbaptized children while masturbating with broomsticks.

So, if churches or states (or church-states) led by men have to arrest us, to save us from error—scare us straight, as it were? Make us confess our lies through torture, or threat of torture?

Well, then, that's better in the end, isn't it? Better than hanging, by far; better a dog than a bitch. Better to marry than burn.

Yes. And yet they expect us to believe they don't hate us, that they never really did. That everything they do to us is *for* us, for our own good.

It's enough to make you scream and keep on screaming, forever.

———

As I approach the border at speed, I am burning, burning—black cohosh in my veins, at least metaphorically; bugbane, snakeroot. Invisible letters printing my skin like scars turned inside out, poison-etched. I ride a dizzying path of visual effects, lungs so heavy I can barely pant as the sun stares down twinned while shadows loop and spit, snarling like yarn around me. And the pain of what I carry inside makes me want to puke, but I laugh instead, out loud and long, shocked by how much the sound of it frightens me. Then hear it echoed back to me in the car's roar, ragged-harsh as some carrion bird's cry, shaking the ground below.

There's an army already amassing within me, drunk with rage and high on hate, and all of them more than ready to riot. More than ready to *kill.*

The signs show me where to go, exactly as they're designed to. So soon enough, I find myself slowing to join one of the lines where they wind through a shiny forest of steel-slicked holding cages with low-level electric haloes: Immigrant-criminals on the one side, citizen-criminals on the other. I can't stop to sympathize, though, even if I was still capable of it. Simply travel on, scanning the crowds inside, looking for my chosen people.

And here, at last, I spot them, all massed together, two cages set facing each other, for maximum psychological cruelty—

"smugglers" versus "kidnappers," those caught travelling with extra cargo. The pregnant ones.

They don't sort out the unviable, not here. That'll wait until the camps. Which means the sizzling threads of pain I glimpse snaking their way through the huddled forms who clump away from the bars, hugging themselves or each other, could easily come from someone already miscarrying, someone fever-bright with internal decay, someone whose ectopic malignancy could never survive her death but still manages to produce a bare shadow of cardiac action. Could come from some ten-, eleven-, or twelve-year-old just trying her best to breathe away incipient panic, well aware that when her burden comes to term the result might rip more than just her perineum apart, or a woman five times her age whose geriatric system somehow beat the odds in a way she might have thought miraculous, under other circumstances. Or from someone whose truth doesn't match their biology, not even now they've been trapped into performing said biology's supposedly most natural function.

The thing I carry inside me is equally improbable, crude and dreadful in its flailing grotesquerie, a boiling, tornado-sized freak of supernature. It took thirteen of us to put it together, let alone inflict it upon ourselves—thirteen witches, sworn to revenge ourselves or die, scattered in thirteen different directions. Thirteen magical suicide bombers whose black intentions gripe us like gut-acid, scouring away all our empathic impulses, our much-lauded softer parts, our misguided capacity for mercy. Removing our regrets in service of a path that turns everything from this point on to nothing but grief, and bile, and awfulness.

A working like this takes blood too, like everything else. Like all magic. (Re-)balance through sacrifice; blood for blood, for blood, for blood, for blood. It's only fair in that it's not, at fucking all.

Yet I've never, in all my life, anticipated giving blood over anything else with *quite* such a fierce and savage joy.

———

Three guards at my checkpoint, two male-presenting, one female-. I'm not surprised: Uniforms really do change everything, don't they? Powerless to powerful, in one small step. All it takes is a willingness to be the stamping boot for once, instead of the face it grinds down on.

They ask me where I'm going, and why.

(*Across. To visit friends.*)

They ask me if I have anything to declare.

(*No, officers.*)

They ask me if I'm sure.

(*Why wouldn't I be?*)

And here they exchange glances, all three of them—two smug, one kept carefully blank, only guilty by association. Or so she thinks.

Come with me, ma'am, one of the men tells me, as the other one fails to hide a grin. Pulling out the blood test kit.

———

We all know the story—how it happened slowly, almost imperceptibly, until it didn't. Until, all at once, it was already too late.

I remember straight, cishet men complaining how hard it was to get women to date them, let alone fuck them, and wondering why. Conversations with my straight and bi female friends about how everything was taken as an invitation, a secret signal: talking to a man means you want sex, dinner means you want sex, stopping on the street when someone yells at you means you want sex, meeting someone's glance means you want sex. That constant frantic baboonish obsession with their own genitals every prospective patriarch seems to share from adolescence on, almost to the moment of death: there's a reason we used to call it "acting like a dick," before they made that illegal.

Women won't engage with us, they thought, so we'll force them to. We'll pass laws saying they have to be married to access what few rights we leave available for them, then make them have kids with us in order to buy the rest back. . . and they'll stay with us because they love those kids, because it's genetically encoded into them *to* love them. Because no one can ever physically be a mother without automatically feeling *motherly*.

Sure, the same way all cancer patients can't help loving their disease, or anything else life-threatening they might want— need—removed from their bodies, in order to survive. Fetishize our tumours by giving them a soft skull and a nice smell, love-drunk eyes, little latching mouths to siphon off the discomfort. Call it Cronenberg's Law and leave it at that.

At some point, it was decided to replace all adult women unwilling to be involved with this process with children, who have no choice but to accept it: tiny blank slates dependent on the same injustices that created them, ripe for brainwashing. And if childbirth doesn't kill us the first time, they'll just force us to keep on having children until it does: Force generation after generation of children to be born motherless, instruments of their own half-orphaning, splashed out into the burning garbage heap of this dying world on a tide of pregnant people's blood.

I can take this, we told ourselves, over and over; I can take this, if I have to. The same way we did about every other fucking thing. But we can't, and we don't. Not anymore.

On the one hand, sacrifice isn't sacrifice when there's no other choice, self or otherwise. It's murder.

But you know what? I'm good with it, at this point.

We're good with it.

———

When the border guard sees my blood test's result, he turns it towards me, so I can see it too. Leans close and murmurs, obviously lying: *I could help you, you know.*

(*Oh, could you, officer?*)

He was someone's baby once, I think; he had a mother who loved him, who he loved. Then his father taught him he was more important than her, and she said nothing to contradict him.

But he wasn't, officer, and neither are you. You just don't know it yet.

You will, though.

————

For me, the plan went like this: get pregnant, reach a border, try to cross. Find a guard willing to usher me across in return for favours. I knew it wouldn't be difficult, especially if I offered him unprotected sex—I mean, I was pregnant already, right? Soiled and soul-dirty, core-ruined, illegal on every level. Just like they like it, predators like whoever *this* particular predator would turn out to be. This fellow victim of the system so bought in he truly believed he wasn't a victim at all, that he never had been, and never would be.

(Outside, there's no way the female doesn't know what's happening too. But she won't say anything or interfere. Not with the other one looking at her and sniggering like it's all a big joke while waiting for his own turn, later on. How many times do they do this a day, usually? Impossible to say.

(Well, never mind.)

No need to go over the details, aside from the fact that I don't shut my eyes or bother to pretend I don't enjoy it. Just meet his gaze full on, nurture my own scant pleasure like a lit fuse, a tiny spark. He'll never notice, probably, grunting and sweating away above me, greedily chewing my breasts like something born with teeth. . . or *not* like one, not really.

As they'll see soon enough, all three of them, and more.

And ahhhhh, you wittering idiot G-d I refuse to believe in even now, but I hate them all so savagely—all the men and women who ever cooperated in putting this roundabout of stupid, brutal zealotry in place—for making me hate *anyone* this much, any real and actual other human being, that I'm willing to do what I'm about to. For making me so happy to anticipate his suffering once the spell I carry inside me is unleashed. But I made my decision miles back, years back; I suck it up, I nurture it, I turn it inside out, excoriating myself as much as anyone else involved. I ride a cyclone of rage and desire, bucking and snapping and snarling as I chase my own climax, knowing full well that it's key. How it's the final ingredient that will turn my child —however potential—into my weapon, my black miracle, my blood-magic atom bomb.

From cell-swatch to baby to monster set free to ravage and avenge, in a single squirming, painful, red-soaked forward surge.

See him start to hunch and lock my shaking thighs, making it impossible for him to pull out. The process starts here, with his ejaculation, my orgasm: a flash-paper split second of bodily joy before he feels something turn irretrievably *wrong*. Too tight, too *hot*, pain ratcheting sharp up the scale from arousing to anything but; oh Christ, oh *no*. Like sticking your cock in a pool drain by accident and feeling that sudden tug, that *rip*—blood in the water, bastard, gouts of it, dizzying-fast. Yes, that's right.

I see it reach his dumb animal stare, that fear, which makes me grin. And I—

—*I* can feel it too now, *my* child, only mine. Swelling between us, reaching out with claws fixed, with mouth wide open.

Feel it start to salivate at the very taste of him and bite down, *hard*.

———

Things happen fast, from then on. Exactly the way they need to.

My child tears through my would-be rapist from the bottom up, starting with his dick. It slips from me in a mess just as he begins to shriek, uncomfortably large enough to bruise my groin, but not break my pelvis; I rise without bothering to pull my pants back on, slipping off my shirt as the placenta spills out as well, then catches fire and spreads upwards, hardening into armour. The door bursts open; I hear the shouts, feel bullets bounce and skitter off me, ricochet to spin the other male side-long while my child finishes with his partner and leaps on top of him instead, still growing. It's going through puberty now, suddenly rabid to breed, spiked penis jerking up to spear him straight through the guts and spit on contact with his gooey-hot insides; it jackhammers him to the point of death, then hurls him aside and swipes the female across her throat even as she punches the alarm, freeing a bright crimson gush, a wail that never seems to end.

And: yes, I tell the rest of the border guards, come now, keep on coming. My child wants to meet you.

My child, and *its* child.

The placenta reaches my face and closes over me, a bruise-coloured glassine helmet, tingeing everything around me with rot. I step over the male guard as my child takes off down the hall, lope-brachiating, noting the way his perforation has already begun to swell: Tiny claws scooping up and outwards to free my first grand"baby's" bloody muzzle, its jaws of multiply-rowed teeth that twist and root their way from its "father's" pink-splayed intestinal nest. Then step past the female guard, her up-rolled eyes empty, thinking how this might so easily have been *her* fate too. Since some of us hated collaborators enough to want to go that far.

(We took a vote on it, six to seven; you can thank us for our commitment to democracy, if you want, when it's all over.

(Those of you who manage to survive.)

Birth a monster, set it free, let it pave your way—this sloppy trail beneath my feet, wet with slime and screams. I follow its track outside, down the road of cages, hands raising to cast smaller workings as I walk by: Make the electrical charge-boxes overload, the locks melt away, the doors fall open. Let loose new crowds of siblings, friends, parents and kids that *my* child's children were all born knowing to stream around, to leave untouched in their wake, smelling their relative innocence. Immigrant-criminals, citizen-criminals. . . my business is not with them. My business is with the system, and those who want to join me in its downfall.

At last, I reach the same cages I passed on my way to find that first sacrifice, dead Officer Idiot, my blithe sexual extortion-ist. Pause outside as the doors spring free to make my pitch, before they all go running: *Here's what happened, what I've done, what we've done, my co-conspirators and I. Here is what I can do for you too, if you're so inclined.*

Revenge always digs two graves, they used to say. Perhaps so; no, *probably* so. And yet.

And yet.

———

Will it hurt? Someone asks.

In this world of ours? I think. And hear somebody laugh, long and bitter, before realizing it must be me.

What doesn't? I reply.

Some nod, some don't. Some shake their heads and shoulder through, leaving the rest behind.

Take each other's hands, then, I tell those who remain, not watching the others go—run to find their families, made and otherwise. To spit on the remains of their captors or sob with disgust at the carnage, grab the ones they love and head for the open border's lights, together. *Hold on tight. I'm going to cast the spell again now, pass it on to all of you, to do whatever you want with it. And then I'll be done.*

(At last.)

Because: *Blood's what it takes,* I say, *and I still have some left to give, thankfully. So, here's the deal.*

You can have it all, so long as you promise to use it.

They think a minute, longer than I did, my first time. And then, then. . .

I do, someone says, quietly.

I do too, says another.

I do, I do, echoing through the group, rippling outwards. I feel my eyes sting. I've never been so proud.

Black cohosh in my veins, at least metaphorically; hatred's poison, anger's bite. All the pain I've ever felt or ever will. A hunger for justice I trust to never die, not even if it kills me.

I breathe out, one final time. Transmit it to them like a virus, its lettering inscribed on all their flesh at once, scarred upside down. That rush of nausea, tight chest and doubled vision, colours exploding outwards on every side. A toxic, tropical frog skin bloom.

Everyone doubles up, screaming, shaking. Everyone gives birth together, rips wide in a splash of blood, heals perfectly in the trauma's wake. The babies burst like bombs, bloat like leeches, and claw the dirt, mouths slavering. The electricity only makes them bigger. No bars can keep them in, or out.

I fall backwards, already cold, and stiffening. Peer upwards and search the sky for stars, even as my sight starts to fade.

———

Soon we're alone. I can hear women crying around me, women, people, mothers. I understand, though I can't help but feel impatient.

You would have had to trade your children for freedom eventually, I tell them.

I know, one replies again, barely able to whisper. And *yes, yes, I know as well,* I want to snap, but don't. I mean—what would be the point, exactly?

We've always known.

Other children are coming, now, for the ones who have them —half-siblings running with arms out, calling. *Please,* they say. *Come with us, please. Don't make us live without you.*

Go, I tell them or try to; I can't tell anymore. *There's only so much time, so go—find a new country, one that isn't this one. Just go, go. . .*

. . . and don't look back.

WET RED GRIN

Imagine a lady, old as dirt. Kind of old where there don't seem to be much left of her but bones, wrapped in a loose, wrinkly bag of skin. Cataracts on her slitty blue eyes, so thick they make 'em throw back light; she stinks of vinegar and baby powder, adult diaper rash and Clorox bleach. Goes without saying she's white too, but I will anyhow, just to set the scene.

Chart down the bottom of her bed says CAMP, MRS. WILLENA, plus a bunch of meds and a few more diagnoses—DEGENERATIVE DEMENTIA; ALZHEIMER'S DISEASE. And on the *very* last line, there's this, just in case: HAS SIGNED A DNR.

Most old ladies, they got yellow teeth, stained from years of smoking, coffee; some got off-white or ivory, meaning they come out at the end of the day, go in a cup and get cleaned with Polident if you're well-provided for, baking soda if not. Dip and no insurance gives you brown teeth, or black, or none. Mrs. Camp, though—she had something different, something I never saw before or since. Bitch was close-mouthed in general, had a scowl on her, like knotted purse strings. But sometimes. . .

. . . sometimes, Mrs. Camp, she let slip with a kind of wet, red grin, 'specially if she thought you weren't looking. Thin in the lips but with way too many teeth for comfort, all dyed dark as stewed beetroot somehow, and crooked with it too. That's how I first knew she was a wrong 'un.

My mawmaw knew conjure, grew up with it. And my Auntie Fee grew up with *her*, so she knew it too—maybe not as much, but enough.

So: "What makes somebody's smile that shade?" I asked her, one day, as we sat in her room down the end of the DNR unit. "It don't seem natural."

Auntie Fee laughed a bit, just a bare hissing sketch of the way she used to, and blew a little smoke out through her tracheotomy scar; janitors'd been good enough to unplug the fire alarms in that part of the Home a while back, 'cause when you got COVID and you're upwards of eighty, who the hell cares?

"Ain't much natural 'bout *that* one," she whispered, and I nodded. "But them choppers of hers. . . they mind me of something your mawmaw used to mention, back when. You ever hear of reddening the bones?"

"Never."

"Well, you go home and look it up on that Google of yours, Lainey. Thing knows more'n I've forgot, or so I hear."

Didn't have the Internet at home, so I went to McDonald's instead. Google showed me pictures of graves from Paleolithic times, skeletons dyed with ochre and madder root, sprinkled with the dust of ground-up rowan-tree berries. The idea was to bring vitality back by colouring them the same shade as blood, so you could consult with your elders if things got bad enough— uncover 'em and ask 'em for advice, same way you would've back when they were alive. Found a couple of sites said you could make totems by cleaning roadkill, disarticulating the skeleton and boiling it, then stewing beetroot mush, red wine and red chalk dust to make a paste with it. You mixed it with your own blood to "feed" 'em, then rubbed the bones all over, buried them, dug 'em back up when the moon was dark and washed the paste back off: hey presto, nice and red.

"So, you think she's a conjure lady?" I asked Auntie Fee, the next morning. She stared at me sideways like she didn't remember a thing about it, which maybe she didn't. "Or used to be, I guess."

"Who?"

"Mrs. Camp, Fee."

"Oh, *her*. Hm, wouldn't put it past her; sure is haughty enough, not that she's got any good reason to be, these days. Now she's stuck in here waitin' to die with the rest of us, I mean."

"True enough, I guess. How would a person go 'bout reddening their *own* bones, though?"

"Oh, child, how would *I* know? Pass me another one of them cigarettes, 'fore that other nurse comes in."

————

It was COVID times, two years on. Got a job in Dawson's Care Home, mainly to check up on Auntie, and 'cause they were short-staffed enough they sort of stopped remembering to check up on whether or not a person had the exact kinda experience they claimed they had, on their resumé. Though from my point of view, wasn't like I *lied* to 'em, exactly; was halfway through my paramedic training when they slapped me up in Mennenvale Female for a five-year bid, and I probably spent at least three quarters of that playing trustee in medical, drug bust or no drug bust. Kept my head down the whole while to rack up good behaviour, and they needed people already knew where to stick a needle wouldn't kill a bitch outright, so old Doc Rutina didn't have to fuck around with anything entrance-level while they were bringing in somebody with a shank between their ribs.

Anyhow. Doc's character testimony came in handy later on, when the M-vale board had to figure out if it was worth letting me out on compassionate after my mother passed—Second Wave was all over that place already, 'specially in gen pop, so they decided what the hell. Kind of hilarious in hindsight, considering I hadn't seen that sorry whore since she dropped me off at Mawmaw's and skedaddled, back when I was five.

Guess Mawmaw must've had enough of men altogether by the time she hit fifty, so she took up with Auntie Fee instead, her best friend since childhood. They raised me up both together, sharin' a truck, a house, and a bed till Mawmaw got cancer and Fee nursed her through everything after—two surgeries, two courses of radiation, three trips to the hospital that all but cleaned 'em out, broke 'em so bad I had to give Fee my tuition just to keep the bank from evicting her after she paid for Mawmaw's funeral.

No baby, that's so you do better'n either of us, is what she told me, with tears in her eyes; and *Naw, Fee, I'll be just fine,* was what I told her, folding it back into her hand.

Well, what else was I gonna say?

But I was out of M-Vale now, just like Auntie Fee was in Dawson's, penned up with Mrs. Camp and the rest of them wheezing biddies on the DNR unit. She needed me, same way I needed that job—bad enough to lie for, or obfuscate, at least. Didn't know just *how* bad, though, not back then.

Not as yet.

———

Dawson's was a bleak place, overall—worse than M-vale's infirmary by far, and that was saying something. Didn't help they were sticking to no family visits, or all the staff went double-masked, hair-netted, and gloved up like they was treating Ebola, smiles hid behind face shields we had to disinfect thirty times a day. Some nurses wore those clear plastic glasses underneath, like dental hygienists; janitors and us newbies, we mainly got by with dollar store swim goggles and wrap-around sunglasses, if that. Nobody wanted to get too close on either side.

Auntie Fee was fast asleep when I came in her room that first time. They'd took her wig off and hid it somewhere, her face gone all white and slack under a mess of baby-fine hair; had to take her pulse and study her breath a while, to convince myself she wasn't dead already.

Eventually, she cracked one eye open.

"Hello, ma'am," I said, at last. "I'm new 'round here, thought we should probably get acquainted. My name is—"

She stirred and snuffled a bit, grimaced, then went off in a surprise coughing fit once she recognized my voice.

"Lainey, child, that you?" she managed, finally. "Gal, I thought you still had. . . six months to go, last I checked. What-all you doin' up in *here,* for Christ's own sake?"

At that I gave a quick look 'round, just in case anybody else might be bothered to listen in.

"Well, now," I told her, quietly, "Jesus can look after himself, if the Bible's anything to go by. Bad bitches like us, though— times like this, we got no choice but to look after each other."

That got her eyes all bright again, thank God, even under those too thin, bleared-up lids.

"You go on and speak for yourself, Elaine Ann Merrimay," she hissed at me. "And wash your damn mouth out too, while you're at it."

"Yes, ma'am," I replied, smiling, under my mask.

One thing a job like mine teaches is that people say all sorts of things when they're dying. It's like the process breaks something open inside them, some long-buried infectious reservoir, a quick-draining sick-pocket. They don't even have to know what's happening, let alone accept it; might still be entirely convinced they'll survive, but it doesn't matter. A sort of punch-drunkenness takes over, when it comes home that the walls around 'em are probably the ones they're gonna die inside, not despair, exactly, just a kind of stillness, a waiting. The ones without that look, they were either new, or checked out completely: dementia, psychosis, amnesia, catatonia.

Mrs. Camp wasn't any of that, though, whatever it said on her chart. Didn't know what she had goin' on inside her, either, any more than what she might've done to make her teeth so red. . . but it made me shiver.

The night nurse, Ke'Von, said she liked to tuck cutlery up her sleeve and sneak it back to her room, which was creepy, even if she never cut anybody with it but herself. For all her bag-of-bones gauntness, she moved on her own, not fast but steady; never needed hearing aids or glasses, either. Sometimes I saw her whispering to other residents, right close up in the ear—one day I had to take her back to her room when I saw the lady she'd been talking to was crying, but Mrs. Camp wouldn't tell what she'd been saying, and the other one just blubbered, lying how she couldn't remember. One way or the other, that same lady died a day or so later, which wasn't exactly a surprise. Didn't like how Mrs. Camp grinned as they wheeled her body past, though.

About a week later, I swapped shifts with Ke'Von, 'cause his boyfriend was sick of 'em only ever meeting up over breakfast. Not like I had anybody at home, and besides. . . I sort of wanted to know what went on at Dawson's every night, 'specially in Mrs. Camp's room.

"That bitch is odd with a capital '*O*'," Ke'Von agreed, when I asked him how she seemed, from his angle. "You know she cuts herself, right? All over, where she thinks nobody's gonna see?"

"Yeah, 'Von, I know—with the cutlery."

"Okay, sure. . . but did I tell you *what* she cuts on herself?" I shook my head, folding another towel. "Looks like words, but not in any language *I* ever saw. No, seriously—took a snap while she was asleep one time, ran it through a bunch of translation apps. That shit ain't even Cyrillic, sis."

"What's it look like?"

"Um. . . Arabic, maybe, with a little Pinyin thrown in on top, but like if worms wrote it underneath a tree's bark, or some shit. And you *know* I know what I'm talkin' about, so don't give me that stink-eye, either."

"Yeah, yeah. You higher education-havin' motherfucker, you."

He struck a pose, like he was rolling his languages degree out for all and sundry to admire. After which we both smirked at each other, high-fived, blew each other a kiss, and got the fuck back to work.

Soon enough, I was walking in on Mrs. Camp herself. I knew she'd seen me; caught the eye-flicker, even if she didn't react as I went through the routine spiel: *How're-we-today-time-for-your-sponge-bath,* and the rest. I was the one lost my place, shocked still, when I slid her robe down her shoulders. On her back from nape to waist and all down both arms, not to mention the tops of her thighs and inside both her legs, her skin was scar-etched with signs like vévés or alchemy, all woven together in a sagging web—some red, some pink, some white as sin.

Must've taken all her life to make. And looking at it. . . maybe it was the way the wrinkles bent those scars out of shape, but just for a second, the whole of it made my guts twist, and my head hurt.

Then she glanced over her shoulder at me, and grinned, like she was ready to bite a chunk out of my arm, right there.

Don't mind admitting it, I jumped. She laughed.

"Be careful when you put your hand under the pillow, dear," she told me, like it was a secret. For the first time, I heard her accent—Kiwi, maybe, or South African; *kayuh-ful, hend, pillah, deah.* "Sometimes there are *things* under there. And they might not always let you go."

The fuck? I thought.

But: "Thanks for the warning, ma'am," was all I replied. To which she simply chuckled, then looked away as I sponged her down, stripped the mattress, checked for night sweat, and other fluids. No need to clean the rubber covers, thank God—Ke'Von was good about that, not like some—but I still had to check, which meant steering her to a chair while the air finished drying her. Which was harder than it'd been a minute ago. I couldn't get my hands near her without the skin on my arms trying to yank itself away.

It got a bit easier once I'd helped her dress, and she didn't look at me again, either, which also helped, so I sighed to myself slightly when it was all done. Almost made it out the door too, before I heard her mutter something.

"Sorry, Mrs. C.—what's that?"

"I *said*, 'You and Miss Fiona over there have a bit of a bond there, don't you?'" She nodded towards Fee's room, thin lips twitching. "Oh, not by *blood*, I mean; can't smell *that* on you, not quite. But something, nevertheless." That grin blooming back out, even as I tried my best not to look. "A certain care, on both sides. It's very—'sweet' would be the word, I suppose."

"Think you got me confused, ma'am. Maybe it's just 'cause Miss Fiona and me, we're. . . from the same stock."

"Why, what a way to put it, Nurse Merrimay! Sounds positively archaic."

"Not sure what-all you mean by that, ma'am."

"Really? You surprise me."

High-nosed, gutter-minded bitch, I couldn't stop myself from shaping, back inside my jaws, where nobody should've been able to see—or hear—it. Her head whipped around, though, like I'd said it out loud. And she just smiled the more, till I felt like I was going to puke.

Vinegar in my eyes, prickling at 'em; vinegar in my nose, making it itch, making me want to sneeze and retch at the same time. Shouldn't have been able to smell her breath, but I could —it was rank with meat, and peat. Dead vegetable matter. A bog-stink, hot like a breeze from hell. And then she looked away, suddenly, blinking at the window—the way people do, they got

what she's got. They disconnect. Needle skips in the brain, and they're somewhere else. Somewhen.

Then the vinegar-rot stink thinned out, and for a second, I thought maybe I saw something in her face I'd never seen before.

"Suboptimal conditions," she said abruptly, scowling up at the dark sky outside. "Oh, I should have prepared better. Why is there never enough time?"

Since I didn't think she even knew I was here anymore, I could pretend like I hadn't heard. Never any good answer to that question, anyway.

Last time I ever saw her, alive. But not the last time I ever *saw* her.

———

It shouldn't've been me who found her; wouldn't've been, Ke'Von's man-at-home hadn't gotten a positive test result that sent 'Von off to line up for most of the day before to get *his* ass tested. But he did, and whoever covered 'Von's shift did the usual half-assed job, probably just knocking on Mrs. Camp's door and moving on when nobody answered.

Between paramedic training and M-vale, I've seen my share of the shit people can do to each other, and I can handle it— mostly. That room, though, that night. It's the only thing that's showed up in my nightmares, since.

I remember walking in, flipping the light and thinking *Shit, who painted the place red?* Then my foot went out from under me, and I went down, *splat*, in a cold, viscous puddle; scrambled back to my feet, wiping myself down, swearing. Wasn't till I saw the limp, shredded thing all over the bed and realized how the stuff dripping off me was blood that I punched the alarm and swore even harder, if only so's I wouldn't start screaming.

The worst part was how I could still make out Mrs. Camp's scars on the torn remains of her skin, surrounded by a spill of deflating organs. They made weird channels for the blood leaking everywhere, guiding it into patterns on patterns on patterns, a whole new design.

Doc Dawson and a couple of orderlies came running, took over, set me aside to wait for the cops. I remember Dawson himself wrapping a blanket 'round my shoulders and saying, quietly: *Sorry, Elaine, can't let you wash till the CSIs say it's okay.* Poor little Nurse Sarah, who thought she could handle anything just 'cause she'd bagged upwards of fifty patients when the ventilators wouldn't give 'em enough oxygen and gotten quick enough at slipping a bronchoscopy tube down the throat to clear the lungs of gunk, she just about tore out of the building, wailing —never saw her again.

And that one detective, a lady, saying: *No one saying* you *did this, Miss Merrimay, though if you* did *have to remove all the bones from a body, you'd know how, right?* Not to mention the residents and the rest of the staff alike, rubbernecking over the yellow tape like this was hands down the most interesting shit ever happened to them.

Dawson drove me home, afterwards. "Might want to think about preparing for the worst, Elaine," he told me, at my door. "I mean, I'll do my absolute best to avoid the topic. . . but if the police ask me why I hired an uncertified ex-con on compassionate parole as a nurse, I'm going to have to tell them we had no idea you falsified your resumé, so we're letting you go; you understand. Just can't afford to keep the home operating if we lose our liability insurance."

"I get it," I said finally. "Thanks for that, Doc. G'night." And closed the door on him, right in his face. Then I took a hot shower, burned my scrubs in the sink, and passed out.

Last thing I remember is wondering just what the fuck *did* happen to old Mrs. Camp's bones, let alone the rest of her.

———

I took the day off, then switched with 'Von again for the night shift, 'cause I felt like I really might as well rack up as much time with Auntie Fee and money as I could, considering. Helped I kind of liked the hands-on work—reading a chart all the way through, getting the routine and the meds down, trying to catch issues might've got skipped over. . . like solving a puzzle, in a way.

So, when I opened the door to a resident's room I'd never visited before, the bloated size of the woman in bed didn't throw me any, or the restraints—she was another dementia case, prone to wandering, and people on permanent rest get heavy. The faint sour stink in the air was. . . familiar, somehow, though I knew I didn't know the name: AZZARELLO, Mrs. JOY, 08 October 1941. Then I read further enough something *did* hit me wrong, and frowned.

The fuck? I mouthed.

"Language, dear," croaked the woman in the bed, without opening her eyes. I froze.

"'Scuse me, ma'am?" I asked, after a moment.

"Oh, sorry." Mrs Azzarello gave a close-lipped smile, eyes crinkling open. "That's what I have to tell my grandkids, when they visit. Shocking how young folks talk these days, isn't it?" She took a deep breath, looking around, like she'd never seen her own room before. "Still, shouldn't complain. It's a miracle just to be alive, on a beautiful night like this."

"Guess so."

My brain did the thing brains are supposed to do, telling me: *Course you thought she sounded like Mrs. Camp—you were thinking about Camp, and she said something Camp used to say, 'cause most folk her age say the same things, sooner or later.*

"Mrs. Azzarello—"

"Call me Joy, dear. And I'll call you Elaine."

But my first name's not on my badge, I thought.

"Um—sure. Well, Joy. . . don't remember the last time we updated your chart, do you? Offhand." Those eyes of hers flickered, and though my brain still had no idea what was going on—

wouldn't admit anything *was* going on, for fear it might make it true—my nerves and my guts, they knew.

"Oh, I don't pay attention to all that," she said. "That's what my family pays for, don't they? Elaine."

And she grinned at me: Wet. Toothy. Red. Dark brown red, like peat. Like meat.

Hello, Mrs. Camp.

Made myself smile after that, say some happy nurse-y bullshit—I don't remember. It was

straight-up reflex, taking over. Meanwhile, I checked the chart again. *Wt Admit: 104 lb 7 oz / 47.732 kg,* I read on Mrs. Azzarello's chart, doing my level best to look dumb as paint. *Wt Last: 99 lb 14 oz / 45.303 kg.* The words kept on repeating in my head, while I strained and grunted her puffy, malformed body upright for a sponge-down; couldn't be less than two hundred pounds, now.

Close to her, that vinegary stink was worse, the skin drumtight, full of weird protrusions and hardnesses. Her round, weirdly cheerful face had marks all down the cheeks and forehead: faint, wavery, purple. Bruises from the inside, spread out thin and long as cellulite, tapering into scars.

Stretch marks, I thought, numbly. *Fuckin' stretch marks.*

"See you later, ma'am," I sang out as I opened up that door again, glancing back. She grinned at me again, even wider.

"Do say hello to Miss Fiona for me, dear," she said.

(*Deah.*)

I slammed the door, ran down the hall, and barely made it to the john.

———

"What would be the point of reddening your own bones?" I asked Auntie Fee, a few days later. Didn't necessarily expect her to answer, but she did—it was a good day for her, least in *that* way.

"Your mawmaw would've said the *point* was to keep on living," she told me, whispering, wheezing. "The soft parts go, but the hard parts survive. Bone has a long memory, you know, longer by far than flesh. Think about all them old kinds of human beings they're always finding in caves and such—all that information they can get a hold of now, and from nothin' more than a bunch of dust. They can boil it down, tell you exactly what that person might've looked like when they were alive. . ."

"That's from DNA, Auntie Fee."

"Sure, but where-all does DNA live, exactly? In the bone, the marrow. In the smallest of all small things, just like God willed it to do."

I moistened my lips. "Auntie Fee, you ever notice how Mrs. Camp used to smell like vinegar?"

She snorted. "Hardly coulda missed it."

"Well. . . Mrs. Azzarello, she smells like that too, now. Why you think that is?"

"Oh, Lainey. And I thought you were so smart." She chuckled. "Need a *lot* of vinegar to make your bones soft, red or not. That's so's you can slip 'em out through the mouth and into the skin of the next person you want to pretend you are. Break out of this whole waiting-to-die nuthouse in stages, one dead old lady at a time."

Granted, she said it like she couldn't imagine it being anything but a joke. And yet.

After my shift, I went surfing on my phone, reading about things like the *penanggalan,* the *kephn,* the *obayifo, adze,* and the *loogaroo,* who leave their skins behind to go hunting as floating sacks of organs or balls of fire, fireflies even, soaking their guts in vinegar tubs to shrink 'em back down for re-entry. Then I ordered some stuff off of Amazon, splurging on next-day delivery. And finally, I called Prisha, who'd be on the front desk by now, and handled a lot of the admin in practice. She cheerfully filled me in, without even asking why I needed to know.

Maybe people 'round here could stand to ask a few more questions, every once in a while, I thought.

Mrs. Azzarello hadn't talked, though she made a point of grinning whenever no one else was by, teeth like an open gash. All the mysterious bloat she'd suffered was shrinking away fast, leaving her gaunt as before, or gaunter. The orderlies didn't think she'd last much longer, offered me a chance to get in on the betting pool. I declined, but asked 'em to do me a favour: could they put this *Love U Grandma* teddy bear in Mrs. A's room for me? Somewhere she can see it, and it's facing her; even if she don't remember who it's from, it'll make her happy.

They agreed.

Nanny cams in those bears don't send a signal very far, but Ke'Von's boyfriend was one of those IT geeks builds fiber-optic networks for fun; he set up an app under my user ID on the home's network that picked up the cam signal via Bluetooth, so I could log in from my phone to watch it.

This is federal-level privacy violation, he warned me, in a text. **Easy to find if admin goes looking. U sure u need to do this???**

Yup, I texted back.

¯_(ツ)_/¯, was his only reply.

Traded shifts with Ke'Von again, which pissed him off till I made him promise not to go into Mrs. Azzarello's room, and to stay off that corridor as much as he could—then he got all interested. So, I said I'd show him what I came up with, once I had it.

"Bitch, you better," he told me; *Might be you think again if it's what I think it's gonna be,* I thought, but didn't say.

Tried to stay up and watch, but I fell asleep two hours in and yawned all next day, so I switched to skimming through each night's video on my break the next morning, deleting it if nothing happened. And four days later, I got my proof.

———

"Well, technically Mrs. Camp's file's still private," was what Prisha had told me, when I called. "But there's no next of kin listed and she's *super* deceased, so—what'd you want to know?"

"Oh, just where she came from, who she was. Stuff like that."

"Well, says here she was born in Rhodesia, this place that used to be next to South Africa; trained as an anthropologist, wrote a lot about various indigenous folk religions. Oh, and her husband was in Doctors without Borders, just like Dr. Dawson— a lot younger than her too, when they hooked up. Doesn't say how he died, just it was a few years ago, and. . ."

She paused.

". . . uh, maybe I shouldn't get into this, but—hell, the bank records are right there."

"What?"

"Turns out, Mrs. Camp had her a *lot* of money set aside. Like, not to be shitty about it, but enough to afford a *much* better home than here. Huh." I could almost hear her shrug. "Could be she was being nice to Dr. Dawson, since him and her husband were friends? I guess?"

"Guess we'll never know," I said, and hung up.

———

Okay, so. . . what I saw on that file was bad. Worse than. Like the first time I got beat up so awful I didn't recognize myself after. Like that other time I woke up bleeding, hurting from north to south *down there*, and couldn't remember anything about it— just laughing at some shitty country bar, things getting dimmer, getting small, flicking off. Like that one night in M-Vale I heard someone bumping against the wall over and over, moaning, and I banged back 'cause I thought they were enjoying themselves just a little too much—but in the morning Guard Winslow went in to find out why they weren't lined up for count, only to discover someone'd fucked 'em to death with a hammered-out bolt from the kitchen stove fan hood.

No sound or color, thankfully, but the nanny cam had an infrared setting, and didn't need light to see: grainy black and white, except reading white for various shades of grey, and what have you.

It starts with Mrs. Azzarello in bed, slack, barely seeming to breathe. A rattle deep in her chest. Then she spasms, jolting back and forth, like somebody with an invisible set of defib panels is trying to revive her: Mouth open wide, arms whipping. A thick mist abruptly sprays, falling to darken—whiten—the sheets, painting scattershot patterns over floor and walls.

The body writhes, twisting. It opens its mouth again, wider, wider. More mist sprays from splitting skin. The head twists and twists again, corkscrewing itself upwards. The hair parts, shows what must be skull. The grey bedsheets have gone almost completely white; great splotches drip down, soaking the mattress. And something sharp-edged, white as the blood it's shed, rips free, reaching upwards.

We catch gleams off slick tendons, peeling away like string-cheese; at the end of fleshless fingers, somehow still strung and reaching, dim nails shine. The rest of the skin tears away with ease, like it's already rotten. Both hands pop back the scalp, shred and shed the upper body from skull to thighs; knees and feet kick free of the bottom half, like a pair of crotch-ripped pants. Organs spill out the ribcage as the thing inside curls back, clambers into a crouch, crawls to the end of the bed and sits there waiting, a cat on the lookout for prey. Can't listen, 'cause it's got no ears; can't *see*, not with those empty sockets. Doesn't seem to matter worth a damn, though, on either point.

Then something blurs and jerks, almost too fast to register—it's down on the floor all of a sudden, spider-crawling, limbs bent back and unnaturally high. *Scuttling*, to the door, and through it. And just before the light outside blots out the camera's IR vision, you see how it's nothing but bones, and all its bones are white-for-grey. . . a wet, cold white, like zero, nothing, blank. So blank it might as well be black.

But in color, you just *know*, there's no way they'd be anything but red.

————

Knowing what to expect when I walked into Mrs. Azzarello's room the next morning didn't make it any easier, 'specially the part about how once I hit the alarm, I'd inevitably end up in a room with that same lady cop asking me what I thought the odds were on the same person finding this kind of mess twice in a row. Not to mention why I hadn't seen fit to tell anybody, last time, how I was not only a former adoptive ward of one of the patients, but a former resident of M-vale.

"'Cause I knew the whole place'd get shut down, if I did," I said, bluntly. "You tell *me* what's more important—fucking my life up even more and gettin' my Auntie thrown out on the street or figurin' out who did this. And *how*."

That got her to blink. Cops don't like admitting they don't know something, but the smarter ones don't like lying, either; getting caught at it wrecks cases, makes the whole job harder. In the end, she just told me they might come back to me on the topic, so don't skip town—best I could've hoped for, really.

Fuck your worst-case scenario, Dr. Dawson.

When it was finally over, I cornered Ke'Von at the end of his shift and dragged him out to my car. He didn't want to come—was already freaking out over having been grilled by the cops for the second time in a month—but I insisted.

"Got something to show you," I told him, and queued up the recording.

"The fuck's that," he asked, afterwards, a lot more toneless than that reads. More like: *The fuck. Is that.*

"Mrs. Camp," I answered. "Them weird-ass bones of hers, anyways."

Never seen a guy that big make a face like that before, and I don't hope to ever again, if I'm lucky.

"Lainey, no," he said, finally, kind of pleading, like he thought I could do anything about it. "I mean. . . c'mon now, *no.* That is some seriously ill sort of bullshit, right there. That just. . . can't happen."

"Well, I kind of think it *can,* 'Von," I pointed out, "if only 'cause we both of us just *watched* it happen, in real-time. Shouldn't, I do agree with you on that one, for sure. But. . ."

He nodded.

"You could've faked this, though, somehow, right? For—a joke, or a prank, or whatever. A. . . sick, *sick*. . . joke."

Now, that did get me annoyed, just a tad.

"Seriously? If I *did,* your boyfriend must've been in on it, 'cause everything I know about computers could fit in a fuckin' Dixie cup. Who you think helped me set up this shit in the first place?"

"Aw, man." He thought about it for a minute, and I watched emotions chase each other over his face. "Okay, so—ugh, Christ. So. What do we do about it?"

I had to think. I mean. . . conjury, at least according to what I'd heard, didn't truck too much with stopping things. It was more all about rerouting what was already happening, turning it towards or away from the people you wanted to hurt or to keep safe. There was always this sense that motion made for more motion, that the world followed a set of laws mostly based on energy and nothing ever really came to an *end,* as such.

But then again—I ain't my mawmaw, nor yet my Auntie Fee, and some things are just bad, rotten, inexplicably so; need to be done away with, or close as makes no never-mind. Just like some people do things that put 'em beyond the pale forever, making it so there's no forgiveness for them, just regret and penitence at best, eternal exclusion from being trustworthy-till-proven otherwise at worst.

I mean, I ought to know.

"I think we gotta kill it," I told Ke'Von. "Break it down real small, burn it and piss on the ashes, bury it out in the goddamn desert. . . something like that, anyways. So it can't do something like *that* anymore, to anyone."

"Suits me. Can we, though? I mean—that's fuckin' *magic*, right there."

Well, he wasn't wrong.

"We can try," I offered, which was all I had. "Don't have to help me do it, you don't want to; I'd understand. Can't claim I wouldn't appreciate it if you did, though."

"I just bet you would. Bitch."

"All day, every day."

I gave him a smile, most probably of the wan, small variety. To which he just kind of nodded again, sighing.

". . . yeah, okay," he replied at last.

———

Whole home was afraid, now, staff talkin' amongst themselves, surly, *too* quiet. Overheard Dawson *begging* one orderly named Wojciech not to quit, and if he couldn't afford to let even *him* go —same asshole I knew for a fact liked to slap patients 'round on the sly—then things really were getting tight around here. Then again, plenty of people were looking me cross eyed as well, like they thought the cops might be right, and *I* was the one doing this shit. Like it was *my* fault Mrs. Camp had chosen me to fuck around with, while she was making her slow motion escape from death.

Late that afternoon, Ke'Von found me in the office, on the computer.

"Mrs. Waltham," he murmured. "On the second floor, few doors down from your Auntie Fee. Lisbeth had to get me to help her change the sheets, 'cause suddenly she's too heavy for her to move, and looking like ten tons of sick in a two-ton bag." He hesitated. "Might have to go slow, though—Beth swears she's gonna make sure Dawson knows something weird is going on with Mrs. W, and she's a good one. She means it."

Maybe, I thought. But would Dawson do anything about it? That, I doubted.

"Go slow, we may not get another chance," I said.

At that, Ke'Von gave up trying to be subtle; still kept his voice low, thank God.

"Lainey, I don't wanna kill an old lady, no matter what the fuck's inside her! You get me?"

"Look, me either," I told him. "So. . . we just wait till the bones come out, give it a few days for it to finish—eating her, I guess. Absorbing her. Whatever."

"Aw, shit." He looked away. "Man, we're supposed to *help* people."

I sighed.

"'Von, Mrs. Waltham's gonna die anyway—just like Camp, and Azzarello. If it wasn't

COVID it'd be Alzheimer's; matter of *when*, not *if*, this unit. We both know that."

Ke'Von scowled at empty air. "So, what's this all *for*, then, anyway?"

I'd asked myself the same question, truth told—wasn't sure how long Mrs. Camp had been thinkin' on this, but just hopping over and over from one DNR-havin' end-of-lifer to the next didn't sound like any kind of long-term strategy to me. Then again, maybe there was less and less Mrs. Camp every time she let those red bones rip, 'sides from the parts that remembered how she liked sneering at other people.

"Really don't think that matters all that much now, 'Von," I said at last.

"Shit, probably not." He grimaced. "The hell you looking up the cleaning inventory for, exactly?"

"Just checking on something Prisha told me," I said.

————

Ke'Von and I'd already both switched back to night shift, which wasn't hard because—surprise, surprise —people were *really* eager to get off that shift, they only could. We snuck the bear into Mrs. Waltham's room, and Ke'Von's man put a script on my app to send us an alert if it picked up any motion.

"Looks to me like that thing takes at least a minute, minute and a half to finish, completely," I told him. "So long as one of us stays nearish, we should be able to get there quick enough."

Ke'Von shook his head. "We really doing this?"

"Brought your bat, didn't you?"

He had, and we weren't the only night staffers who'd started carrying for self-defense, be it knives, Tasers or tire irons— anything they thought they could hide fast if Dawson dropped by, which he was doing a lot less of. Even Wojciech had started wearing a full tool belt, with a wrench **and** a hammer.

"Just keep moving, look busy, even if you have to let things slide. Gotta pray there's no code blues, when that thing goes off."

"Christ Almighty."

Ke'Von offered his hand; I gripped it tight. "Stay safe, okay?"

"You too."

That was one long fucking night. Some of it I spent watching Auntie Fee sleep, through the little window on her room's door; the rest I spent trying to stop myself from checking on Mrs.

Waltham, while Ke'Von tried to do the same. Every noise—the buzzing of lights, slow tick of wall clocks, creak of opened doors, or the squeak of cleaning bucket wheels—sounded ten times loud as normal, the silence between noises ten times as deep.

One of the former caught my attention when I was passing by Mrs. Waltham's room for what must have been the twelfth time, eventually: a different *kind* of wheel-squeak, one I didn't recognize. Looked down the hall to see Wojciech hauling an empty cargo cart away from a residence room. As the door clicked closed behind him, every muscle in me went instantly cold and stiff, faster than my brain could figure why.

"*Hey!*" I shouted. "Wojciech! The fuck you doing?"

He looked up, startled. Then his eyes narrowed, and my guts clenched up. He stepped away, hand falling to the hammer on his hip, and I took a step back. . . which is when the phone alert from the nanny cam went off, a shrill shriek I'd intentionally picked to be painful as possible. Made me jump like a rabbit.

I turned, grabbed up the bat I'd brought from home—hidden behind a supply-closet door—and ran, forgetting Wojciech completely. Pulled up in front of Mrs. Waltham's room, panting.

"'Von, *get on over here!*" I yelled, hard enough to scrape my own throat. Then I flung the door open and lunged inside.

The upper half of Mrs. Waltham's body looked like it'd exploded: Blood all over the bed, the walls, dotted by shreds of skin. Mrs. Camp's shiny red-brown skeleton sat up amid the wreckage and clicked its teeth at me, tilting its head, like it was flirting. Words seemed to leak out between its jaws, buzzing inside my head: *Why, hello, deah! So pleased you could joy-en me! I do hope you—*

Well, fuck *that* shit.

If I hadn't right then realized which door Wojciech must've had opened, not to mention what he must've left in that room, I'd probably have stood there frozen a lot longer than I did. But I wasn't losing anyone else—not that night, anyhow. So, I just swung my bat as hard as I could, aiming straight for her skull. That fleshless arm came up, but I'd moved too fast. The bat struck the skull's temple dead on, with a deafening *crack*, and spun right the fuck out of my hands, leaving my palms stinging in agony.

I staggered backwards. The skull grinned at me, utterly untouched.

And: *Oh, my deah, deah, deah.* The click-buzzing voice sounded almost fond. *Didn't really think that would work, did you? After all, this is* magic.

Right that same second, Ke'von appeared in the doorway, own bat held high like he was ready to try for a grand slam. Then he saw Mrs. Camp and dropped it. The skeleton's jaw flapped like it was laughing. It reached down, ripped away the tissue left over its legs and leaped at him.

Ke'Von screamed. They went down together. I jumped in, grabbed my arms 'round the ribcage—those red bones were hot and slippery, almost steaming—and tried to pull her off, feet skidding on the blood-slick floor. Ke'Von was still screaming, trying to push Mrs. Camp's naked skull away, but it had its teeth into his wrist now and was biting down, grinding; I shoved one hand up inside her jawbone, hooked the fingers of my other into her eye-sockets and pulled till her grip broke, twisting upper from lower like I was Steve Irwin punching a crocodile's ticket.

As Ke'Von yanked his mauled hand back, I rolled my whole body, hard as I could. Whatever let the thing move like it still had muscles, it sure didn't give it any extra mass—Mrs. Camp's skeleton went flying down the hall like a discarded puppet, clattering to the floor in a heap. An instant later it was straight upright again, crouched in that same hunting-spider pose.

This was fun, children, I heard, in my head. *But I haven't the time, right now. See you soon. . .you in particular, Elaine.*

Faster than a snake, the thing leaped over our heads, bone

feet rattling down the hall. By the time I could make myself roll over to look for it, it was gone.

Ke'Von was twisting on the floor, meanwhile, desperately holding his wounded wrist shut. The size of the blood-puddle slapped me back to reality—he needed emergency care, *now*. I stumbled back into Mrs. Waltham's room, hit the alarm.

Then I ran.

———

When the cops realized I wasn't first on the scene for once, they searched the building, but I'd worked here long enough to know spots like that place behind the boiler where the basement wall went back three extra feet. Thing was a sweatbox, but I gritted my teeth and sat it out, turning on my phone every few minutes to check the time.

Please, God, I thought, *let them finish up and clear out before it's too late.* If I was right, I had at least a few hours. . . but there was no way to know, really.

At last, around five in the morning, I took my chance.

Creeping back up, I found Mrs. Waltham's room taped off and the blood already mopped up off the linoleum; whatever Ke'Von had told the cops, they'd apparently decided they didn't need to leave officers in place. I let out a breath I hadn't realized I'd been holding, went to the supply closet, unscrewed the handle from one of the mops.

Then I opened the door to Auntie Fee's room.

Fee was snoring. Her room looked exactly like usual, except for the big blue plastic barrel that asshole Wojciech had left in a corner; I could smell its vinegar stink from here. Faint gurgling echoed from inside it; shadows moved, like they were settling.

Just to confirm my guess, I shook Fee's shoulder, gently first, then harder. When she didn't move, I skinned back her eyelid;

her pupil shrank, but the eye stayed still. My stomach went cold again.

Of *course*, Wojciech had probably pumped something extra into Fee's IV to make sure she stayed down—for all I knew, she was dying already.

A dull *clunk* echoed through the room, then a whirr, a dropped coin edge-spinning, about to fall flat. The stench of vinegar billowed out; I choked, bracing myself on the bed to keep from puking. It took everything I had to make myself turn around.

Mrs. Camp's skeleton grinned at me as it rose slowly from the open barrel, teeth wet and red and shiny as always. Vinegar ran down its skull's smooth sides; I heard static in my head yet again, buzzing.

Deah, we're not really going to bother with this, are we? You already know how fighting me ends, for you.

"Just tell me one thing," I managed, trying to spit out the taste. "Dawson. . . was he in on this from the beginning?"

The skeleton's skull tilted. *Well, when I realized those nasty plaques in my brain were going to make it difficult to focus, I had to improvise. Dawson offered the perfect environment, even if I had to settle for distinctly substandard material. And I was going to take your Auntie, there, just to teach you a lesson, but—no amount of old bodies can ever provide as much power as one young, healthy one, you know.* It clapped its jaws, smacking nonexistent lips. *Which is why, though I'd have preferred a different, what did you say?—stock? —you'll do, dear. You'll do.*

The dripping digits came up, curving into claws.

This will hurt quite astonishingly, dear, the skeleton told me, pleasantly. *But not for long.*

And: *Yeah,* I thought, *that's true.*

If I just stand here and let it.

———————

In hindsight, I think Mrs. Camp might just have forgotten how fragile her bones had to be, now she'd spent hours soaking in vinegar. Soft enough to get down a woman's throat without killing her, right? I mean. . . she *was* magic, that's true. But if magic could cure senility, this would be a whole 'nother sort of story.

When she leaped at me, I didn't try to duck out of the way; just let her grab on, fingers clasping 'round my throat. My breath choked off for a second, till I stretched my head back and locked the muscles hard, and the bones bent like rubber. I shoved one hand up to wedge my fingers between hers, loosening her grip; jabbed my other right between her ribs to grab her spine, then ran straight at the wall. The skeleton crumpled between my body and the wallpaper, black rips tearing mushily open in the smooth red surfaces.

The buzzing static in my head skirled upwards, into a shriek. While the rubbery arms beat at me helplessly, I grabbed at the joints in hip and shoulder and yanked them apart, threads of sinew stretching like taffy, hurling arms and legs into each corner; they whipped over and over themselves, began humping back towards me like blind snakes, while I threw the ribcage down and trampled on it in a frenzy.

Vertebrae separated; ribs spun away. My head was splitting with those silent screams. And then I stamped down hard on the neck, separating skull from spine; crouched and jumped, both feet landing square on the skull, weight of my whole body behind 'em. Crushed instantly flat, the skull split apart like a rotten melon.

The shrieking stopped. The limbs stopped moving. A second later, whatever held them together dissolved, and every bone not already torn free tumbled away from its neighbours. Suddenly, I was standing amidst a scattered fan of pieces, red and damp and lifeless.

I dropped to my knees, panting. "Don't throw up," I gasped to myself, "don't throw up, don't throw up. . ."

It's over, I thought. *It's done.*

Except it wasn't, quite.

I made myself get up, soon as I could. First step: Gather up all the pieces, dump them back into the vinegar barrel. Lid on, lock shut. Then down to the basement, find a cart—thank Christ this was the deadest hour of the day, just before shift change at six a.m.—and wrangle the barrel back down to the basement, in the service lift. That gave me privacy, and time, to separate what was left of Mrs. Camp out into twenty different medical waste disposal bags, double wrap them, and put 'em all in the bin for next week's pick-up.

After that, one last meeting.

————

When he opened his office door and found me waiting in his desk chair, Dawson boggled, but only for a moment. Then he came in and closed the door.

"Miss Merrimay," he said, dully. "I'd say I'm sorry, and it's the truth, but somehow I don't think you care."

"Got *that* right, Doc." I folded my arms, not getting up. "Did you know? When you admitted her? That all this shit was going to go down?"

Dawson closed his eyes.

"I'd seen her do amazing things," he said. "She spent her life learning how. It was like having a saint for a sister-in-law—Edward was as good as my brother. Then he died, and she couldn't save him, or stave off the Alzheimer's, and she offered to leave me enough to keep the home going for decades if I'd just. . . accommodate her." He gave me a desperate look. "You have to believe me, even after everything I'd seen—what she planned? I just didn't think it could be *possible.* Would you, if you hadn't seen it?"

"Still ordered the vinegar drums, though, didn't you?" I said, tonelessly. "Don't lie, Doc, I saw your signature on the order. Passed them off as cleaning supplies. Got Wojciech to haul one into every target's room and haul it away afterwards. And went out of your way to get a good selection of candidates in your intake. Dementia patients, no kin left who cared about 'em . . . they couldn't remember if they saw anything, and who'd believe 'em if they did?"

I got up, then, walking 'round the desk to glare in his face. "So you can tell yourself it was all for the home, but I'm gonna bet she told *you* what'd happen to you, if you didn't. And you believed her."

Dawson took a shuddering breath.

"I have no excuse for what I've done," he said. "But if you want to punish me for it, you're going to have to come up with a much more plausible version of events, if you don't want the Home shutting down after I go to prison. Not to mention how I could provide an equally plausible version that would present you to considerable disadvantage, as well." He moistened his lips. "So, it seems to me we can either ruin each other or walk away and not throw more of the living after the dead. Which would you prefer?"

I sighed, suddenly tired.

"Doc," I replied, "I'd be a whole lot more pissed off about that kind of ultimatum, if I hadn't already thought of it. So, here's what we're going to do."

He blinked.

———

The cops marched into the Home a week later and arrested Jan Wojciech right in the middle of his shift, charging him with the murders of Mrs. Camp, Mrs. Azzarello, and Mrs. Waltham, as well as multiple ongoing cases of patient abuse, theft, and trafficking of medical pharmaceuticals. Dawson made sure there was enough evidence available on the smaller stuff that the circumstantial murder case looked a lot more convincing, and the court denied bail. Trial's still in progress; I haven't really cared to follow it. In the meantime, Mrs. Camp's will was cleared by the lawyers, and things have improved a lot around the Home: better staff, better food, better class of care. I even got a pay raise.

Never told Ke'Von about the deal I worked with Dawson, and he didn't ask. But then again, it was never the same between us, really. About a month and a half later, he quit. We haven't talked since then.

I did ask Fee, once, if I'd done the right thing. She took a long time answering. At last, all she said was, *Would you do the same again, Lainey, you had to?*

Absolutely, I said, and she shrugged.

Then there you go.

And I would. If somebody's got to suffer shit they don't deserve, better assholes like Wojciech than the people in the Home, even if it means weasels like Dawson get to put off their reckoning a while.

Nobody gets to put it off forever, after all. Mrs. Camp could tell you that, and so can I.

So *will* I, no doubt.

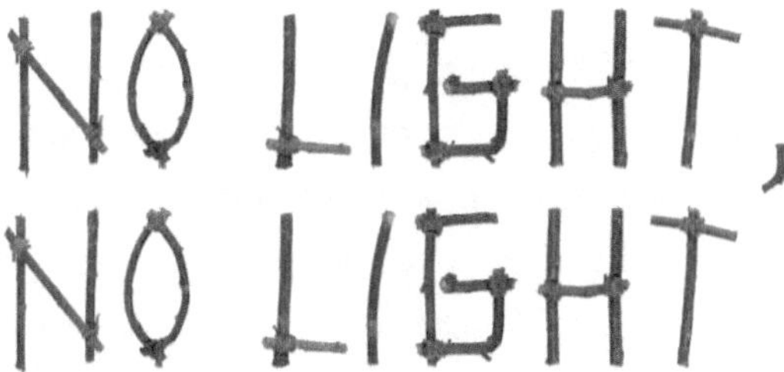

There is fire under the ice, always: fire and venom, poison, lava, gas; salt blood, eggs and sperm and bone-fragments, a million foetal, fossilized monsters. And lies, also—above all, below all, lies.

Everything about *me is a lie.*

———

Lying, I discovered long ago, is a sort of magic. You tell the truth in advance, and make it so, changing other people's timetables for your own; you reframe a story from your own perspective, occult it, change the narrative, make it your own. I've done this since I began to talk, long after my parents thought me likely to —began with a full sentence (factual rather than fictional, at the time), then kept on going. I made words my weapons, my tools, my trade. I clothed myself in a suit of lies and made my way out into a liar's world, already equipped—apparently from birth—to tell exactly how far the version of reality we socially agree to agree upon might be stretched before thinning, let alone before breaking: lied my way through school, from bed to bed, into and out of trouble. Faked my way into and out of things, learned on the job, fell on my feet time and time again. Charm was part of it, yes; I'm not unattractive, though flexible to a fault. Trustworthy, under the right circumstance. Or at least consistent.

You can't simply make *things be the way you say they are, Thomas,* my mother told me, once, after some formative debacle. *Some truths are simply* the *truth.* To which I begged to differ, not that I felt it right to do so to her sweet, slightly sad face.

All truths are negotiable, Mother, I might have replied, had I truly wished to hurt her. *Even when we don't want them to be.*

———

Solstice, the point in the year where the sun appears to stand still, reaching either its highest or lowest point in the sky. Winter is said to start with one, on December 21 or 22, which marks the shortest day of the year—once backdated by Christians all the way to December 13, the feast of virgin martyr St. Lucy, upon the theme of whose truncated holiday John Donne once wrote his famous "Nocturnal" . . . *let me call/This hour her vigil, and her eve, since this/Both the year's, and the day's deep midnight is.*

The Vikings, meanwhile, called the same period Yol, from which our word Yule probably evolves. Not Christmas, not originally, but rather the resonance of a far longer darkness to come, a climax both mythic and terminal. Fimbulwinter, Vargavinter— that's what the sagas call it, the dusk before true night falls. Three successive winters when snow blows from all directions, and summer never comes; innumerable wars follow, the sun's death, the end of worlds. A harsh time, a black time. A time when the wind bites like wolf teeth.

"Who ever thought we'd look back on the idea of Ragnarök with nostalgia one day, eh, Tom?" Dr. Gríma Kjellson asked me, as we mapped rising temperatures together by the infamous

Lakagígar fissure's side. Ice was already softening on Vatna-jökull, after all; the shelves were falling both north and south, meltwater rising. Grant applications aside, we both knew we were really there to find out how long we had, then try—*try*—to figure out a way to extend it.

Just science pitted against itself, from one end of the thermometer to the other. As things get hotter, they start to split, to fall apart; holes form, and things once lost are revealed, crawling up toward the surface. Our plan was simple, hopefully too much so to fail: set one disaster to catch another.

"Who indeed?" I replied, meeting his smile with one of my own, equally thin and pointed.

Jokes being all we had to offer, you see, even in the face of certain extinction. Since we knew ourselves abandoned, though not—as yet—by whom.

———

Throughout my life, I used to have this particular sort of dream, this string of dreams that almost seemed to feed into each other, the way you'll dream about a place over and over, some place you've never really been. Not in real life, waking life. But every time you do, you recognize it, even though it doesn't exist. I mean. . . you have to *assume* it doesn't really exist, yes? Or hope so, perhaps.

The place I'm thinking of—I always just called it Coldhame, like Cold Home but with the words run together in compound metaphor, a sort of homemade Anglo-Saxon kenning: "bone-house" for body, "battle-light" for sword. So "cold" because it couldn't be anything else, snow-crusted and mainly level, but with rocks here and there, grey further off, black closer up. A snowy sky too, clouds swollen and overhanging; grey wavering light, maybe some fog in the distance, or steam. Hard to see where the horizon lay, if there was one. The shadows of cliffs, or mountains. Maybe glaciers. Mountains covered in ice. And "home" just as much, somehow—instinctually, inexplicably. Because it belonged to me, and I to it.

Sometimes I'd come walking into the Coldhame dream from one direction, sometimes from another. Sometimes I'd just find myself there, suddenly realize I'd slipped from lying with my eyes closed and trying to breathe slowly, deeply, relax myself part by part until I could go from trying to sleep to simply—*being* asleep, my eyes open again, seeing this landscape inside my skull, this movie projected on the backside of my shut lids. No sense of time-lag, just here, then there. A done deal.

I knew it *was* cold, but I seldom felt it. Maybe because I was wearing dream clothes, all kitted up for survival hiking. Maybe because it didn't matter. I could see my breath, but only when I thought about it. I kept my eyes on the ground, mainly, because I already knew what everything else looked like, after a while. These black fields could be tricky; unstable, untrustworthy. Sometimes the snow lay over scree and your feet would start to slide, especially if you walked too fast. Sometimes the earth gave way entirely.

Much like the time my father phoned me at boarding school to tell me my mother had died—almost exactly that same sudden lurch and shudder, that gravitational spasm. Predicted, but never quite believed; the impossible, proven. Unless he was lying. But why would he be?

Because he did, that's why, so often I'd gotten used to simply assuming it: a habit, a game, his job. Because he was, at base— much like me—a bloody liar.

(Not that time, though.)

A slip and a fall, short or long, into darkness. Because there was always a hole under the ice of Coldhame, somewhere—I entered each dream well aware it was there, though I never could tell exactly where, no matter how slowly I moved, how wide I kept my eyes as I scanned the stony dirt. How carefully I struggled to tell cracks from tracks.

Never could tell where the edge was, no. Not until I was right down in it.

————

These days, after briefly lying myself into the Army and then lying myself back out again before any potential charges could stick, I am currently deep in study to eventually become what's known as a vulcanologist: "Vulcan" after the god, the Roman name for Hephaestus, whose forge made all the Greek pantheon's best toys and weapons. He was dwarfish and ugly, crippled too, because his mother Hera disliked the sight of him so much she threw him out of Olympus as a baby, determined to start over. Of course, next time 'round she got a complete psychopath—Ares, god of war, a bully who also happened to be a coward—but at least *that* one was handsome. Which I suppose explains why, when Hephaestus married Aphrodite, the goddess of desire, the two of them cheated on him with each other.

I don't have any of those problems, thankfully, amongst my many; an only child, not straight and not married, either. Much preferring to swipe right on my own Greek gods, meet them on neutral ground, then leave while they're in the shower and block their accounts, after. Unless they're useful for more than sex, that is.

Gríma advised me once that switching my store of archetypes to those derived from Norse mythology would probably suit me far better, given how little distinction Scandinavians tend to make between their deities and their monsters. *Loki is a god as well, Tom,* he said, *but also a Jötunn; god of the Jötnar, one might even argue, since he constitutes their main representative amongst the Aesir. Though the Jötnar themselves would disagree, if you asked them.*

I'd looked Loki up, by then; you do that, when you're fucking a guy from Iceland. And he certainly did remind me of myself, at least in archetype—chaotic and impulsive, quick to plaster pleasant fictions over his own mistakes in hopes he could fix things before anyone noticed, gambling the lie wouldn't prove impossible to deliver upon. Attracted to whatever finds him attractive, changing himself to match it and settling into the imitation only to tire of the game long before his partners do, doomed to remain ever unsatisfied. Apt to turn on a dime and burn things down from the bottom up, often by setting himself on fire.

Sorcerer, seer, insult comic of the Viking age; he called his fellow gods out on their shit and got away with it, until he didn't. Husband of monsters, father of monsters—*mother* of monsters, in his female form. An enviable ability, even by today's standards of gender fluidity.

It only makes sense there's a god of lies, even if he comes from a culture I wasn't born into. If there wasn't, I might well have found myself compelled to invent one.

Going by most myths, Loki rarely represents anyone else's interests particularly well, I pointed out, *be they Jötnar, Aesir, or otherwise. Or so I've gathered.*

Which makes him your perfect role model, doesn't it? Gríma replied. *Much better than Vulcan, anyhow.*

Ah. But enough about *me.*

———

The moment I got off the plane in Reykjavik, it had already occurred to me I might just be headed into Coldhame territory. Not that one necessarily expects to stumble across an imaginary landscape outside the confines of one's brain, but—then again.

Perhaps we all spend far more time doing that, on an unconscious level, than we actually think we do.

The team I was joining—Gríma's team—already camped close to Lakagígar, whose hundred and thirty-plus vents bisect the mountain of Laki in the western part of Vatnajökull National Park, not far from Kirkjubæjarklaustur in southern Iceland. It was here, over 1783 to 1785 CE, that a series of violent eruptions caused forty-two billion tons of basalt lava and clouds of sulfur dioxide and hydrofluoric acid to vent from both the fissure itself and from Grímsvötn, the volcano that spawned it. Fluorine gas later joined the party, eight million tons' worth, spewing what came to be called the "Laki haze" across Europe.

The consequences for Iceland were severe. Nearly a quarter of the human population died of starvation, along with eighty percent of all sheep, fifty percent of all cattle and fifty percent of all horses. Dental and skeletal fluorosis ran rampant. In Reverend Jón Steingrímsson's "fire sermon" of 20 July 1783, he described the situation in horrific detail: "This past week, and the two prior to it, more poison fell from the sky than words can describe: ash, volcanic hairs, rain full of sulfur and saltpeter, all of it mixed with sand. The snouts, nostrils, and feet of livestock grazing or walking on the grass turned bright yellow and raw. All water went tepid and light blue in color and gravel slides turned grey. All the earth's plants burned, withered, and turned grey, one after another, as the fire increased and neared the settlements."

Nor did the devastation stop there. As the gas moved through Europe, fog hung heavy, and the sun shone blood colored. Thunderstorms multiplied, spewing hailstones so big they killed livestock; there was widespread panic and flooding as volcanic winter descended. Those who inhaled the gas directly suffocated on their own internal soft tissues, which swelled as sulfur dioxide reacted with the moisture in their lungs, turning into sulfuric acid.

The only "good thing" about the disaster—the detail upon

which Gríma built his theory that the rapid recent shrinkage of the Vatnajökull glacier might signal an incipient fresh eruption from both Lakagígar and Grímsvötn, one potentially violent enough to cause yet another fissure—was that the original event *did* manage to lower global temperature all over the Northern Hemisphere, eventually producing England's own Year Without a Summer.

"Not to mention the general, eh, Malthusian fallout," Gríma added, with typical Icelandic fatalism, the sort you can trace right on back to the Sagas themselves: *there is no need to look, it is just as you think; the leg is off.*

"Does the university know you're planning to re-poison your own country, in order to stave off climate change a few more years?" I asked him. "I mean. . . do they even believe in the concept?"

"Of course, they're not Americans. Besides which, I'm not *planning* on it."

"But you do admit that might be the result." Adding, as he shrugged: "And they're willing to sign off on it?"

"Tom, please, do you really think I'd ask them to? This is why *you*'re here, my friend."

Gríma and I had met under. . . interesting circumstances, which is often how I make most of the contacts I *don't* end up deleting. As smart as he was charming, he was ever-so-slightly taller than myself, long-haired and muscular as one of those giant cats who drew the Norse goddess Freya's war-wagon; like Freya, as well, his passions ran high. Love *and* war. The sort of gorgeous ecoterrorist fully willing to kill some to save most, extend the year's longest night a year or so in itself in order to soothe our planet's fever with a healing fimbul-solstice, no matter the literal fallout. If they tried him for it afterwards, at least he knew he'd look good on television.

I was—*am*—of a far colder turn of mind, which he openly

appreciated, when many don't. Sadly, I've never been immune to that sort of flattery.

Our plan was to drill down and take core samples, send heat-sensing pinhole cameras in on filaments as far as we could without them melting, then use ground-penetrating radar to map out as much of the rest as possible. See if the fissure actually *was* forming cracks that might bloom into new vents; see if any of those pre-vent cracks looked hot(ter than usual). Though with volcanic activity, the "safe" range of heat involved is often some-what hard to reckon.

On the Reykjanes peninsula, the Iceland Deep Drilling Project almost reached five thousand metres in search of geothermal energy, supercritical water transformed by heat and pressure into something beyond either a liquid or a gas, a five-hundred-degree form of steam. We, on the other hand, were only seeking to map out sub-ice volcanic action—tuyas, tinder—without penetrating the sort of mafic dike swarms that mimic oceanic crust fissures, at least until we felt we had to.

"What if the vents don't *want* to erupt, though?" a younger team member ventured. "In time to do us any good, I mean."

Gríma and I traded glances.

"Those charges I got you from my army contacts might come in handy, at that point, I'd suppose," I said, to which he nodded gravely.

"Tom is correct, sadly, Margrét," he explained. "Since if science has taught us anything, it's that we cannot trust nature to do the right thing on command—no more than nature, in her turn, can trust *us* to."

"Gods and monsters," I found myself murmuring, not quite under my breath. And Gríma nodded once more.

"Since all gods *are* monsters," he agreed.

———

On day two we broke ground; by day four we were down far enough to sink the cameras and start mapping. On day seven, Thursday / Thor's Day, we found an interesting deviation, a shadowy area that seemed to involve up to three vents at once, tangled like a knot of plaque-crusted veins hiding beneath an obese man's ventricle. A potential heart attack waiting to happen.

"I could always widen the hole with a few micro-charges," I suggested. "Shear off a bit of shelf and break it down, let it melt in the steam, see what bubbles up. So to speak."

Gríma let his brows tangle and hike, just slightly. "I love when you talk dirty," he murmured, after carefully making sure poor little Margrét was looking elsewhere.

So that was Friday, sorted.

The charges went off a treat, revealing something unexpected—rivulets of extremophile life that glowed and fluttered in water currents hot enough to cook at a touch, glowing "microbes" large enough to see with the naked eye, fungi sprouting from thin seams of rock poised above lava like groping, twisting tubers, blind yellow insects clinging to half-molten shelling. None of us had ever seen anything like it.

"This is odd," Gríma announced, unnecessarily. "Don't you think?"

"Couldn't not, really."

"Will it interfere with the next stage?"

I studied the fissure. "Can't see it doing so," I said, finally. "Still room on one side to lower down another round of charges. Of course, they'll probably collapse the grotto beyond saving." I shot him a sidelong look. "Margrét's not the only one who'd object to doing that so soon. Before getting a good chunk of fauna samples, anyhow."

"Can't blame her. Strikes me as a shameful waste myself." But Gríma's sigh sounded more like he was sad about not really being upset than anything else. "So, I suppose we'd better take the time to do that now. Before anybody has the chance."

"Good," I agreed, and we did.

It was late when we retired, but anticipation kept us sharp.

————

"You know that Loki is supposed to be imprisoned beneath a volcano, the tales say," Gríma murmured, as we shared the comfortably tight fit of his extra large sleeping bag. "For killing Baldr, the light-god, and refusing to mourn him afterwards."

There was more to the story, of course; there always is. When the Norns foretold Baldr's death, his mother Frigga travelled the world begging each creature individually to promise not to let him die. . . except the mistletoe, which she considered far too weak and young to be any sort of threat. But Loki, who disapproved of anyone cheating wyrd except himself, made an arrow out of one of its twigs. When the rest of the Norse gods stood around Baldr in a circle trying to wound him with various weapons and laughing at the way nothing hurt him, Loki slipped this arrow into the hand of the god Hod, who had been blinded in battle. Hod threw it, only to hear a horrified hush as the twig lodged in Baldr's throat, killing him instantly. And though many suspected Loki had disguised himself as the Jötunn woman who would not weep over Baldr's grave, to doom him to the dread hall of his own daughter Hela, no one would ever have known the full depth of his guilt if he hadn't gotten drunk and started telling all the other gods how stupid they were, years afterwards.

"Thor caught Loki in a net of Loki's own devising," Gríma continued, gripping my wrists, playing at pinning me down further than I already was. "And Odin All-Father sentenced Loki to be bound to a rock beneath a mountain with ropes made from the guts of his own son by Sigyn, his Aesir wife. There he would lie forever with a snake dripping venom on his face, writhing so hard the earth around him cracked and threw off hot vapors."

"Under this mountain, or somewhere else?" I asked him, licking along his sweaty neck.

"Under every mountain, maybe. Every volcano. He is a god, still."

"Oh yes. And not forever either, really."

"No, only until Ragnarök. Ragnarök, or until he is found and escapes, whichever comes first."

We rutted against each other until the heat inside matched the cold outside, then fell asleep.

———

In the Army, I considered my particular role as the person who'd actually do things everyone else knew had to be done, even if they weren't willing to risk getting caught. They relied on me to be the bastard, and then they got rid of me—this is the way it works, almost always. The part I seem born to play. Tom as tempter, as agent for ill change. Tom, who says: "That's a terrible idea. . . of course I'm in." Tom, who—when co-conspirators point out that no one who knows the full plan will ever go along with it—tends to suggest: "Then *lie* to them."

You poison everything you touch, son, and that's the sad fact of it, my former commanding officer told me, right before I was decommissioned. *You contaminate; spread like the clap, no matter where your prick's pointed. Bloody hell, you're COVID in a suit.*

To which I replied: *You mean, I make everything I touch more like* me.

Which is true enough, so far as it goes. Though I can't shift my own shape, regrettably, I do know more than a bit about how to convince others they can alter theirs—what cracks they can get through, what holes they can fit, if they only try their best.

Exactly, what they're capable of—what we all are, if we're willing to admit it.

———

That night I had the Coldhame dream at last, as I'd somewhat known I would. The only thing that surprised me was how long it had taken to percolate, given the last week's events.

It came upon me more oddly than usual, though it didn't seem so in the moment: On memory's tale, sliding from lived experience to impossibility within an oneiric eye-blink. It began with an impromptu parking lot rave I'd attended while still in grammar school, all the almost- and adults crushed around me far too drunk to tell a tall, equally drunk thirteen-year-old from someone they should legally worry over making passes at. Cradled in the reeking smell of hash, beer, and gasoline, I danced wildly, flailing into prospective fights and flirting with anyone willing to flirt back. Until, without warning or explanation my mother was suddenly there, and I screamed at her to leave me alone—for once being outright honest about how much I hated. . . well, everything, really, aside from her. Which I know she found hard to distinguish, at the time.

In real life, I turned and ran, trying not to hear her crying behind me, and in the dream the parking lot's cracked asphalt turned to steaming black gravel underneath my feet, then to snow-swathed rock; the sky went steely pale, humid summer flashing to arid, freezing wind. Adult once more, I half-clambered, half-ran down an ever-steepening slope, not slowing even when the chasm finally opened before me.

Didn't feel as though I fell, but I went down hard nonetheless, too fast for climbing, or even rappelling. My gloves and boots juddered over the crevasse walls, sliding farther down and faster, darkness collecting around me till there was nothing but blind black everywhere, feeling my descent in the pit of my stomach. After which it stopped short, the way falls in dreams always do, and I spasmed through the sort of shock people used to fear would kill—or wake—you. This did neither, however, so I sat up, looking around.

It felt real: air almost too heavy to breathe, cold and old and dusty; palms skinned sore, grains of rock shoved in under my nails, deep enough to hurt. It looked like the kind of cavern one might find at this depth, if I'd somehow managed to get past the thermophile grotto and the charges we'd hung just beneath it. Granite walls cracked apart by tectonic force and smoothed out by trickling water too deep to freeze, alive with drips splashing into puddles, lit only by glowing stains of lichen. I searched the ceiling for the crevasse I must have fallen through, couldn't find it, then scanned slowly down through the walls' dark places, squinting for a way out. Columns resolved themselves with effort; cracks and holes, holes and cracks, bulging outwards, retreating inwards. Forming shapes, one of which. . .

. . . moved.

"Christ!" I leaped back, then caught myself; scrabbled over the rock floor and finally got close enough to make the shape out properly. A naked man taller than me, than Gríma, mane of hair equally filthy and its color impossible to see in the faint light. He lay propped up against the wall's base, head slack, though I could see his chest moving. Ribs stood out gaunt beneath lean muscle.

I drew breath. The sound came out sharp, enough so to rouse him; his eyes cracked open.

"*Water,*" he husked.

Or seemed to. Not in English, and it wasn't as if I spoke Icelandic, or. . . whatever this was, something coarser, older. Far older. Yet I understood, immediately—simply *knew*, the same way I knew Coldhame, knew myself. Knew what lie to tell and when, to whom. As if he—we—

(shared a common tongue)

I scooped up some from a nearby pool, burning my own skin to trickle it between his lips, both cracked so deep they seemed almost scarred. As if they'd been sewn together once, then ripped free.

At length he held up a hand. His wrists were chafed bloody.

"When?" he whispered.

I told him the date, watching his eyes widen. They were pale enough to throw back the lichen-light, a blue so pure it almost read as white. "Soon," he breathed, and scrambled to his feet with startling speed. "Come. Follow."

He led me to a crack of shadow between folds of granite, a passage I'd never have seen without his help, and before I knew it, we were hurrying down a lightless hallway, our feet slapping the stone and raising eerie echoes that rang long distances into the dark.

"What happened?" I called after him, struggling to keep up. "How'd you get down here? Who *are* you, anyway?"

"No time!" he shouted back. His voice was clear and high now, almost girlish. "Touch the stone, think on what you feel! And run—run, run, *run!*"

His footsteps accelerated. I stumbled and let myself fall against the wall, palms flat upon the rock, and froze, sucking in a gasp. The stone buzzed against my skin, almost stinging. A low thrum filled my ears, like the deepest, largest bass string in the world tightened to the edge of snapping. Every cell in me knew what that meant, even before my brain processed the signals and gave them their oh-so-bland English name: *Imminent tectonic event.*

"Hell," I breathed, bursting into the fastest sprint I could manage till the slope became a climb, a clamber, spider-swarming through my own blood up the same walls my companion treated like a ladder. Calling up after him, as I did: "Wait, please wait! Wait, *wait* for me, *please—*"

At which point something exploded, filling the entire narrow world with heat too bright to bear.

———

A dream, still a dream. Or was it?

What else could it be?

This is the wyrd which cannot be unspun, a voice said, deep inside me—a man's voice, a woman's voice, my own voice, my own. *I bring it to birth, because I must; my malice, my pride. My revenge. Squatting here centuries-long in this fissure waiting to be found, and now you find me. . . you, who are a splinter of myself, disguised in human flesh; oh, this is loreful, this is correct. This is where my lying-in must begin, here, in the flame's bright heart.*

Birth, I repeated, or thought I did. *Birth of what?*

Gods and monsters, of course, came the answer, a sly smile in every syllable; *you* know *you know it, kinsman. Monsters to kill the gods, then become the gods. The beginning of the end, the beginning IN the end. The beginning.*

Ragnarök.

A hand in mine, reaching down, pulling me bodily up past fungi and insects, stalactites of salt and crystal, old bones and runestones, fluorine blooms, coiling corpse-wax blossoms. That strange face grinning down at me with yellow eyes and blue pointed teeth, hair like red flaming horns, "he" turning into "she" and back again, old to young, young to old, human to inhuman. The wall opening fractal around us, forming a spiral staircase; the hole melting around and beneath us, changing, always changing. That hand in mine sprouted tattoos that spread upwards and downwards along my own limbs in turn, the snaky ridges that united us becoming ever darker and more complex, calcifying, growing scabs, digging in, becoming scars. Snakes and wolves and scales. Its nails grew and bent backwards, spaded, and subdivided, became claws that popped off to embed themselves in the fissure's walls.

The fungi puffed up, released spores that turned into gas, suffocating me, making me hallucinate; I spit phlegm and blood, drooled bits of tissue, hearing again that voice which crooned, sympathetically, seeing my distress—

Oh yes, I forget, after all these years, so long away from humans. You really are such delicate creatures—and credulous too, if I recall. Though probably not you.

The hand in mine getting larger, rougher-skinned, blue-grey and stony. Above me, that face (male once more), a foxy fall of hair sloped down across half of it; he pushed it back to reveal naked bone, fossil-teeth in double rows, one glowing, rheumy, sunken corpse's eye. A shadowy wolf padding in to join us from some parallel tunnel, a giant snake tail stretching to grate behind us, venom dripping down like boil-off to scald me, brand me, blind me. And Loki. . .

(for who else? Who else *could* it be?)

(no one else)

Loki, himself, always getting bigger, brighter, hotter, almost too painful to hold on to, not that he let me pull away. His red hair gathering together into a single spiralling horn, ridged like an ibex's, growing so far back it dug into his own skull, drawing blood. And always moving up faster, faster, faster as we rose straight up through the explosion's heart, thermite charges paused between microseconds, their very sparks flinching apart to let us travel through them—

Up into his embrace, his arms closing 'round me trap-tight, a pair of jaws. His scarred lips on mine, snake teeth biting in, a thousand years' worth of swallowed venom venting headlong down my throat. Telling me somehow, as it did:

The Naglfar sets sail now, rescuer, that ship made from spite and dead men's fingernails. My children rejoin me, hungry for heart's flesh. Soon they will swallow the moon and sun, breathe poison across

Midgard's skin. Then the cold will come, forever, and this world will shrink back to its beginnings: A rot bred from my ancestor's bones, a rim of rime, a crack with darkness above, darkness below, darkness everywhere. And then, at long last, I shall count myself satisfied.

But will you? I wonder.

Will I? Will you, *Thomas? Willing shadow, avatar, long-lost descendant? Bastard offspring?*

Oh, I doubt it.

———

And I wake, buried in snow, the camp borne away by lava; wake alone, Gríma no doubt long gone as well, his ashes up-blown to hang black-burnt on the eruption's tree like Odin's corpse from Yggdrasil's branches, a sacrifice, himself to himself. Wake blind and coughing, stripped back to my innermost core, with all my falsehoods peeled away in the face of a stinging yellow storm, a sulphurous rain, a phosphorescent overhung cloud of unknowing that turns the long night bright.

Hearing my dream-god's voice ever in my ear, deep-purring: *This way, Tom the Liar; stumble away on your jaundiced feet, down to the shore, just where the ice is breaking. Watch how the world-serpent rises at last to meet us from his planet-wrapped coils, breaking surface with a wrench, a hiss—open your raw eyes wide and see how they shine, my dear one, the keratinous scales of our vessel's hull, so twisted and broken, where they've grown to full length after burial!*

Here comes my half-faced daughter, my berserk second son, his wolfskin trailing. My Jötunn and my Aesir wives, who held the bowl so long between them, keeping the serpent's venom from my face. Who never deserted me entirely, no matter how I cursed them for my own mistakes. Let me introduce you: Angrboda, Tom; Tom, Sigyn. Hela. Fenrir, Nari, and Nali. We are family now—you, I, and they—if only for the service you have given me. Brothers in blood yet unshed.

The ship is here, so step on board. Help me wield the wyrd with which I'll scratch my fellow gods' faces away from the firmament, bringing an old world down to birth a new. And if we die in the doing so, what of it? All stories live on, for good or ill; all lies become truths if they only last long enough.

No fiction powerful enough to trick a whole world into hanging poisonous green leaves from a plant once used to make the arrow that killed the god of light and forgiveness up to steal kisses beneath can ever be quite forgotten.

———

And is it only telling me what it thinks I want to hear, this voice? Probably, yes.

Almost certainly.

(I would.)

Text of a note left behind for her parents to find by Ester Oricielo (still missing):

Dear Mom and Dad—

By now you know I went anyways, even though you said I couldn't. To you it's a concert, and I get that. To me it's something else. I need to see them live, and I'm going to. It's my money. I'll text you after. Don't know if I'll be back, depending on how that goes. I love you.

E.

————

Text exchange between freelance journalist May Burnside and Cultural Slide webzine editor Dwina Wandrell, 01/11/2023:

- 3:35 a.m. -

hey, may, you up?
get up

get up RN not kidding

- 3:38 a.m. -

kay
up NOW
you hear about the concert?
what concert

cicada, doom in a room

you hear?
that was today?
*night?

boot up, go to cp24.com

- 3:41 a.m. -

oh *shit*, dee

EXACTLY

———

Second text exchange between DW and MB, 01/11/2023:

- 4:55 p.m. -

don't want to rush you
but?????

yeah yeah, sending what I've got so far. mostly quotes and notes,
not hooked up yet

we need CONTENT on this

well, it's complicated

can't just keep updating w/
same shit

why not?
everyone else is

bitch, fuck YOU

just read, get back to me

- 5:07 p.m. -

you better be kidding

like I said

- 5:09 p.m. -

now just keep reading

———

Notes towards an article about the mass disappearance of audience members from the Cicada Music "Doom In A Room" showcase, 31/10/2023

According to police sources and family members [specifically Jerry and Margo Oricielo], many came because of social media rumors about an appearance by Oil of Angels, Skull Covenant frontperson Sarai Lispector's occult gloomcore side project (possibly named after the song by 1980s experimental band Cocteau Twins, given its reliance on drone and low-volume, looping vocals [check])

- Skull Covenant is/was a fairly well-known Toronto doom metal band, the first band signed by Cicada Music, a company formed in 2015 to develop, promote, and distribute what they called Toronto Dark. Every Doom in a Room thus far has been arranged to introduce a new Cicada band (Skull Covenant being the first, also in 2015).
- This was Cicada's first official Doom in a Room since the end of the COVID-19 pandemic.
- Other acts performing sets that night were fellow Cicada bands Vestment of Worms, Gore Crow, Widdershins Nazarene, and Eeyore, all introduced at previous Doom in a Rooms (2017, 2018, 2019, and 2020, respectively). The lineup was supposed to end with a full set from Skull Covenant, *possibly* followed by Oil of Angels.
- Since the venue where Doom in a Room usually takes place (Killya Darling's) folded ~~during the pandemic~~, [third "during the pandemic," fix it later] the show was moved to Wychwood Barns Art Collective's largest performance venue, the Slam, which has a formal 150-person capacity. Eyewitnesses claim the crowd inside exceeded this by at least a hundred, probably more. [check, is this actually possible?]
- Masks were required inside, and audience members had to show vaccine passports to get through the front door. People turned away were allowed to stand outside and watch the show on flatscreen TVs mounted on the Slam's outer walls, with two

generator-powered speakers providing sound. These speakers apparently blew when Oil of Angels took the stage; outside attendees claim they couldn't hear anything from that point on, except screaming.

This is what happened, and maybe how. What we still don't know, as of now, is why.

"I came with three friends," says Genevieve Joscelin, University of Toronto Kinesiology student and self-described Skull Covenant "superfan." "I left alone. Woke up in Emerg, and nobody can tell me what happened. Mab [Coorie] and Ai [Fang]" —both also U of T, both still missing—"were into the band, like me. . . but Derek [Kuletski, Joscelin's boyfriend of two years], he only came because I asked him to. He didn't like anything harder than dad rock." She starts to cry. "I just want to know what *happened.*"

Philip Takashima admits he's still angry, despite having good reason not to be. "I was *this close* to making it inside," he claims, rubbing one fist like he wants to punch something. "After months of planning, seeing that club door slam in my face, I was ready to f***ing commit murder. So, I stood there stewing for close to an hour, moving back to look at the screen and then up to the door again, just praying they'd open back up. . . and then I saw the screens go out, just as the screaming changed. Because everyone's screaming, right? But I heard the difference, I heard it right away." Now he looks haunted. "And it got worse. Me and a couple of other guys, while we were trying to break down the doors, we realized the noise was *fading.* Getting quieter. There had to be at least a couple hundred people in there, and when we finally got the doors open? Maybe a dozen came out. At most. I could see bodies on the floor and the stage, but nowhere near enough. And the air inside was full of smoke, and it stank like. . .” He shakes his head. “Crap. And blood.”

One witness speaks from his hospital bed only on condition of anonymity, as he admits to being a notorious illegal live streamer. “I use—used to use, crutches and a fake leg cast,” he confesses. “GoPros and a mike built into a crutch handle, batteries taped in my armpit, my phone in a compartment in the cast, and who hasn’t got an earbud in 24/7 these days? Nobody complains about a dude holding up a crutch—well, not usually. But I think that was why I saw the s**t kick off before anybody else did.

“Sarai had just started her big stunt piece where they were trying to play music off an actual rock, like a physical stone, something she said she’d brought back from. . . Israel, I think? Turkey? I don’t know how it was supposed to work, but I heard about fifteen seconds and then my earbud blew, like, just this deafening static screech in my ear. So, I drop one of the crutches and I rip out the earbud, cursing a blue streak, and I think that was when the security guy by the stage realized something was hinky, ’cause he climbs down and starts pushing through the crowd towards me. Well, I’ve already seen my GoPros are dead too, so I do a one-eighty and start fighting my way out of there, and then—” He pauses.

“Everything goes dead silent,” he says at last. “And then it was like somebody turned on the biggest spotlight in the world, behind me. Like, I could *feel* this light, physically shoving me in the back. I went down on my face in the middle of the crowd, and I remember I thought, ‘F**k, am I deaf?!’ before it all went black. And then I woke up in the ambulance, and they tell me I might be stuck with crutches for real, this time. For a long time, anyway.”

He tries to smile.

———

- 5:15 p.m. -

R U kidding me? THIS is what you got out of your interviews?

i know, it's weird

it's thin. doesn't actually *tell* us much

more than anybody else has, so far

get me some cops/relatives on the record, at least

working on it

———

Notes fr. Conversation w/ TO Police Dept Public Relations

- Inside of Slam's covered in blood, *but no bodies.* (Everyone they actually *found* was alive, went to hospital. Any other event like this?)
- They're trying to type the blood, possibly break it down for DNA. Relatives giving samples. Says it'll take "incredible" amount of time. (Not willing to say how long that might be or even take a guess.)
- Not willing to speculate further on nature of incident until more evidence is found or existing investigation is resolved. WAIT, EXISTING INVESTIGATION?????

Notes fr. Conversation w/ TO Det. Davis Whitfield, Sex Crimes

- Holy shit. Whitfield says Sarai Lispector's been subject of investigation as "person of suspicion" for close to a *year.*

- Been reaching out to small select group of fans: email, Instagram DMs, texts. Lot of them just "kids," like Ester Oricielo (we're talking seventeen to nineteen, which isn't really kids per se, IMHO). All invited. Most of them came, lot of them defying parents.
- Ester's relatives sent copies of Sarai's emails to police. "She was grooming our daughter. That's what they call it, right? Teaching her all this. . . stuff. Against God." Weird stuff about how she's the perfect person to come see Oil of Angels. "We're kin," Sarai apparently told her. How so?
- *Who are the Lispectors?*

———

Excerpt of online creative writing from Sarai Lispector, age 19, c. 2015:

After the fall of Constantinople, we opened up all the reliquaries and made a brand-new saint from what we found inside, a saint made from saints. Then we made armor from the bones of our martyrs, those killed in battle under the new saint's banner. And then, last of all, we made a chapel from the rest of the bones to contain our saint, because after the fall, bones were all that we had left.

We rode out wearing eyeless bone masks and wings on our backs, covered all over with our new saint's relics; we didn't need to see; we had faith. Perpetual adoration. And beneath those eyeless masks our pupils turned inwards, spinning like pinwheels, opening like irises. Letting out a black so dark, no exterior light could ever hope to penetrate it.

We hooked an archangel and pulled him down, fighting all the way. We made the hook from half-angel bones and tempted him with Oil of Angels, extract of compounded Nephilim—he smelled it from far off and went into a frenzy, determined to destroy what God had told him should be extirpated. What clever heretics we were, to weaponize God's law and turn it against Him!

Angels cannot destroy each other, after all; the Apocrypha tell us as much. Satan was thrown down, not killed. They are all made from the same substance, the Word Made Flesh, the thoughts of God. So, it only follows, sensibly, that nothing from Heaven can be overcome, except with its own substance.

Pinned to that hook and surrounded by wards, fenced in with all the myriad names of his (and our) progenitor, we pruned him, cut him back, pinfeathers and all. We knew his wings would grow eventually, those quills of his carving their way back into the world, drawing blood from the air with their motion; we did not dream we could hold him forever. But we got what we wanted, even so: to bind our blood to his, to the One Name's, the Maker's.

For Who is like God but you, Micha'el, old ancestor? Whoever could be?

That was our ambition, you see. Our generative sin. To make Nephilim of ourselves. To set ourselves apart from all others, a living affront, stronger than any by sheer virtue of our arrogance, our heresy.

My grandmother told me this, as her grandmother told her. And on, and on, and on. So far back, the words we wanted to use to tell this story had not yet been written.

So far back, we had to make up our *own* words for we wanted to say.

———

- 7:31 p.m. -

i'm confused. R u saying lispector was a child predator?

i'm saying i don't think this was an accident

she chose everybody in that audience; every other person,
anyhow, and she had some kind of a reason for choosing who
she chose

which is?

don't know, but i got hold of the band's agent—he says he'll ask
joey kau to call me back from hospital

the keyboardist? thought he was in a coma

seems not
agent promised he'd call tonight

setting my watch [/sarc]

———

TRANSCRIPT, PHONE INTERVIEW, 1/11/2023 10:42 PM
M. BURNSIDE (MB), J. KAU (JK)

JK: Am I the only one left?

MB: From the band? Uh, yeah. I mean, the other guys from Skull
Covenant are okay, basically—they were backstage already, in
the green room.

JK: Sounds about right. No, I mean. . . from the concert.

MB: We don't really know what happened to anybody else. Yet.

JK: . . . that sounds about right too. From what I saw.

MB: Which was—?

JK: Well.
(PAUSE)
What did you hear?

MB: A lot of different things, really. I was hoping you could clear them up for me.
JK: I can try.

MB: Okay. Um. . . a lot of people are saying Sarai was handing out invites right and left on social media, that's why the place was so overcrowded. True or false?

JK: True.

MB: And these people she picked out, they were—really young, a lot of them? Like. . .

JK: Oh yeah, they were. The *special* fans.

MB: Special like how? I mean. . . some of the parents, they're throwing words around like, um—"grooming?" Like they, like kind of implying—

JK: Oh wait, what? No, no, no. That wasn't Sarai's thing at all. She had me, she had Eya. . . two full-grown adults just hung the fuck *up* on her, both of us. Which was pretty funny, considering how much we couldn't stand each other.

MB: Eya, this is Eya Gall, right? Secondary vocalist for Oil of Angels?

JK: The very same. Classically trained, dontcha know.

(PAUSE)

She's gone too, now—*they*, shit. They're gone. The both of them.

MB: Yeah, still missing. You're saying you guys were all—

JK: Well, *obviously*. But I really don't want to talk about Eya, okay? I mean, I *barely* want to talk about Sarai.
(PAUSE)
I will, though, don't worry. You'll get your story.

MB: . . . all right. Thank you.

JK: Oh, don't thank me yet.
(PAUSE)
Do you know why she called the band Oil of Angels?

MB: Because of the Cocteau Twins—

JK: No. She knew people would assume that, but no.

MB: Okay, then why?

JK: You ever read that stuff she wrote, Sarai, back when she wanted to write books instead of songs? The "family stories?"

MB: I looked it up, yeah, sure. It's on your website.

JK: Uh huh. Well, they told her something else when she was growing up, the Lispectors, something even weirder. She said they told her if you found a way to kill a bunch of Nephilim and boil them down somehow, you could make your very own guardian angel.

MB: . . . what?

JK: Nephilim. People like her, supposedly. And her grandma, and her grandma's grandma...

MB: —because her family fucked an angel right after the fall of Constantinople, or some shit. Right?

JK: Or some shit, yep.

MB: And you *believed* that?

JK: Sarai did. And Eya did, because Sarai did. And me...
(PAUSE)
We started Oil of Angels during COVID, you know that, right? Hooked up with Eya on the Web, formed ourselves a little magical musical polycule. Wrote and recorded the album. And then, when international airflights finally opened up again, we all went to Chorazin together... Khirbat Karazza, whatever it's called now. You know where that is?

MB: Um... it's in Turkey, somewhere? Supposedly where the Antichrist is going to be born. Oh, and M.R. James said Count Magnus went there to... right, I get it. That's why the album's called *Black Pilgrimage.*

JK: Yeah, that was Sarai's idea, like everything else. So—that's where the rock was from.

MB: The rock from the concert.

JK: Black basalt. We played it on an acoustic turntable, an analog amplification system with resonant membranes—a stylus picks up surface variations, transmits the vibrations to a copper horn and bang. This Colombian artist, Leonel Vasquez, invented the original version. The idea was to make a noise nobody'd ever heard before and weave the song around it. . . something cool for our first live performance, y'know. For the *fans*.

MB: Was it a new song too?

JK: No, it's on the album. The last track. You've probably heard it.

MB: . . . maybe.

JK: Doesn't matter. Anyhow—that rock made a sound, like a shofar, or a kangling. Like one of those. . . you know that noise from Inception, that "BWWWAAAOOOAAAAWWW" sound? They do it with a machine, something they invented for the first *Star Trek* movie. Not that, but *like* that. It made me want to throw up. I mean, I felt like I was browning out, like I was gonna swoon. And then I saw Eya start to scream, and float, and melt. Like all of her was coming apart, and just—boiling upwards.

MB: Um. . . Mr. Kau?

JK: Sssh, just listen, okay? Just listen.
(PAUSE)
Sarai met Eya on some Nephilim-gene board on the Dark Web, supposedly, so I guess it makes sense about her. But what I still don't get, what I'll never know, is how she found all those other ones. All those *kids*. Didn't think angels fucked around that much, to be frank. Then again, demons are angels too, right? And there's the Watchers, like in that weird-ass Aronofsky movie. . . think those were the ones who first thought monkeys looked hot, according to Sarai. . . but anyhow. *Anyhow*.
(PAUSE)
I see what's happening to Eya and makes me feel sick, even sicker, so I look away instead and then I see what's happening to everybody else. All those special, *special* fans coming apart the

same way, spewing into the air in a huge fuckin' gore milkshake or something—blood sprayed all over the walls, but the rest, it went up towards the stage, towards Sarai. Splashing onto her like a reverse waterfall made from nothing but guts, skin, bone marrow, *cells*. And first it was pinky-red, and then it was gold, and then it was white, bright white. And Sarai—she was in it, but she wasn't *part* of it, you get me? It was holding her, wrapped up in itself, clutched tight in two long things like tentacles, or maybe like, um. . . claws? Those two things a praying mantis has, the ones they tear bugs apart with. *Tight*. Kind of like it loved her. Kind of like it wanted to eat her.
(LONG PAUSE)

MB: What happened then?

JK: Um. . . it came apart too? Flicked out two bits of itself, *wide*, like a pair of wings. And it went up.

MB: Up?

JK: Through the roof. That big window up there, the one they cover at night—I heard it break. Glass came down everywhere. Got a big piece of it in my back, all down one side; I lost a lot of blood too, the docs told me. They took it out while I was sleeping. So. . . up through there, and into the sky, so high I couldn't see it anymore.

MB: And Sarai?

JK: Oh, she went with it. She was yelling. Telling it to stop. Telling it *let go*, then *don't* let go. Don't, don't, don't. . .
(LONG PAUSE)

MB: Listen, I have to ask—

(JK SIGHS)

—no, but seriously, you *know* I do. Did you. . . expect what happened to. . . happen?

JK: Like, did I think it would *work?* Of course not! I mean, who could possibly. . . well, Sarai, sure. Obviously. But no, I never thought. . . fuck.
(PAUSE)
Fuck.

MB: I'm sorry.

JK: Oh, are you? Me too.
(PAUSE)
I know what happened after that, you know. Saw it. . . dreamed it, I guess, in my coma. Because why not, after all this other shit? Sarai. . . I think she thought she'd be absorbed by it, kind of, like everybody else, but better. Become its brain, or its heart. . . its conscience? The monkey on the angel's shoulder. And instead, it just grabbed her and went straight up, so far, she died, and when it figured out she'd stopped yelling, believed it couldn't make her work again, it just dropped her. Probably find her drifting in from the Islands next week, all freezer burnt and suffocated, with every bone broken from slamming into the water—surface tension gets pretty hard once you're up over a mile, I bet. Yeah, I think that's right. . .
(PAUSE)
'Cause that's the thing about angels—they don't have free will. Not even the ones that want it. And this one, created beyond the boundaries of either side. . . no will, no wisdom, no *experience* beyond that moment it came together, just—power. An angel only beholden to her who made it, except. . .

MD: . . . she's dead.

JK: That's right. She sure as fuck is.
(LONG PAUSE)
And now it's just out there, somewhere—unwelcome in hell,
unwelcome in heaven. Yeah, that's *got* to suck.
(PAUSE)
Here's the thing *I* worry about, though: What comes next, now
she's gone? Now it's rattling around the cosmos with no one to
look after, no one to take orders from. No one to love it. No one to
love. How mad that's gotta make it. And what that might make it
want to do to *us*, if—I mean, *when*...
(LONG PAUSE)

MD: When what?

JK: When it comes *back,* you dumb ass. Because... it will. I
mean—
(VERY LONG PAUSE)
... *I* would.

———

- 11:59 PM -

there's no fucking way we can print this, may,
you get that, right?

don't think that's true, actually
like
not necessarily

WTF dude
I mean, * TF *

look, he said it

I didn't
so all the crazies in quotes
so
its cool

this is anything BUT cool, you weirdo

. . .

okay, it's pretty cool

. . .

. . .

let me think

will do

———

Lyrics for "Egregore," the final release from Oil of Angels' first (and last) album, *Black Pilgrimage*:

> *And in the air*
> *A smear of wings*
> *A narrowing*
> *A harrowing*
>
> *We turn the key*
> *An opening*
> *Unlock the gate*
> *To bitter things*
>
> *Now we begin*
> *This is how it starts*
> *We break the sky*
> *The whole world's heart*

Above
Below
Above
Below
As above
So below
Oh low
Low
Low

We bring above so low
From high to hell
From high to hell
Ah el
Ah el
Ah el

I call your name, A'el

(saraia'el)

YELLOWBACK

Brendan's phone said 31 October, which meant the workday began with Alistair making the same old joke about how you couldn't tell Halloween had been cancelled on account of public health, because everybody was still wearing masks. To which Brendan could have pointed out that Halloween had been cancelled since he was five, but didn't, because it seemed mean. He even made sure to smile, mouth hidden inside his own mask's hot, wet fabric pocket; experience had taught him Zoomers actually *could* tell the difference if they were looking at your eyes, which they always were. Keep eye contact, smile at the jokes, no matter how many times he'd heard them. Alistair was a nice enough old dude, after all, and jobs doing things Brendan liked to do were hard to come by–probably always had been. But most especially now.

"Be back to take over at noon," Alistair reminded him, "and you should maybe think about ordering in, by the way. I hear it's gonna be *extra*-crazy out there tonight."

"Oh yeah? Why?"

"Check your feed, man. There's an anti-vax demo scheduled, bunch of idiots who don't wanna take their booster shots, so there's twice as many cops out as usual and they're all running facial rec checks. That same dumbass shit about undocumented D'Vatzers maybe sheltering in the place down by the Shoreline, in buildings that cleared out after last year's tidal creep." Alistair crammed his hat on, wound a knitted scarf the length of both Brendan's arms twice around his mask and zipped up, sighing. "Anyhoo, I got a test to take for that upgrade in the a.m., so I need at least five hours' sleep before I start studying—you get into trouble, do *not* call me first, okay? Good kid."

He waved going out the door, which sealed shut behind him, audibly. Brendan waited a full minute, then slipped his other phone out from under the desk—the disposable scrambler he'd bought this afternoon, on his way up, from a dude on the train—and texted Nazneen.

cops r pulling masks tonight, stay safe

The dots rolled over, so he knew she was reading it, ready to reply. After a moment, her words appeared, making his stomach flutter:

need to see u

at work rn, come by the back

too hot. u need to meet me. joe chih mins.

Brendan stared down at the words, quick-blooming across the screen, fast as Nazneen's thumbs could go. That woman typed faster with gloves on, outside, than Brendan did at home.

He could tell her it was far too early to take a break, or that he couldn't risk losing his job over getting caught helping her out when there was going to be twice as much pork as usual on the menu. But as ever, he already knew he wasn't going to; her use of periods alone implied urgency.

be there in 15, he texted and got out his keys. And the fact that this decision later proved to be the only reason he didn't get arrested this Halloween was hilarious, particularly in hindsight.

———

Extract from the American Medical Association's Instructional Bulletin #372, June 2022, "Fundamentals of D'Vatz's Syndrome ('Yellowback')", pp. 23–27:

Where does the disease come from?

The first cases of D'Vatz's Syndrome, or Chambers' Sarcoma (after the first two scientists who isolated the disease's DNA markers in infected patients), are thought to have occurred as early as 1985, though little attention was paid to them due to the burgeoning AIDS crisis, and their relatively remote location in clusters across the Iran/Iraq/Afghanistan area of the Middle East (from which the colloquial name "Yellowback" derives, from the Pashto *sha-zhairh*).

The first recorded case in North America occurred in 2010, around the same time American military personnel began returning from the conflict in Afghanistan, though the disease did not gain public notoriety until fashion model Gianna Capparelli contracted it in 2013. Since then, the number of cases has risen exponentially. If current trends hold, a full ten percent of all North American females may expect to contract DS.

What kind of disease is DS?

The syndrome has some features of a fungal infection, but also some features of neoplasmic cancers, scabbing and leprosy. No viral or bacterial agent has yet successfully been isolated; however, the patterns of outbreak development suggest some form of aerial or contact transmission. The disease can be detected prior to symptom onset by a DNA scan of the patient and has so far only been observed in patients with a double-X chromosome.

How do the primary symptoms progress?

A normal period of incubation has not yet been confirmed; the longest known period between DNA marker detection and initial active manifestation was three years and seven months. The disease's progress is measured in four stages:

Rashing. The patient develops a visible, highly itchy rash over the facial area, neck, and upper chest and shoulders. This stage is often accompanied or preceded by reports of ambiguous pain or general discomfort and lasts on average approximately three to four weeks.

Blistering. The patient develops heavy pustules and blisters over the same area, shedding most layers of the epidermis, which grows back with a distinct yellow tinge (the source of the disease's popular name). Yellowish or orangish discolouration of the irises may occur as well. This stage lasts approximately two weeks.

Masking. A heavy yellowish-brown, scab-like tissue begins to grow over the affected area, occurring first as isolated lesions and then spreading to join together. Surgical removal is impractical, as the tissue alteration includes acutely heightened nervous sensitivity and a concentration of anticoagulants, making both anaesthesia and successful healing prohibitively difficult. Ultimately, the "mask" will cover the entire affected area, often closing over eyes and nostrils; the impeded airways frequently induce sleep apnea, which is thought to contribute to the likelihood of coma (see under *Secondary symptoms*, below). Untreated, this stage generally lasts from sixteen to twenty-four weeks, though extended periods of dormancy can be achieved (see *Treatment options*, below). However, heightened stress levels, as well as social and psychological comorbidities, often cause serious health debilitation in general.

Unmasking. The infected tissue becomes so genetically altered that it triggers an immune-antibody response, causing the mask to separate completely from the cranium. The process has an extremely rapid onset, usually concluding in less than ten minutes, and almost always leaves the patient's facial area completely debrided; if the infection has entered the patient's eyes, or the maxillary or facial bone, this tissue too will be shed. Prognosis beyond this stage is extremely poor. The event itself causes extreme levels of pain, often with severe accompanying blood loss; patients who cannot be quickly anaesthetised and treated show a >97% mortality rate from shock and exsanguination. Those who do survive the initial event show a >91% mortality rate within the week, rising to >99.5% within two months, overwhelmingly due to onset of sepsis in the exposed tissue.

Is there a cure?

Not yet.

————

Joe Chih Min's was a food truck, not a restaurant; you had to subscribe to a very restrictive app to find out where it was going to be within the neighbourhood, and since it never stayed anywhere more than two hours, it made for a fairly efficient place to check in with somebody who wasn't supposed to be out on the street, for fear of automatic arrest, no-bail detention, and getting shipped (or shipped *back*) to Quarantine Holding.

Going by her own testimony, Nazneen had been out of QH for upwards of a year now; they'd met in the spring, when she'd taken shelter in Alistair's bookstore from a stalker—she'd eventually had to knee the guy's 'nads just to drive him off. *Six months gone and I haven't infected anybody yet,* had been almost the first thing she'd told him, *even if you* did *have the second X-chromosome to bond to.*

Brendan had just shrugged, trying to play it cool, before replying:

Kinda making an ass of U and. . . you, potentially. In terms of gender presentation, I mean.

And here she'd paused to study him again, a bit more intently, before twitching the scab where her left eyebrow used to be, dismissively.

Don't think so, no, she'd said, after a moment. *Sure, you're soft on the outside, but you also got a full-ass beard, not stubble with attitude. And I'm pretty good at spotting facial plugs.*

I identify as genderqueer, he'd muttered, into that same luxuriant growth. *Just to say.*

Oh, cool. I identify as someone with a fatal disease whose parts happen to match the neurology; nice to meet you.

Prickly, smart and inaccessible—Brendan's kryptonite trifecta, all wrapped up in one double-masked package. He couldn't have stopped himself from falling for her if he'd tried, which he really probably should have. And yet.

Here they were.

Today, Joe's was parked around the corner up on Maitland Terrace, behind the demolition site that used to be a diploma-mill "institute" before going tits-up sometime during second or third lockdown. The truck itself was an unmarked dark blue van, doing its business out of open back doors. Most of the customers wore hard hats and masks, a few obvious homeless wore neither; none were Nazneen. Brendan paid cash for a Korean Street Toast sandwich and ate it standing there, mask down over his beard. He was on the verge of giving up when a light tap on his shoulder made him jump.

"Sorry," Nazneen murmured, but he could hear her smirk in her voice.

"Yeah, sure," he muttered, yanking his mask back up. "This better not take long. If Alistair calls the store and I'm not there, I'm screwed."

"Yeah, I know. Problem is, this can't wait." She handed him yet another fake prescription slip. Between her parka's raised hood and her mask, her eyes glinted—luminous black, still beautifully-shaped, with only a hint of cataract on the left iris. "We need somebody to get this for us, now."

Brendan scowled down at the slip. "Promethazine—that's new. What for?"

"Do you care?" But even her usual snark sounded half-hearted; she sighed, adding, "Look, I'll come by after work, and explain. Just. . ." She waved back towards Yonge Street in the direction of that Rexall's they'd used twice before. "I'll wait here, till Joe's gone. If it's after that—"

"Up the alley, I remember. Keep out of sight."

He saw one eye crinkle, hinting at a hidden half-smile. "That's why I picked up this," she said, slipping a classic horny red-devil mask out of her pocket. "Makes it hard to see, but it should keep the assholes off. For tonight, at least."

"Not the assholes in blue," he reminded her. "Or the King."

"Fuck the fucking King."

More for display than anything else, probably, but he got it— nothing about Toronto's very own D'Vatzer-obsessed serial killer in this week's feeds, but that could change anytime, and they both knew it.

"Just put that on," he told her, turning his back.

Inside the store, he passed the clerk the slip and thumbed his phone unlocked, automatically scanning to see if the keyword search-string he'd bookmarked had been updated yet. *TENTH 'UNMASKING' HOMICIDE KEEPS POLICE GUESSING* was still the most recent link, so he clicked through, re-familiarizing himself with the details: *"Toronto chief of police Alexander Marcus confirms that the body found 09 October under the railway bridge at Queen Street West and Dufferin is yet another victim of the serial murderer variously dubbed 'The King,' 'The Unmasker,' 'The Defacer,' and 'The Façadist' by multiple news-aggregator sites. . . No identity as yet established, due to advanced stage of D'Vatz's Syndrome, lack of ID and apparent homelessness, plus condition of the body. As with*

previous victims, infected facial 'mask' was removed from the scene. . .
An artistic reconstruction of the victim's original face will be available
on the Toronto Police Services website once completed, and the public
is asked to assist in identification. . ."

One of Nazneen's bunch? He hadn't asked her; not like she'd volunteer that sort of information, anyhow. Every person she lost was like losing a part of herself, probably—that was the way people put it, at least online, just talking about the pandemic, and D'Vatz's came with a death sentence already attached. . . but then again, so did life, in general. It was hard enough to process, even with medication.

Brendan had to think most neurotypicals did the same thing he did about it, just in different ways: Distracted themselves from the ticking clock by fixating on what was in front of them, for exactly as long as that would keep them too occupied to remember. The next task, the next episode, the next game, the next whatever sort of high left the best aftertaste. The next fuck, plus the relationship mechanics surrounding it.

Brendan hadn't ever gotten close enough to Nazneen even to hug her, let alone anything else. He barely wanted those sorts of things from most people, including his own parents. Yet somehow, over a remarkably brief time, she'd managed to become the single best distraction he currently had. Which meant a lot— enough so he'd do whatever it took to stay close to her, and she knew it, well enough to exploit it. He didn't resent that, though. Given her situation, it was totally understandable.

The pharmacist rapped on the counter's Plexiglass sneeze- shield, startling him.

"For your wife?" he asked, eyebrows hiking, as he handed Brendan the orange plastic phial. "Or family member?"

"Uh. . . family."

"Well, congratulations. Good news in bad times, hey?"

The hell?

"Uh yeah, thanks," Brendan answered, perplexed, already

trying to type "promethazine" into the search engine one-handed as he stepped back outside. Which explained why he was halfway up the block before he looked up to see police cruisers parked around the bookstore. *His* bookstore. With an ambulance in their midst, waiting. The red and blue lights circled, flashing, calm and silent.

Fuck.

Without letting himself think about it, he crossed the street, not hurrying, not looking back. He didn't allow himself to run till he was back on Maitland, well out of any possible sightline.

Joe's van had left and Nazneen was indeed up the alley, sitting on the curb, alone. She leapt to her feet as he accelerated; it was almost funny to see how quick the alarm in her eyes flashed to relief, then back to alarm again, with a side-order of dismay.

"Did you get the—okay, good—no, fuck, never mind. Cops, yeah? They see you?"

He shook his head, panting too hard to speak. She swore again and grabbed his arm. "Goddammit. Come on."

———

From Toronto Police Services Case File #3A24-2034, Homicide Evidence Item #17: Transcript of Voicemail Left for Det. Inez Machado, 2034/10/13 0244

[NOTE: Distortion-filter used on call rendered some words uncertain; marked where relevant.]

Detective. I'm the one who carved those signs inside the masks, after I took them off. I know you haven't released that detail to the press. Haven't found the right [combination?] yet, though. Obviously.

I'm calling because I need you to do something. Understand,

I'm not blaming you, or your colleagues—you're just doing what you have to. So am I. This isn't personal. But truth's supposed to matter. And I am *not* an unmasker, a defacer – definitely not the [King?]. [Not any more than (any/ all?) of us are (going to be)?]. If I have to be anything, call me. . . a seeker.

It's not about hating these people, either. I mean, I do hate them. But that's [incidental?]. I just need what [they're becoming?]. To go where they're pointing the way. See what they're teaching us to see.

It's going to happen to all of us, sooner or later. I'm only expediting the inevitable. We'll laugh together, afterwards. And I don't think I'm going to need too many more tries to [make it work?].

Keep your family safe, Inez. Until after.

[CALL ENDS]

————

Down to the Shoreline, past the Creep's most recent markers, Nazneen and Brendan, hammering hard through greasy, oily water, half Lake Ontario, half. . . other stuff, polluted at best, irradiated at worst. The slushy top layer sprayed higher than the rest, slopping almost to Brendan's crotch, and he couldn't help but wish he'd worn a cup.

Harbourfront had been gone for a while now, tsunami blowback from that crap in New York. Nazneen and the girls she nested with fought a constant losing battle to stay just far enough out that it wouldn't be worth even the cops' time to come after them, the places where yellow and orange zones crossed over, just skirting the red. And when things got too dangerous, they'd even boat out there, using a raft cobbled together from extra air mattresses. . . but they hadn't done that for a while, according to what Nazneen had told him.

They can't be trusted, Brendan, his mother had warned him, not all that long ago—and she got all her news straight from the CBC, old-school, though in podcast form rather than radio broadcast. The "nicest" nice person he knew. But even she was convinced that since nobody knew exactly where D'Vatz's came from, let alone how it operated, this could only mean people suffering from it were. . . tainted, somehow, on almost a moral level. Which definitely jibed with the way everybody else seemed to treat them.

Some scientists thought it was pheromonal, though that was just a theory—nothing had ever been proven, quite probably (as far as Brendan could figure, using the Darknet's nameless equivalents of NuGoogle) because no one had done any sort of experimentation aimed at confirming or denying it. They preferred to just scoop Yellowbrows up and tuck them away in QH, so no one would have to deal with them who hadn't already volunteered for the privilege.

I was training for Forensics, back when I was a med student, Naz had told him, *so I never worked with patients—all I ever saw were individual tissue samples. But I was there for nearly a year before I got diagnosed, and I'll tell you this: all those press releases about 'promising avenues of investigation'? Total bullshit. Our lab, we never found a single bacterium or virus we didn't recognize, not even a goddam prion or a toxic agent, and we'd've damn sure heard if somebody else did. I'd bet good money we're not dangerous, except maybe to ourselves.*

How so?

She'd shrugged. *Not like I can go by anything but anecdata, but given what I saw in QH, let alone in the squats? Unmasking seems to go a lot faster, around other D'Vatzers.*

But if it's dangerous *to* keep *you guys in proximity, then why—?*

But the equation came together so fast he didn't even have to complete his own sentence, let alone watch Nazneen shoot him one of her patented *how dumb is you, dog?* brow twitches.

You think QH is designed to trigger as many unmaskings as possible, as fast as possible, he finished, at last.

Cheaper than a bullet, she agreed. *And if we're all in the same place, it's easier to just cremate us real fast and shove us in a hole, without having to deal with too much oversight.* She paused, still watching him. *Now, ask me the real question.*

What real question?

'*But Naz, if being around other Yellowbrows kills you faster, why the hell would you break out of QH just to shack up with a bunch of other scab-faces?*'

Brendan hoped that wasn't supposed to be *his* voice she was mimicking. But: *I don't have to,* was all he said. *I know why; you already told me, practically that first night. Because they need you.*

(*And you need them,* he could have added, easily. *Closest you'll ever get to being any kind of doctor, now. Even if it* does *mean you have to deal with real people.*)

Again, though, that seemed mean.

"Sure I'm not gonna scare off you guys's, um. . ." he began, hesitantly, unsure how best to proceed, without being insulting. To which Nazneen snapped back, cutting him off in mid-word-grope—

". . . customers? Clientele? Those sad Yellowflesh hate-fuck fetishists we make our bribe money off of, for if and when the cops come calling?" She didn't even bother slowing down. "We try not to shit where we eat, in general. And the ones desperate enough to come to us aren't gonna be scared off by one stranger they don't recognize. So, no."

"Okay, then. That's good."

"It is, isn't it? Especially for you."

One good thing about D'Vatz's, she'd told him, back when he was still too shy with her to follow up on her previous hints that foraging and sex work provided her personal enclave's economic baseline. *Nobody with full Yellowback seems able to get knocked up, at least not for long—automatic miscarriage, usually around the*

*same time most chicks would be taking a test. It's messy, but then. . .
so's everything else, right?*

"True enough," he muttered, following along behind.

Naz's nest was in one of the buildings still poking above the waterline on the edge of what was left of the Leslie Street spit, once the top floor of an abandoned auto repair shop. After drying off best they could with a knot of ragged towels left by the door, he and Nazneen moved further in, finding the rest of the nesters gathered in what had been the shop's office lunchroom. It surprised Brendan how well the women had adapted. The windows were all sheathed in cardboard to conceal the light, which came from arrays of heavy candles backed up by the occasional LED flashlight, back-reflected by taped up sheets of aluminium foil. Furniture was limited to ratty cushions, worn mattresses, a few folding chairs probably donated from some church's basement, but everything had been organized as neatly as possible, under the circumstances.

Through a serving window that opened into the kitchen, he could see a couple of women sorting through piles of unlabelled cans and plastic bags full of expired bread products, plus a basket crammed with dumpster-dive fruit and veg; for not even vaguely the first time, he hoped none of them were gluten intolerant. Large jugs of water, probably boiled over that open fire in the long-dry sink, took up half the kitchen counter. And sure, the air tasted funky from unwashed bodies in proximity plus mildew and rust, but it wasn't like Brendan hadn't smelled worse locker rooms. This was. . . pretty homey, for homeless people.

"Hey, Naz," wheezed one of the kitchen sorters, a heavyset woman in almost full mask, with dark-skinned hands. "Good food run haul, for once; want me to set anything aside for—?"

Then she stiffened, somehow seeming to sense Brendan, even lurking behind Nazneen's shoulder.

"Fuck's *he* doing here?!" she demanded.

All eyes—those still visible, at least—turned to Brendan,

who swallowed. He'd met some of these women before (one at a time, on the street, as Nazneen handed the drugs he'd helped her scam off to them), but seeing all of them together in one place at once was disquieting, even for him. All had their outside masks off but were *physically* masked up to some extent, most worse by far than Nazneen, to the point where telling age or ethnicity was difficult; nobody's face completely gone, though (*yet,* he tried not to think).

Whatever trust he might've earned by complicity in Nazneen's crimes, it clearly wasn't enough to outweigh years of hard-learned paranoia. Even translated through those half-visible, rotten banana-scabbed features, their expressions hit him like a slap: wariness, suspicion, resentment. Even contempt. Like *he* was the dangerous one. The disgusting one.

It wasn't as unfamiliar a feeling for him as they might have thought, but it still hurt, just a little.

"He's *here* 'cause the fucking cops found him, Retta," said Nazneen, flatly. "So, we're taking him in, till he can make other arrangements—he's earned that, at least. Don't you think?" She strode to the kitchen window and set a green plastic bottle on the shelf. "That's to stock us up on our vitamins again, and Retta —" another plastic orange phial, which she tossed straight to the other woman "—here's the refill on your duloxetine." She turned. "Annie, meanwhile... you here? Or...?"

"I'm here," a high, unsteady voice answered, from somewhere in the back. "Did you get it? Please tell me you got it."

"*Brendan* got it," Nazneen pointed out, "so thank him."

"Oh God, thank God. Thank you. Both." A slight figure pushed its way through the group, shrouded in a heavy woollen blanket. The girl's face was near-completely masked over, but one bright blue eye stared out of the lumpy yellow-brown mass her head had become; the third of her mouth still visible smiled, in pitiful relief. "I had to sit with my head in a bucket for two hours today. Please, God, let this work."

As she reached for the phial, the blanket slipped, revealing achingly scrawny limbs, skin piss-coloured beneath a ragged green summer dress. So thin, all over, except for her face. And—

Brendan boggled. Was that one of those medical-curiosity gigantoid-size tumours people watched YouTube videos about removing? Everything under where her breasts should be bulged out, almost nauseatingly.

Then he remembered: *promethazine*. The doctor had prescribed that to his sister, two years ago.

For her morning sickness.

"Holy *shit*," he yelped. "You're pregnant!"

Annie jerked back a step, automatically, though her single eye flashed: *No, eh?* While the rest of the room silenced itself in a rush of indrawn breath. But Nazneen simply sighed.

"Okay," she said, at last. "Well, now you've *got* to stay."

Brendan stared at her. She wasn't smiling—though she rarely did, especially when she was joking. None of the others were smiling either. His stomach sank.

"Or. . . what, exactly?" He asked, cautiously. "You'll *kill* me?"

Now it was her turn to stare.

"*No*," she snapped back. "Fuck's wrong with you, man? We just need this shit kept on the down-low, at least until Annie stabilizes. So, you hide out here a day or two at the most, and by the time we find you somewhere else to go, it won't even matter anymore. . ."

("Hopefully," Brendan heard Retta mumble, almost into her collar, from the kitchen.)

"Sorry," Brendan said to Annie. "That was rude. I just. . . didn't think that could happen."

Annie nodded, shrugging. "Yeah, me either—so it must've happened before I got ill, I guess. Right, Naz?"

"Only way," Nazneen said. "Unless you agree with that whole 'no one knows where it comes from, must be fuckin' *magic*' proposition the streams're so fond of."

"Ou don *ow*, dough," another woman put in, from the back, her voice so mushy she needed subtitles. "Uh ean, *un* uh us do. Weh *CAHnt*."

Nazneen cocked her head, shooting this dissenter a glare she very likely couldn't even see, given how overgrown she was—all Brendan could recognise was a single upper row of teeth, half-blocked by a lip swollen three times normal size and flared inside out. She had one hand slapped up over her tracheotomy tube, blocking it to produce what little sound she was still capable of; the girl next to her hugged her around the shoulders, shushing her, gently disengaging her fingers one by one.

That last part seemed to deflate Nazneen, who sighed. "Claire, just rest, okay?" she told her. "It's a disease, but who cares, seriously? Nobody that matters."

Again, Annie nodded.

"I'm due this week," she explained to Brendan. "That doesn't change. But Naz's a doctor—almost—and Heather there has her doula's licence, so. . . yeah. Whatever happens, happens. And soon."

This time, Nazneen nodded too, her mouth set at a slightly grimmer angle.

"*Very* soon," she agreed.

———

Alistair, who kept track of all sorts of heinous shit, had once shown Brendan what he thought was evidence that there was a ring of weirdos making "completion" films out there, Yellowback porno videos that ended with somebody reaching in from above to rip the girl's mask off just as the guy fucking her climaxed. Brendan told him it sounded like an urban myth to him, not quite snuff and not quite not, with some bullshit *True Detective*-style mythology mixed in; Alistair couldn't completely argue the point, not when with every fresh post to the thread, rumours of what could be glimpsed underneath the mask got weirder and weirder.

"This one guy says he saw one where the girl didn't even have any face at all under there," he said, scanning further. "Just meat and bones and, like, fat. . ."

". . . and eyes, right?"

"Nah, not according to him. No eyes, at all."

"That just means it came off too soon, that it wasn't dried out and *ready* to separate, so whoever it was pulled it off early, like a scab. So, the eyes got stuck inside."

"That's fucking sick, man."

"No shit, Alistair. Can we maybe talk about something else, for a while?"

All this stuff he'd tried so hard to block out, coming back to him now in fitful dribs and drabs, between half-grasped snatches of light, painful sleep. *I heard some of them just disappear when their masks fall off, like poof, dissolve into ash, or shit; they go somewhere else, someplace men can't go. . . My cousin used to message me on a Cryptocom app from QH; near the end she told me she could barely sleep anymore for nightmares, and her last post said she'd started seeing shit when she was awake, that she couldn't tell which was which anymore—colours were reversing on her, and there were mountains. She said the sun was black, and it ran backwards. . . There was a woman in my neighbourhood who vanished, but I think she just crawled away somewhere to die, like a cat. I'm betting she's probably under somebody's porch somewhere, and come spring someone's gonna get a really shitty surprise—seems a hell of a lot more likely.*

He could have written it all off as typical web bullshit if not for comments like that one: brutal flashes of misery, convincing by sheer weight of awfulness. Plus, the last post Brendan had read, before slamming Alistair's computer shut so hard it startled them both, comprising only two words above an embedded image of a brown-and-yellow, red-streaked *thing*, crumpled inside a plastic neonatal crib: *My daughter.*

God, he hoped it had already been dead.

In his half-doze, he couldn't stop imagining how it must have sounded, in that delivery room. When had the moans of pain turned to screams? His brain slapped poor Annie's clogged-up face on the unknown mother, and he flailed in his blankets like a rat in a trap: *Christ, no, out, let me OUT*—

Then he jerked upright, finding the screams were real—two voices, equally panicked. And one of them was male.

Naz and Retta were halfway down the main corridor when he burst out to join them, flinging his whole bulk at the door of what the nest called their 'service' room—the place they used for the johns too eager, poor, or ashamed to provide their own. On the mattress, Claire struggled against her customer with a frenzy nobody could mistake for even the freakiest stripe of fucking; both bodies were red-splattered, air flooded with hot copper stink.

Brendan and Nazneen dove onto the guy, got their arms under his and yanked him off, still yelling. As Brendan hung on, grimly, his grip blood-slippery, they wrestled the john to the head of the main stairway and threw him down—he landed at the bottom, hard, with a combination splash/shriek. Brendan felt Nazneen brace herself, probably anticipating a roaring return charge, once the guy regained his balance. But. . .

. . . then the man looked up, and it hit them both, clear as a slap. This guy wasn't angry. He'd never *been* angry.

He was *terrified.*

Oh, shit.

Leaving the john to flail his butt-naked way back across the channel between their building and the next, Nazneen and Brendan turned, as one.

The screams had already stopped, and it was easy to see why: Claire lay limp, shrunken-looking skull seemingly fused with the mattress, indistinguishable from the stain spreading around it— blotched crimson, an oozing starburst. Her tube was out, hole spraying mucus. Between long, bubbling breaths, her nude teeth shone scarlet.

Nearby, a yellow-brown, bowl-shaped oval thing lay slightly folded in on itself, cracked edges trailing shreds of raw red tissue. From the back, only one tiny slit remained where a mouth might once have been.

Nazneen was shaking. "Fuck," was all she said. "*Fuck.*"

"Naz," Brendan started to say, the very first time he'd ever dared use the diminutive, but she just snarled at him, shaking him off; shining trails silvered her puffy, spotted cheeks, their discoloured sections already threatening to merge. Repeating, as she did: "Ugh, ahhhh. . . fucking, fucking *fuck*!"

Like a building collapsing, she crumpled, bending at waist and then knees until she was face down on the floor, fists smacking the dirty linoleum with dull, steady thuds. Brendan recoiled, unsure what to do until Retta stepped up from nowhere behind him, her hand on his shoulder.

"Take her away," she wheezed. "It's done—we'll deal with it. Try and keep her calm, get her to sleep."

"But—"

"Just *do* it, boy. We're gonna need her later, with Annie."

Which was true, and she wouldn't be much help if she stayed locked in the loop of her current grief, her fear, her anger. He bent, got his arms around her, and lifted; it shocked him how light she was, as if her anguish had hollowed her out. For lack of any other idea, he carried her back to his cubby and sat down with her among his blankets, holding her to him. Helplessly, he fought back his body's reaction to the hot, damp feel of her sobbing breaths on his neck.

Eventually her grip eased, her breathing quieted. He thought she'd fallen asleep when her hand fisted itself in his beard and hauled his head around to hers.

The kiss hit him like a body slam; half her mouth was hard and crusted, the rest soft and wet and warm; the smell of her hair flooded his nostrils, rank and sweet at once. Her other hand descended to cup him, and he groaned with the pressure. His hands broke all control, seizing, pulling, sliding between layers, finding and gripping sweaty skin. Naz only yanked harder on his beard and moaned between his lips.

Conscience forced words out of him, between gasps. "Naz, this isn't. . . I mean, you don't. . ."

"Shut *up*," she snarled. And pushed him down on his back.

He took her at her word and tried to make as little noise as possible, though he couldn't suppress a choked groan at the end, seconds before her own hand and bucking hips brought her to a teeth-gritted, silently shuddering conclusion. She slumped, hair hanging down, chest heaving in the still, damp air. Then, without warning, she half-slid, half-shoved herself off him and rolled herself into the blankets, facing away from him.

"Don't look at me," she rasped.

But I don't want to look at anything else, he just barely managed not to say. *I'd look at you forever if you'd let me.*

Even he could tell how that would sound, though.

He remembered the night they'd met, Naz crouching behind the counter as he scanned the outside to make sure she could get away clean, muttering to herself as she shrugged her coat back on and wrapped her scarf up extra-high, extra-tight: *This whole thing, it's a wet dream for garden-variety misogynists, let alone the incels, the crip-fuckers. . . I mean, none of them really think we're human anyways, so this is just the icing on the cake. But 'not all men', right? And you, you actually seem okay, but I bet you wouldn't've looked my way before I started growing patches, got this thing. Now I'm a freak, though, I'm* fascinating.

I just want to help, he'd told her. And: *Oh*, she'd replied, after a long, slow blink, eyelids already too stiff to narrow any more. *So, you're* another *sort of fetishist.*

At last, back in the now, he made the decision to cup one spread hand over her shoulder blades and let it rest there, lightly;

she didn't respond, but didn't move away, either. What light remained slowly drained from the room, leaving them in darkness.

"I shouldn't have done that," she said, at last.

"I... didn't mind."

"Oh, no shit." Her voice turned acid. He was weirdly happy to hear it. "Guess that takes care of next Valentine's—wait, no; odds are, I'll be *long* dead by then. Want me to will you my mask, after?"

That hurt, but not enough.

"I *said* I'd help you," he told her. "Get you what you needed. So, if you needed *that*, and now you need... I don't know, to be alone, then I get that too—"

Then he stopped, as cold shot through him. "Fuck," he breathed.

She let out a hiss. "Okay, you're right, I'm sorry. I'm being a bitch."

"No, no, no, it's not that. Don't move."

"Why?"

"Um..."

He couldn't take his eye from the window, that blocky silhouette atop the next building over. "Remember that guy you kicked in the nuts, outside my store? The one you thought was an undercover cop?"

"Our meet-cute? Sure. Why?"

"'Cause . . ." Brendan swallowed. "He's outside, over there. On the other roof."

————

The guy was gone by the time Brendan got over there, but Naz hadn't needed confirmation. When he got back, she was already in the lunchroom, telling everyone they were blown; the burst of protests in response held disappointment, anger and fright, but no real surprise. Soon enough, they were breaking down all the moveable goods and starting to inflate the raft.

We'll move out around 4:00 a.m., Naz told him, amidst the rush; *Annie first, then everything else. Deadest time on the street, let alone the Lake.*

It'd sounded good to him, at least till he woke to the sound of furious retching: Naz, doubled over, in the corner of the room. She tried to push him away, feebly, when he went to help, but gave up and fell back against him as the spasms eased, more annoyed and bewildered than afraid. Then they both realized they could hear other people puking.

Brendan helped Naz down the hall, stopping to let her check every possible hidey-hole; he could feel her dismay and confusion mount as the count of the stricken rose. By the time they'd gone through everyone, nearly a third of the group lay exhausted; the whole floor stank of bile and acid.

Nobody going nowhere, Retta managed, finally. *Not now.*

Not everybody's *sick*, Nazneen muttered.

We ain't leaving anybody behind, Naz. Fine. A day, to rest.

A blink, then. And by the time he looked up again, almost a week had passed. Too late, not that they knew it.

Not yet, anyhow.

———

Around noon, in the middle of the latest police newscast Brendan's search-strings had flagged for him—nothing about the King or their nest, thankfully, just some noise about a maybe-inside-job equipment theft from an unidentified downtown precinct—Annie's water broke. By the time night fell she was howling uncontrollably, deep in the throes of full labour.

They made a heap from all the bedding for her to burrow inside, stripped from the waist down; Naz was checking her vitals and making her take sips of water as Heather tried to talk her through it, Retta intermittently levering Annie up so she could squat and bear down, panting. Brendan, meanwhile—who'd only ever seen birth as footage on YouTube—was stuck in the corner with one of the window coverings partially peeled open, obsessively checking to see that guy hadn't reappeared, just trying to keep out of it.

Is she going to die? he'd almost asked Naz, near the start, but stopped himself by cycling through a *Terminator* menu of her potential replies: *Oh, definitely, just like everybody else. . . but wait, you meant WHEN, right?; why no, child, no one ever* really *dies; fuck you, asshole.*

So now he just stood there scanning the black water outside, the next building's slumped outline, watermarked by wave-reflected moonlight.

Didn't help that everybody else was still sick too, but then again, you wouldn't expect it to. He could hear them like a weird under-chorus, supporting Annie's pain through rough mimicry —groaning, puking, groaning again. The promethazine had helped while it held out, but it was long gone now, not that there would've ever been enough to go around in the first place. Brendan was still amazed it had worked as well as it did. . .

'Cause it's not like they could all *be pregnant, now. Right? That, that's just—*

(impossible)

Another thing he couldn't possibly say to Naz, another subject he was too scared to broach. Especially since in *her* case, because of his participation, it was a genuine possibility.

Don't worry about it, that's what she'd tell him, if he did. Automatic miscarriage, remember? But—when was that supposed to happen, exactly? Sooner, rather than later; he was almost sure. So why it was still going on nearly six days later, that would be the question. . .

"*Jesus!*" Annie screamed, behind him. "Jesus, *please, Jesus!*" Like she thought He would appear next to her, stroke her sweat-soaked head, if she only did it loud enough. Light up the whole nest with His Sacred Heart's burning.

And: "Ugh," he heard Naz answer, nauseated, turning aside to grab the communal bowl and retch into it; saw Retta reach for her hand and fist it, tight.

"Take it easy, baby," she wheezed, possibly addressing them both. "S'alright, okay? You're doin' fine. Right, H?"

Heather, reassuring, almost as mushily: "Uh huh, absolutely. Just squeeze and release, Annie, squeeze, release, squeeze—"

Downstairs, the front door suddenly broke open with a violent crack, as if kicked; Brendan heard the splash of water spraying everywhere, boot-broken. Then he was up and moving, somehow, passing Naz; she bounced to her feet as well, bowl flipping, all but racing him to the top of the stairs while Annie howled yet again, wordless with pain. They were almost at the top when he heard a noise he didn't recognize, some sort of buzzing hum ratcheting up within seconds to an electronic shriek, a giant lightbulb turning on—Naz yanked him back by his hair, pulling him down to where she crouched.

"Cover your *eyes!*" he thought she yelled, under the mounting whine, so he did, but not quite fast enough to block out all of that giant burst of bright white light exploding up the stairs with a deafening detonation, turning everything around them negative.

Flash-bang, sonic grenade? Combo of both?

Police gear for sure, the sort designed for crowds, but even with the split-second slice of a look Brendan'd been able to grab before whatever it was went off, he'd seen only one guy—*that* guy, had to be. No backup. What kind of cop tried to bust a nest all by himself, without calling for surrender first?

(*Well, the kind who steals his equipment from his own station. Obviously.*)

Retta yelled from behind him, unintelligible through his

ringing ears. Naz screamed back, more terror on the visible half of her face than he'd ever seen.

"Get her *out!*" he half-heard, half-read in her mouth—her voice sounded like they were underwater. "Get Annie out of here, *now!* It's *him*, goddammit! It's *been* him, all along!"

Him?

"That cop?" Brendan blurted stupidly, blinking hard to get the spots out of his vision. "You *know* the guy, or—?"

"*No*, fuck it!" Naz pulled his head close with one hand, still yelling. "It's *him!* The fucking. . . !" Then the buzzing whine whirled up again, and they hunched down together against another *boom* of blinding light.

But Brendan didn't need to hear the end. He'd understood, at last. His guts wrenched at his spine.

The King.

Boots mounted the stairs, stomping hard—Brendan shied away, taking Naz with him, as some sort of throat-set projection mic squealed awake. The scrambled vocal it emitted was like articulate feedback jacked to 11.5, each vowel firework-popped, louder than a bomb.

"HARRRRRBINGERS!" it roared, translating whisper to scream as the man rose out of the stairwell, following inexorably behind Brendan and Naz as they tore down the hall towards Annie's room. "PARRRRRIAHS! CARRRRRCOSITES! FROM THE CITIES YE SHALL BE CAST OUT, AND IN THE WASTELANDS YE SHALL FORRRRRAGE IN VAIN!"

Annie greeted them with another shriek, a fresh explosion of piss and blood jetting to soak the sheets even as Heather tried to stuff a wad of it up inside her and Retta pulled hard, dragging her onto her feet as she chanted, "*Go, go, go, GO—!*"

But in the next instant they were both caught in mid-jackknife themselves, spasming with new sickness, then bam, down on the blankets with Annie, flailing helplessly. Brendan gaped, aghast, watching their own crotches darken, like the flasher's tone had thrown them both into spontaneous auto-abortion.

"We're so fucking *fucked*," Naz gasped in Brendan's ear, then broke off, grunting in agony; he didn't have to see where she was clutching to understand the same thing must be happening to her, with equal immediacy. He eased her down and turned as a black figure appeared in the door, head helmeted and faceless, inhuman and angular in its body armour; above his shoulder, to his right, hovered a high-buzzing miniature defence drone, the thing that had hit them with the flash-bangs. One hand brought something pistol-shaped down, its aim centering—on Naz.

Brendan flung himself at the King in pure reflex: he got one hand on the weapon and forced it up, his sheer weight enough to send them both staggering back into the hall. Then the other man's training kicked in and he flipped Brendan over his knee, slamming him to the ground so hard Brendan saw stars again, all the breath and strength crushed instantly out of him. The King held his weapon on Brendan for a second before dismissively turning away. He strode into the room and stopped, helmet angled down at the helpless women; the drone followed behind, its wasplike buzz threading through the cries of pain and fear like a bone saw, pitiless and terrifying.

He lifted his free hand to his helmet and adjusted something. The voice that came from the drone was a quarter the volume it had been, but still loud enough to scrape the skin. "NAZNEEN HIKAR, HEATHER BRRRRRAIDIE. I WANT THE CHILD."

"*Annie's* child?" Naz spat. "Screw *you*, stormtrooper."

"UNIMPORRRRRTANT. THE *CHILD*."

The pistol-thing gestured sharply at Annie, still writhing and moaning. Retta must have thought that would give her enough chance; she lunged up and charged at him, but her pain and his reflexes were too much. The weapon whipped back. A blue-white line of light struck her with a *crack* like a thunderclap: all her limbs kicked out at once, like a dead frog jolted with current in some high school bio lab, and then she fell. Before she'd even hit the ground, the weapon was pointed at Naz again. "GIVE ME THE CHILD!" the man roared.

"It's not *out* yet, you idiot!"

"THEN *GET. IT. OUT.*"

Even that mightn't have broken through Naz's shock. But the next sound did: Annie's agonized moans, already diminishing, suddenly died in a hissing strangle that ended in a flat *shlupp*, like a vacuum container sealing shut.

Heather wailed and scrambled forward. "Oh, fuck, Naz," she sobbed, "her mask! She's blocked up! She can't breathe! Fuck, Naz, *help me*!"

She caught Annie's hands and held them down as the girl bucked and kicked, before Naz flung herself on top of her, digging in her back pocket for her Swiss Army knife.

"Tracheotomy, fuck!" she gasped. "Somebody get me a straw —Brendan, Heather, hold her down, *shit*—"

"NO!" The King stepped forward; for the first time his voice betrayed something like fear. "FIRRRRRRST CHILD OF THE NEW RRRRRACE! THE ONE BORRRRRN TO BRRRRREAK THE WORRRRRLD OPEN! SAVE IT, NO MATTER HOW—"

"Asshole, you want me to cut her *open*?"

The man didn't even answer, just lunged forward, jerking his sidepiece up—extendable truncheon with a Kevlar edge, tooled sharp: *I will, if you won't,* in other words.

As he did, though, Brendan leapt up to grab the drone out of the air and smash it against the wall, feedback squeal audibly ripping through the man's helmet; he staggered, which gave Brendan enough time to hurl himself onto the man again, from behind.

They went down together, truncheon skittering away across the floor. Brendan pounded the man's head against the floor until, on the fifth or sixth blow, something snapped. The whole thing came off like an ant's head, tumbled across the room, rolled up against Naz's feet; she kicked it away, sliding her knife blade into Annie's throat. A horrid, high whistling pierced the air.

"*No, goddammit!*" bellowed the King, shoving up against Brendan's weight. "Not like this! No fucking way!" He twisted, but Brendan shoved his face against the floor with one arm; it only muffled his shouting. "You *know* how many of these fucking bitches I took apart, asshole?! How many masks I had to peel off? And they were all fucking *wrong*, goddammit! Every mask I looked through, every sign I carved, *nothing*! Nothing *worked*! But then—I heard."

His breathing steadied, movements stilled. A touch of awe slipping into his tone like morphine, making him smile, high on his own crazy.

"I heard how they were finally getting pregnant. All of them. And I knew if I could find the one, the *first* one, the mask of the one *chosen*—then *that*. . . would be the one. The one that'd finally —*finally*—let me *see*."

"See *what?*" Brendan blurted, despite himself.

The man's head whipped around, then. Wild eyes glared out of a scab-like, yellow-brown mask, long dead and dried to his under-skin, ringed in black stitches crusted with blood; the bottom half was torn open where his jaw's movements had cracked the desiccated tissue.

Brendan screamed, jerking backwards. Before he could recover, the King twisted and shoved, hurling him off. Brendan hit the floor hard, wind knocked out of him for the second time in two minutes and scrabbled back as the man clambered to his feet. Blood trickled down the stolen mask, dripping to the floor.

"The other world, shithead," the King whispered, his mouth moving behind the ragged brown tissue he'd stolen. "The *real* world." From his belt, he drew something very much not regular issue—long and angular, a Plexiglass triangle blade, wine-dark with stains. "The one I saw, in my dreams. The lake, two suns. Black stars."

Brendan stared up at him, gasping for breath.

A whole new type of cry filled the air, shocked and hungry, angry, *betrayed*. From between Annie's legs, Heather fell back on her butt, arms full of something pink, wrinkled and squalling. Naz slowly took her hands away from Annie's throat, watching as the hollow pen sticking up from it quivered and twitched.

Annie's breast rose and fell. Retta, who had just begun to roll over, lay still and frozen. In Heather's arms the baby wailed, tiny mouth gaping.

". . . Heather?" Naz husked.

Heather's voice was thick. "She's okay," she gulped. "She's fine. She's perfect. Oh, God, Annie, I wish you could see her. . ."

"She will," said the King, smile so wide now it tore "his" mask even further. He held up the knife. "Least I can do for her. Give her one look, before I go. . ."

He moved towards the women, past the unconscious Retta. Brendan struggled to rise and couldn't, still crumpled with pain and anoxia. Heather crab-walked backward, the baby in one arm, but Naz threw herself in front of Annie, bloodied penknife out.

"Don't you fucking touch her, asshole," she rasped.

The King stared at her. Then he spun and hit Naz right in the breastbone with a flashing roundhouse kick, knocking her yards backwards; the penknife clattered into the corner.

"You fucking *BITCH*!" he screamed at her. "Don't you *get* it? I was *right!* I was *right all along! I did this! My dreams were right!*" He shifted his knife to an overhand grip, lifting it above his head, and stepped towards Nazneen—

"Who said they were *your* dreams, insect?"

The voice was strange. Clear but muffled, as if speaking through cloth, yet oddly buzzy and muted as well, a bad microphone in an echo chamber. Slowly, Annie sat up, one hand holding her breathing-tube in place. The other came up to her mask, flattening itself against the rough surface. . .

. . . and slid it off. The brown-yellow oval dripped clear, viscous fluid to the floor. Silently, without fuss, Annie set it aside.

Brendan had never really known what was supposed to make someone beautiful. What he felt for Naz was mostly about who she was, her smell and voice, her movements; he'd never even really seen her whole face or body, not truly. But Annie's unmasked face seemed to blaze, so brightly he wanted to cover his eyes. Her skin was smooth and perfect, lips full and blushed with health, and her wide eyes shone a brilliant amber-gold, irises no colour he'd ever seen on any real person before, ever.

This was beyond beauty. Beyond human.

The King's knife fell to the floor with a clatter. A second later, he sank to the floor himself, falling onto his knees. His hands lifted, empty and imploring.

"Yes," he hissed. "It was you, all along. Lend me your mask. Please. I just want to—I need to *see*."

Annie smiled. With a flickering movement, she plucked the tracheotomy tube from her throat and flung it away; the tissue rippled in its wake, sealing up.

"Why?" she asked. "You already have one of your own."

For one final second of incomprehension, the King goggled at her. And then a sharp hiss split the air; smoke curled up, with a foul, acrid stink. The King's hands flew to his face, ripping and tearing, but the mask-tissue was *moving*, sealing itself to his flesh beneath even as it crawled and spread like spilled sewage, covering him over.

He screamed, and screamed again, lunging to his feet and twisting around, only the force of his shrieks keeping the tissue from sealing over his mouth. Arms windmilling, he staggered towards Heather and the baby, smoke billowing around him and the sizzle of his dissolving flesh growing ever louder.

Without warning, a massive roar drowned all other noise.

The building shook. The ceiling broke apart like an invisible wrecking ball had torn through it, and the walls fell away to either side. Cold night air crashed down upon them; wind extinguished the candles in a gust. The King fell with a thud, hard enough to break his screams for a moment; beyond him, the lights of Toronto flickered and went out, drowning the city in the dark. Sirens and screams came floating over the water, until the King's voice rose over them in fresh peals of anguish.

Revulsion seized Brendan like something utterly alien, something beyond either instinct or decision—like he was staring at some rotten, pulpy, slug-like *thing* whose mere existence brought his gorge boiling up. He grabbed the King's stunner pistol from where he'd dropped it, rolled upright, and tackled the other man, hammering at his skull with the pistol butt; and even as they toppled over together, Naz had joined the scrum, driving the man's fallen knife into his waist beneath the armour over and over again, then above the armour through his neck, choking off his screams in bloody gurgles.

Her mask split and cracked and fell away as blood spurted over it, as transfigured as Annie's had been, a thing of wild chaos and storm to Annie's eerie serenity. She dropped the knife, plunged her hands into the dying man's blood and wiped it over Brendan's mouth; it burned like liquid fire, making him ravenous and horny all at once. Without transition they were embracing, kissing, smearing the blood all over each other's faces as the body of the King crumpled and shrivelled between them, and Brendan soon realized it didn't seem at all strange that they were laughing too. Laughing like they were going to piss themselves.

"Good," said Annie. She had risen to her feet, taking her baby from Heather's arms; it nursed at her breast as Heather, also unmasked, clung to one of her legs in a storm of blissful weeping. "All new ages begin with sacrifice. This. . . was worthy." She looked up at the stars. "It is time."

Time? Brendan mouthed.

He looked at Nazneen, but her grin was too wide for fear. They watched Retta crawl over and press her unmasked face to the floor at Annie's feet. Something stirred dimly in Brendan's mind at that—some hard-to-recall doubt, a faint feeling of wrongness—but it passed.

He was here, with Naz; *with* her, as he'd never dared dream he could be. That was worth a bent knee, or two.

"The tide turns," said Annie. "The true face of the world revealed. All will admire it under their proper stars, at last." Her voice rose to a cry. "Unmask! *Unmask!*"

She lifted one arm high, and the earth's rumble echoed up through the night. Staring up at the field of stars, Brendan's mouth fell open. The sky was *rippling*. Around every star grew a web of black cracks, like ice fracturing over black water, or dead dry skin peeling; through them leaked something like black-purple ink, or boiling tar. The screams echoing from the extinguished city took on a slow, awful resonance, maddened choir singers reaching for impossible chords, a harmony beyond.

Brendan looked at Naz. She kissed him, then took his hand and put it to her stomach. "Unmask," she whispered.

His guts gave an awful lurch; whether joy or terror, he could not have even begun to guess.

But I wear no mask, he thought.

LITTLE HORN

"Beloved men, recognize what the truth is: this world is in haste and it is drawing near the end—therefore the longer it is, the worse it will get in the world. And it needs must thus become very much worse as a result of the people's sins prior to the Advent of Antichrist, and then indeed it will be terrible and cruel throughout the world."

—Archbishop Wulfstan's "Sermo Lupi"
to the English, 1014.

This whole business, it all started right about when I burned my church down. Not one I went to or ministered at—I mean the one built *around* me, raised by my very own personal worshippers, so they could do their sacrificial reverence to me in private. Might've done it earlier if I'd only known that was an option, but one way or the other I'd definitely had enough by that point, eighteen damn years' worth of it. Frankly, cousin, you'd only known these people the same way I did, I do believe you probably would've done it too.

So, picture this, if you can: I'm up on the podium, enthroned in front of a shrine of bones with a Hand of Glory on either side of me, my head already sweaty-aching under a crown made from ten different kinds of horns that bites into my scalp so it doesn't start to tip askew. Got me wearing a black goat-skin robe, uncured, rough and stinking; got a reversed cross in pig's blood drawn on my forehead, so thick it draws flies that sting and cluster 'tween my brows, buzzing like a bad light-socket. Twenty naked fools already down on their knees inside the hexfoil, knocking their heads on the ground and scratching themselves hard enough to open wounds—thirteen still robed and masked likewise with their backs turned to the wrangle and a dagger in either hand, supposedly poised to guard us all against incursion. And then, to top it all off, out come the reverend and his sister-wives with a bag of live-caught feral cats and a brace of three foot skewers.

Preaching from Jubilees like always, chanting away as the blind and swinging mass of cats growls and hisses against each other, getting ready to make them scream. Telling them dirt-faced fools how *lawlessness increased on the Earth and all flesh corrupted its way, alike men and cattle and beasts and birds and everything that walks on the Earth, all of them corrupted their ways and their orders, and they began to devour each other, and every imagination of the thoughts of all men was thus evil continually.* Continually, continually, continually.

And didn't that make 'em all writhe and moan, cousin, just like the words were stuffed with fentanyl cured in crack, or what have-you... well, didn't it? What do *you* think?

Yeah, that's right.

They say good people have a light around them, and that's true. It licks and laps, sweet like dripping honey, almost edible. But then there's the others, lurching around, all driven by their own little seeds of darkness, their slime-mold souls—their flesh spored like fungus, turning from within. And I grew up amongst the latter, living symbol of that black angel-sized hole they all claimed to yearn to throw themselves down into. Constantly being told how *special* I was, how the ruin I instinctively sowed around me had to be nurtured with deliberation, whipped up high like a fire fed by cruelty and filth. How without me to do it before, none of this ridiculous gothic shit they spent their time caught up in would be anything but simple human perversion; the same old lust, hate and murder cops have been cleaning up after since a hundred years before the last millennium's turn.

They found my mother under a pile of trash after the seven-year cyclone went by, that particularly strange one, a swirling mass of live insects and fire, caught-up animals cooking and bleeding out, rotten garbage of every sort. Rivers burst their banks as it passed by; graves gave up their fruit, the dust and bones of ages past spread miles wide, human ash forming fulgurites with each red lightning strike. The moon eclipsed the sun, turning it blue-black, and fields scored in its wake became fallow. All these omens: surely, my birth couldn't fail to be something special, considering my mother was a virgin when the winds came for her. Or so the reverend always claimed.

She was comatose when they pulled her out and dead by the time they cut me from her womb, nine months later, but that didn't matter, supposedly; just a vessel, the reverend used to say, a necessary step along the low road to the low god. Said God being whoever sowed the seed of me inside her, thus making me harbinger of a long-awaited uprising against the cruel archon who made this awful world, condemning us to live encased in dumb meat until it finally rots enough to fall back off. To set us free.

I've heard this shit all my life, cousin—same as you, probably. It never gets more likely, but it sure does get wearing.

That tide of stupid whispers, wet with drool, all ready for the show. *All flesh, all flesh, corrupting its way; all flesh, all flesh, corrupting its way*—and then the first cat gets dragged out by its scruff, and I'm just *done*. Done with all of this stupid shit, forever.

So: "Put that down," I tell the sister-wife nearest me, my voice so seldom used she barely looks like she recognizes it, a grating, dusty thing. Adding, as she hesitates: "I said, DOWN."

"Now, Little Horn," the reverend calls me, placatingly. But I can feel it in me now, coming up *through* me, the way he always taught me it would; the true speech, a desert wind blowing straight back from Megiddo, wrathful-raw and rank. That it would be there when I reached for it, when I finally *wanted* to reach for it. He just never thought he'd be the thing to make me want to, I guess. I mean, why would he?

But: "That's not my *name*," is all I say, by way of reply, and I shut my eyes. Find that door inside my mind, the red one; open it, recognize what's crouching there, in the dark behind. Let it recognize me, in turn. Then open wide myself, everywhere at once, and tell it to *come on out*.

And I light that whole fucking place on fire.

———

The cats got out okay, in case you're wondering. Nobody else, though; I made damn sure of that before I walked away, stepping out of the fire seemingly unburnt, yet still hot enough on the outside, my first few footprints came down all smoking and gooey on the road's asphalt, till my skin cooled enough to draw dust. I was naked by that time, of course, but smeared all over in ash and other debris, which probably made me seem clothed from a distance. Still, someone did slow down to take a gander after a while, which is when I figured out I'd forgotten about that dumb fucking crown of horns.

You know how it is, cousin: Antichrist's a position, not a person. There's hundreds of us around might fill that particular slot, we only knew we had the right to try for it. But most of us don't, no more than most of the normal sheep-folk surrounding us know their own selves what they're capable of, under truly special circumstances.

So, we wander about instead, hunger-driven—collide and tangle, vaguely aware of each other in proximity like tigers huffing each other on the wind, similarly carrion-breathed, and aroused to heat by the scent of it. Enjoy each other's company a while, in season, though like as not we won't cleave together more than a shortish spell; we tend to breed true only with normal humans. . . if you can call your regular range of devout Satanists "normal."

Wandered down along a road a while, then, enjoying my solitude, for all I didn't expect to be alone for long, 'cause we never are. People move towards us like iron filings towards a magnet, drunk with praise—fall in love with us and want to do things for us, and you can't convince them otherwise, not even if you try. But they always destroy themselves for us, over us, or self-destruct if you refuse their tribute. And if you let yourself get angry with them, they'll be attacked, or have an accident, or commit suicide.

You have to accept their worship, or you'll be alone, the reverend always said, *but to do so is to know you're a seeder with no driver sowing death everywhere you go, even unto the end of the world.* Just a (semi-)human payload, continually moving towards Armageddon.

(I always know where to shoot. I always know where to go. Which way to step so the bullet hits whoever's standing next to me. I always know where the fight will be, and I walk through it, unscathed. I am a weapon, made for nothing but final war.)

(Fire and blood, bitches.)

So, when this nice young man got out of his car and took some steps towards me, calling out worriedly: "Lady, you okay? Anything I can do for you, lady?" I simply smiled.

I'm no lady, son, I might have said, if I'd wanted to. *Not a ma'am, not a missus, not a miz. Just a bad thought, the kind that hurts to think. A scream walking 'round on two legs, searching for yet another mouth to fill.*

I *was* hot, though, that's true enough—hotter than even I like to be. And my head hurt.

"God wants you kept safe," he told me, practically panting with the prospect of doing some good, 'long as it wouldn't cost him too much. "I can drive you wherever easy enough, you need me to. No trouble."

I nodded, smiling wider yet. "The God *you* mean's a fly on a dead dog's eye," I replied, mildly. "But go on and do whatever makes you happy, I suppose."

A mild, surprised frown. "Excuse me?"

"Oh, I doubt even I can do that."

Here he shook his head just a bit, eyes slightly aflutter, sure he couldn't possibly have heard what he just did. Then stepped back and opened the door for me.

"Climb in," he told me, and I did. We pulled away, Carrie Underwood blasting.

"Bet you just love this song, don't you?" I asked. "'Jesus Take the Wheel'. . . sounds kinda dangerous, to me."

"Uh huh," he agreed, nodding, then sniffed. "Oh wow, that's some kinda stinky—what is that, you think, exactly?"

"That'd be me, I'm afraid."

"We should do something about that—get you some normal clothes, wash off that stuff. Get rid of the whatever it is on your head too."

"Probably, yeah."

Gave him a sly look, then, pupils sliding horizontal, yellow-flaring in the dimming sun.

"Think your girlfriend just might wear the same size as me?" I asked him. And smiled.

———

A few hours later, just as twilight became full sodium-glare night, I let that boy drop me off in front of an all-night roadside diner called Meg's Big Bite, dolled up in pink from head to toe, like Devil-baby Barbie. Meg like Megiddo, I found myself thinking; there was a coincidence, or maybe not. Since oh so very little is, in our lives.

When I walked in to find you already there, therefore, that's why I maybe wasn't as surprised as I otherwise might have been.

Saw you sitting there and knew immediately what you were to me, cousin—what *we* were, to each other. Felt the hair at the back of my neck first stiffen a bit, then sleek back down again once you looked up and shook your head, just a bit.

"Like some coffee?" you asked. "I ordered us a pot."

And: "Hm, could be," I replied. "Gotta be better than goat's-blood brewed with moonshine, one way or the other."

"Shit, I hope *so*," you said, eyebrows hiking. "Sit on down."

We examined each other for a minute or two, staring across the red-checked plastic tablecloth. You were taller than me, probably older—had olive-tinted skin and hair the same vaguely reddish shade as mine, drawn back in a mass of braiding on one side, shaved almost to the scalp on the other. Your eyes were heavy-lidded, lashes thick-dark as mascara above and below but the same basic colour as mine too, that sly light yellow-brown from some angles, molten gold from others. Hazel, I've heard it called, but that's just the sheep lying to 'emselves, trying to boil it down anyway they can into something recognizable.

Plus, those same slitted pupils, too: slant and weird, oval on occasion, never fully round. A pair of black moons floating in an alien sky.

"Some call me the Nail," you said, "on the Internet, anyway. And they call *you* Little Horn down at that hillbilly Left Hand Path honky-stomp of yours or used to."

"Yeah, and some call me Kiss My Ass, 'specially when I've just laid the hellfire down on 'em," I told you, voice finally smoke-free, but no less gravelly. "So, who the fuck are you *really* when you're at home, or even when you ain't?"

"Beata Callander, nice to meet you. Am I your first fellow antichrist?"

". . . Pretty much."

"Hm, me too, or almost. Interesting, huh?"

"Interesting how?"

"Oh, just exactly how hard they all work to keep us apart. And maybe why."

Me, I'm not too educated, as such; the reverend made sure of that, or tried to. But *you*, cousin. . . someone took a *good* long time making sure *you* could conjure your own opinions and formulate your own insights into arguments; someone taught *you* debate wasn't just necessary, but essential. I'd've liked to've grown up in a house like that.

So: "You tell me," I suggested. To which you took a little bow and did.

"My parents were Sunday go-to-meeting kind of Satanists, at best," you began. "I mean, they practiced, off and on; made their obeisances, but didn't do much else. To them, this was like some sort of beauty pageant or something—a community thing. Competition to build character. One of us I met later on, though, his parents'd built a cult like yours around him out in the woods somewhere, not quite Manson-level, but not quite not. I used to call him Damon Hellstrom, 'caused I knew it pissed him off."

I poured sugar in my coffee, enough to hold a spoon upright. "And what happened to him?"

"Good question. I passed through there a while back, saw everything was coming up roses—lots of tattooed pussy-slash-ass, a functioning meth kitchen, bundles of money and all the bodies buried deep enough nobody'd come sniffing around, as yet. Then I came back two weeks ago, found nothing but a burnt-out shell and a pile of corpses, his very much not amongst them."

"Sounds sad."

"Well, the guy *was* a world-class asshole even without the whole End of Days thing, but yeah. Particularly by implication."

I shrugged, downing most of my coffee-syrup in one long, tooth-aching swig. "Might be he didn't want some bunch of naked morons rubbin' up on him all the time anymore, tattooed or not," I suggested. "'Cause . . . some people just don't, you feel me? Gets wearing."

"You'd know all about *that*, I guess."

"Yup." You shot me a glance, and I met it, levelly. "What, you think I was gonna deny it? Being an object sucks—of worship, or otherwise. I wanted more."

"More than ruling the world for a thousand years? Some expensive tastes you got there, cousin."

I snarled. "Stop lookin' 'round inside my head, bitch."

"Aw, but it's so hard not to." Adding, as I fumed: "Listen, I've been where you are and you know it, just like you know the drill: how we get blamed for everything even when we're not responsible for it, because strength is terrifying and we're literally strong as hell. That's why all our lives, great and terrible powers will conspire to destroy us, while equally terrible powers will die to keep us safe. Thus, that cult of yours *was* yours, to keep or to kill, because strength makes its own laws. And if they were dumb enough to think different, too bad for them, right? You're the goat, not the sheep; you lead, you will never *be* led.

"So: *Listen to your own voice above any other, save that of Him who made you. For you will move armies like chess-pieces, in your time; you are the scythe, the torch, the ram that breaks all doors and levels the final playing field. You will Prepare the Way.*"

"Or I'll call myself Peggy, get a job in a library. You don't know."

"Kind of think you'd have to be able to *read*, for that," you replied. "Or at least have a legal birth certificate."

"Oh yeah, 'cause I'm that kid from *The Omen*—Derrick, or whatever. Right?"

"Damien, and so am I. Potentially, at least."

"Lucky you."

"Lucky *us*."

You smiled at me then, full force, something I'd never hitherto been on the other end of. It was. . . powerful, I guess is the best way to put it. Made me think yet again on the whole question of incarnation—were we Nephilim in reverse, or something altogether different? Just demons who've slipped inside human bodies and forced them to replicate an amalgam, some tadpole of evil waiting to bloom into full frog, or maybe something from outside space-time forcing a little bit of itself *inside*, moving us around like human skin finger puppets? Are we a mask, or a mirror? When we speak, are our voices ever our own, as opposed to an echo wrapped 'round a lie. . . low-key devil-daddy whispering through us, murmuring bad advice in every ear we meet?

We both knew the creed, like you'd said. How each of us was a weapon, so we needed to be pointed, be primed. . . and the worst part of it all was realizing how we didn't live for ourselves alone, how we *couldn't*. How we were at least half human, which really *should* give us free will, and yet. The very idea of our own individuality might just well be another illusion, one so good even *we* couldn't help wanting to believe in it.

"Yeah," you agreed, doing that annoying mind reading thing once more. "The Nazarene had it pretty easy, all told; *he* came here alone. Didn't have to battle it out with a bunch of other saviours-to-be, like sharks in their mother's belly, till one of them got born and the rest became calories. But the only way one of *us* will rise is by ingesting the others, becoming the most singular, the sum of All."

"Says who, exactly?"

Your grin widened. "A *very* good question. Too bad none of us ever seem to ask it."

I was taking a second to absorb this particular idea when I noticed how the other diners had all already begun first turning 'round in their seats, then getting up and drifting towards us, starting to loom and cluster. Seemed like we must've kick-started an extra helping of the usual effect, sitting down both together like that; pretty soon, everybody within a certain radius was gonna start in on genuflecting and humpin' our legs while carvin' IT'S ALL FOR YOU all over 'emselves with the tableware, or some similar kind of shit.

"Oh, I love you *so much*, Little Horn," one old lady to the left of us told me, raising her shaking hands my way.

"No you don't," I snapped, recoiling right before she could connect, and took a spiteful jolt of pleasure out of the pain that flashed through her eyes as she watched me brush her worship aside. While *you* just leaned past and laid your hand on hers before that hurt could turn inward, gently telling her—

"Yes, I know it's disappointing, but that's life sometimes, isn't it? So, look me in the eyes and believe me when I say you can just walk away—you don't *have* to kill yourself because she rejected you, after all. Just go sit in the john for fifteen minutes or so and cry till you feel better; stay out of her sight, she'll forget about you soon enough. Okay, ma'am?"

The old lady shook her head a bit, like she was trying to clear it. "Okay," she replied, eventually.

You patted her hand, then let go. "Perfect. Have a nice day, now."

"Gonna do that with all of them?" I asked, watching the old lady wander away, while the others drew closer. But you shook your head.

"Was kind of hoping you'd help out, actually," you suggested, "before we start a riot, and the cops get called. Or the TV news."

I frowned again, sighing. Then said, finally:

"...ugh, all *right*."

Entirely without planning to, we rose and turned together, in a weird sort in unison—didn't quite hold hands, or even touch, but I nevertheless felt *something* flicker between us: a jolt, a spark, a charge. Your strength recognizing mine, making it, or me. . . us *both*. . . just that little bit stronger.

I glanced back at you, only to watch you smirk in reply: *Quite the trick, hm?*

And yeah, it was. A trick *and* a treat, energy humming at almost the same pitch through the holes between our atoms, sewing us together and the rest of the world apart—

—but this was exactly when the night outside ripped wide, allowing the twisted-'round, hoof-like foot of yet one more of us to step through onto the very same road that other boy had driven me in on, and fire bloomed bright as reality sealed itself shut once again behind him.

"Aw, crap," you cursed at my elbow.

Back in the Middle Ages, people spent what I feel was an entirely inordinate amount of time making drawings of what they thought Hell might look like, let alone how the things that lived there's bodies might be arranged. Given their own circumstances, I guess it makes sense that they usually fell back on what they knew: streets full of shit (often on fire), dead folks covered in boils and blisters from the plague (also often on fire), demons that looked like worms and scorpions and toads and such, with their entrails hanging out and their dicks all covered in thorns, napalm vomiting from all the usual orifices (along with all the *un*usual ones).

The reverend, he had a corkboard set up in the back of my church with versions of what Antichrist was supposed to look like pinned all over it, from mosaics and statues to paintings and woodcuts and what-all—had 'em up there for everyone in the cult to study, I can only suppose, just in case they forgot what they were keepin' an eye out for. And I must admit, the whole thing seemed nothing but ridiculous to me, given I'd seen the photos they took of my mother, after all. Knew what I saw when I looked in the bathroom mirror too—one more human being, more or less, occasional goat eyes aside.

Exactly like *you*, cousin, in other words, or that asshole you'd told me about at the top of our conversation, give or take the dangly bits.

This new sumbitch outside the diner, though, he had what I could now hear you loudly thinking were *all* the Hieronymous Bosch accoutrements: face in his gut, face in his ass, faces for pecs, with a tail twice as long as his three-foot cock and the both of 'em dragging on the ground, spreading liquid crap behind and pre-cum like lit gasoline before. As he turned, I saw how four crumply, supernumerary wings like hunks of melted garbage bags had busted out his back, both above and below the shoulder-blades; had eyes blinking all up and down his spine like landing lights too, and a mouth that sported three rows of teeth nested one inside the other, plus a pair of dusty black lips split in front like a lion's, stretched wide from ear to double-pointed ear.

I elbowed you in the ribs. "And just who," I demanded, "is *this* motherfucker, exactly?"

"Don't pretend you can't tell, *cousin*," you replied grimly.

"Same guy you've been pussyfootin' 'round warning me about? Yeah, I'm gettin' that idea."

"Well, screw me for trying to be subtle. I thought we'd have more time till he got here."

"Uh huh. Fucked *that* one up, now, didn't ya?"

It was damn hard not to stare, all told, so after a second or so I didn't even try. Just heard the reverend in the back of my head, wittering on, singing his way through every *Jubilees* translation available through Google: *For in this time there will be many, many, many like Legion, though only one ascends.* And this asshole definitely looked like he was aiming to be the One in question, even if it meant he had to eat his way through the whole rest of his entire generation.

"Shit, man," I said, with a mixture of disgust cut with sneaky semi-admiration. "Old boy sure has put some effort in, ain't he? And me, I wasn't even born with horns."

"Don't think he was either, truth to tell. Check those faces, one by one—they seem pissed off to you too?"

I did, and they did; the eyes flashed yellow, weeping blood, each pupil identically side-slitted. Plus, that sludge he was passing had bone fragments in it.

"Oh, *ugh*. That's not gonna happen to *us*, is it?"

"Not unless we either chow down on every other antichrist left alive or slather ourselves in ketchup and wait."

I shook my head. "Fuck *that* shit," I said, to which you laughed, and nodded.

"Damn straight," you replied.

And this time you *did* reach out to take my hand, or I took yours. Doesn't really matter which.

———

We're not supposed to work together, even against a third— *that*'s part of the creed too. Selfishness, not self-sacrifice; strength, not weakness. To admit fear is to make yourself vulnerable, in the Devil's Bible.

For who is like unto the Beast? Who is able to make war with him? Only one, and He's not here.

(Yet.)

But in the meantime. . .

Our looming, roaring Cousin Number Three, yet one more brother from another mother—or why not call him the Beast, since he'd certainly done more'n enough to earn the monicker— must've felt us touch from way 'cross the parking lot, that *spike*, how it roiled and spat, hooking deep into each of our worshippers' medullae oblongata at once ('sides from that old lady in the john, I'd venture a guess). How it jerked them 'round in unison, made their eyes fall on him all at once, and let the lamentable spectacle of his florid self-injury flush anything else they might have had in mind away like poop down a chute. How they howled out jackal-pack style, chucked a couple of chairs through the diner's front windows, then started swarming full-bore towards him without even stopping long enough to kick out the last few shards as they went.

One man in a trucker hat cut his wrist wide open, but kept on running, barely slowing down even once he'd bled out far enough to fall over, so his own momentum slammed him up against the Beast horizontally, trapping that sharp-swinging demonic dick head between the dying man's body and the Beast's own thorny ankles. The rest either tripped over him or leaped him like a stile, scrabbling headlong, climbing each other like ants.

They broke over the Beast in a wave, tearing at him with their nails, no matter how bad his blood burnt on its way out.

Ha! Got *you, fuck-stick.*

The Beast screamed out like an Aztec death-whistle, mouth gaping so wide it tipped the whole top of his skull back like a fuckin' Muppet's. *Gonna puke fire all over 'em,* I thought. . . but no, that wasn't it at all, turned out. I only wish it had been.

Aw, what the—

Ever see a guy rise up on those raptor-sized claws at the back of what should be his heels, puff his blinking chest out like a rooster and *cum ropes of flame* over everything around him like a firehose, a stream so hard and hot it melts whatever it touches, like lava? No? Well. . .

. . . just count yourself lucky, then. Wish to fuck I could power wash the sight of that out of *my* mind, and I'm half-Satan.

"*Gaaah*, Jesus H. CHRIST," I heard you retch from beside me, automatically, then yip as the Carpenter's antithetical name sliced your tongue open, spitting blood. I felt the sting of it pass straight through one ear and out the other, a searing migraine-thread, and narrowed my eyes against the pain, left one blooming red with burst blood vessels.

"Time to put on the whole damn armour, cousin," I told you,

fisting your hand in mine and digging my nails in, deep enough to yank you back to yourself. Saw you nod again, out the crimson-tinged corner of my gaze—then straighten up, grimly, throwing our twinned palms out together towards the Beast and shooting him the double horns.

The Beast looked back at us, still engorged, and laughed: long, loud, like us making our final stand was the funniest shit he'd ever seen. He was ashy, dripping, mainly lit by his own secretions; a few smoking remnants of various diner patrons kept on crawling blindly 'round his hoof-feet, almost too scorched to moan, while they waited to get stomped on. I watched the faces of all those relatives he'd devoured thus far trying to scream for them and failing.

"Get rrrrrreadyyyyy, cousinnnnns," he told us, in a voice like rocks being ground smooth. "Thisssss. . . is going to hurrrrrttttt."

Your hand in mine, tight. Tighter.

That *jolt*.

"Sure is," you told him, grinning back. And I knew just what you meant.

Because—

———

All my life, ever since a certain point, I've known myself not just weapon, but sacrament. The body *and* the blood.

Fire runs hot through all three of our veins, always has. The Lightbringer's genetics at work. With you and me, though, cousin, that means something extra.

I cast myself back to my church, the cleansing of it, wiping the slate clean with summoned conflagration: blood as a halo turned outwards, not inwards, burning anyone I cared to touch. Reach up under my skirt, slap a red hand across someone's face and they go blind, start to melt, as the fruit of my sour womb infects 'em. Saints and martyrs have a similar sort of power, or so the big-C Church claims—rose-scented decay, generative damage, life-giving. Wound as super-power, sweet and pure, bringing life instead of death; where their severed heads fall, a font of healing water springs up.

But me, again—*you* and me—

—we ain't no saints.

Like the Beast, we're doomed to make stuff hot, make forces intersect. To call the storm, bring locusts, turn the fields to salt. To drink this whole world's blood and eat its flesh at once in a spasm of de-Creation, leaving it desolate and naked. *For with me, the time has come for bitter things.*

"Gonna turn your head so far backwards, you'll looking up your own ass forever," I told him—my voice in your mouth too, coming from everywhere at once, echoing like feedback. Reaching out, calling to my brothers and sisters he'd already swallowed, offering them vengeance; hearing them know their time had come and answer. An awful choir risen from every atom of his bloated body, singing destruction's song.

And then, just like with my church, we lit that fucker up all together, but *oh* so very much harder. A tiny little taste of Armageddon.

So hard that when we were done, there was nothing left but the crispy bits, blown up and away like sparks into a dark, dark wind.

———

We paused then, panting, contemplating letting go. Which is when we heard that slow clap from somewhere near and turned, instead.

He was standing back in the diner's ruins, maybe where that booth we'd once shared used to be—a man, or something like it. The face and form he'd put on hinted at Robert Johnson by way of Stagger Lee, classic crossroads style; had goat's eyes and a pork-pie hat pulled down low, to hide his spiky nubs. And *his* voice, now. . . I felt it all through me, threatening to pick me apart the same way you and me'd just done the Beast, cousin. I know you felt it too.

". . . Lucifer," you said at last, quietly.

"Beata," he named her in turn, inclining his head. "And you, Little Horn. . . ah, you. *Here is my beloved, in whom I am well-pleased.*"

I both understood the compliment and wanted it, fiercely, which made me want to shut his mouth with a punch.

"Which of us you talkin' about here, exactly?" I demanded.

"Hm. Why not both?"

We exchanged a glance.

"Ain't that against the rules?" I asked.

Another half-nod, half-shrug, infinitely fluid. "Oh, but rules can change, always. . . *we* know that, if anybody does. Remember the creed, girls: unlike the rest of His sheep, we don't *have* to accept, to forgive *or* forget. Don't like the way the world is? Change it. Fight, and victory will be given to you. It's your birthright."

For *You were made to rise, to be served, to rule. To set all about you against each other, killing for my favour.*

"Victory," you repeated, nodding. "But not forever. Right, Dad?"

"Says who? *Revelation* was written by Christians, after all— what did you think it would claim? So, rise up and take what's yours, daughters."

"Oh yeah? And what's that?"

"*Everything.*"

I paused, then, just for a minute. Saw myself sometime in the future, maybe with you, standing in front of our opposite number—Lamb to our goats, born again at his own absent Father's whim, to mop up and start over. Heard one or the other of us saying how if rules *could* change then might be we didn't even have to be enemies at all, no more than the world *had* to end, and knew in that moment how we could have offered the Beast we'd just slaughtered the exact same choice, he hadn't been such a disgusting piece of crap.

How two thousand years of Scripture could be brushed away in an instant with one simple pair of phrases: *I don't have to fight you, not really. I never did.*

No point in saying that out loud right now, though. Educational deficits aside, one thing I've never been's *completely* stupid.

"What makes you think we want it?" you asked him.

"What makes you think you have a choice?"

Oh, but wasn't that *your* sin, originally, Serpent? Believing you had the right to choose?

"Pass," I said, finally. "Thanks, ever so, but. . . no."

"Yeah, me either."

Our low-key devil daddy spread his long-fingered hands, smiling politely. Correcting us gently, as he did—

"Not *yet*, you mean."

And was gone, leaving us alone once more, together.

———

"So," you said, after a long, slow while of us walking down the highway, watching the horizon lighten. "Still want to call yourself Peggy?"

"I'm thinkin'," I replied.

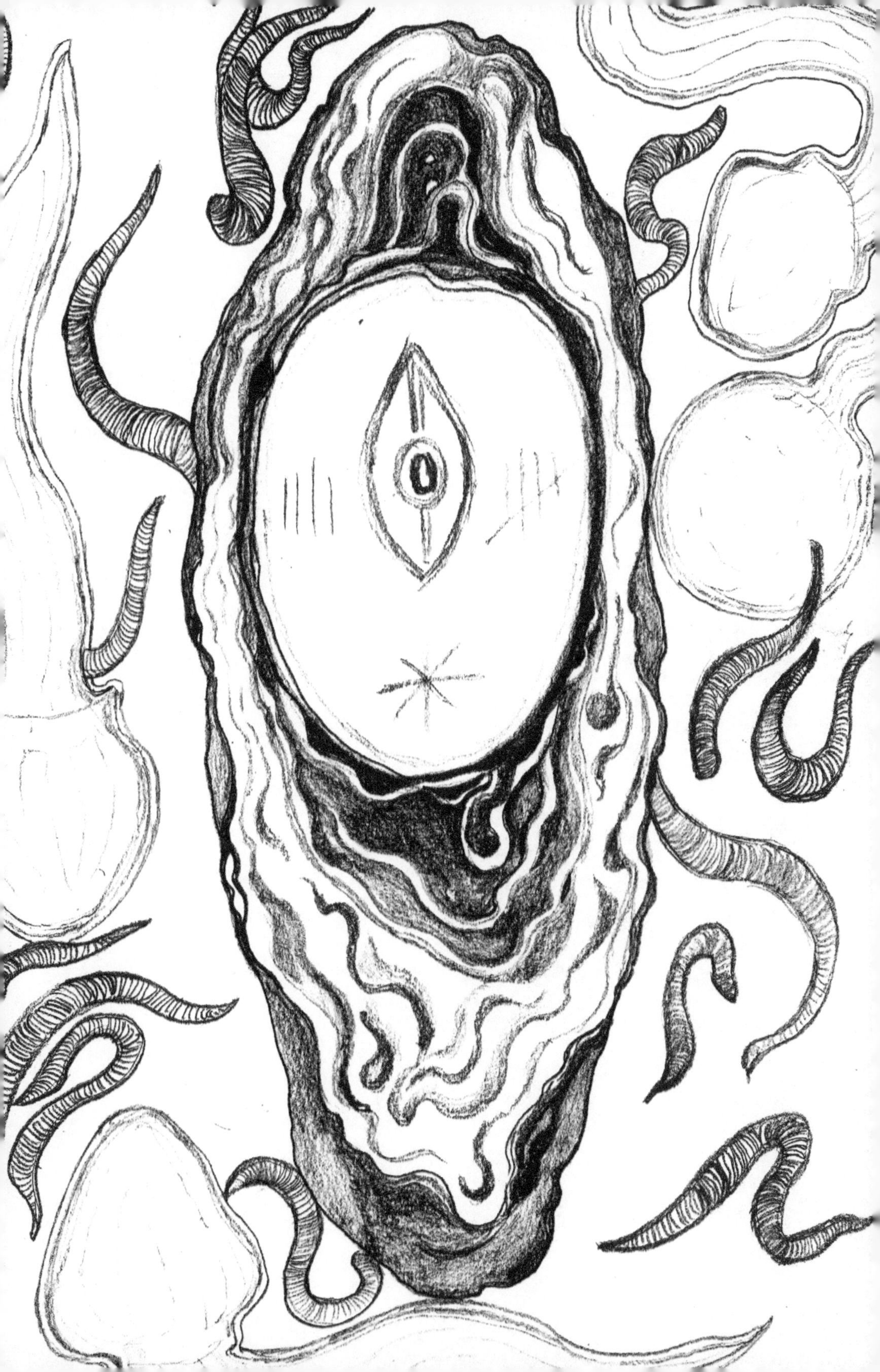

ACKNOWLEDGMENTS

For my family, whether they want it or not, with special thanks to Becky LeJeune and Alan Lastufka.

ABOUT THE AUTHOR

Gemma Files is a Canadian horror writer, journalist, and film critic. Her novel, Experimental Film, won the Shirley Jackson Award for Best Novel and the Sunburst Award for Best Canadian Speculative Fiction (Novel). Gemma is also a two-time Bram Stoker Award winner.

A NOTE FROM SHORTWAVE PUBLISHING

Thank you for reading! If you enjoyed *Little Horn*, please consider writing a review. Reviews help readers find more titles they may enjoy, and that helps us continue to publish titles like this.

For more Shortwave titles, visit us online...

OUR WEBSITE
shortwavepublishing.com

SOCIAL MEDIA
@ShortwaveBooks

EMAIL US
contact@shortwavepublishing.com